Dani Atkins was born in London in 1958, and grew up in Cockfosters. She moved to rural Hertfordshire in 1985, where she has lived in a small village ever since with her husband, two (now grown-up) children, one Siamese kitten, and a soppy Border Collie. She has been writing for fun all her life, and has been writing for a living since 2014.

You can find Dani on Facebook at www.facebook.com/daniatkinsauthor

Twitter @AtkinsDani

OUR SONG

This is the story of two couples who, by fate and circumstance, find themselves in the same intensive care unit one night. Ally is married to Joe, and one selfless act has led to him lying in a hospital bed. Charlotte is married to David, who also lies in a nearby room. Over a period of twenty-four hours, the two women take a journey into the past, with long-buried insecurities and resentments bubbling to the surface. For David was Ally's first love, and she has always felt that Charlotte was instrumental in their split. As the clock ticks through the long night, and their husbands fight for their lives, will Ally and Charlotte be able to put the past behind them?

DANI ATKINS

OUR SONG

Complete and Unabridged

CHARNWOOD
Leicester

First published in Great Britain in 2016 by
Simon & Schuster UK Ltd
London

First Charnwood Edition
published 2017
by arrangement with
Simon & Schuster UK Ltd
London

The moral right of the author has been asserted

A catalogue record for this book is available from the British Library.

ISBN 978–1–4448–3386–7

Published by
F. A. Thorpe (Publishing)
Anstey, Leicestershire

Set by Words & Graphics Ltd.
Anstey, Leicestershire
Printed and bound in Great Britain by
T. J. International Ltd., Padstow, Cornwall

To Ralph,
For being the music to my song

1

There were many things that might have changed the eventual outcome of that night.

He could have taken his car to work, instead of leaving it for his wife to use. But then she wouldn't have made it to the school Christmas concert on time. And he knew how important it was for Jake to have at least one parent in the audience when he made his stage debut in the Nativity play. He was that kind of father.

He could have gone to the pub with the other tradesmen. But if it came to a contest between spending time drinking with his workmates, or going home to his beautiful wife, there was no choice. None at all. Even after seven years of marriage he never wanted to miss a single moment of time that could be spent with her. He never would. He was that kind of husband.

He could have ignored the children's pleas for help as he crossed the parkland. He could have told them their dog would find its own way back to safety from the middle of the frozen lake. But once he'd seen the look of terror on the animal's face, as it struggled to pull itself out of the hole, he knew he'd have to rescue it. He was that kind of man.

★　★　★

The girl couldn't have been more than nine years old; the boy looked even younger than his son Jake. They had burst through the trees beside the pathway like two barrelling cannon-balls, grabbing on to him and talking, or rather shouting, incoherently. For one crazy moment, he thought they were trying to rob him. He even imagined himself going home and telling his wife that he'd been mugged by some primary-school children, and by the way, darling, how was *your* day? But it wasn't his money they were after, he quickly realised that, although for several moments he was no closer to understanding what they did want of him, because they were both crying hysterically.

'Whoa, slow down there. What's wrong?' he asked, directing his question at the young girl.

'Please, can you help us? Marty and Todd are in trouble. Can you come?' The girl was tugging on his arm and trying to pull him off the path and through the narrow copse of snow-covered trees. The man knew this park well, he'd visited it many times as a child, played football matches here as a teenager, and used it regularly as a shortcut to and from the housing development site where he was currently working. There was nothing beyond the trees except a large boating lake which bordered the park. He felt a chill run through him that had nothing to do with the falling temperature.

'Calm down,' he instructed, resisting the surprisingly strong pull on his arm. 'Take a breath, tell me what happened. Who are Marty and Todd, and where are they?'

The girl answered, tears coursing down her face as she spoke so fast it seemed as though each word had run straight into the back of the one which came before, like a verbal pile-up.

'Marty is our big brother. We were playing with Todd by the lake, and I told Marty that it wasn't safe, but he said it was okay and then Todd ran backwards and he ended up in the middle of the lake and it was okay for a minute because it's all frozen over but then it cracked and he fell in and he couldn't get out, so Marty went to help him, and then he fell in as well.'

'Show me where they are,' the man commanded, already breaking into a run and heading towards the trees. The children, slightly calmer now they'd found an adult to take charge of the situation, were close at his heels. 'Are you here with anyone, a parent or someone?' he asked, his words emerging sharp and staccato from his mouth, accompanied by a cloud of billowing vapour. Mentally he was already berating the adults who had allowed these children to be in such danger. He would never in a million years let Jake go to the park without either of them being with him. His over-protectiveness drove his wife crazy at times, but just look what could happen when you let them go out by themselves. They ended up falling into a frozen lake.

Hang on, boys, the man silently urged. *I'm coming.*

The man burst through the trees and onto the edge of the frozen lake. Instinctively he threw both arms out to either side and braced them, to

3

prevent the children running alongside him from skidding down the small snowy incline and onto the ice.

'There they are!' exclaimed the girl, extending a trembling arm as she indicated two spots some fifteen metres from where they stood, where the thin ice had cracked open and Marty and Todd had slipped through into the freezing water.

The man's eyes darted between the two holes in the ice, rapidly assessing the situation. It was bad, but thankfully not as bad as he'd first feared. From the furthest hole there came a volley of short sharp yelping barks, as Todd saw the return of his human family. But it was the other hole that concerned the man, where a young boy, who looked about eleven years old, was struggling to keep his elbows on the edge of the precarious jagged rim of ice. He was crying and clearly terrified, yet he still kept glancing behind him at the other hole, where his pet was splashing in the freezing water, trying to stay afloat.

'Hang on, son. Keep your elbows on the ice and try not to kick too much. I'm coming to get you,' the man urged, pulling off his heavy parka jacket and throwing it down on the snow-covered bank.

The boy's face was alabaster-white with fear, the freckles on his nose, a distant memory of summer, stood out like brown splatters of paint on a blank canvas. 'Pl-please get Todd f-first,' the boy begged through chattering teeth. 'He's been in the water longer than me.'

The man didn't reply, not wanting to agitate

the boy further, although he did spare another glance at the dog struggling frantically in the ice-cold water, trying to reach the jagged edges of the hole, which resembled razor-sharp teeth set in bone-white jaws. The jaws of death. The man shuddered.

'People first, dogs second,' he said as he stepped carefully off the bank with its powdery white snow, and onto the slippery glass-like surface of the water. Cautiously he lowered his weight onto one foot, preparing for instant retreat if the ice should groan or crack beneath him. It stayed silent and solid so he pressed on.

Fifteen metres. It felt more like fifteen miles. After two or three steps he could feel a change beneath the soles of his heavy work-boots. What had initially felt skating-rink solid, now had a definite spongy spring beneath his weight. He paused, glanced back at the two children on the bank, and gave them a quick reassuring smile. Very slowly he lowered himself down, first into a crouch, then onto all fours before finally sliding forward until he was completely horizontal on the ice. Spread the weight, he told himself, rapidly trying to recall what other advice he might have picked up over the years for people attempting this kind of thing. The only one that seemed to come to mind was: *don't do it*. He blew the air noisily out through his mouth and gritted his teeth.

He crawled slowly on his stomach to the boy, fighting the urge to hurry, knowing the ice was capricious and cunningly deceitful. It felt like hours, but it could only have been minutes

5

before he was close enough to grab hold of one of his woollen-mittened hands in his own.

'Hold on tight,' he instructed, wrapping his fingers firmly around the young boy's bony wrists for better purchase. 'We'll have you out of there in no time.' It was a promise he prayed he could keep. He braced himself, and even the dog fell silent, as though he too had realised the importance of the moment. The man pulled as hard as he could, trying to ignore the worry of dislocations or injury on the sharp edges of the ice. They could be fixed. If the boy slipped from his grip now and sank beneath the icy surface, he might be beyond his help.

The boy flew out of the water like a fish on a line. From the bank he heard the younger children cheer in delight. The man gritted his teeth. They weren't home free yet.

'C-can we g-get Todd now?'

The man shook his head briefly as he began to inch them backwards towards the bank. 'Let's get you back on land first. Then we'll worry about your dog,' he replied, hoping the lie would pacify the lad until he had got him to safety. The boy was a sodden dead weight, despite being thin and gangly. There was no flesh on him, and the danger of hypothermia in a body this slight was all too real.

There were very few moments in his life when the man had felt such relief as he did when he finally pulled the boy off the ice. Perhaps the closest had been in the delivery room, when he was told the two people he cared about most in the world were alright. The man plucked up his thickly quilted coat and wrapped it around the shivering boy, rubbing his hands briskly up and down the length of his quivering frame, to bring back the circulation.

'Are you okay? Can you breathe alright? Is anything hurt?' the man questioned, already pulling his phone from the pocket of his quilted jacket.

'No. Just cold,' said the boy through blue-tinged lips. 'Thank you. You're going back for Todd now, aren't you?'

The call connected to the emergency services, and he held up his hand to stall his reply as he requested an ambulance. But his eyes gave away his answer unknowingly. He always had been a terrible liar. The two younger children huddled around their brother, all three looking towards the remaining member of their family, who was still in peril. They spoke hurriedly in urgent whispers, yet still the man was slow to realise what was happening. It was only when he saw Marty shrug off his enveloping coat that he realised his intentions.

'You're not going to help Todd get out of the water, are you?' the boy asked, his voice shaky. Three young faces looked up at him, each urgently pleading for him to deny it.

'He's a dog,' the man said, already realising the futility in trying to make them understand.

'*Of course* he's a dog,' replied the youngest child with a disparaging look, his voice scornful. 'But you got Marty out, why can't you get Todd?'

Their eyes bored into him, like miniature

Spanish Inquisitors. The man looked back to the ice and realised the animal's valiant efforts seemed to be diminishing by the moment as he grew increasingly colder and weaker. Large chunks of ice broke off beneath his scrabbling paws whenever he got close to the edge, plunging him back into the freezing depths time and time again.

'He'll find his own way out,' the man said, with a reassurance he did not feel. 'Dogs are clever like that. Just give him a minute.'

The boy he had just rescued looked at him with unmistakable disappointment. 'You *have* to help him, or he's going to drown or freeze to death,' he declared, with dire and unshakeable certainty. 'And if *you're* not going to get him out, then I will.' He moved towards the edge of the frozen lake.

The man caught him easily. His cold bony body struggled against the restraining arm.

'Or I will,' said his determined sister, stepping much closer to the edge of the ice than was wise.

'Or me,' added the youngest.

The man gave a sound of desperation. He could stop one of them, but not all three.

'Todd!' cried the wriggling boy in his arms. The children gasped in unison as their pet slipped beneath the surface of the water. After ten agonising seconds his small furry head reappeared, and that was the moment when the man knew he had no choice, because he'd seen the look of defeat in the animal's eyes. He was giving up.

'Damn it,' muttered the man, looking around

for another solution, another adult, another option, but there was none. He knew what he was about to do was a really bad idea, but what was the alternative? The ice had held him before, it would do so again. He hoped.

He turned to the three children who were now all crying. He laid a strong and steady hand on the shoulders of the older two. 'Okay. Listen carefully. I'm going to try and help Todd, but I will only do this on one condition.' Three bobbing heads already promised they would gladly agree to whatever he asked of them. 'No one, and I repeat *no one* is to take even so much as one single step onto this ice. No one except me. Is that understood? Whatever happens, you three are to stay right where you are until I get back. Promise?' Their eyes were wide as marbles with terror, but once again they nodded. The man took one last hopeful glance over his shoulder, but he didn't really expect to find anyone else walking by the lake at this time of day. He glanced skyward. It was going to be dark in less than fifteen minutes; if he was going to do this crazy thing at all, then he didn't have much time.

He stepped back onto the ice.

★ ★ ★

The taxi dropped him off at the corner, a short walk from the department store.

'Is here okay, mate?' The man glanced up from the screen, where he had just been checking his emails. The Oxford Street pavements were

9

heaving with last-minute Christmas shoppers, which was only to be expected given that the holiday was less than a week away.

'Yes, that's fine,' murmured the man, snapping shut his phone case and distractedly pulling a note from his wallet. He never even glanced at the fare displayed on the cab's meter, just handed over his money, with an automatic 'Keep the change'.

The cabbie smiled at the generous tip, and quickly pocketed the money in case the man might have selected the wrong colour note by mistake. 'Happy Christmas, mate,' he added, as the man straightened from his window. The man just nodded, his attention now all on what had caught his eye when they'd pulled up at the corner. Outside the department store he was bound for there was a small brass band, or orchestra or ensemble (he never *did* manage to work out what the difference was). Whatever it was called, there were people with an assortment of musical instruments, positioned in a large semi-circle behind music stands, following the wildly enthusiastic arm gesticulations of their conductor. The sound of Christmas carols filled the street, drowning out the London traffic and making even those who chose not to stop and listen walk past with a nostalgic smile.

He began to walk towards the store, hampered by the flow of the crowds. But after only twenty metres, an uncomfortable tight and breathless sensation hit him like a small fiery comet right in the middle of his chest. It was so sudden and unexpected he drew to an abrupt halt, causing a tattooed pierced man in a leather jacket walking two paces behind to cannon right into him.

'You can't fucking do that in the middle of the street,' the tattooed man snapped, clearly not at all affected by the wave of Christmas good cheer that was infecting the assembled crowds from the music.

'Sorry,' muttered the man, more worried by the disturbing recurrence of this unexplained symptom than he was by the man's anger. He was definitely coming down with something. This was the third time this had happened in the last couple of days. He reached out and laid a supporting hand on a nearby lamppost and waited for the feeling to pass. It was cold; the forecast had threatened snow showers for the afternoon and evening, yet he suddenly felt incredibly hot. He had to resist the urge to tear off his expensive woollen topcoat and the jacket of his suit. He lifted his free hand and ran it across his mouth and upper lip, and wasn't surprised at all to feel the small beads of perspiration that had broken out there. Bugger it. He must be coming down with that flu bug that had been doing the rounds at the office. Just his damn luck to catch something right before the Christmas break. Well, he still had just over a week before they were due to fly — that should give him plenty of time to get over it. He smiled, and patted his inside pocket where the airline tickets to New York — his wife's surprise Christmas present — were hidden. She had been wanting to go back for ages, but he'd always made an excuse and put it off. But what was the point of working as hard as the pair of them did, if you couldn't just blow the schedule, and treat yourself once in a while? He smiled again, imagining the look on her face when she saw what he had done. He'd booked them into the fanciest hotel, got great seats for a Broadway show and was prepared to sit by patiently and let her sight-see or shop to her heart's content. And if that wasn't true love, then he didn't know what was.

In less than a minute the weird feeling in his chest had passed. He reminded himself to pick up a packet of paracetamols when he was in the store and slipped once more into the flow of foot traffic. There was a throng of people around the musical group, some were even singing along. It made reaching the glass revolving doors of the store a more lengthy procedure, forcing him to stand and wait his turn for several moments. His back was to the group, he wasn't a musician — far from it — but when the trumpet notes sounded out loud and clear behind him, he instantly recognised the instrument. He felt once more that familiar compulsion, which even after all these years he could never resist. His head turned and his eyes went straight to the person playing the gleaming brass instrument. It was involuntary, a reflex; he did it every time he was at a show, a concert, or any live performance. It was as though the strains of the instrument called him like a siren song which he was powerless to ignore. He'd done it for years, he probably always would. His eye lifted to the face of the musician playing the instrument on the

12

bustling London street. It wasn't her. It never was.

The curtain of hot air blasting down from the overhead vents as he entered the store made him feel like he was entering a greenhouse. The smell of a hundred different perfumes and cosmetics swirling above the shoppers in a cloying cocktail of fragrances just compounded that. For a moment he regretted his decision to come shopping in the middle of the day, but his diary was full of meetings and appointments right up until the office officially shut down for the holiday season, and this was the only free time he had over the next few days.

He was propelled away from the entrance on a wave of shoppers and went with the flow, until he found the section he was looking for. There were undoubted advantages in being over six foot tall, and being able to see over the heads of a crowd was definitely one of them. He managed to successfully weave among the ditherers and browsers, avoided being sprayed with some cologne he had no interest in sampling, and found the counter with the jewellery concession he wanted.

He was looking for one last Christmas gift for his wife, to join the collection of glossy bags that were already hidden at the back of his wardrobe. They were both guilty of going a little over the top for birthdays, anniversaries and, of course, at Christmas too. It would be easy to say that they did this because they were over-compensating for the thing that was missing from their lives, but the truth was much simpler than that. He just liked spoiling her.

He stood before the sparkling array of designer jewellery that was securely locked away within a glass cabinet. He'd been quietly pleased with himself for having remembered her casually commenting that she liked this particular range a few months ago. But he hadn't been expecting there to be such a vast selection to choose from. He was going to need some help.

'Can I help you?'

He looked up and smiled at the female assistant, who in turn took in the tall, extremely good-looking man with the piercing blue eyes standing at her station, and returned his smile with added interest. The man genuinely didn't notice the way she stepped a little closer to the counter or the slight dilation of her pupils as she looked at him. He wasn't arrogant or conceited, but her reaction wasn't unusual. Women were drawn to him; he'd never had to work hard in that department. *Except for once*, a voice he tried never to listen to reminded him. He doused the spark of the memory, the way you would a fire, instantly and thoroughly before it had a chance to catch. Damn that trumpet in the band, he thought irritably.

'Yes, please. If you could. I'm looking for a gift for my wife.'

The disappointment on her face was just visible before she dipped her head. 'What exactly were you thinking of? We have some lovely necklaces and bracelets that have just come in. Would you like to start there?' The man nodded with a small helpless shrug, and the assistant laughed. 'Don't worry, we help lots of husbands pick out a special gift for their wives. I'm sure we'll find something that's just perfect for her.'

Fifteen minutes later he was no closer to making a decision. He absently ran a finger inside the collar of his shirt as he bent low to study the jewellery laid out on a blue velvet cloth. It seemed to be getting incredibly warm in the store, and he wondered if the heat had just been ramped up. In addition, the high-voltage lamp hanging low over the counter to showcase the jewellery was beating down with scorching intensity on his head. He had broken out in a hot sweat, drenching his entire body in clammy perspiration, and really wished he'd stopped to buy himself those paracetamols before doing his shopping. He was sure he would have felt better by now, if only he'd have popped a couple of those.

He had a sudden pressing desire to get out of the overcrowded, over-warm and over-priced store. He wanted — no, *needed* — fresh air, cold fresh air. He could feel a pulse pounding rapidly in his neck, and when he spoke it was a real effort to draw up enough oxygen to breathe at the same time.

'I'll take that one,' he said, jabbing his finger randomly at one of the necklaces.

'Certainly,' said the assistant lifting it up from the surrounding items. 'Would you like it gift-wr — ' She broke off, her voice suddenly full of concern. 'Are you feeling alright?'

He tried to find a reassuring smile, but the effort triggered a curious shooting pain in his jaw. 'I'm fine,' he lied, bracing one arm on the counter, because all at once he didn't trust that his legs were up to the job of supporting him. 'It's just a little warm in here.'

'Can I get you a glass of water or something?'

The man nodded his reply, wanting to conserve the breath in his lungs, which seemed to be struggling to do their job. *What kind of flu is this?* he thought worriedly.

He never even heard the woman ask one of her colleagues to fetch a glass of water, because he was far too concerned with not keeling over right there in the aisle, and making a total spectacle of himself in front of the hordes of shoppers.

'There's a chair over there,' the assistant volunteered, lightly touching her hand to his elbow and gesturing to a red velvet-covered seat beside the adjacent counter.

'No, that's okay,' he answered, unaware his words were coming out through lips that were rapidly turning more blue than pink. Now she was *really* worried.

'Would you like me to call the manager? He could make an announcement and see if there's a doctor in the store?'

'God, no,' said the man fervently. 'It's just a touch of flu. It'll pass in a minute.'

The woman looked highly doubtful and glanced around to see if his water had arrived. But there was no one to be seen except the shoppers, bustling and jostling against each other like koi carp at feeding time.

'Here,' the woman said, diving beneath the counter and producing her own handbag. 'Have

16

this, I haven't opened it yet'. She pulled a small bottle of water from the depths of her bag and passed it across the counter.

'Thank you,' muttered the man weakly. It was a struggle to break the seal with one hand still occupied supporting his weight, but eventually the flimsy plastic tag snapped free, sending the bottle top flying through the air. He never did drink from it, though, because as he shakily lifted the bottle to his lips, a heavy crushing pain suddenly constricted his chest. It felt like a solid steel belt was being cinched tighter and tighter around him. Grey spots danced before his eyes and his hand simply released the bottle, splashing a small torrent down onto the jewellery display. The man hit the floor at just about the same time as the small plastic container.

Ally

They say the sense of smell is the most evocative of all the senses for conjuring up emotions and memories. I think I agree with that. Because for me the smell of chicken nuggets will forever be intrinsically bound up with bad news. Actually, perhaps I should clarify that, not chicken nuggets, but *burnt* chicken nuggets. They were under the grill, one side golden brown, the other side almost there when the knock came at my door. For a second I thought he had forgotten his keys, but then I remembered him separating them from the fob that held the car keys that morning.

I could see two silhouetted shadows beyond

the frosted glass of the front door. I glanced around for my purse. It was a little early in the evening for carol singers, and the shapes standing on my doorstep were quite tall, but these days when they were out of school uniform most teenagers looked like adults. They weren't teenagers, and they weren't carol singers either. But they were in uniform. As soon as I opened the door they both reached up and took off their hats, in perfect unison, as though they had practised it like synchronised swimmers in the police academy. Why do they do that, some abstract part of my mind wondered, even while I could feel one hand rising to my throat, as though preparing to stifle a cry. My other hand was already gripping the door jamb for support.

'Mrs Taylor?'

I nodded.

'Mrs Alexandra Taylor?' And why did they do that? Why two questions instead of one? Why waste time when it was obvious I was the person they'd come calling for, by the blood that was rapidly draining from my face.

'What's wrong? Is it Joe? Has something happened?' What a stupid question; of course something had happened. It was there in their eyes, in the hats tucked neatly beneath their arms, in the pause they took before answering.

'I'm afraid there's been an accident,' the taller and slightly older officer began. I looked at the second man standing beside him, as though he might have different news, but he was just look-ing uncomfortable and decidedly nervous. I could tell this was the first time that he'd done this.

18

'But *I* have the car,' I said stupidly, because that was always my fear when the roads were icy.

'Not a car accident,' the policeman said gently, as though the bad news might somehow have diminished my mental capacity. Actually, it probably had. 'May we come in?' I wanted to say no, because I didn't want any of this to be real. I wanted to shut the door — slam it even — in their young sympathetic faces and tell them they had the wrong house, the wrong woman, the wrong man.

I staggered back into the hallway and they followed me, one of them reaching out to grasp my elbow to steady me.

'Joe. What's happened to him? What sort of an accident? Is he . . . '

'Your husband is alive. He's been taken to St Elizabeth's hospital. Our latest information is that his condition is listed as critical; and he's still unconscious.'

The smell of burning breadcrumbs filtered from the kitchen into the hall, permeating the almost incomprehensible words.

'The paramedics successfully resuscitated him at the scene, but obviously we're unclear at this time how long he wasn't breathing.'

Joe, not breathing? This had to be some sort of horrible mistake. Joe did good breathing. A little noisy at night sometimes, but I kind of liked that. He was an *excellent* breather.

'I don't understand. What's happened to my husband?' I cried, gripping the officer's blue-jacketed arms as though I wanted to shake the answer out of him.

'I'm sorry, we should have explained. I am afraid technically he drowned, Mrs Taylor,' was the totally inconceivable reply.

Somewhere, far in the distance, the kitchen smoke alarm began to peal.

Charlotte

'*Raging Poppy* or *Scarlet Harlot?*' asked the manicurist with a small grin. I studied the two bottles on the table in front of me. My hand hovered back and forth above them, before plucking up the darker red shade. 'I think a trip to the Big Apple deserves a bold colour like this one,' I decided, handing it over.

'You're *sooo* lucky,' she sighed, shaking the varnish as vigorously as any cocktail bar tender. 'I'll be surprised if I get anything more than a supermarket toiletry set from *my* boyfriend. He'd never think of surprising me with a holiday.'

I wriggled in my seat, a little embarrassed that I had blurted out my secret to a girl I hardly knew, who I only saw on my regular visits to the salon. But I had to tell somebody; I was so excited, I just wanted to share it, and I couldn't risk it getting back to David that I'd found the one email he had forgotten to delete confirming the itinerary for my surprise Christmas present. And it wasn't like I was deliberately snooping or anything; I had literally stumbled across it while looking for something else. '*I am not the kind of wife who goes rifling through her husband's inbox. Truly, Your Honour.*' I smiled as I visualised myself held up for charges in the dock. Perhaps once . . . but that was a very long time ago; another lifetime, another me. A small niggling memory emerged from nowhere to pierce my bubble of good humour, dragging me back to a night not that long ago. Just a month or two back, in fact, when the sound of my husband mumbling in his sleep had woken me in the middle of the night. I stiffened involuntarily, causing the manicurist to brush bright red varnish onto the skin around my perfectly oval-shaped nail.

'Sorry,' I murmured. She looked up and managed to hide her look of irritation as she fixed the problem.

I'd been lucky that they had been able to fit me in at such short notice, but I was a regular, so they'd juggled around some appointments for me. At least I didn't have to worry about getting time off work. That's the benefit of owning your own business — the boss is always very reasonable about stuff like that.

I didn't doubt for a minute that David had executed the planning of this holiday down to the last smallest detail. He was a master of organisation in everything he did. He had to be with his job. So there would be no missing documentation, no lapsed travel insurance, no out-of-date passports. But he was still a typical man, who simply wouldn't get the necessity of a mani, pedi and of course a good Brazilian before any self-respecting woman could go away on holiday.

Not that I intended to let him know I'd found out about our post-Christmas trip to New York. He would be crushed if I ruined the surprise, especially as he'd obviously gone to a lot of effort to give me this perfect present. I wasn't going to do anything to spoil the moment for him. Which meant I had spent quite a bit of time in front of the bathroom mirror over the last few days, practising my totally surprised and delighted face, until I was sure I could convey exactly the right blend of astonishment and excitement.

I found myself smiling yet again, as I sat waiting for the first coat of varnish to dry. The manicurist was right: I *was* a lucky girl. I caught a glimpse of my reflection in one of the salon's many mirrors, correction — woman, not girl. When your last birthday took you out of your twenties, you probably couldn't justify hanging on to the title of *girl* for much longer. I looked again at my reflection, and wondered if David was right, that I didn't look my age. My naturally blonde hair was cut in a sharp and stylish style that feathered around my face and followed the line of my jaw. It was subtly highlighted to look as though I had just returned from a fortnight in the sun. I had the time and money to spend on make-up, manicures, spray tans and facials. I knew I looked years younger than many of the women I passed in the street, women who were probably around the same age as me. Women who looked stressed and harried by life as they pushed prams along the pavements, hurrying to get to child-minders or nurseries, tugging impatiently on the hands of small children who seemed totally devoid of any sense of urgency. Lucky, lucky me.

Halfway through the second coat of varnish, the soporific piped background music was interrupted by a jarring ringtone coming from the direction of my feet. I glanced down and saw the sides of my tan leather bag vibrating gently, as though a tiny creature was trapped within it.

'I'm sorry,' I apologised, 'I meant to put it on silent.'

'It's no problem,' assured the manicurist, pausing with her brush in the air before continuing. 'Do you want to get it?'

I shook my head. 'No. It can go to voicemail. I'll just ignore it,' I said.

But the phone wouldn't stop. A few moments after the caller would have been directed to leave a message, it rang again. I frowned at my bag, as though that might be enough to make them go away.

'Are you *sure* you don't want to answer it?' the girl questioned.

I looked down at my brilliant red fingernails, fanned out on the table like the wing tips of an exotic butterfly. I couldn't touch anything for at least ten minutes without ruining them.

'No. Whoever it is can wait,' I declared. But apparently they couldn't, because my handbag remained silent for less than a minute before the phone within it started ringing again.

'I am *so* sorry about this,' I apologised.

The girl stopped to screw on the lid of the clear varnish she had just started to apply. 'Don't worry. It happens all the time. Would you like me to answer it for you, as your nails are still wet?'

There's something a little unsettling about watching another woman go through your handbag, and I was much happier when she had finally extracted the phone and held it within her palm. She peered at the display. 'It's David,' she read 'Is he your — '

'Husband, yes,' I said, biting my lip. He probably assumed I was still at the office, because I hadn't told him I was taking a few hours off to prepare for a trip I wasn't supposed to know about.

'Would you mind just telling him that I'm tied up and that I'll call him back in twenty minutes or so?' David didn't know all the members of my team, so with luck he'd think he was talking to one of the juniors.

'Of course,' she replied, pressing the button to accept the call.

'Don't say anything about where I am,' I whispered just as she opened her mouth to speak. 'And nothing at all about New York,' I added in a panicked rush.

I sat back, feeling guilty, as though I'd been caught out cheating on him or something, which was totally crazy. As if I'd ever do anything like that.

'Hello. No, this isn't her, she can't come to the phone right now, I'm afraid.' A small silence followed, and because I was studying her carefully while she lied to my husband on my behalf, I saw the precise moment when she became aware that something was wrong. The realisation flooded over her face like a blush.

'What is it, what did he say?' I asked urgently.

The manicurist held out the phone to me. 'It's not him, it's some woman.'

There was no reason to think of her name, but in that brief millisecond as I leaned across the table, it was the only one that crossed my mind. The manicurist held the phone to my ear.

'Hello, who is this?' I heard the stiffness in my voice.

'My name is Marie, I work at Sunderson's Department Store. Am I talking to Mrs Williams?'

Even as I heard myself confirming that she was, my brain was scrolling, computer-fast, down a list of possible reasons for this call. It settled on the only one that seemed logical. David must have lost his phone and this woman had found it somewhere. I liked that solution; it made sense.

'Mrs Williams, your husband asked me to call you — '

'He did? I'm sorry. I don't understand,' I interrupted, my theory falling to the floor where it promptly shattered.

'He was in the store, shopping for — well, that's not important — but he . . . he wasn't feeling very well.'

In the time it took for me to jerk my hand up, snatch my phone from the manicurist — smudging all my nails in the process — a series of snapshots flashed through my mind: David pushing aside his meal last night, having scarcely touched it; David needing to stop between flights to get his breath climbing the stairs to our flat;

25

his face as he kissed me goodbye that morning, his colour a little paler than usual.

'Is David there? Can you put him on the phone please?'

'I can't do that right now, Mrs Williams,' the assistant said with a small choked noise, which bizarrely made it sound as though she was crying.

Fear slid over and around me like a cloak. 'Why not? Where is he? Is he there?'

The woman hesitated before replying. 'Yes, he is, but he can't get to the phone right now.'

'Why not?'

'Because the paramedics are with him,' the unknown woman using David's phone continued. 'They're lifting him onto a stretcher right now.'

'Paramedics? Why does he need paramedics?' There was genuine panic in my voice now. 'Why is he on a stretcher? Please, tell me what's happened to him.'

I could hear someone talking in the background, and the woman took a second or two to reply. 'They've just told me they're taking him to St Elizabeth's and that you should meet them there.'

'Why are they taking him to hospital? I don't understand. He's just coming down with the flu or something.'

The woman sounded almost apologetic to have to be the one to break it to me. It was beyond wrong that I was the last one to know. 'I don't think it's the flu, Mrs Williams,' said the woman kindly, 'I don't want to alarm you, but I think your husband may have had a heart attack.'

2

Slow motion. Everything was happening in slow motion. Almost as though *I* was the one under-water. But it wasn't me, was it? That had been Joe, under the water in the middle of the frozen lake. What had he been doing there? How on earth had it happened? The policemen hadn't been able to tell me, which seemed ridiculous, almost negligent in fact. Surely they must have known it would be the first thing I'd ask? Someone should have made it their business to find out.

'Mrs Taylor? Are you alright?'

What a stupid question. Of course I wasn't. 'Yes, yes . . . I'm just . . . I'm . . . '

I felt as though I had literally been plucked out of my calm peaceful evening and dropped into the terrifying depths of someone else's nightmare. This couldn't really be happening, could it? The senior officer had doubtless dealt with many shocked relatives in his time, because he seemed to know exactly what needed to be done. He laid steadying hands on my upper arms and spoke in a firm and measured voice. 'Take a second. Breathe. Then let's get everything sorted out here so we can drive you to the hospital.'

'I . . . I've got the car, Joe's car. I can drive myself.'

'I don't think that's such a good idea,' said the

27

policeman gently. 'You're not in the right frame of mind to get behind a wheel. And besides, we can get you there a lot quicker. No one is going to stop *us* for speeding.'

He was right, the important thing was to get to Joe as fast as possible. He needed me, but even more than that, I needed him, always had and always would. I grabbed my handbag and looked around for my coat, totally incapable of seeing it hanging on the line of hooks on the wall.

The second policeman, who I hadn't even noticed had disappeared, emerged at that moment from my kitchen, and from behind him belched a smoky haze smelling of burned food. 'I've turned everything off, but your dinner was just charcoal,' he advised.

'It's not mine, it's my son's — ' I broke off horrified. 'Jake!' I cried, as though I'd left him in a pram and absent-mindedly gone home without him. How could I have forgotten that he was sitting in the lounge watching television, waiting for dinner, waiting for his dad to get home, waiting for the comforting routine of normality which had shattered in tandem with the ice beneath Joe's feet.

'What do I tell him?' I asked the two men, as though the uniform they wore gave them all the answers. 'Should I take him to the hospital with me?' I saw the undisguised look of sympathy on their faces.

'Is there someone who could stay with him, a family member or a neighbour perhaps?'

My parents were an hour's drive away, and Joe's had retired to the coast several years ago.

We were planning to stay with them in the summer and Joe had already vowed that this was the year he would teach Jake how to swim. '*It's a life skill, and he needs to know how to get himself out of trouble in the water,*' he had declared. A sob tore its way out of my throat. Both officers tactfully said nothing while I fought to regain control.

'Alice, she lives next door, she might be able to help.'

'You go and explain things to your boy and I'll knock next door,' volunteered the officer. 'Which way, left or right?'

As my feet took me unsteadily towards the lounge I could hear a familiar theme tune as Jake's favourite animated TV show began to play.

'Jake,' I began, my voice nowhere near as steady as I wanted it to be. I didn't want to scare him, but it was almost impossible not to, seeing as I was totally terrified myself. *Not breathing.*

'Jake honey, will you turn that off for a minute?' His head spun around as though I had just made the most ridiculous request imaginable. 'I need to talk to you.'

'Can't it wait, Mum? This is my favourite episode,' he said, with that particular wheedling whine that only those under the age of eight can pull off effectively.

I glanced at the screen. 'You've seen this one already, and I need to talk to you. I have something important I need to tell you.'

Reluctantly his small stubby fingers jabbed on the mute button. 'Is this about Father Christmas?' he asked, in an anxious tone. 'Because Tommy Jackson in my class said his mum told

29

him that he wasn't real. You're not going to say that, are you? He *is* real, isn't he?'

I looked into his trusting blue eyes and felt something slice through me. *Don't you do this to us, God,* I said almost belligerently, *don't you break his heart, don't you dare.*

'Yes, Jakey, of course he's real,' I said, using the nickname he had only recently told me he was now much too grown up to be called. I knelt down beside him on the slightly worn carpet and tried to pull him onto my lap. He offered a token resistance, squirming eel-like for a moment, all bony little arms and elbows, before nestling in the familiar dip of my body.

I raised a hand and smoothed back the long dark hair from his eyes. He needed a haircut. I'd been meaning to book him one for weeks at my hairdresser's, but I knew he was hoping that Joe would take him for something far more trendy — which I would probably hate — at the local barber shop. I squeezed him a little tighter than I should have.

'Jake, I have to go out for a little while,' I said gently.

He stopped trying to see what Bart Simpson was silently doing on the screen and turned to me in surprise. 'Now?' he queried. 'But it's almost supper time.'

I nodded and had to swallow several times before I could continue. 'I know, sweetie, but Alice from next door is going to sit with you and I'm sure if we ask her she'll make you something nice to eat.'

'But where are you going? You never go out at this time. You're not teaching a lesson are you?'

He knew my schedule almost as well as he knew the programme times of his favourite shows. I gave private music lessons three evenings a week, but mostly the students came to our house. It was easier that way.

'No Jake. I have to go to the hospital.'

'Why Mummy? Are you sick?' he shot back, his voice full of worried concern. *See God, see what will happen. Take it back. Take it all back right now before it's too late. Let there have been a horrible mistake; let it have been another Joe Taylor who had done something so ridiculous as to try to cross a frozen lake. Not our one.*

'No Jakey, It's not me. It's Daddy. He's had . . . he's had a little accident and he's gone to hospital so they can make him better.'

'What kind of accident?'

'He . . . he fell on some ice.' Not quite a lie, but certainly not the whole truth. Jake didn't need to know that. Not yet.

'But he's alright, isn't he?'

Not breathing.

'Oh I'm sure he's going to be just fine,' I said, the lie burning my throat, my tongue and my lips on its way out. 'But I need to go and see him and . . . and they don't let children in the ward he is in.' I added another lie to the pile. 'So Alice will stay with you, and after I've checked Daddy is okay I'll come back home and tell you how he is.'

I heard a click and looked up. Alice Mathers, my next-door neighbour, was standing in the doorway. She was still wearing her fluffy pink carpet slippers and an old-fashioned apron with a frilly edge that she always wore when cooking.

31

She was trying very hard not to cry, and was mostly succeeding.

'Hello, Jake. Do you mind if I come and sit here with you?' she asked, crossing over to the two of us. She didn't say a word to me, she didn't need to. She picked up my hand and squeezed it tightly. 'Go,' she mouthed.

My own eyes began to water and for just a moment we stared helplessly at each other. 'I don't know how long I'll be,' I apologised.

She shooed my words away. 'You'll be as long as you need to be,' she said brusquely. 'Don't you worry about us. We'll be fine.' She glanced at the flickering animation on the television. 'Jake and I will just see what mischief this Bert boy has got himself into, and then we'll fix something to eat.'

'Bart. His name is Bart,' Jake corrected with a giggle.

My smile was watery. Alice was great with him. She had three grandchildren and the youngest was about the same age as our son, so she always knew just the right things to do and say.

'Okay Jake, I'm going now,' I said, hugging him tightly and kissing him on the cheek. He squirmed away and jumped with gusto onto the settee cushions as though it was a trampoline. Joe was always telling him off about that.

Not breathing.

'Bye Mummy. Wish Daddy better.'

I nodded fiercely.

'Phone from the hospital,' whispered Alice giving me just one brief hard hug. It was as though she knew my brittle nerves couldn't withstand a lengthy one. 'Joe's fit and strong, he'll get through this,' she said huskily. I bit my lip so hard I could taste the coppery tang of tiny bloody droplets when I swallowed.

The policemen were waiting for me in the hallway. 'All ready?'

'Yes, please can we hurry?'

But before I was out of the door I was stopped by a cry from my son. 'Wait Mummy, wait.' He thundered up the stairs, and across the upstairs hall, making the entire ceiling vibrate from his pounding little feet. He reappeared moments later and barrelled down the staircase and into me. My arms flew around him as he thrust a very dog-eared and much-loved plush toy lion into my arms. It was the toy he still needed to sleep with; the one we had to hide when friends came round to play, or during sleepovers. But the one that had to be carefully packed in every holiday suitcase, and tucked firmly under his arm and beneath his chin each night.

'Take Simba to Daddy. He always helps when I feel sick. Simba will make Daddy better, I know he will.'

I cradled the small, slightly grubby toy in my arms all the way down the path, into the waiting police car and through the streets which flashed by in a blur as we raced towards the hospital.

Charlotte

I jumped to my feet. 'I have to go.'

I was halfway to the door before I realised I

had picked up none of my belongings and had absolutely no idea where the hospital was, much less how I was going to get there. Fortunately the salon staff sprang into action, and one of them even went out into the lightly falling snow to hail me a taxi, while the girl who had been painting my nails retrieved my coat, and helped me into it.

Still in a daze I pulled three twenty-pound notes from my bag and thrust them into her hand. 'I don't know if that covers everything,' I said.

'Don't worry about it. We can sort it all out next time,' she assured, walking me to the door. 'And try not to worry, I'm sure your husband is going to be just fine. My dad had triple by-pass surgery after his heart attack last year, and he's doing really well now.'

I know she was trying to reassure me, but as I ran towards the waiting black cab, I found her words more worrying than comforting. Her father was probably in his late fifties or early sixties, but David was only thirty-one. He took good care of himself, ate sensibly, didn't smoke and used his gym membership two or three times each week. Heart disease shouldn't be knocking on our door for many more decades, if at all.

Infuriatingly the traffic was heavy and the roads were congested on the route to the hospital. We'd been stuck in a bumper-to-bumper jam for nearly five minutes, and if I'd had even the vaguest notion of where the hospital was located, I would have fled the cab and run full pelt through the snow-flecked streets to get to him. Instead I leant forward and rapped on the glass partition.

'I need to get to the hospital really quickly. Is there another route you can take?'

'You're not having a baby back there, are you?' quipped the cabbie with a cheeky grin. He had no idea that his irreverent jest was going to be my tipping point, but he got it soon enough as he witnessed my face contort as the tears I had been trying to suppress managed to find a way out. The irony of his words was as black as the paintwork of his cab.

'My husband has had a heart attack,' I replied, the tremor in my voice matched only by my trembling lower lip. 'I really need to get to the hospital urgently.'

'Blimey love. I'm sorry. I was just kidding with you. I had no idea this was a real emergency.'

He sat up a little straighter in his seat and gripped the wheel more firmly beneath his nicotine-stained fingers. I guess there are two things cab drivers are just itching to hear: *Follow that cab* and *It's an emergency*.

'You might want to buckle up, back there,' the driver advised as he swung the cab down a narrow side street.

I scarcely noticed our breakneck journey through the winding London streets. My mind was too full of David. How could this be happening to him, to us? Every time I closed my eyes I tried to imagine my strong and energetic husband rendered so weak and incapable that he had to be lifted onto a stretcher and into the back of an ambulance. It was incongruous and my fear-frozen brain just couldn't equate that image with the man who had carried me over his shoulder and into our bedroom just last week, dropping me squarely into the centre of our queen-sized bed. 'I thought we were going out?' I had said, watching as he tugged off his tie, quickly cast aside his shirt and unzipped his custom-made suit trousers. 'I've lost my appetite,' he had growled hungrily, as he lowered himself on top of me. 'But luckily only for food,' he had added, nibbling at the curve of my neck in the way that he knew drove me absolutely crazy.

How could he have gone from that passionate strong man to someone who had to be carried out of a department store in less than seven days? It made no sense.

I don't think I have ever been more grateful to see anything than I was to spot the first blue road sign with the large white letter H in its centre. 'Two minutes more,' the cab driver confirmed, glancing back at me over his shoulder, which considering the speed he was driving he probably shouldn't be doing. We pulled in at the main entrance to Accident and Emergency and, as thankful as I was that we had finally arrived, I was strangely reluctant to step out of the cab. Once I left it and walked through those sliding glass double doors it was all going to be real. David would be a patient; a sick person lying in a high metal-framed bed; a name written up in scrawling handwriting on a whiteboard in a ward. He wouldn't be just mine;

it would no longer be just the two of us.

'I can't really stop here,' prompted the cab driver regretfully. 'This bay is only for the ambulances to drop off.' As if in confirmation one pulled in directly in front of us, its siren still wailing.

'Sorry,' I said, reaching for the door handle with a hand that was visibly trembling and stepped out into the cold afternoon, surprised to find that the day was already turning dark.

A paramedic ran around to the back of the ambulance that had just arrived and flung wide its doors. I felt my entire body stiffen in fear as I craned my neck, trying to see who was about to be lifted from within it. A small clutch of medical staff burst out of the building and slid into action in the way I had seen on countless television hospital dramas. Only this time it wasn't just make-believe. This time someone's life really was hanging in the balance. Was it David's? I felt sick and giddy and that wasn't just because I was holding my breath fearfully as the patient was lifted down and then speedily trundled through the snow and into the hospital.

As they ran I caught a few snippets of their rapidly barked-out assessment. 'Hypothermic male aged . . . ' ' . . . frozen ice . . . ' ' . . . vital signs . . . ' ' . . . core temperature . . . '

The only thing I could make out of the heavily cocooned figure, swaddled in red blankets on the stretcher, was a thatch of sandy-blond hair. It wasn't David.

'Are you going to be okay on your own? Have you got someone meeting you here? Would you

37

like me to park up and come in with you?'

The cab driver's kind words almost set me off again. 'No. Thank you though, that was really thoughtful of you. But I'll be fine.' I added a mental postscript, *or I will be as soon as I know he's okay.*

It was the first time I had ever seen a London cabbie look apologetic for the size of the fare, but I paid it without a second thought. 'Good luck to you and your husband,' he said gruffly and patted my hand awkwardly as he passed me my change.

I could still feel him watching me as I walked through the doors into the Accident and Emergency department. It was only the sound of an approaching siren, heralding the arrival of another new casualty, that prompted him to re-start his engine and pull away.

My legs were trembling so much as I approached the main reception desk it felt like I'd just spent half an hour on a cross-trainer. But no amount of exercise had ever made my heart pound so much I could scarcely hear past its throb in my ears, or cover the palms of my hands in an unpleasant sweaty film. Fear was the only thing that could do that. And I was terrified. My torture was prolonged just that little bit longer because both of the receptionists were busily engaged on telephone calls and although I was only kept waiting for a minute or two, by the time one of them did replace her handset and look up, my anxiety levels had rocketed right off the scale. *Was I already too late?*

'I'm sorry to have kept you waiting. Can I help you?'

At last. The shaky voice that came out of my throat was so far removed from my usual tone, I could scarcely recognise it as my own. 'I had a call to say that my husband — David Williams — was being brought here by ambulance. Could you tell me where I can find him, please?'

I'm sure the woman wasn't being deliberately slow, but it seemed to take her an agonisingly long time to type David's name into the hospital's computer system and begin her search. 'Sorry, we have a new IT program that we're still getting to grips with,' she explained, as she waited for the screen before her to respond. I was good with computers, it was part of my job, and it was all I could do to stop myself from yanking the keyboard towards me in an attempt to speed up the process myself. I wasn't usually this way, but stress can do funny things to a person when someone you love is in danger.

Finally her screen flickered back with an answer. I stared intently at the woman as her eyes scanned the information. Lines of text were reflected in the lenses of her spectacles, but there was no way I could decipher them. What wasn't hard to make out however was the sudden sobering of her face as she verified David's status. It was suddenly getting much harder to breathe.

'Mrs Williams, your husband was brought in with a suspected MI. He was brought into A&E and is currently about to be moved up to ICU.'

Did no one use full words in a hospital any more — was it all just acronyms? But I still understood what she was saying, far better than I wanted to.

'Can I see him?'

She frowned, as though what I was asking presented a problem, and beneath the fear and terror a spark of anger flared. No one was going to keep me from David's side, no matter what hospital rules or protocol I broke to get there.

'Normally we ask relatives to wait until the patient has been transferred and settled into the Intensive Care ward,' she explained. Then she saw my face. 'But let me see if I can get someone to take you through to triage before he's moved.'

'Thank you,' I murmured gratefully.

The receptionist picked up the phone and punched some numbers into the keypad. I strained my ears, trying uselessly to hear whatever was being said, which was made much harder by the arrival of a family group at the desk beside me. I glanced up at a husband and wife who had their arms protectively around their three young children, each of whom was crying noisily.

'Let me just ask this nice lady if she can tell us anything,' said the man to the oldest boy, who had a blanket draped around him, and strangely was the one making the most noise. 'It's not your fault, Marty. You're not to blame, but you need to hush now.'

He most certainly did, I thought, briefly wondering if it was an elderly relative they were here for. Then all thoughts of the group beside me were instantly abandoned as my own receptionist smiled gently. 'Okay, good news, Mrs Williams. Someone will be out in just a moment to take you to him.'

'Thank you. Thank you so much,' I said on a small broken sob. I caught a look of sympathy on the face of the mother from the family group beside me. We were all victims in this place, and while none of us were actually wounded ourselves, we were all in pain.

I followed a nurse young enough to look like she was wearing a dressing-up outfit for a costume party through to the area where David had been taken. I'd always felt far happier when the medical staff looked old enough to have been doing this for more than just a few months. I was hoping whichever doctor was looking after David was positively ancient.

If it hadn't been for the nurse who was walking directly in front of me, I would have walked straight past David's bed. But in fairness when I had last seen him, just eight hours earlier, he hadn't been hooked up with wires, tubes and electrodes to a series of extremely scary-looking machines. He also hadn't been that particular shade of grey that is seldom seen on human skin. There was another nurse stationed at his bedside, who was partially blocking me from David's view as she adjusted the thin lines of plastic tubing that fed into his nostrils. I was glad I had a moment to compose myself and swallow down the disappointed hope that all that had been wrong with him was just a bad case of indigestion. They didn't expend this much effort for something that a couple of antacids could have fixed.

I edged past the nurses. 'Hey, you,' I said. His eyes were closed, but they flickered open

41

when he heard my voice.

'Charlotte,' the voice that was pretending to be David's replied. I knew all of his voices: the professional one; the impatient driver one; the thoughtful son phoning his mother one, and *my* one, the deep sexy burr thickening and lowering his tone when he spoke just to me. And this weak and thin strain wasn't one of his at all. I reached for his hand, hesitating when I saw something that looked like a clothes peg attached to one finger, and then lifted it regardless. His fingers curled around mine, but there was no strength in them.

'Look at you; I leave you alone for just five minutes and find you in bed surrounded by a load of women. Typical.' The nurse on the far side of the bed gave me a quick glimmer of a smile, but the one at the foot of the bed who was scribbling something on David's chart raised her eyebrows, as though my frivolity offended her. *Okay, I don't like you*, I decided. You don't know either of us, nor the deep threads of humour that ran like strands of steel weaving through our relationship, binding us closer together than I could ever have imagined it was possible to feel.

I lifted his hand to my lips and it felt heavy, like I was doing all the work. *Like it was lifeless.* I tried to stop the thought from showing on my face. I kissed his knuckles and I knew my eyes were over-bright and glittering with tears. I furiously blinked them back. 'What happened to you?'

'Your husband collapsed with chest pains,' came the response from the foot of the bed. I

42

ignored her. That much I already knew.

'I just came over really breathless and dizzy,' David supplied, his words an obvious effort as he struggled to breathe and talk simultaneously. Something he'd been able to do just fine only a few hours earlier. 'This damn flu bug is a real killer.' He saw the horror in my eyes and gasped out a reassurance. 'Not literally, sweetheart.'

I saw a look flash between the two female professionals. Neither of them thought this was the flu, and nor did I. 'Have the doctors told you what's wrong yet?' He shook his head, and I could see how much even that small manoeuvre exhausted him.

'He's been scheduled for tests, but first we need to get him upstairs to ICU and stabilised. They'll be able to give you more information as soon as the results are back,' advised Good Nurse.

As they spoke, the nurses began making preparations to detach David from the fixed monitors in the ward and move him onto portable units. The fact that his condition was so precarious he needed to be continually monitored wasn't lost to me. If anything, my anxiety levels were now even greater than they'd been before. A beefy-looking orderly turned up and stood by the bed in readiness for David's move.

'I can come with, can't I?' I asked, not for a moment expecting the answer would be *no*.

'No,' said Bad Nurse, and she didn't even glance my way or offer a reason.

Good Nurse filled the breach. 'I'm so sorry, but for the safety of your husband we can't do that. We aren't allowed to let relatives accompany patients while they're being transferred to the ICU.' She at least sounded genuinely apologetic, but honestly what did they think I was going to do? Get in the way of the stretcher and make it crash? Then I saw the level of professional concern being directed at the man who meant everything to me, and realised they were worried about David *crashing* in a totally different way. Should anything happen to him during the move, they didn't want to be hampered by panicking family members.

'Okay, I understand. But will someone let me know the minute I can come up?'

'Of course we will.'

I looked down at David who, even as sick as he was, looked surprised at my lack of resistance. I wasn't usually one to back down from a confrontation, a fact we both knew only too well. But any comment he might have been about to make was forgotten when he caught sight of the right-hand side of my face.

'What happened to your cheek? You're bleeding,' he asked in wheezy concern.

I raised my fingers gingerly to the area he was looking at with obvious anxiety. It made my heart ache that *he* was the one lying on a stretcher, yet he was still stressing about some silly scratch on my face that I couldn't even feel. I ran my fingertips across the smooth skin of my cheek and felt the lines of dried crusty residue on them. I gave a watery smile.

'Manicuritis Interruptus,' I said, showing him the hand of smudged nails with the same blood-red colour as the marks on my face. He gave a small laugh, or tried to, but it ended in a terrifying moment of watching as he struggled to catch his breath. Whatever those damn tubes up his nose were doing, they certainly weren't giving him enough oxygen. I have to say this for Bad Nurse, she was quick enough when she pulled them free and rapidly replaced them with a full oxygen mask. It was probably less than a minute before David was breathing more comfortably again, but it felt like much longer.

'We need to get him upstairs now,' said my least favourite nurse, but I agreed. *Take him anywhere you want as long as it has all the necessary equipment to make him better, to make him David again.*

'Let's just take this off for a moment so you can kiss him goodbye properly,' said the Good Nurse kindly, lifting the elasticated straps away from David's nose and mouth. I didn't like the words '*kiss him goodbye*'. It sounded terrifyingly prophetic.

I bent down and very gently pressed my lips to his. Our eyes locked as I slowly broke contact. '*You take my breath away*' — the memory of him saying those words to me, just two nights ago suddenly filled my head. We had just made love, and I was lying in the strong circle of his arms, my head resting on his hard muscled chest, listening to the pounding of his heart gradually slowing down. His words had been romantic and tender at the time, now they just sounded like yet another dreadful prophecy.

'I'll be up as soon as they let me,' I promised,

holding his hand even as the bed began to be wheeled away.

'I love you,' said David, his voice muffled and distorted by the mask.

'I love you too,' I replied, as the orderly gave one more push on the bed and our contact was broken. I smiled at him as they wheeled him out of the bay, down the corridor and through a set of double swing doors. I waited until I was sure they were out of earshot, then standing on the tiled rectangle where his bed had stood, I burst into loud and terrified sobs.

Ally

I'd never been in the back of a police car before. Well, why would I? I've never broken the law, never been arrested, never even protested or demonstrated about anything when I was at university, although I knew plenty of people who did. All I could think of as we hurtled through the dark December afternoon was how much Jake would have loved this. He was really into police cars, fire engines and flashing lights and sirens, well at least that was this year's fascination. Last year it had been all about dinosaurs, before that . . . I shook my head and rubbed the bridge of my nose. What did it matter? I was only trying to distract myself from the real reason why I was tearing through thirty-mile-an-hour zones at twice that speed, going through red lights at junctions and overtaking vehicles on the wrong side of the road. Jake would have loved it, every bit as much as I, most definitely, did not.

But the officer had been right, we reached the hospital much quicker than I could ever have achieved. They drove straight into the ambulance bay, the rotating light on the car's roof illuminating an eerie blue sphere around us. I was out of the vehicle even before the driver had pulled on the emergency brake, moving too fast on the slippery pavement. Luckily the second policeman had jumped out almost as quickly, and grabbed on to my elbow when I lost my footing on the dusting of snow in my haste to get inside. Joe was here, somewhere in this monolithic block of concrete and glass he was close by, and his nearness pulled and drew me like an enormous magnet.

'We can come in with you, if you'd like?' the officer volunteered.

I shook my head, aware that a couple of off-duty nurses were glancing our way in curiosity. It had been a far from inconspicuous arrival. 'No, I'll be fine from here, thanks,' I replied, virtually tugging my arm free from his hold. More interest from the nurses. I probably looked as though I was resisting arrest. As grateful as I was to both of them, I wanted nothing more from them, with their solicitous protocol, their sympathetic eyes, and their too-young-to-be-policemen faces. Just being around them made me feel vulnerable, like a victim.

The automatic doors glided silently apart and I dashed through them, heading for the reception desk, anxious not to lose any momentum. A middle-aged woman with large framed glasses looked up from her paperwork as I approached.

'Can I — '

I never even let her finish. *Not breathing*. 'I'm here for Joe Taylor. I think he's in Intensive Care. The police said he'd been in an accident,' I gasped out all on a single breath. My voice shook, actually not just my voice, my entire body was trembling with tension like the latent thrum of electricity in a pylon. Unconsciously I hugged the soft toy Jake had pressed upon me more tightly against my chest. I could smell my child on the flattened and slightly discoloured plush material: a combination of a little bit of bubble bath and talcum powder and a whole lot of Jake. It gave me the strength I needed, like adrenaline into a vein.

The receptionist's eyes were kind behind the moon-shaped lenses of her glasses. 'Let me check for you. He's probably been taken to PICU,' she said drawing her keyboard closer towards her as her fingers rattled in my husband's name.

'P, Q,' I repeated, as though this was an algebra test and that was the answer.

The woman looked up from her typing. 'PICU,' she repeated. 'That's our Paediatric Intensive Care Unit.'

'Paediatric?' I said confused, and then realised her easy mistake. I don't suppose many thirty-year-old women stood before her clutch-ing cuddly toys if they weren't coming to see a child. 'No, it's my husband I'm here for. Joe Taylor. He's thirty-six. I was told he fell through some ice . . . ' My voice trailed away. It was still such an impossible scenario I couldn't quite believe the words I was saying. I nodded down at the toy I was clutching. 'This is our son's. He wants me to give it to his Daddy.' My voice broke and a few determined tears squeezed past my barrier to trickle down my cheeks. Almost seamlessly the receptionist whipped out a concealed box of tissues and passed them to me. I guessed they were needed here on a fairly regular basis.

It seemed an eternity before Joe's details popped up on the monitor. I wondered if the receptionist had ever played poker. She most definitely should take it up, because I could glean nothing at all from her face. 'I'll get someone to come down and talk to you,' she said, already reaching for the phone.

'No. Wait. What does that mean? Is he . . . is he okay?'

'All I have are his admittance details. I can't give you any medical information,' the woman said gently. 'But one of the ICU team will be down to speak to you in just a moment.'

I paced. Fifteen steps to the corner with the vending machine, eight to the Ladies' toilet, twelve to the double doors with the word Triage stencilled on them, and then nineteen more back to the reception desk. My circuit took me past a family waiting in a morose huddle on the uncomfortable plastic chairs. The children looked distraught, and it made me even more relieved that I hadn't subjected Jake to this awful twilight period of not knowing. Kids got scared enough in hospitals as it was, and seven was far too young to have to sit and wait to find out if your father was going to live or —

'Mrs Taylor,' my head shot up at my name and my eyes flew towards the softly-spoken doctor who had just emerged from the lift. His glance ping-ponged between me and the woman with the three children.

'Here,' I said, hurrying towards him.

He smiled, introduced himself and I instantly forgot his name. 'I'm one of the team who are currently looking after your husband,' he explained.

A long shaky breath left my body, like steam venting from a valve. *Looking after your husband*, those four words filled me with relief. Until that moment I hadn't realised how very afraid I'd been that Joe was already beyond help.

'How is he? Can I see him?'

'In a little while I hope to be able to take you to him. Right now my colleagues and I are working very hard to stabilise his condition and to bring his temperature back up.'

As he spoke, the doctor placed a gentle guiding hand on my back, leading me towards a small side room. I didn't want to go in there with him. It looked like the kind of place you were taken when they had bad news to break. The room held a single desk and two visitor chairs. Neither the doctor nor I chose to sit down.

'Have you been told exactly what happened to your husband?'

50

I shook my head. 'Not really. I know he fell through some ice, but I've no idea what he was doing on the lake. I was told that he had to be resuscitated, but if he's breathing then why isn't he awake?'

The doctor's voice was grave. 'At the moment he's breathing with the help of a machine while we try to warm him up.' His tone implied this was altogether more urgent than just covering Joe up with a thick pile of blankets. I wanted to tell him Joe was *never* cold. Not even in winter. We had constant battles over whether the bedroom window should be open or closed, which usually ended with me huddled beneath the depths of our maximum tog duvet, while Joe would have cast aside all the covers. I wanted him to know Joe, to understand him, I wanted him to be more than just a case or a condition, I wanted him to be a real person to the people who were trying to keep him alive.

'I believe relatives deserve to be told the whole truth, Mrs Taylor,' the doctor continued solemnly. Suddenly my knees felt weak and I regretted my decision to stand. 'Your husband's condition is still extremely critical. He's not out of the woods yet.' I looked away, unable to focus on the doctor's face, afraid if I saw even a trace of compassion on it, I would shatter into a million pieces like a thin pane of glass . . . or ice. I focused my attention on a long peeling curl of paint that was hanging from the wooden doorframe.

'But . . . when you get him warm, and he can breathe by himself, he's going to be alright, isn't he? Joe's strong, and fit. He *can* make a full recovery, can't he?'

The doctor missed a beat before replying. I couldn't help but notice that. 'Let's just concentrate on one thing at a time. We've got a long and difficult night ahead of us.'

Charlotte

A police car was just pulling up outside, its siren dying on a long lamenting wail, as it bathed the reception area with a circling strobe of blue light. I was grateful for its diversion as I ducked quickly into the adjacent Ladies' toilets. I splashed cold water on my face and used the rough paper towels to scour off the dried nail varnish from my cheek. The resulting bright red skin made it look as though someone had just slapped me. Hard. It was a look I'd seen there once before, many, many years ago. But it wasn't an angry slap that I was reeling from today, this was a sucker punch, coming out of nowhere to fell me, giving me no time to prepare or defend myself.

I stared at the terrified young woman in the water-spotted mirror in front of me. She looked terrible. Her eyes were red, her nose a shiny beacon and her blonde hair was totally awry. No way was she the same Charlotte Williams who had left her smart London flat that morning, secretly excited about a surprise trip her husband had been planning for her. That woman was gone, and right now I wasn't sure if she was ever coming back.

More for distraction than vanity, I dug around in my bag and pulled out the colourful purse which housed my make-up, intending to repair some of the damage. But my hand shook so much that I fluffed far too much powder onto my cheeks, making me look like a scary geisha, and my mascara wand trembled in such unwieldy fashion, I was in real danger of taking out an eye. I threw the bag down into the sink where it clattered noisily, its contents spilling out in a colourful cascade. I tried to remember the relaxation techniques from the yoga classes I had taken a while back, drawing the air slowly down into my lungs, holding it for a moment and then slowly releasing. But what had felt easy and achievable when I was sitting lotus-style in a mirrored dance studio, wasn't so easy to reproduce in a hospital toilet. I watched the rapid rise and fall of my chest in the mirror above the sink, and heard the erratic sound of panic lacing each indrawn breath. I sounded like I'd been running, maybe even pursued by something dangerous. But in reality the only thing I was trying to get away from was my own fearful imagination. I had just enough layman's medical knowledge to be truly terrified of what might be wrong with David. I scooped the assortment of cosmetics back into my bag and headed once again to the reception area.

There was no one waiting at the desk, and the two receptionists were busily engaged in conversation and didn't initially notice me.

'Did you see the way she was holding that toy lion?'

'I know, it almost broke my heart.'

'And when she said why she'd brought it.'

'I know. It's so hard not getting emotional. No matter how many years I've been doing this, whenever a young child is involved it always gets to me.'

I felt a sharp familiar stab as I accidentally eavesdropped on their conversation and quickly pushed it away. There was more than enough trauma and angst to get through right now, I didn't need to go actively looking for more. I shuffled slightly and the small movement made them look up.

'I'm sorry to interrupt, but they've taken my husband up to Intensive Care and I didn't know where was the best place to wait for him.' By best, I meant closest, which I think they realised.

'There's a cafeteria two floors below the unit, you could wait there,' the bespectacled receptionist suggested. 'We'll let them know where to find you. You look like you could use a good strong coffee,' she added kindly. It would have been rude to point out it was going to take a lot more than just a shot of caffeine to fix the way I felt. In fact, the only thing I could think of that could possibly make this horrible day alright would be David and me walking out of here arm in arm this very evening. Something cold ran from my neck all the way down my back, because I knew that there was no way that was likely to happen. At least not tonight. *Or ever?* whispered an ominous voice in my head.

'There are some forms we need you to complete,' added the other receptionist, pulling a small bundle of papers from one of the stacked trays on the desk. 'You could take them with you and drop them back down here when you're done.' I took the sheaf from her outstretched hand, glad to have something to occupy myself with while I waited.

The cafeteria was like a ghost ship. I guessed the afternoon tea crowd had long since departed when visiting hours had finished, and it was still too early for the evening meal rush. I took a cup of something brown and unappealing back to one of the sticky-topped cafeteria tables. It could have been either tea or coffee in the ceramic container; the taste didn't give it away. I've always been the kind of person who sends food back in restaurants when it isn't hot enough, I've never been shy about complaining when something is inedible. David often teased that I had probably had *The Customer Is Always Right* tattooed on me. A fact we both knew to be untrue, because he was familiar with every last inch of my skin, had touched it, caressed it, kissed it. My hand shook slightly as I lifted the cup to my lips and drank the horrible drink without thought or comment.

I completed the forms the best I could, but there were still a lot of questions I had to leave blank. Most of them were to do with family medical history and childhood illnesses. David's mother would know the answers to all of those, but I really didn't want to phone her until I had some positive news. She would insist on taking over the moment she knew David was in here. She'd demand to speak to the doctor in charge, and when that wasn't good enough she'd continue like corrosive acid burning her way through whatever obstacle they put in her path until she'd got the chief consultant of the whole hospital on the end of the phone line. Maybe I *should* call her? She certainly knew how to get things done. I shook my head, hoping she would eventually forgive me for my decision. It wasn't that I didn't get on with my mother-in-law, but she wasn't exactly a warm or approachable woman, not even towards me — and *I* was the girlfriend she'd approved of! Put it this way, even after five years of marriage I still felt more inclined to call her Mrs Williams than Veronica.

I glanced at my watch. David had been gone for over half an hour. How long did it take for them to transport him up a few floors and push his bed into position? Shouldn't someone have come to find me by now? What if they'd forgotten where I'd gone? What if some other emergency had taken precedence over his case — perhaps that patient who'd been brought in by ambulance when I first arrived?

I wasn't usually given to the type of panic I could feel coursing through my veins like a virus. In fact I could only recall one other time when I'd felt this threatened, this vulnerable, and it had been David himself who'd come to my aid back then. This time I was on my own. There was no one I could call to come and sit with me; no one to tell me that everything was going to be alright. Oh sure, we had plenty of acquaintances, couples we socialised with, but I had no one I would call a true close friend. *David* was my friend; *David* was my person. I felt as lost as a missing twin as I headed for the lifts and pressed the button to summon the carriage to take me back down to Reception.

Ally

Shell-shocked, I followed the doctor back into Reception, blinking away the tears from my eyes and trying to pretend they were due to the bright fluorescent lighting. His honesty and candour had ripped away any shred of hope I'd been clinging to that this was all just some stupid mistake. I'd never felt so scared or so helpless in my entire life. Or alone.

An insistent buzzing noise, like an angry insect, sounded from the pocket of the doctor's lab coat. 'Excuse me,' he apologised, withdrawing his beeper and scanning the small green backlit screen. I found myself holding my breath as I studied his face for a clue or a sign. *Please be good news*, I thought desperately, *Please, please, please.* He looked up and I told myself there was comfort to be found in his small but encouraging smile. 'We're in luck. I can take you up to your husband right now.'

'Oh, thank you,' I said on a grateful sigh, hurrying beside him to the lifts.

'He's in our ICU for now, that's on the fourth floor,' he explained.

I nodded.

The lift seemed to take for ever to come. My eyes darted impatiently between the digital

57

read-outs above both shafts, willing one of them to reach ground level. They crept with excruciating slowness down through the numbers, stopping at virtually every floor in the entire building. I burrowed my fingers tightly into the fur of Jake's small toy, to prevent them from jabbing repeatedly on the call button. I was on the point of suggesting that we take the stairs when both carriages pinged almost simultaneously. I shifted my weight from foot to foot like a sprinter on the blocks, to see which door would open first. The right-hand lift won by a whisker and we stepped inside it just as its neighbour arrived at Reception.

'I'm afraid you'll only be able to see him for a few minutes,' explained the doctor, 'but there's a Relatives' Room just down the corridor, so you'll be able to wait close by.' I nodded, willing to agree to just about anything at that point. Perhaps if I promised not to get in their way, they'd let me stay with him.

I saw almost instantly that there was no way that was going to happen. Joe was in a small room that was crowded to capacity with a frighteningly large number of individuals dressed in white coats and blue scrub outfits. Everyone was moving at speed, and as they rushed around his bed I couldn't even see the man they were all busy trying to save. In my mind I was flying to his side at a run, my feet scarcely touching the hospital linoleum as I rushed to reach him. In reality my footsteps hesitated and faltered the closer I got to the room.

The doctor had tried to warn me on the lift

journey up what to expect, but I hadn't been listening, not closely enough, because nothing he had said had prepared me for this. I saw Joe in small terrifying glimpses to begin with as a doctor or nurse stepped to one side or the other to allow someone access to a piece of equipment or their patient. It was like a well-orchestrated ballet as they ducked and slipped fluidly behind and around each other as they worked.

We reached the glass door to the room and still all I could see was a blanketed form in the bed. He looked about the same size as Joe. A nurse straightened up from adjusting an IV drip and I saw a shock of familiar hair on a starchy hospital pillow. Just this morning that same hair had laid beside me on my own pillow, his lips had whispered, 'Time to get up, hon,' in my ear, just as they'd done a thousand times before. But they weren't whispering now. They wouldn't be able to, because there was a long plastic tube emerging from his mouth and disappearing off to a piece of machinery beside him.

'Oh Joe,' I whispered.

The doctor accompanying me laid his hand gently on my shoulder as my eyes darted around the room, trying to take it all in.

'What's his temp now?' fired out someone in staccato urgency.

'Still only up to eighty-one,' came the reply. Someone made a small hissing noise, so I knew that wasn't good news.

'Push another adrenaline.'

'How many is that?'

'Let's try warmed peritoneal lavage,' suggested

someone, 'because if we don't get this fella warmed up soon he — '

The doctor beside me cleared his throat noisily. 'This is Mrs Taylor, everyone. Is there any way we can give her just a moment with her husband?' Every head in the room turned towards me, every eye was full of sympathy. That couldn't be good.

They parted like the Red Sea, clearing a path to the bed. Part of me wanted to ask them all to get out of the room to give us some privacy, and another part wanted to scream at them to keep doing whatever they were doing, don't stop, don't rest, not even for a second.

Thankfully they had no intention of desisting from their efforts as I walked on shaky feet towards my unconscious husband, but they did fall silent in their tasks and moved with a hushed deference around us. I think I preferred their frenetic energy, their stillness made it seem as though they were giving up, as though the fight was already lost.

I reached Joe's side and tried to find some part of him, a hand, an arm, an anything, that didn't have something either attached or inserted into it. There was none.

'Hey Joe, it's me,' I began on a voice that trembled on every word. 'It's Ally,' I added, because his eyes were closed. I looked down at him, feeling certain that whatever state he was in, wherever this accident had taken him, he would hear my voice and open his eyes. My own eyes grew hot and gritty as I stared unblinkingly at his face. Gone was the wind-burned colour that never left his skin, not even in the middle of winter. Gone was the warm pink of his lips. His face was a mottled mosaic of greys and blues. I had never seen that colour on a person before, at least not on a living one.

But Joe wasn't dead, his chest was moving rhythmically up and down, in tandem with the small bellows-like machine beside him that was doing all the work. I reached out my hand and then looked up hesitatingly, unsure.

'Can I . . . can I touch him?' Several heads nodded in reply. He was cold, so very cold. My fingertips ran over his cheek and the chill of him penetrated the pads. 'Joe, wake up. Please wake up,' I said, leaning down so my head was only inches from his. A chill emanated up from him; it was like standing before an open fridge. When the tears from my eyes fell from my own face and landed on his I almost expected them to freeze there.

'We need to — ' began a voice behind me, before someone silenced them rapidly.

'Let her have a minute. She needs this time.' I closed my eyes against the hidden implication behind those words. They were allowing me time to say my goodbyes.

I reached for Joe's hand, ignoring the drip in the back of it, the tubes leading from it and the fact that it looked like a lifeless frozen mannequin. I gripped it, hard enough to hurt the delicate bones in my own fingers. 'You have to wake up now, Joe Taylor. Because you have people here who love you and need you and . . . and Jake needs his daddy because you know

61

I'm no good at all that boy stuff, and I don't know how to teach him how to play football, or how to change a tyre on a car, or how to shave . . . or any of that kind of crap. So just wake up now please, and stop scaring me like this.'

'We really need to — '

I looked up with eyes that didn't know how to stop crying. 'I know. I have to go.' I bent back down to the icy effigy of the warm and loving man I had fallen in love with so many years earlier. I kissed the side of his mouth, my lips grazing the plastic tube protruding from it. My eyes scanned the room, sweeping over every last one of the team of medical professionals. 'Don't stop,' I begged them. 'Please don't stop. Bring him back to me.'

I turned and as I got to the foot of the bed I gently placed our son's toy against the metal rail, standing it upright as a small furry sentinel and protector. 'Look after him,' I said ridiculously to the stuffed toy. Not a single person laughed, not one.

Charlotte

I stepped out of the lift, at a rate worthy of a competitive race walker, or at least a seasoned London commuter. My path to the reception desk was momentarily blocked as two uniformed police officers crossed in front of me. They scanned the sparsely populated reception area, spoke briefly to the staff behind the desk and then strode towards the family with the crying children. I wondered fleetingly if whoever they were here to see had been involved in an accident. I wanted to feel compassion for them, but right then all of my sympathies were diverted a lot closer to home.

'Ah, Mrs Williams,' began one of the duo of receptionists as she saw me approach. 'We were just on our way up to get you,' she said, while simultaneously relieving me of the partially completed forms. 'Your husband is still being settled into the unit, but they've said if you'd like to go up you could wait in their Relatives' Room. At least that way you'll be closer at hand.'

'Yes. Absolutely. The closer the better,' I agreed.

The Relatives' Room was small and oppressive, like a tomb, I thought darkly, a small gloomy NHS tomb. The Relatives' Tomb. They should rename it. Then again, perhaps not. It wouldn't give much hope to the countless desperate relatives who had sat exactly where I was now sitting. Possibly even on this self-same uncomfortable plastic armchair, with its wooden armrests with the chipped varnish. How many sweat-drenched palms had it taken for the varnish to be eroded like this? How many prayers had this tiny room heard, I wondered? More than a church confessional, I guessed. How many had been answered? Not all of them, that was for sure. Not every relative who sat within these walls got to leave and go home with their loved one. People died on this ward, there was no point pretending otherwise. They didn't call it Intensive Care because they'd run out of ideas of what to name it. Only sometimes — however hard they tried — the care just wasn't going to be intensive enough.

Not that I thought for a moment that that was going to happen to David. He was sick, that much was obvious, but people didn't die of an illness that just sprang up out of nowhere. You had time to prepare for the big life-threatening kind of diseases, didn't you? Death didn't just turn up unannounced and sweep you away on a rolling tsunami. You got a warning, time to prepare. *Didn't you?*

I shuddered. It must be the room, making me think this way. The claustrophobic green walls and the small grimy windows that looked out on absolutely nothing except the grey concrete slab of another building. Even the door felt morgue-like, with a tiny porthole set within it instead of a proper pane of glass. It was certainly as quiet as a tomb too. In fact, the whole ward was. But then only two of the eight glass-walled rooms were occupied. The one at the far end — the one I had mistakenly thought was David's — was teeming with medical staff. They were bustling and flurrying around the patient within it, their faces unsmiling, full of concern. In panic I had gripped on to the arm of the small exotic-looking nurse who had led me through the ward, feeling her bird-like delicate bones beneath my fingers. 'Is that David's room? Is that my husband?' I had asked, my voice thick with dread.

'No, no, no,' she had assured me, her voice a sing-song melody, her large dark almond eyes soft and kind. She looked wrong in her drab nurse's uniform; she should be draped in a rich and vibrant silken sari. She shouldn't be here in this setting, and neither should David, nor I.

'Your husband's room is at the far end of the corridor,' she said, but when I'd tried to turn that way she had guided me (with surprising strength) in the opposite direction. 'The doctors are with him now,' she explained. I walked with my head craned, eyes fixed on the bay where my husband was being examined. Not that I could see anything, as venetian blinds had been pulled down for privacy. It didn't look as though the poor chap in the other room cared much about privacy, one way or the other. He didn't appear to be conscious and was hooked up to so many bits of machinery his room looked more like it belonged in a mission control centre than in a hospital.

After twenty minutes the glaring bright fluorescent lights in the small waiting-room had begun to hurt my eyes, so I'd switched them off, preferring to sit in the dim light of just one small side lamp and the weak twinkling fairy lights wound about a small, tired-looking artificial Christmas tree. The tree sat on a low table positioned against the wall, and was about a quarter of the size of the one we had in our flat, and nowhere near as elegant. I changed the colour theme of our decorations each year. This Christmas it was silver and ice blue. In January I'd take down the decorations and donate them all to a charity shop and start all over again next December. David had called me on that, just once, during our second year of marriage. 'Don't we want to keep them?' he had asked, gently removing me from the small stepladder and taking over dismantling the uppermost branches. 'When I was a kid I really enjoyed looking out for my favourite glass ornament every year . . . ' His voice had trailed away, and he'd said nothing more. But he'd given me a long hard squeeze before reaching for the roll of bubble wrap to carefully protect each delicate glass ball.

This tree, sitting in the hospital room, held little cheer. The decorations were tattered, and the metallic paint on most of them was chipped. It looked sad and old, and I knew just how it felt. I resolved to give our own decorations to the ward when we took them down in January. Hell, if they just got David better, I'd buy them the biggest Christmas tree imaginable every damn year. I touched my fingers against the tiny silver star on the top of the small tree and wished very, very hard.

Ally

'Are you sure you don't want me to get Stan to drive us to the hospital so we can be there with you?' I shook my head, a pretty stupid thing to do when you're on the phone. 'Don't worry about the snow storm,' Alice continued, 'Stan's a good driver and he says he'll be happy to take us.'

I looked around me, momentarily confused by my neighbour's words. I was standing just outside of the hospital's main entrance, where I'd come to phone Alice, as promised. I hadn't been sure where I was allowed to use my mobile phone within the hospital, but just in case there was any truth in the medical urban myth that they interfere with patients' life-support systems, I'd taken myself as far away from Joe's bed as possible to make the call. But until Alice had mentioned the weather, I hadn't even noticed it was snowing, and quite heavily at that.

I looked up at the falling white flakes, illuminated and backlit by the orange glow of the sodium arc lights ringing the parking bay. They gave the drab concrete area an ethereal air, which felt at odds with the turbulent churning feeling squirming inside me.

'No, Alice. Stay where you are. I don't want Jake seeing Joe like this. It would terrify him.' I knew that for a fact, because I was twenty-three years older than my young son, and it had scared the life out of me. I shivered violently, only then noticing that I'd come outside without my coat, and had absolutely no recollection of where I had left it. I was barely capable of looking after myself right then, Jake was far better off staying at home in the capable hands of my good-hearted neighbour. When the medical team restored Joe from his cryogenic state back to the warm — in every sense of the word — man we both loved, I would bring Jake straight to his father's bedside, whatever time of the day or night it was.

'Okay Ally. Whatever you think is best. Don't worry about Jake. Stan and I are happy to stay

67

here all night if needs be.'

'Thank you so much, you're being so kind and — ' My throat constricted, preventing me from saying any more. Alice gave a small harrumphing sound of dismissal, which turned into a cough followed by several moments of discreet nose blowing. When she next spoke there was an authority and pragmatism to her voice which was probably for the best. Sympathy would have been my undoing just then.

'Now what else can I do for you? Do you need me to call anyone? Your parents? Joe's?'

I swallowed noisily. As much as I would dearly have loved the weight of both of those calls to be lifted from me, they were mine to make, no one else's. 'No, I'll phone them, but I thought I might wait until the doctors have some more encouraging news.'

'Good idea,' confirmed my friendly neighbour, who was probably about the same age as Joe's parents, but seemed decades younger. The thought of how Joe's parents would react to news of his accident was a real concern. Neither of them had been particularly well recently, and Joe's dad had given up driving several years ago, so even without the impending blizzard, there was no easy way for them to make the five-hour drive that evening.

'Can you just put Jakey on?' I asked, using the time it took my son to run from the kitchen, where he had been playing with Alice's husband, to the hall telephone to compose myself. I breathed in deeply, inhaling small snowy particles which stung my lips, turning them cold,

68

but nowhere near as cold as Joe's had felt.

'How's Daddy? Is he all better yet? Are you coming home now?'

I breathed in some more snow, which coated the lies I was about to tell like a frosting of icing sugar. 'Daddy's doing just fine, sweetie. They're giving him some really horrible medicine, but it's going to make him all better very soon.'

There were probably whole chapters written in child psychology books about why you aren't meant to lie to your child in this kind of situation. But sod that. I would protect my son from anyone and anything that I thought would hurt him. That was the only type of mother I knew how to be.

'Tell him to hold his nose, then it won't taste so bad,' recommended Jake wisely.

My eyes began to water, and it had nothing to do with the sharp icy crystals stinging them. 'I'll do that. Good idea.'

'And come home soon, because Daddy was going to read me the last chapter of my story for bedtime tonight, and no one does all the voices right except him.'

My fingers tightened fiercely on the small handset pressed to my ear. It was a precious lifeline, my only link to a rapidly disappearing normality and far removed from this terrifying world, where doctors gave you time to say goodbye to the man you love, while a machine pumped oxygen into his lungs.

'I promise we'll both be home as soon as we can. Be a good boy for Alice and Stan.' I know you're not meant to make promises to a child which you don't know you can keep, but you're also not supposed to tear their world apart either. On balance, I could live with the choices I'd made.

I spent most of the lift journey back up to the Intensive Care ward trying to convince myself that my decision not to contact our families was the right one. If I was being honest, part of me was scared that once I let word of the accident out, I would set in motion a terrible chain of events. I stared miserably at my distorted image in the polished chrome of the lift's control panel and wondered if I was already too late. The dominoes were already beginning to fall and there was nothing I could do to stop them.

One of the nurses found me staring through the glass walls of the room where the team of doctors were still busily working on Joe. I couldn't tell from their activity or the looks on their faces if his condition had improved or worsened, and I was too scared to ask. She cupped my elbow and led me away from the room, virtually having to drag me when I resisted the pull of her arm.

'There's nothing you can do out here,' she said gently.

'I just wanted to stay close by. So he knows he's not alone,' I added. I glanced up at the crowded room. Joe was far from alone.

The nurse patted my hand comfortingly. 'As soon as there's any change, I'll come and get you. I promise. In the meantime, you can wait far more comfortably in here,' she advised, coming to a stop outside a door with a glass porthole set within its wooden panel.

I wondered in what universe the nurse might imagine that I would be even remotely concerned about whether or not I was comfortable while my husband's life hung in the balance. This was, without a shadow of a doubt, the very worst night of my entire life. I reached out my hand and opened the door to enter the Relatives' Room. And that was the moment when my night suddenly got a whole lot worse.

Charlotte

My ears were attuned to the sound of footsteps travelling briskly up and down the corridor. Each time they approached I could feel my heart increase its rhythm and my mouth immediately went dry in anxiety as I forgot how to swallow, forgot how to breathe. Each false alarm stretched my fragile composure until it was gossamer-thin and in danger of ripping to shreds at the smallest provocation. The silence took on its own tempo and sound as I continued to strain my ears, trying to make out anything that was taking place in the infuriatingly muted ward outside. Footsteps approached again, only this time they didn't hurry past on some mission but paused and lingered at the threshold of the room. I froze. I'd been waiting for so long to talk with the doctors, but now they were here I suddenly wanted to barricade the door and prevent them from entering. I looked up as the chrome handle inched downward and the door swung open.

Ally

I was expecting the room to be empty. The nurse hadn't said there was another occupant. But there was. Her face was turned to the door and her eyes locked on mine. There was no moment of uncertainty or any lack of recognition. It had been years since we'd last met, but I knew the contours of her face as well as I knew my own. She was the woman who had changed the course of my life.

There was a moment of simultaneously shocked silence. She was the first to speak.

Charlotte

'You?' I saw the nurse's eyebrows rise several centimetres, as Ally's mouth dropped open in shock. 'How did you know he was here? Who told you?' I continued.

The nurse's glance darted between us both, clearly baffled. And she wasn't the only one.

Ally shook her head, as though she was in the middle of a really confusing dream. 'I . . . I was at home . . . the police told me. Why are *you* here?'

I didn't even register her question. A million suspicions, ones I thought were so deeply buried that they'd never crawl their way back to the surface, suddenly returned. 'How did they know how to reach you?'

'They found my number in his wallet. I'm confused. Just what are you doing here, Charlotte?'

72

For a moment her words rendered me speechless. Was she delusional? Was she having some sort of breakdown? I could think of no other reason for her to challenge me. She was the one who didn't belong in this room. She was the intruder.

'The same as you, apparently,' I replied, wanting to sound indignant, but the words came out laced with pain. *He carried her number on him? After all this time?*

The nurse, perhaps not the sharpest tool in the box, looked from Ally to me, as a dawning comprehension crossed her features. 'Oh, so do you two know each other?' she asked guilelessly.

There was a long moment of stony silence.

'We do. Or rather we did,' answered Ally quietly.

I waited until the nurse had left us alone, before turning once more to the woman whose existence ran like a dangerous fault line buried deep beneath the bedrock of my marriage. 'Please go home. You don't belong here,' I pronounced.

Ally's features contorted, and her eyes filled with tears, but even through her pain I couldn't help noticing that she still looked pretty. 'I have no idea what you're talking about, but *of course* I belong here. The man I love is fighting for his life, where else should I be except right here?'

'He's not your husband. He's mine,' I cried, my voice breaking as the tears I hadn't wanted her to witness began to fall.

Ally's eyes widened incredulously. *Yeah, right, like she didn't know we were married.* 'David?' she asked tremulously, and I hated even hearing

73

his name on her tongue. 'David's *here?*'

She reached out a hand to steady herself on one of the chairs. She looked totally shocked, and for the first time I began to feel uncertain. But I was determined to stand my ground, even if the soil was shifting and sliding beneath my feet. 'David's *here?*' she questioned again, her voice dazed. 'Here? In this hospital? In this ward?' I gave a small sharp nod, still a beat or two behind her in putting things together. 'I don't believe it. How is that even possible? I had no idea.'

And suddenly I *did* believe her. No one could feign that look. I watched her run her hands through her shoulder-length glossy brown hair, as she shook her head from side to side in total disbelief. Her eyes went to mine and within them I saw a reflection of my own incredulity as yet again fate had pulled us inexorably and inescapably back together once more.

'It's not *your* husband I'm here for. It's mine,' Ally confirmed.

I liked maths, I always had, but even I couldn't begin to fathom out the odds against finding myself sharing the same hospital waiting-room with the woman who owned a piece of my husband's heart, a piece I'd never been able to reclaim.

Ally

I lowered myself slowly onto one of the hard plastic chairs. What were the chances? A million to one? A billion? Neither of us spoke for several minutes, robbed of words by the sheer enormity of the situation. You think you're in control of your life, you think you're the one making all the decisions and then something like this comes along and you realise you're just a tiny chess-piece being moved around on the whim of something or someone much larger. Free will? I wasn't sure I even believed in that any more. I broke the silence first.

'So what's wrong with him? What's David in here for?'

'Heart attack.' Charlotte fired the words like bullets. They found their mark and I flinched from their impact.

'Really? Isn't he far too young for that?'

She fixed me with an eye-narrowing look, as though I was being deliberately confrontational by daring to question her. Her hand went up to rub tiny invisible lines from her forehead, and I couldn't help wonder if that smooth unlined face was just down to good genes, or if she'd had some help. 'Yes, well, I'm not sure yet. I'm still waiting to speak with the doctors,' Charlotte conceded.

We fell into an uncomfortable silence. There was so much between us that was volatile and incendiary, the smallest spark could lead to an inferno, something I suspected neither of us were capable of dealing with right then.

As much as I didn't want to converse with her, I found it almost impossible to stop myself from covertly studying Charlotte. We had chosen seats as far apart from each other as the small room would allow, and although the lighting was dim, it was still bright enough for the stylish haircut, the statement silver jewellery and the impossibly high heels to make their intended impression. I was pretty certain her sharply cut designer dress had cost more than my entire annual clothing budget. I was dressed in a plain black jumper, with jeans tucked into my black boots, it was my uniform as a working mum and a look I favoured, and besides which, Joe liked me in jeans. A sudden memory sprang up of his strong work-roughened hands running down the length of my denim-covered thighs. A small sound tore free from the rock-hard lump lodged in my throat. Charlotte's head jerked up at the noise, but although she looked in my direction she made no move towards me.

'So, your husband . . . John, isn't it?'

'Joe,' I corrected, stupidly irritated by her mistake.

'What happened to him?'

'He fell through a frozen lake.'

Charlotte's perfectly threaded eyebrows rose upwards. It was — I knew — a completely understandable reaction. 'What was he doing on a lake?'

'I have no idea,' I replied, cutting short her fledgling attempt at conversation. She gave a small shrug, which confirmed her lack of real interest in my husband's condition. Her thoughts were only of David, there was no change there. None at all.

We both jumped when footsteps approached the door of the Relatives' Room. It was impossible to tell which end of the corridor they had come from: Joe's room or David's. The door opened and a white-coated doctor stood at the threshold. It wasn't a face I recognised from the team of medics who had been working on Joe. The doctor was flanked on one side by a nurse and on the other by a much younger man with a stethoscope hanging casually around his neck.

'Mrs Williams?' questioned the older doctor, his eyes going from Charlotte to me in enquiry.

'That's me. *I'm* Mrs Williams,' Charlotte replied with particular emphasis, as she jumped to her feet.

My fingers curled unconsciously into the palms of my hands as phantom words from the past echoed back to me, words I had no business remembering.

'Mrs Williams. Mrs Ally Williams. It's going to happen, you know. One day, a few years from now.' David's arm had tightened around me, pulling me closer against his warm naked body. I had pushed playfully against him, my hand finding very little resistance in the taut firm muscles of his toned abdomen. 'Shut up, you,' I had replied, burrowing my head against his broad shoulder, using it as a pillow. The bed in his student accommodation was narrow and not particularly comfortable, but neither of us had seemed to mind.

'You can protest all you like,' he had said teasingly, threading his fingers through my long brown hair and gently raising my head so I could look into his eyes. 'But you'll see. One day, I'll have my way.'

A small pink flush had flooded my cheeks. I never quite knew if he was being serious or not when he said stuff like this. 'I think you just 'had your way' quite effectively . . . twice,' I had informed him primly.

'Want to go for a hat trick,' David had asked, pulling me up on top of him, 'Mrs-Williams-to-be?'

* * *

'Would you like to come with us, Mrs Williams? We have an update now on your husband's condition.'

I was glad to be left alone in the room, glad Charlotte had been led away by the group of doctors for a private consultation. I told myself I didn't care whatever it was they were saying to her; I told myself it had nothing whatsoever to do with me; I told myself my interest was only in Joe, and no one else. I sat in the small darkened room, surrounded by my own lies.

My eyes kept going back to the weakly flickering lights of the small Christmas tree on the table. There'd been another Christmas tree on the night we had met, a magnificent one. It had been almost as tall as the marquee it was standing within, and was only just visible through the arch of fairy lights twinkling at the entrance as I hurried along the path. But I hadn't had time to stop and admire it, for I'd been late, I remembered. Suddenly the sole of my new cheap black shoes, the ones I'd had to rush out to buy that afternoon, had skidded like skates on the ice-slickened path and I had begun to fall . . .

3

Ally — Nine Years Earlier

'Whoa. Steady on there!' His voice had come from out of nowhere in the darkness, just as his hand shot out to grab my arm, catching me before I fell spectacularly arse-over-tit in front of the long snaking line of students queuing up at the entrance to the Snowflake Ball.

I think my feet did that silly pin-wheeling thing that you usually only see performed by cartoon characters, before I finally got some traction and regained my balance.

'Thank you,' I gasped, already feeling a flush of embarrassment on my cheeks. I looked up but I couldn't make out anything of the man who had caught me.

'Not got another girl falling at your feet, David?' called out a disembodied voice from the other side of the path. 'It's starting to get really old now, mate. Why don't you back off and give the rest of us a chance?' The lairy comment ended in a burbling gurgle of laughter, the guy clearly delighted by his own wit. Me, not so much. Especially as his words had drawn the attention of several students who were waiting in the queue to surrender their ball tickets for the event the Student Union had billed '*The seasonal event you can't afford to miss*'. I hadn't actually agreed with that tag line; for me it was more a case of it being '*The seasonal event you can't afford to attend*'. Not at seventy pounds a ticket, and hardly anything left of my student loan for the term. If it hadn't been for a desperate friend begging a favour, and a trumpet player with a bad case of flu, I definitely wouldn't be standing in front of the enormous marquee, in my cheap slippery-soled shoes, with a stranger's hands gripping tightly on to my arms. Still gripping in fact, long after I was out of danger of falling.

'Thank you,' I repeated, in the direction of my rescuer, who was still a tall shadowy shape in the darkness.

'You should take more water with it,' he said teasingly.

'I'm not drunk,' I retaliated, although I wasn't entirely sure the same could be said of his friend, nor perhaps of him, for all I knew. Anxious to leave, I pulled my arm free from his hold with a little more force than I should have used, and almost lost my balance yet again. Once more his hands steadied me. I heard someone laughing in the queue and could feel the heat rising like mercury in a barometer in my already flushed cheeks. I hated being the centre of attention or making a spectacle of myself, and right now I was in danger of doing both those things.

'I was only joking,' the man — who I assumed was called David — replied. 'The path is really slippery here, it must be quite difficult to walk on in high heels.'

Except that I wasn't wearing heels. My new shoes were shiny black patent flats, worn with a plain black pencil skirt and a cheap Primark black blouse. I looked more like I was going to a funeral than a ball, but then I *was* one of the performers and not a guest, I had to keep reminding myself. It was like a modern twist on the fairy tale. *Cinderella, you can go to the ball . . . except you have to play in the band when you get there.*

'You're sure you're okay? I didn't hurt you when I grabbed on to you, did I?' He had a lovely voice, a voice made for singing, my musician's ear instantly decided. It was rich and had a depth of tone that made you think of hot molten honey. I blinked the fanciful notion away just as my rescuer's friend shouted out once again.

'David, it's fucking freezing out here. Just get her number and come over here or the rugby guys will have drunk all the champagne by the time we get in.'

I glanced over my shoulder in the direction of where the comment had come from and then back at the man before me. 'No. I'm fine. Thanks again. Sorry, I have to go,' I said ducking past him to veer off towards the rear entrance of the marquee. I was already fifteen minutes late for reporting in to the leader of Moonlighters, the university band who were providing the live music for the ball. He was probably having kittens, thinking I wasn't going to show up.

Just as I was about to disappear into the darkness, someone within the marquee flicked a switch and the row of trees lining the path suddenly materialised like magic, each one wreathed in sparkling white LED lights threaded through their branches. That was the first moment when I saw him properly, illuminated and backlit by the radiance of a thousand twinkling lights. He was, without question, the most dazzlingly good-looking person I had ever seen in my entire life.

The atmosphere at the rear of the marquee was the usual frenetic madness which you expect before a big performance. True, I was more familiar with classical recitals than big jazz bands, but the buzz and barely reined-in aura of panic was still easily recognisable. I knew the band-leader by sight only, but I would have been able to figure out who to report to because he was the one who looked closest to having a stress-induced heart attack.

I wove through the bustling performers and tapped him on the shoulder. 'Hi, I'm Alexandra Nelson — Ally,' I amended. He spared just a millisecond to nod distractedly and then continued scanning the crowds, looking for something or someone. 'I'm depping for your sick trumpet player,' I added. His hands latched on to my shoulders and for a moment I wasn't sure if he was going to shake me for being late or kiss me with relief. Thankfully he did neither.

'Thank Christ, I thought you weren't coming.'

'Sorry,' I apologised, 'But I got — ' I didn't get the chance to finish my sentence as a large folder of music was thrust at me. 'I bloody well hope you're as good as Tom says you are, because we're on in ten.' I gave a noisy gulp and looked down at the weighty sheaf of sheet music in my hands. 'So please tell me you're the best sight-reader in the entire music department.'

I wasn't sure if I could legitimately claim that title, but this was no time for false modesty. I glanced down at the music with a confidence that I hoped wasn't misplaced. 'Don't worry. I can handle this.'

He nodded, apparently satisfied. I thought of the universally acknowledged tough auditions to get into this elite band of musicians, and knew mine would probably go down in Moonlighters' history as the easiest admittance ever. But with their biggest performance of the year just minutes away, and a room full of students who had paid a large amount of money for their evening's entertainment, what else could he do? Besides, I was only playing with them for just this one gig.

'Just follow the rest of the band. We throw in some moves on a few of the big numbers.'

My heart sank a little. This was a world away from the University Philharmonic Orchestra in which I usually played. This wasn't the type of music I typically performed, nor the kind of people I tended to socialise with. *Moves? What moves?* I hoped to God he didn't mean actual dance moves, because that was *definitely* not me.

'You'll be fine,' he assured either himself or me, and I could almost see him mentally crossing *Missing Trumpet Player* off his list of problems which needed to be sorted out in the next ten minutes.

I shrugged off my thick quilted jacket, sat down on one of the large storage boxes used for transporting the amplifiers, and ran my eye down the set list. We would be playing three sets, of forty-five minutes each, over the course of the evening, and the music was largely well-known jazz numbers — the kind popularised by artists like Michael Bublé. My parents would have loved it; they would certainly have enjoyed it far more than the scores of recitals and performances they had dutifully sat in the audience for over the last fifteen years, since I had taken up music. The fact that they'd never missed a single one of my performances was testimony to their love and pride in my accomplishments, rather than a love of the musical content. It had taken me a long time to appreciate that my love of classical music must have skipped a generation. It was my grandmother who I really wished had still been with us to attend those concerts. It was *her* musical gift that ran through my veins, as much a part of my genetic make-up as my brown hair, green eyes and generous curving lips. Lips which I should be getting warmed up, I realised, as I snapped open the clasps of the black leather case which held my trumpet.

The marquee was amazing. The high vaulted ceiling was a canopy of folded pleats, into which had been set an entire Milky Way of tiny glowing lights. There was almost too much to take in during our sedate single-file walk up onto the stage. But I could see at least two giant ice sculptures and an enormous chocolate fountain positioned to one side of the venue. There was a wooden boarded dance floor immediately in front of the stage and the remainder of the vast space was taken up with a sea of large circular white-linen-covered tables, all festively decorated. An excited roar went up from the assembled ball-goers as we took our positions. I was playing First Trumpet and walked to my designated position — top row, behind the trombonists, who in turn were behind the saxophones. There was a familiar fluttery feeling deep within my stomach. A strange intoxicating cocktail of terrified nerves and mounting excitement. There was a moment, just one, right before the first song began, just as the band-leader glanced at his assembled musicians to check we were all ready, when I thought — as I always did — *What the hell am I doing here?* Then the leader flung his hands dramatically upwards and I raised my trumpet to my lips in readiness and lost myself, as always, in the magic of the music.

The first set flew by. We had a twenty-minute break, just enough time to down a bottle of water and sample a few of the sandwiches that had been provided for us in the small makeshift 'green room' at the back of the marquee. It wasn't what the diners in the marquee were eating, but then they *had* paid for the privilege of a hot gourmet meal and the six bottles of wine that I'd seen on each of the tables.

I didn't bump into David again until our final break. The rest of the band, not surprisingly, all knew each other really well and were chatting together in companionable clusters. I felt a little awkward among them, which was ludicrous, because out on stage I could feel the strains of the music we were making drawing us together into one cohesive living musical entity. I wasn't shy, but I'd always been one of those people who preferred to watch quietly from the sidelines. Perhaps it was the result of being an only child to parents who were a good fifteen years older than those of my classmates. Or perhaps it was just the way nature had made me. People who didn't know me well often mistakenly thought I was standoffish or distant. Neither was actually the case, but it took me a long time to open up to strangers, and even though I was now in my second year of university, I had made a whole load of acquaintances and very few close friends.

I wandered out through the makeshift curtain separating the musicians' backstage area from the main marquee and saw him straight away. He was standing beside one of the tables to the left of the stage, chatting and laughing with a couple of its occupants. For no reason that I could see, he suddenly turned in my direction as though he had been summoned by name. He said something to his companions, clapped one of them on the shoulder and then straightened up and began to weave his way towards me. For one stupid moment I thought of pretending I hadn't seen him and diving back through the curtain, an area which was out-of-bounds for the ball guests. There was no reason for this sudden fearfulness. He certainly didn't look menacing as his eyes held mine, and he made his way confidently towards me through the crowd of guests, some of whom were beginning to look decidedly inebriated. David looked devastating in a dinner suit, which fitted him far too perfectly to have been a rental, as though he'd just stepped out of an advert for the type of glamorous jet-set lifestyle no one actually lived. He had undone his bow tie and it was now loosely draped around the unbuttoned collar of his crisp white shirt. I never could understand why that should look so sexy and attractive, but it had never looked more so than it did on him and made my throat constrict in a way I couldn't quite control.

'Hello, Drunk Girl. So you're a musician,' he said, his mouth curving in an easy smile. 'You play the cornetto.'

Despite myself, I could hear the amusement in my voice as I corrected him on every count. 'I told you before, I wasn't drunk. And that's an ice cream, not an instrument. And it's not even what I play anyway. I'm a trumpeter.'

His eyes twinkled, even more brightly than the lights glinting down on us from the ceiling, and I realised he had once again been teasing me. 'You play very well,' he complimented. 'How long have you been with Moonlighters? I don't remember seeing you at any of their shows before.'

I glanced down at my narrow banded wristwatch, a gift for my fourteenth birthday, which was still keeping perfect time seven years later. 'Just under two hours, actually,' I replied, 'I'm depping.'

'Of course you are,' he responded with a knowing nod, then bent his head so close to mine that I caught the fragrance of his spicy aftershave. 'What *is* that, exactly?' he added on a whisper.

I smiled. I was so used to speaking only with fellow musicians or my housemates, who were also music students, that I tended to forget that not everyone was familiar with the vernacular. 'Standing in for someone who's sick,' I explained. 'This isn't really the type of music I normally play.'

'Heavy metal more your thing, huh?'

I glanced up at him through my lashes. He was quick-witted and sharp, and suddenly I felt like I was swimming in waters way out of my depth. 'I play for the University Philharmonic,' I said proudly. 'But I don't suppose you've been to many of our performances?'

He smiled, and I noticed his eyes crinkled up at the edges when he did so, making him look even more breathtakingly good-looking. 'Now, why would you think that?'

I gave an embarrassed shrug, regretting my comment and not making things much better when I added, 'I don't know, you . . . your friends . . . you're not the kind of crowd we usually get in our audiences.'

'You sound a little prickly and defensive about your musical tastes, Tipsy Person.'

'Still not drunk,' I corrected. 'And I only meant that it doesn't seem like your type of music. I doubt you could even *name* three classical composers.'

'Ah, a challenge,' he said mockingly. 'I do love one of those,' and suddenly I wasn't sure if he was just referring to the names of the musicians, or something else altogether. Nevertheless his brow furrowed attractively (*and how was that even possible?*) in concentration. 'Erm, Beethoven, Bach . . . and . . . er . . . '

'Bartók, Berlioz, Bertini, Bizet, Brahms — '

'Wow, it's all about the Bs with you, isn't it?'

'Bollocks.'

'And another,' he said jokingly. 'Do you take everything so seriously, Intoxicated One?'

'Do you take *nothing* seriously?' I countered.

'It's all about balance,' David replied. 'And this *is* a party. You're allowed to have fun. All work and no play . . . ' he left the words hanging in the air.

'Gets you a First,' I finished, unwittingly revealing my three-year educational blueprint.

I was actually quite grateful for an excuse to step out of the sparring arena when I heard the sound of a small bell tinkling lightly from the green room behind us. 'I have to go, we're back on now.'

'What time do you finish playing?'

'Not for another forty-five minutes,' I replied, already turning to go. But his hand reached out to lightly clasp my wrist, preventing me from leaving.

'Join me for a drink at our table when you're done,' he invited unexpectedly, inclining his head towards one of the noisiest in the room. I looked at the table he had recently vacated. His large group of friends were laughing uproariously at something, apart from two couples who were indulging in the kind of public display of affection that usually prompted someone to yell '*get a room*'. Everyone looked as though they were well into the party spirit and they were certainly dressed for the event, in expensive-looking prom dresses and dinner suits. As I watched, one of the waiting staff approached their table carrying a tray loaded with four bottles of champagne. The group cheered raucously at its arrival. I wondered, for the first time, if David himself might be a little drunk, although I could detect nothing in his manner to indicate that he was.

I shook my head, and gave a small tug, releasing my wrist from his grip. 'Sorry, we're not allowed to,' I lied, improvising wildly. 'We're not permitted to socialise with the paying guests.'

'How Dickensian.'

I shrugged. 'It's the rules.'

His eyes twinkled mischievously. 'They're made to be broken.'

'Not by me, they're not.'

I was shaking my head gently as I disappeared through the gap in the curtain to rejoin the other members of the band, never realising for a moment that I had just met the man who was going to change my entire life.

Charlotte

'I'm sorry? *What* kind of virus did you say?'

The doctors had brought me to a small room behind the nurses' station. There were no papers on the desk, and no name on the door. It was a bleak room and that had seemed horribly

91

symbolic. The senior doctor, who looked to be in his mid-fifties, had a thick russet-coloured beard that was threaded with strands of lightly greying hair. Distractingly he looked more like a lumberjack than a consultant. The younger doctor quietly shut the door, closing out all sounds of the ward behind us and the consultant invited me to sit down. When I'd declined he had been quietly insistent, 'Please, Mrs Williams, take a seat.' That was when I began to feel truly afraid. Was what he was about to say so alarming that I literally wouldn't be able to stand after he'd delivered his words? Perhaps.

'Viral cardiomyopathy,' supplied the doctor. He reached across the space between our chairs to lay a stilling hand lightly on both of mine, which were twisting together in origami knots of anxiety. That small human gesture was when I knew we were in real trouble here. I forced my hands to be still.

'But you can give him something for it, can't you? If it's a virus you can still treat it, can't you? With antibiotics . . . or something?'

I glanced over at the younger doctor who had accompanied us. He was fiddling awkwardly with the end of the stethoscope hanging around his neck, and I suddenly realised why he was here. It was to learn how you delivered really bad news to a patient's relatives. Well, he'd have to learn it at another time, with another patient, because I just wasn't going to accept this diagnosis. I looked back at the senior consultant who was regretfully shaking his head from side to side.

'Viral cardiomyopathy occurs when viral

infections cause a condition called myocarditis, which results in a thickening of the myocardium and dilation of the ventricles.'

I shook my head impatiently. 'In English please,' I said.

For the first time I saw the man behind the physician; he was there in the softening of his gaze as he met my eyes. 'In layman's terms your husband — '

'David,' I supplied.

'David,' continued the doctor, 'has caught a virus that has attacked the muscles of his heart, damaging them.'

I swallowed visibly. 'So how are these muscles fixed? How do you make them better again?' He was silent. 'What are you saying to me? That they *can't* be fixed?'

The doctor inclined his head slowly, I guess to allow me time to absorb the words that were set to alter the course of my future. Only I didn't realise that then.

'In real terms David is going to suffer from increasing shortness of breath, fatigue, and dizziness. We need to carry out further tests, and explore ways of alleviating some of his discomfort. But at this point you have to be aware that he is going to have to radically adapt his lifestyle to his condition as we try to find a way of slowing down the deterioration.'

'And if you *can't* slow it down?'

The doctor looked like he really wished I hadn't asked that question, but he must surely have known that I would. 'Let's cross that bridge when we come to it, shall we?'

I shook my head emphatically. 'No,' I said, surprising both of the medics with my vehemence. 'Let's cross it now. I need to know. Is he . . . will he . . . ?' For all my show of strength, there was still no way I was ever going to be able to get that question past my terrified lips. I tried it another way. 'Is . . . is his condition life threatening?'

It took seven seconds, I counted each one of them, for the doctor to deliver the very worst news I had ever received. 'It can be.'

Ally — Nine Years Earlier

I made a concerted effort not to even glance in the direction of his table for the last set. Even so I imagined I could feel his eyes on me, boring through the darkened room like lasers. When I wasn't actually playing, I kept my gaze determinedly fixed on my music stand, feigning concentration. Our last number, *In the Mood* by Glenn Miller, was one of the band's signature pieces, and almost before the final notes rang out, the crowd rose to their feet and began to cheer in a deafening standing ovation. It was worlds away from the muted applause I was more accustomed to, and surprisingly I rather liked it. Buoyed up by the audience reaction, my cheeks felt warmly flushed as I bowed low alongside the other performers and left the stage.

Amid the back-slapping and congratulations in the green room, it was easy to pass unnoticed as I gathered up my belongings, stowed my trumpet back in its case and slipped on my jacket. I was cinching the belt tighter around my waist when the band-leader came up and threw his arm around my shoulders, his earlier stress now completely dissipated by the successful performance. He thanked me at least five times (I counted) for helping them out.

'I really enjoyed it,' I said, and was surprised to find that it wasn't just a polite lie. Maybe David-whoever-he-was had been right. Maybe I *was* in danger of taking myself too seriously. Maybe I did need to lighten up a little.

'Honestly, you should try out next time we audition,' the leader urged. 'You'd be sure to get in.'

I gave a whimsical shrug, still a little on a high from the show. 'Maybe I will. Anyway, I'm happy to have helped you out.' I turned to go.

'Look, we usually finish off at one of the campus bars after a gig. Why don't you join us?'

It was my second unexpected invitation of the evening, and unlike the first one I found myself wavering for a moment before turning him down. 'I'm sorry, but I can't. I have to catch an early train back home in the morning. Maybe another time.'

★   ★   ★

I stepped out through the flap at the back of the marquee. The temperature had dropped quite dramatically during the evening, and my breath now billowed out in an icy plume, like chilled dragon flames. I glanced around, the whole area appeared to be deserted, but I was used to

95

walking at night on my own. I adjusted my hold on the handle of my trumpet case, suddenly regretting my decision not to wear gloves. I had taken no more than two steps from the marquee when his words pierced through the darkness, halting me.

'I knew it.'

I recognised who it was immediately. I had a good ear, and his voice was quite distinctive. So there was no reason to be afraid, no reason for my heart rate to have suddenly increased fourfold within my chest. I slowly turned my head and saw him leaning up against one of the sparkling illuminated trees, a glass of champagne in each hand.

I hesitated for just a moment before stepping towards him. 'Knew what?'

'That you'd stand me up. That you'd go scurrying off before the stroke of midnight, like Cinderella, clutching your trombone.'

'It's not a — ' I stopped and shook my head. He was playing with me, I realised that. I was amusing to him, an interesting diversion, a piece of light entertainment, and I still had absolutely no idea why.

'You didn't come to my table,' he scolded me gently.

'How do you know, if you were waiting out here?' I countered.

'Touché,' he said with admiration, and held out one of the glasses to me. I was going to say no, really I was, but instead I found my chilled fingers reaching out to take hold of the delicate stem.

'I knew you wouldn't come,' he said quietly.

'Did you?'

'But I also knew that deep down you *really* wanted to.'

'Did you?' I repeated, not bothering to disguise the obvious scepticism in my voice. 'You're very sure of yourself, aren't you?'

He grinned at that. 'Not at all. For instance, right now I'm not sure if you're going to drink that glass of very palatable champagne, or throw it all over me.'

'People only do that in books or films,' I informed him. 'In real life it's a waste of a perfectly good drink.' I raised the glass to my lips, preparing to sip, but his hand came out to stop me.

'Not so fast, Wasted Girl. We should make a toast.'

'One of us may be wasted, but I'm pretty sure it's not me,' I informed him. True, his speech wasn't slurred and he seemed perfectly steady on his feet, but they'd consumed quite a few bottles on his table, and it was hard to believe he hadn't joined in.

He tutted disapprovingly at my comment, then raised his glass aloft, nodding at me encouragingly to do the same. Slowly I held up my hand with the champagne flute.

'This is ridiculous,' I muttered.

'Sshh. You'll ruin the moment.'

I bit my lip. Definitely drunk, I decided. I would just play along. Take a sip and then get home. I still had a lot of packing to do before leaving in the morning.

'To us. To a long and happy relationship.'

'I'm not drinking to that,' I protested.

'I don't think it's legally binding,' he offered on a conspiratorial whisper.

I shook my head, wondering how I had got into this stupid situation in the first place. It was completely out of character for me.

'Go on,' he urged. He really wasn't going to let this one drop, it would seem.

'Okay, whatever. To us,' I said on a rush, and swallowed down an enormous gulp of champagne, and passed him back the glass. 'Thanks, now I really *do* have to go.'

'Then let me walk you,' he suggested, taking both our glasses and placing them at the base of one of the trees.

'Don't be daft, you don't even know where I live.'

He gave a shrug which looked both boyish and charming. 'Can't be that far. Anyway, I have a thing about letting pretty young woman go wandering off into the night unaccompanied.'

I dipped my head, letting the fall of my long hair hide my look of sudden embarrassment. I wasn't good with compliments and was pretty sure he was still just toying with me. 'At least let me walk you to the main road,' he suggested, and despite all my good intentions, I agreed.

It was only a few minutes' walk and when we got there I was pleased to see there were still plenty of small clusters of students milling around. 'I'm fine from here,' I assured him, feeling suddenly awkward under the bright orange glow of the street lamps. 'You should probably go back to your friends at the ball now.'

'I'd like to see you again,' David said, handing me back the trumpet case that he had taken from my hands as we walked. 'What are you doing tomorrow?'

'Going home, back to Hertfordshire,' I told him.

'How about meeting me for coffee before you leave?'

I shook my head, but he wouldn't let it go. Somehow I got the feeling that not many girls turned him down when he asked.

'I really think you're going to need some caffeine to sober you up after the night you've had,' he declared solemnly.

I could feel my lips starting to curve. He really was very funny and I was drawn to him in ways that were starting to worry me a little. 'I tell you what,' I suggested. 'If you *really* want to see me before I go, I'm going to be stopping off at the campus coffee shop at half-past-seven in the morning.'

'Half-past-seven!' he exclaimed, in the tone of someone who had genuinely thought there was only one of those a day, and it was definitely in the p.m.

'I have a nine o'clock train to catch. That's the only time I'm going to be around. If you want to see me, then that's where I'll be.'

Just then a loud rumbling sound came up the road. I glanced up, and with mixed emotions saw that it was my bus. I dug into my pocket and pulled out my pass as the doors hissed open to let me board. I turned back to David who was standing on the pavement, his face a little conflicted.

'I don't even know your name,' he said, as I

flashed my pass at the weary-looking bus driver.

'If you turn up tomorrow, I'll tell you,' I promised, just as the driver — right on cue — pressed the button to close the doors, effectively putting an end to our conversation.

David stayed on the pavement watching me through the grimy windows as I walked down the length of the bus, found somewhere to sit and settled my trumpet case on the seat beside me. Of course he wouldn't be at the coffee shop the next day. That much was obvious. He was at a ball, and the party was only just getting started; he was probably a great many hours away from going to bed. I was certain the last thing he was going to do was get up early after a night like that, to go and meet some random girl he'd been teasingly flirting with that night. He probably wouldn't even *remember* meeting me by the time morning came around. It was, most definitely, the last time I was ever going to see him. As the bus slowly pulled away from the kerb, I waggled my fingers at him through the window in farewell.

But the following morning, looking decidedly the worse for wear, he was sitting in the coffee shop, his eyes fixed on the door, waiting for me.

Charlotte

'Can I see him now?'

The doctor nodded. 'Of course. He'll be going up to Radiography shortly, as we need to run a few more tests, but you can sit with him until they're ready for us.'

I didn't even bother asking the name or the nature of these further investigations. The names would scare me, and whatever they were trying to discover would frighten me even more. The click of my heels on the shiny linoleum was all I could hear as I followed the doctors to David's room, that and the faint strains of Christmas music coming from a small radio playing quietly at the nurses' station. It seemed almost irreverent for everyone to be looking forward to the imminent holiday season, while all I could see in the days and weeks ahead of us was something dark and fearful.

I threw a glance over my shoulder at the other occupied bay in the ICU unit. At the far end of the corridor, Ally's husband was still surrounded by a group of worried-looking medics. It served as a reminder that ours wasn't the only uncertain future that night.

'I should warn you, Mrs Williams,' the russet-bearded consultant began, turning to me as we reached the glass-walled cubicle where David lay. 'We've given your husband a very powerful sedative, in preparation for the tests, so you may find him rather woozy.' I craned my neck, like an onlooker at an accident, trying to see beyond the width of the doctor's broad shoulders for a glimpse of David. But the man was as broad as a small garden shed, and I couldn't see past his white-coated frame.

'I understand,' I said, anxiously stepping through the gap he left when he finally stood aside and allowed me to enter the room.

There were two nurses in David's room, but I never looked their way as I walked towards the bed on rubber-jointed legs. I don't even remember lowering myself onto the plastic moulded chair positioned beside him. I just found myself suddenly seated. I could hear the doctor asking questions, I heard the nurses reply, but their words were distorted, just unintelligible sounds, like a record played at the wrong speed. For a moment I wondered if they were even talking in English. Admittedly it was hard to distinguish anything above the small hitching sound that someone was making. It wasn't until one of the nurses passed me a small square box of tissues, and squeezed my shoulder gently, that I realised the sound was coming from me.

The wall of monitors surrounding David looked like a bank of television screens, each one showing a program I didn't want to watch. They reduced David to a compilation of blips, charts and read-outs. It was all these professionals could see of the man I loved; it was all they knew of him. But there was more — so much more — about him that they didn't reveal. Things that not even the woman sitting in the Relatives' Room down the corridor knew. Those secrets were mine. They were a wife's.

David was sleeping, but not in a way I recognised. His body wasn't curled on his side, there was no hollow for me to be drawn into by his powerful free arm, to cradle me tightly against him through the night. There was no hand, gently caressing my hip bone as I snuggled back against him, or tenderly cupping the fullness of my breast, as he slept.

His head moved fitfully upon the starchy hospital pillowcase, and the nurse closest to him gently touched his shoulder. 'Wake up, Mr Williams, you have a visitor.'

David's eyelids fluttered, and I was torn with a need to see the beautiful blue depths of his eyes, and the fear that if he opened them he would read every last worry stencilled on my face. 'Your wife is here,' the nurse urged softy.

'Wife,' David repeated, his voice thick and muzzy with medication. 'No, she's not here. She's in New York.'

The nurse looked at me quizzically, but I just shook my head. Somewhere in his dream, my 'secret' Christmas surprise was weighing on his mind.

'I'm right here, David,' I said entwining our left hands, hearing a small satisfying metallic sound as our wedding bands brushed against each other.

'New York,' he repeated, his words a gasping breath.

'Hush now,' I soothed. 'Save your strength. New York can wait, until you're better,' I murmured, no longer caring that I had ruined his surprise.

'No,' he said, struggling to break through the drugs, to make me understand. 'By the tree, in New York. With the lights. They were playing our song.'

'Do you know what he's talking about?' whispered the nurse. I nodded, my eyes filling with tears as I shared his memory.

'On the ice,' David continued, his voice lost in our past. 'By the tree.'

The tears were running down my face, too fast now to stop.

'There was music, beautiful music.'

I gave a watery smile. 'There was. I remember it. I'll *always* remember it.'

'She plays, you know . . . she plays music. She's in a band.'

Ally — Nine Years Earlier

'Are you ready, love? We don't want to be late.'

Reluctantly I scrambled off the bed and opened my bedroom door to call down to my mum in the hall below. 'Just putting on my shoes,' I lied, glancing down at my feet in the black patent flats, the same ones I'd been wearing one week earlier on the night of the ball. For the twenty-third time (and seriously worried now about my newly developed OCD tendencies), I checked my phone's Inbox to see if I could possibly have missed a message. Nothing. I switched the phone's ringer off and slipped it into the pocket of my festive red tunic dress that I was wearing over thick black tights. I gave a quick glance at my reflection, ran a comb through my long chestnut-coloured hair, fought the urge (and won) not to sneak one last glance at my phone, and ran down the stairs to join my parents in the hall below.

Neither of them were wearing coats, but they were hardly necessary as we were only going as

104

far as our next-door neighbour's house for a glass of Christmas morning sherry. It was a tradition we'd been indulging in for as long as I could remember, certainly it pre-dated the time when Max and I were permitted to drink at all. But over the intervening years we had gravitated from orange squash in a beaker, to fizzy Pepsi clunking with ice, to tumblers of frothy Snowballs, and had finally reached the giddy alcoholic heights of a glass of amber-coloured cream sherry. To be honest, I'd have been quite happy sticking with the Snowballs, but then I never had been a particularly sophisticated drinker.

We walked the length of our short crazy-paving path, took a sharp right and walked up the identical path of our neighbours. There was a large ivy wreath on the door that practically obscured the knocker, but Max's mum had been lying in wait in the hall and flung open the door with a cheery 'Merry Christmas! Come in! Come in!'

We followed her into the small front room that was a mirror reversal replica of our own. Decorations were looped like bunting from the cornices of the room, and the entire bay window was taken up with a Christmas tree flashing so fiercely I only hoped no one with serious epilepsy happened to be passing by. Christmas music blared out from the CD player, and I felt a funny little twinge as I recognised the exact same song that had been playing in the coffee shop when David and I had met there seven mornings ago. Seven mornings, seven afternoons, and seven nights. And not a single text. What does that tell you, you stupid idiot, I told myself angrily. Just forget about him.

A figure unfurled himself from the settee beside the roaring fire and threw a very large and disgruntled ginger cat off his lap before getting to his feet and enveloping me in a huge hug.

'Happy Christmas, you,' he said, holding me tightly against his long lean body. He held me at arm's length and surveyed what I was wearing. 'You look like one of Santa's Helpers,' he observed.

'That was so the look I was going for,' I replied.

'Sit, sit, sit,' commanded Max's mum, as though we were pupils in a dog training class. She busied herself, bustling around the room with plates of Devils on Horseback, Pigs in Blankets and other curiously named Christmas fare.

'In her element, as usual,' observed Max, pulling me back down onto the settee he had just vacated. 'So did Father Christmas swing by your place?'

'Absolutely,' I confirmed, taking a small glass of sherry from the tray Max's dad was carrying. 'New boots, CDs and lots of smelly stuff. How about you?'

'The daft bugger managed to get a sewing machine down the chimney this year,' Max informed me, sounding inordinately pleased.

'Wow! The expensive one you showed me in the catalogue?'

'Yep,' he agreed, pulling Flatbread, the

decidedly overweight ginger cat, back onto his lap. 'I still feel a bit guilty. It's way more than they usually spend.'

I gave his hand a squeeze, noting that it no longer felt like the hand of a boy; it was now that of a man. 'When you're a rich and famous dress designer you can buy them a mansion. That'll square things up.'

He grinned and ruffled my hair in the way he knew I hated. Max was my closest friend; the only one I had missed like an ache when I'd left home to study music at university while he'd gone to college to study fashion design.

'So,' he asked, stuffing an entire Pig into his mouth, 'has Prince-Ever-So-Charming been in touch with you yet?'

I shoved him on the shoulder. 'Stop calling him that. I really wish I'd never told you now. Especially as it doesn't look like he's going to call anyway.'

Max put his arm around my shoulders and drew me to his side in a quick hard squeeze. 'Then he's too stupid to deserve you. You're just going to have to end up with me after all,' he teased. From the encouraging glances I saw his mum and dad exchange from across the room, I knew that for them that would be the best outcome imaginable. For Max and I . . . not so much.

'Not that I want to take his side, or anything,' Max added, virtually inhaling a Devil from the servietteful he was guarding preciously from a very hungry-looking cat, 'but you have to admit you didn't exactly make it easy for him. You *could* have given him your number.'

I pulled a face, but I knew he was right. For some perverse reason I had intentionally made it ridiculously difficult for David to contact me, almost as though it were a test. I still found it hard to believe he'd actually been waiting for me when I'd walked into the warm coffee shop, pulling my heavy suitcase behind me.

There had been small smudgy circles beneath David's eyes, yet even they couldn't mar the head-turning perfection of his face. If anything, he looked even *better* in daylight, dressed in shirt and jeans, than he'd done the night before in a dinner suit.

'Good morning,' he'd said, pulling out a chair for me at the small table. 'I've got you a coffee.' He slid a polystyrene cup towards me.

I was shaking my head in pleasant disbelief as I slid into the seat and undid my quilted jacket. 'I really didn't expect you to be here. I felt sure you'd still be asleep.'

He gave a half grin, which made a pulse at the base of my throat forget its normal rhythm and start to race. '*Still asleep* hasn't happened yet,' he admitted ruefully. 'By the time Survivors' Breakfast came around there really didn't seem much point.'

'You must be exhausted.'

'Nah. I can cope with late nights,' he admitted. 'We've had a few of those over the last three years.' I didn't doubt it. The students in any university fell into a multitude of categories, ranging from the studious geeks who practically lived in the library, to the hardened party-goers who would be hard pushed to tell you where the library was. I suspected that David and I hovered near opposite ends of that spectrum. I was here to get an education so I could get the job I wanted in life. I suspected his path in life was already secure, whatever class of degree he came out with.

'So mystery girl, are you going to tell me your name now, seeing as this *is* our second date? It's about time I knew, don't you think?'

'This isn't a date,' I corrected.

'I bought you coffee,' he said, nodding at the container I was sipping from.

I immediately reached into the copious shoulder bag that I'd dropped beside my chair and pulled out my purse. 'I'm sorry,' I said feeling my cheeks grow instantly warm. 'What do I owe you?' On the few dates I *had* gone on at university, all the bills had been split clean down the middle, and I didn't have a problem with that at all.

'Put your money away,' David chided, looking genuinely appalled that I had thought he was asking me for payment. 'Let's start again, shall we?' he continued, and held his hand out to me across the table top. 'My name is David Williams, I am a third-year Economics student, I come from Hampshire, I like rowing and skiing and meeting strange tuba-playing girls at Christmas balls.'

'That sounded like a *University Challenge* introduction, until the last bit,' I said, trying not to laugh, as I briefly allowed my hand to be held by his.

'The last bit was the best bit,' he said seriously, and my stomach flipped weirdly at his words.

'So,' he prompted, giving me a warm encouraging smile.

'My name is Ally — short for Alexandra, and I play the trumpet.'

'That's *it*? That's all I'm getting? What am I going to say when people ask me about my new girlfriend? I'm going to look ridiculous when I have to say I don't know anything about her.'

He was doing it again, pretending this silly little flirting game was actually going somewhere, and I wasn't slick or skilful enough to know how to deal with it.

'I doubt anyone will be asking, because I'm *not* your girlfriend.'

'Not yet,' he said, with a confidence that threw me completely. 'But you will be.'

There was a promise in his words that thrilled and scared me in equal measure. But I was determined not to be just another notch on his bedpost, which I was worried was what this was all about. Had one of his friends dared him to pursue me? Had they even had a bet on it? The thought made me feel more than a little sick, but somehow it rang true. Let's face it, people like him went out with girls who came from the same kind of background as them. Where I came from, polo was a type of mint with a hole, for his friends it was a game everyone they knew played.

'So is that really *all* you're going to tell me?' he said disbelievingly.

I nodded. 'This was fun, but let's not drag it out, shall we. Thanks for the coffee, but I really

110

have to go now, if I don't want to miss my train.'

'I don't know what you think of me, but I'm *not* the type of guy who plays games,' he said and suddenly there was far less humour in his eyes. 'I'm interested, Trumpet-Playing Ally. *Really* interested.'

I got to my feet, biting my lower lip nervously. If I didn't know better I would have actually believed he was sincere.

'Give me your number,' he asked, pulling his phone from his pocket ready to add it to his contacts.

I shook my head.

He looked exasperated.

'Your surname then,' he asked.

Again I shook my head.

'Jesus, you really are going to make me work for it, aren't you?'

'I'm not playing hard-to-get,' I said, getting to my feet. He went to stand too, but I laid my hand on his shoulder to stop him, almost losing my train of thought as I felt the strength of his broad muscles flex beneath my palm. 'I just think there's not much point in making this into something that it's not.'

'I *will* find out your number, and I *will* call you,' he promised solemnly.

I smiled at him as I pulled on the retractable handle of my suitcase and tilted it onto its wheels. 'Okay. You do that and maybe I'll believe you're actually serious,' I said, as I began heading towards the door.

'You'll be hearing from me,' he called out across the practically deserted coffee shop as I

111

twisted the handle, letting in an icy gust of December air.

Only now, seven days had passed, and I hadn't.

Charlotte — Six Years Earlier

It was cold, in the way only New York can be in the depths of December. I was wrapped up warmly, but despite the layers, the scarf and warm fluffy hat, the Big Apple was biting back with determination.

We were only here for four days, and David had planned this, our first trip away together, with almost military precision. He was determined that everything would be absolutely perfect. And it had been.

He'd surprised me with tickets for my birthday present. He'd booked the flights, hotels, and even secretly contacted my boss and secured the time off work, all without me suspecting a single thing. I'd got a little teary when he had handed me the envelope with the airline tickets, in the classy French restaurant where he'd taken me for dinner.

'But this is next week,' I had said, examining the date on the tickets.

He had smiled at me across the flickering candlelight. 'It is.'

'But what about my work?'

'Sorted.'

'And yours? You said you were going on a business trip next week.'

He raised his glass of champagne and took a sip. 'Well, that just proves you can't believe everything I ever tell you, Birthday Girl,' he said, his eyes twinkling.

Something I hadn't wanted to intrude on this perfect moment, nudged me from the depths of my subconscious. This wasn't the time to let her in, so I shut the door on my fears, as I'd done so many times before.

David and I had been dating for eight months. Just eight months. There might be those who thought we'd been together much longer than that. But they'd be wrong. They'd been wrong all along. It was a long time after Graduation before David and I met again, at Mike's wedding of all places. Mike, the perennial player, the guy you could never see settling down, had met his German girlfriend, fallen in love and proposed within an astonishingly short period of time.

I'd been surprised to receive a wedding invitation. Although David and I had exchanged the occasional text and email, I'd had no contact with anyone else from the house since the day we had all worn our black gowns and thrown our mortar board hats high into the air for the obligatory photograph.

To be honest, I hadn't even been sure I would go to Mike and Marietta's wedding, because there were some memories that were best kept securely hidden under lock and key. And those last months, after the '*Ally Incident*' — as it had forever been named in my mind — was one of them.

But, even while *Good Charlotte, Sensible*

113

Charlotte, I've-Moved-on Charlotte was planning to decline, *Hopeful-Romantic Charlotte* had already sent back her acceptance card. And thank God I did, because that was the day when a new and wonderful part of my life had first begun, in a pink-festooned wedding marquee, when David had crossed the wooden floor to the table where I was sitting, held out his hand, and asked me if I would dance with him. The song was an old classic, Roberta Flack's *The First Time Ever I Saw Your Face*, and it was still playing when he'd bent his head to kiss me. I had kept my eyes open until the very last second, still looking for a trace of her, or the grief she had left behind in his eyes. But there was none.

It had become 'our' song, and it was only a long time later that David confessed that it hadn't been random chance that the song, with the lyrics that told our story with such heart-touching accuracy, had been cued up to play. He'd requested it. It was the first romantic thing he had ever done for me. But it wasn't the last.

* * *

New York had been an exhausting whirlwind. David had been before, but it was my first time and he was determined I should see it all. By the third day of our stay I was beginning to flag. We had managed to squeeze in the Empire State Building, a very chilly boat tour around the island, and a visit to Chinatown already that day, and I wasn't sure I had the stamina for the late afternoon trip to the Rockefeller Center that was next on our itinerary.

'Would you mind terribly if we didn't do it today?' I asked, as we grabbed a late lunch in a diner that looked so familiar I was sure it must have featured in a movie I'd seen. But then I'd felt that for the whole trip — practically everywhere we went, it felt like Hollywood had taken me there before.

David had been studying his map, plotting the course to our next destination. He folded it carefully before looking up. There was a hopeful look on my face. 'We could always just head back to the hotel . . . and fool around?' I suggested, feeling sure he would definitely agree to any plan that ended up with us in bed together. And the feeling was far from being one-sided. Each time he held me against him, I trembled like it was my first time. And, amazingly, it just kept getting better and better.

But surprisingly, he *didn't* agree. 'I thought you said you were tired.'

'No one is ever *that* tired,' I flipped back at him with a smile.

There was a light burning in his eyes, a light I recognised, it was the one that always lit a companion fire deep within me. But this time he doused it. 'Actually, I'd really been looking forward to this afternoon,' he said. 'Are you sure you're not trying to cry off because you're scared I'll out-skate you?'

I smiled and took another bite from the foot-long hot dog that I was determined to finish. 'That's never going to happen. I skate

115

better than I ski, you know,' I said confidently, wiping traces of ketchup from my lips with a paper serviette. 'I was just wondering if we could switch it to tomorrow, that's all.'

David shook his head, and there was a look of disappointment in his eyes. 'Our schedule is pretty full for tomorrow, and I've got tickets for the four-thirty session today. We'd probably have to queue for ages if we want to change it.' It was his trump card; he knew how I hated to queue in the cold.

'Oh well, never mind. Let's go today, as planned,' I said, getting to my feet as he paid the bill. 'Just remember when you're nursing all those bruises later on, that you turned down my naked body to get them.'

He smiled, and I thought there was a small glimmer of relief on his face. 'Actually, I'm looking forward to having both the bruises and you in my bed later. You just might have to be gentle with me,' he teased, looping an arm around my neck and pulling me towards him for a quick kiss.

★ ★ ★

The rink was crowded, but the moment we glided out onto the ice I was glad he had persuaded me to come. There was something truly magical about the place. I wasn't sure if it was the enormous Christmas tree, twinkling in the dark afternoon with a thousand coloured lights, or the gilded statue of Prometheus, or the bubbling illuminated fountains. Perhaps it was a combination of all three. We weren't the only ones to be captivated by our surroundings. There was a similar look on virtually every stranger's face as we skated past: a warmth, a camaraderie, a feeling of Christmas and excitement.

David was actually far more proficient on the ice than he'd led me to believe, confessing with a wry grin that he'd actually been on the ice hockey team in the first year of university. He took my gloved hand in his and skilfully manoeuvred us past the families, the couples, and the many tourists who had all flocked here for the same reason we had done. Or so I thought.

Christmas music played through the many speakers positioned around the rink, and the festive atmosphere was infectious, not just amongst the skaters who bumped, jostled and stumbled all around us, but also in the thousands of onlookers watching the rink from all sides.

Our ninety-minute session was drawing to a close when the first soft flakes of snow began to fall. I looked up at the night sky, beyond the two hundred flagpoles with the United Nations flags that ringed the rink, and watched the falling flakes. I could feel them settling gently on my upturned face, jewelling the tips of my eyelashes like crystals.

'You look like a snow queen,' David whispered, skating up behind me.

'Aren't they meant to be wicked and evil?'

'You're not wicked,' he whispered into my ear. I could think of at least one person who

117

wouldn't agree with him, but the last thing I was going to do was let her intrude on this perfect moment. I already carried her around with me far more than was good or healthy. Far more, perhaps, than even David did, I acknowledged for the first time. And wouldn't Freud have an absolute field day with that one.

★ ★ ★

'Will all guests please clear the ice for ice resurfacing,' boomed a request from the address system, marking the end of our session, and although I was sad it was over, I was secretly looking forward to getting inside in the warm.

'Let the crowds go first,' suggested David, sliding his arm around my waist and steering us out of the throng of skaters shuffling towards the exits. 'Come on, we'll sneak in one last circuit now that it's emptying.' We glided away from the crowd, and without the threat of mowing down less experienced skaters beneath our blades, we were able to build up speed.

There were fewer people left on the ice, and I glanced anxiously at a red-jacketed official as we whistled past him at the edge of the rink.

'Shouldn't we get off now? They're going to tell us off in a minute.'

'We're fine,' David assured me.

The snow was falling a little harder now, settling on the ice, covering the scores left by a thousand skaters, making the surface look clean, fresh and pristine. A new beginning. I smiled at the fanciful notion, and felt David's grip tighten on my waist as we skated around the perimeter in perfect harmony.

'Close your eyes,' he said gently.

'What? While skating? I don't think so. I'll fall.'

'No you won't. I won't let you,' he said, and there was a huskiness in his voice that wasn't there before. 'Do you trust me?'

'More than anyone in the world,' I said, suddenly strangely choked and emotional.

'Then close your eyes.'

I did as he asked, letting his body keep me safe, his eyes guide me through the darkness.

'I love you,' he whispered into the curtain of blonde hair billowing back from my face as we skated. He'd said the words before, many times, but there was something in them that felt different this time.

'I love you too,' I replied, turning my face to his and opening my eyes. The rink was now completely empty except for the two of us, but I didn't see that. I couldn't see anything beyond the expression on his face as he looked at me. If I live to be a hundred years or more, I swear I will die with the memory of that look burned into my heart.

The speakers, which had been silent as the rink emptied, now gave a small crackle as the opening strains of a song began to play. I recognised it from the first poignant guitar chords.

'It's our — '

But I never got to finish that sentence, because he had brought us both to a halt directly in front of the sparkling Christmas tree, and with both my hands in his, he went down on one knee before me.

I know now that a rousing cheer went up from the thousand or so onlookers, because I've seen it on the DVD they gave us, but I never heard it. I heard nothing at all except David's words as his brilliant blue eyes, so full of love, looked up at me.

'Charlotte, I can't imagine a life without you in it, and I don't want to. The last eight months have been so incredible and wonderful. I love you so much, and I will spend the rest of my days proving that to you.' Very gently he tugged the glove from my left hand. 'I want to dream with you, make memories with you, grow old with you. Please let me do that. Please say you'll marry me.'

There was a ring between his fingers; he held it poised above my finger. Waiting. I could hardly speak, but I forced my reply past the emotion that threatened to choke me, because he had earned the right to hear my words.

'Yes, yes, yes. A thousand yeses.'

David's eyes were sparkling, more brightly than the stars above us, as he slid the diamond in place. He got to his feet, and pulled me into his arms. 'I promise I will never leave you, never hurt you, never do a single thing to make you regret saying yes,' he whispered huskily. He kissed me then, with such warmth and passion that I was surprised the ice beneath our feet didn't melt clean away.

Charlotte

The door opened, and a tired-looking orderly stood in the frame. 'Patient for Radiography?'

'Yes, that's us,' confirmed the nurse, moving to the bank of monitors and beginning to prepare David for transportation. 'If you would just like to say goodbye to your husband, Mrs Williams, we will take him up and let you know as soon as we get back.'

'I can't go with him?' I asked shakily, getting to my feet.

'I'm so sorry, but no,' she apologised. 'Regulations. But we'll come and get you from the Relatives' Room the very moment he is settled again.'

The orderly was standing behind me, impatiently shifting his weight from one foot to the other, clearly anxious to go. Somewhere there was probably a wife and family waiting for him to come home. For a moment I envied him the simplicity of his life. The nurses were working swiftly, in clockwork precision, as they unhooked, unplugged and disconnected equipment I had a horrible feeling I was soon to become far more familiar with than I could ever have imagined.

I bent down low, and although David's eyes were still closed, I had to believe he could hear me. 'I'll be waiting for you. Right here.' I kissed his lips, tasting the saltiness of my tears as they fell onto them. 'I still remember the promise you made me six years ago. I just hope you do too.'

His eyes opened then, weakly, as though even that was too much effort. Very slowly he nodded.

4

Ally

The noise of the door opening jerked me back from my memories as though I'd been sucked out of a vortex. A very different Charlotte entered the room. This one walked slower, her feet hesitant as though they barely remembered how to do it. With unseeing eyes she felt her way along the back of the row of chairs and sat down heavily. She positioned herself at an angle, facing away from me and looking out sightlessly on the window with no view. I saw her slide a hand into her expensive-looking handbag and withdraw a small bundle of tissues which she concealed within her clenched palm.

She looked shell-shocked, and despite myself and everything I had sworn to feel or not feel over the years, it simply wasn't within me to remain silent.

'Is . . . is everything alright?' That had to be a strong contender for the most ridiculous question anyone had ever asked. It was patently obvious that nothing at all about this night was alright, for either of us.

Charlotte, turned her head slowly, as though having to retrain the muscles and bones in her neck to obey her command. Her eyes, the ones he had elected to look into every morning instead of mine, were bright with the tears she was struggling not to shed.

'Fine. Everything is just fine.' Her lips visibly trembled as the lie slid off them.

Nervously I twisted the thin gold band on my wedding finger. I could taste a coppery tang on my tongue, and realised I had unwittingly been gnawing on my lip as thoughts of the past — of David — had dragged me from the place I belonged. *Joe* was the one who should have been occupying all my thoughts, all my energy, no one else. And yet David, and all that happened between us ran like a vein of ore through my rock-solid marriage to another man. Strands of unfathomable serendipity were stretched like piano wire through my life, and tonight past and present were welded together in a fiery forge. How many times over the years had I secretly asked myself that one unanswerable question: *Where would I be now if I had ended up with David and not with Joe?* And now, I had my answer: right here, in this drab, sad little hospital waiting-room. Right here, sitting in the dark, waiting to learn if the man I loved was going to make it through till morning. The only question was . . . which man?

Ally — Nine Years Earlier

David had phoned eventually, at just about the most inconvenient moment imaginable, just as I was about to join my family at the table for Christmas lunch.

'I have left messages on the mobile phones of

practically every bloody person in *Moonlighters*, but not a single one of them knew who the hell you were. Some of them didn't even remember you *being* there. You were like a bugle-playing Cinderella, running away at midnight. I started to think I must have imagined you. Then eventually I discovered that the only person who knew your name was halfway up the Himalayas on his Christmas break. And incidentally, who does that?' David finally paused for breath.

I managed to erase the smile from my voice before replying coolly. 'I'm sorry. Who *is* this?'

There was a brief pause, but he was better at this game than me. 'Very funny, Orchestra Girl,' he said, and I just knew he was smiling. 'Let's see if you're still laughing when I pass you my mobile phone bill.'

I pursed my lip. Max had been right. I *had* made it inordinately difficult for him. But if it had been a test, even an unintentional one, there was no denying that he'd passed.

David rang me every single day of the Christmas break — confirming what I already knew about both his determination and his ability to pay for the calls. I suppose in old-fashioned terms you could call it a type of courtship. We got to know each other far better over those weeks during our late-night phone calls, than I think would ever have been possible had we been face to face.

Yet when January and the new term began I was nervous all over again when he suggested meeting up.

'When are you back?' he had asked, and I

rolled over in bed to glance at the calendar in the dim light of my bedside lamp. It was gone one o'clock in the morning and this call, like so many others, had stretched into the early hours, long after my parents had gone to sleep.

'Saturday the tenth of January,' I replied on a whisper.

'Is it a secret?' he had whispered back. 'I promise not to tell anyone.'

I gave a small giggle into the darkness. I still found him incredibly funny. I had probably laughed more with him during these calls than I could ever remember having done before. He was tugging out a different, more light-hearted Ally from somewhere within me. And I rather liked her.

In the end, we had arranged to meet at one of the campus bars. I'd turned down his offer for dinner — too intimate, or for him to meet me at the train station — too coupley.

My heart had been pounding with increased tempo when I'd entered the bar and then even more so when David had looked away from the person he'd been talking to, and slowly turned around to face me. I don't remember weaving through the crowds to reach him, have no recollection whatsoever of crossing the length of the room. The raucous laughter around me faded away, and in my ears was a strange whooshing sound. It sounded vaguely like waves on a shore, which seemed apt because I felt as though I was being pulled towards him as surely as the tide is drawn by the moon. Invisible and powerful forces were at work here. I reached his side, and stood before him nervously. What if the connection I felt to him had only existed down the lines of a telephone? What if in real life the differences that I had thought were so insurmountable really *were* too wide to bridge? David reached down and clasped my hand and suddenly a million little pieces fell into place like tiny microscopic cogs within an intricate timepiece.

I was vaguely aware that several of his friends from the ball were standing nearby. One of them, a guy with some ridiculous, slightly rude-sounding nickname, passed David a pint of lager from the bar.

'And who's this then?' he asked. His accent was pure home counties, far posher than David's deep and melodic voice.

'This is Ally. She's with me,' David declared, looking down at me with a confident smile.

And from that moment on, and for the next ten months, I was.

* ★ *

Not that I was ready to acknowledge that, at least not right then. I liked him, there was no point in denying that, but I just couldn't see us as a good fit . . . and he could. He'd held my gloved hand tightly in his as he had walked me home from the bar that first night. He totally disregarded my insistence that I was perfectly capable of walking home alone — I did it without a second thought at least three times a week after music practice sessions.

'There are some pretty strange characters hanging around town at this time of night, when the clubs and bars start to empty,' he observed darkly, tugging lightly on my hand to bring me a little closer to his side.

I looked up at him, with the lower part of my face mostly buried beneath a long scarf which I'd wound — Egyptian mummy style — several times around my neck. 'And are we perfectly sure you're not one of them?' I teased.

He laughed. 'Nah, you're safe with me.' I buried my nose in the folds of wool and considered his words. Physically, I knew he posed me no threat, but emotionally . . . well, I wasn't so sure.

Twenty minutes later we arrived at the small, slightly shabby three-bedroom house I was sharing for my second year. It wasn't much to look at from the outside, but then my expectations had been small, and so had my budget. David studied the unlit house as we stood on the pavement beside the creaky gate with the peeling flakes of paint, both of us shivering in the cold January air.

'Is there anyone else home? Your housemates?' he asked, and for just a moment I wondered if he was expecting me to invite him in. Because that *definitely* wasn't going to happen. But his tone had sounded more concerned than anything else.

'Probably not,' I replied, my breath wafting up from the enveloping scarf in small billowy clouds. 'Elena spends most of her time at her boyfriend's place, and Ling practically *lives* in the music department.'

'Maybe I should wait until one of them comes back,' he suggested.

'Maybe you should go home,' I countered.

He shrugged, and I was pleased to see he wasn't going to push it. Very gently he took hold of the two trailing ends of my scarf and tugged me slowly towards him.

'I find myself worrying about you quite a lot, Bugle Girl,' he said, disarming me totally by how close his face was to mine. So close that the vapour of our exhaled breath met and mingled in a way that struck me as curiously intimate. David's head lowered slowly; he was giving me plenty of time to pull away or tell him to back off. I did neither. Very gently his hands went to my face, his fingers slipping into the folds of wool, easing down my scarf to allow him access to my lips. His mouth felt chilled, but as my lips parted beneath it his tongue was warm, gently teasing a response from mine. I hadn't been kissed in over seven months, and it was pleasing to discover I still remembered how to do it.

I had lain awake for a long time that night. I heard one of my missing housemates return, and charted her progress through the house by the sound trail she left behind. Whistling kettle in the kitchen, creaking stair treads leading to her bedroom, bathroom extractor fan going on and then off, until finally the house was in silence. And still sleep eluded me.

I had a strange fluttery feeling inside me, as though somewhere within me a small winged emotion was beating on the walls of my resistance. I didn't want to get involved in a relationship, and certainly not with someone who was so far outside of my comfort zone that I felt like a trespasser in another world. But there was something about David, something that pulled me like a magnet, something that . . .

A small buzzing noise interrupted my thoughts and my room was lit by a neon green glow as my phone received an incoming text.

'Are you awake?'

I smiled in the darkness and drew the phone back under the duvet with me.

'Well I am now' I typed beneath the covers.

'Sorry. Just wanted to check you were OK. I had fun tonight.'

I stared at the screen and ran my fingers over his message, my lips suddenly tingling as I remembered his mouth on mine. I had felt a little awkward with his friends, though not because they'd been unwelcoming, but just because they were so different from the orchestra crowd I usually hung around with. They were the BNOCs I acknowledged, the Big Names on Campus, and I was the girl who would happily remain anonymous for her entire university career, as long as she got a good degree at the end of it. Was there any way to straddle both worlds? Could he do it? Could I?

'Can I see you again?' he messaged. Before I could reply, another text was added to that one. *'Tomorrow?'*

My fingers took over, even while my head was still trying to work out just how many shades of foolish this whole thing was becoming. *'OK'.*

Two letters, blinking up to me in the dark folds of my bed, daring me to take a chance, step out of my safe and secure world and run without caution through a minefield. I took a deep breath and pressed *Send*. Surprisingly I slept far better that night than I had done in weeks.

★ ★ ★

The early days of 'us' were a free-fall of emotions. We disagreed about so many things it was a wonder that we had ever got together at all. That was certainly the unspoken question on the faces of David's friends whenever we went out with them, which admittedly wasn't that often. Even something as innocuous as super-market shopping was a cause of dissent. I'd worked for one of the major chains during my gap year, to earn extra money for university. I knew when to shop to grab the best bargains and bag the lowest marked-down prices on fresh produce. David would shop at any hour of the day or night, whenever it occurred to him or he ran out of something. He too had taken a gap year before starting university, but as his had been spent working in Africa with orphaned elephants, it offered less transferrable skills for grocery shopping.

'You'd be far better suited with one of the girls your mother keeps trying to fix you up with whenever you go home,' I had told him during an afternoon walk through the frosty crisp grass on the campus green. David had been waiting for me outside the lecture hall, leaning nonchalantly against the brick wall, his eyes warm and twinkling as I emerged with a throng of music students. It was almost impossible not to be aware of the sidelong glances of envy darting my way from some of the females around me. I'd never had that before, and I couldn't decide if I was flattered or irritated.

'I've had it with girls like that,' he had replied, casually throwing an arm around my shoulder and taking my heavy bag from my arm. 'All they talk about is which ski resort they're working at next season, or how well their horse did at the local trials. I want a girl who can *spell* gymkhana, not compete in one,' he said with surprising vitriol in his voice.

I was silent for a few moments, my eyes riveted to the frozen blades of grass beneath my boots.

'You're spelling it, aren't you?'

'Maybe,' I admitted.

He had laughed. 'And *that's* why I love you,' he had said, before moving on to talk about something else, leaving me spectacularly a hundred miles behind him. *Love me?* Did he love me? Or had that just been an inconsequential figure of speech? We had certainly never spoken of it — it was far too soon to even be *thinking* those kind of thoughts. We were too new, still stepping delicately in and out of each other's lives. Mostly we had figured out a workable balance. I still spent two or three evenings a week rehearsing in the faculty or locked away in one of the music practice rooms, determined to perfect my playing not just for me, but for the lost grandmother who had passed on this baton to me.

On those nights David mostly hung out with his own crowd of friends. His *RAH* friends, I teasingly called them.

'You *do* know what that stands for, don't you?' he had asked, kissing me and then gently biting on my lower lip as I went to pull away.

'Hey, if the Burberry cap fits,' I had mockingly replied.

★   ★   ★

It was an argument, or rather a silly squabble, that had surprisingly taken our relationship on to its next level. It was a Saturday evening and we were queuing to buy tickets for the cinema, but even while we were standing in line, we couldn't agree which film we were going to watch. I had wanted to see something arty with an Oscar-winning soundtrack and David's choice was something where Bruce Willis was going to save the world. *Again*. Couples in the queue around us were staring with open curiosity as we eventually got to the counter, intrigued to see which of us would be the one to cave. David pulled a twenty-pound note from his wallet.

'One for Screen One and one for Screen Two,' he said, settling our deadlock in a way I certainly hadn't been expecting.

We took our tickets and parted company at the doors with matching looks of childish determination. It was such a silly thing to have disagreed about, and such a waste of a Saturday night. We

132

both knew we'd taken things too far, but neither of us knew how to backtrack. I was about to give in when he had said with a note of resignation, 'So, I guess I'll see you out here when the films are over,' before disappearing into his blackened theatre.

I made it through the adverts, and the trailers and even the first ten minutes of my film, before I jumped to my feet in the darkened auditorium, earning a sharp hiss of annoyance from the people in the row behind me. Mumbling 'excuse me' after 'excuse me' I stepped over legs, bags and popcorn containers to exit the aisle and then sped down the dimly lit steps and out of the theatre. What did it matter what the hell we watched? The important thing was being with *him*, not about who won the debate or who could change the other's point of view.

I burst through the double doors, and ran straight into him, on his race through them to join me. The cinema attendant looked up at the sound of our collision, then rapidly averted his gaze as David's arms tightened around me and his mouth hungrily sought mine. We didn't speak our apologies, we let our mouths and tongues do that for us. I don't even remember leaving the cinema foyer. I have a vague recollection of David hailing a taxi, even though my house was only a fifteen-minute walk away. The cab driver shook his head tellingly as David pulled yet another large note from his pocket and didn't even wait for his change.

My house was in darkness. Ling had gone home for the weekend and Elena, as usual, was out. David had released his hold on me only long enough to allow me through the front door. Now with it pulled shut behind us, his arms came back around me as we stumbled into the shoe-rack in the hall, tumbling trainers and boots all around us as we attempted to reach the bottom of the stairs without breaking our kiss. Something hit the floor with an almighty crash. Ling's bike, I thought distractedly, stepping over the spinning wheel and reaching the first tread of the stairs. David took my hand and gently began to lead me up the worn carpeted steps.

He paused when we reached the dimly lit hall, unsure of which way to go. In the seven weeks we had been together, he had never been across the threshold to my room. And that wasn't the only boundary he had yet to cross. Despite some fairly intense and passionate make-out sessions, we had never taken that side of things any further. I knew that he'd slept with other girlfriends before me, from things he'd inadvertently let slip, but so far he'd been the one pulling back and keeping our relationship on a slow simmer, even though I was ready to boil. Inexperience silenced the question that burnt my tongue every time he stopped an intimate moment from escalating into something more. Why was he stopping? I'd seen the look in his eyes every time he had pulled away from me. I may be naïve, but I was pretty sure he wanted to carry on.

It was one of the few times I really regretted that my best friend in the whole world was a boy. Maxi would be no use at all to me for a sounding board, and I didn't feel comfortable discussing that side of my relationship with David with him.

'That's my room,' I said, and my voice was so husky I scarcely recognised it as my own. David's hand paused on the handle, and he turned back to me, his free hand cradling my cheek.

'Are you sure you're ready for this? We can stop now. It's never too late to change your mind.'

I felt the skin beneath his palm grow warm, but I kept my eyes fixed on the piercing blue intensity of his. 'I don't want to stop. But . . . this is all new . . . for me, I mean. I . . . I don't know what I am doing here . . . exactly.'

The pad of his thumb lightly caressed the inflamed skin of my face. 'Don't worry. I do,' he said softly, pulling me against him for a kiss that began in the hall, travelled to the bed and kept going even as he gently tugged the clothes from my body.

I'd heard that the first time isn't meant to be all that good. I'd heard that girls are often left disappointed, frustrated and completely unfulfilled. I'd heard wrong.

★   ★   ★

David was my first. My first everything. My first proper boyfriend, my first love, my first lover and my first — my only — broken heart. I'm not sure when it all started to go wrong. No. That's a lie. I could pinpoint the markers like pegs on a map marking a journey which was going to take you somewhere you never wanted to go.

Charlotte — Six Years Earlier

I twisted the engagement ring on my finger, as the lights from the shops flashing past our taxi window caught its facets and threw up a starburst of brilliant prisms. David reached across and covered my hand with his own. 'You're not nervous, are you?' he asked, turning in his seat to study me.

I smiled away the concern on his face. 'About meeting your mother? No. Not at all,' I assured him. And I wasn't lying, I really wasn't. His mother might have eaten Ally alive all those years earlier, but I wasn't an easily intimidated university girlfriend, plucked from the baby pool and dropped in at the deep end. I could swim with sharks, if I had to. I came from the same ocean as David. His mother wasn't the one who was bothering me.

Still, it was impossible not to remember the conversation I'd had with Ally after her one and only disastrous visit to David's family home. Of course that was back in the days before everything got ugly, back when Ally and I were still friends.

'*You can't imagine how awful if was,*' *Ally had said, her arm working as though powered by a motor, as she vigorously beat flour, eggs and sugar in a bowl. Her face was pink from her exertions, speckled with white freckles of flour. She said she found baking therapeutic, and from the array of muffins, cakes and pastries, covering just about every kitchen countertop, she must have needed a lot of therapy.*

'How bad could it have been?' I'd asked, picking up a muffin and hopping up to sit on the only clear worktop left in the kitchen.

'How bad?' she had asked, her voice going up at least one octave. 'I'll tell you how bad. I was wearing the same bloody dress as the catering staff. I spent half the night politely telling the party guests that I couldn't get them another canapé or glass of champagne, and I actually had no idea where the bathroom was!'

I nibbled on the edge of the muffin, which was really still too warm to eat. 'But that wasn't exactly David's mother's fault, was it?' I reasoned.

Ally stopped her frenetic beating and eyed me meaningfully for a moment as though questioning my loyalties. I felt the guilt burn inside me, like acid indigestion, and had to concentrate on swallowing my bite of muffin. She was right to question me, just not for the reason she thought.

She blew several wayward strands of hair back from her face and returned to beating the mixture into submission. 'Perhaps not. But everything else was. It was all done so subtly that David didn't even see most of it. But everything she said was a put down. She didn't even try to disguise the fact that she clearly thought I wasn't good enough for her son. She might as well have given me a sash with 'Gold-digger' on it to wear.'

I'd said nothing, wondering just how much of the perceived slight had been real and how much had sprung from the tiny chip, well more of a notch than a chip, that Ally unknowingly wore on her shoulder. Not that I was dismissing her claims entirely. I'd met plenty of women like that over the years; most of them were close friends with my mother.

'And she even tried to stop David and I from . . . you know . . . '

I was extra careful to make sure that my smile stayed in place as I asked, 'She did? That was a little Victorian of her.'

'She put me in a room over the garage, despite the fact the house has more bedrooms than a small hotel.'

'Oh well. It was only for one night.' I could hear the tightness in my voice, and hoped Ally was still too irate to notice it. I had enough difficulty appearing nonchalant about their . . . enthusiastic . . . love life. I certainly didn't need to be discussing it in detail.

'Yeah, it was. But David came to my room in the middle of the night anyway, and unknowingly tripped the burglar alarm. We were kind of in the middle of . . . things . . . when the police turned up.'

Despite the seam of jealousy that ran like a guilty secret beneath my skin, I burst out laughing. Ally laid down her wooden spoon, and for a moment I thought she was crying at the memory, until I realised she was actually laughing too, so hard that tears were running in small rivulets through her flour-stained cheeks. 'It was kind of funny,' she conceded.

★   ★   ★

138

'Charlotte? Earth to Charlotte.' I jumped at the sound of David's voice, noting with surprise that the taxi had pulled up at the steps of an exclusive London club. 'We're here. You were miles away,' David said, taking hold of the lapels of my coat and gently drawing me closer towards him. He kissed the tip of my nose. 'What were you thinking about?'

I lifted my head, and met his eyes, thankful he couldn't read my thoughts. 'Nothing important. Nothing important at all.'

★ ★ ★

'Of course I'm delighted, darling,' Veronica exclaimed, her voice more cut-glass than the delicate goblet in her hand. 'It just seems a little . . . rushed . . . that's all. You two have only been courting for eight months. I wondered what the hurry was.'

A snort of laughter erupted from the opposite side of the table, as David's red-headed brother mimed picking up a telephone. 'Hey Mum, it's the 1950s calling. They asked if they could have their word back,' Robert said, his eyes twinkling warmly.

'Yes, Robert. Very funny,' said his mother dismissively. 'But despite what you think, you don't want people to wonder if there's a reason behind this sudden announcement and short engagement. You wouldn't want anyone thinking Charlotte is in the *family way*, would you?' she asked her eldest son.

David and I exchanged a look of total

astonishment, literally stunned into silence. Thankfully not something that affected his younger brother. Again he mimed picking up the phone. 'And the attitude too,' he said into an imaginary receiver. 'Okay, right, I'll let her know.'

'You are hilarious,' said his mother, without cracking a smile. Robert winked broadly at me and I smiled back.

And suddenly I remembered how I had almost slipped up when Ally had said to me all those years ago.

'The only good thing about the whole weekend was meeting David's younger brother, Robert. He was really lovely.'

'Yes, he's good fun, isn't he? I mean . . . he sounds like he is,' I had quickly corrected, biting my lip at how close I had come to inadvertently revealing that I had in fact met both brothers many years earlier.

'Charlotte and I might only have been dating for eight months, but don't forget that we shared a house in our final year at university. We've known each other a really long time. No way is this a rushed decision. In fact, I've never been more sure of anything in my entire life.'

Robert made a mock gagging sound and pantomimed throwing up in the silver bucket currently housing the expensive bottle of champagne.

His mother's eyes narrowed as she icily commented, 'I really don't think you are my child at all, Robert. I believe there may have been some dreadful mistake at the hospital.'

Robert shrugged nonchalantly, and I knew

140

that without his intervening banter the evening would have been far more frigid. Veronica Williams turned in her seat to look at me. 'I do hope my grandchildren — when they arrive — ' she added hastily, when it looked like David was about to speak again, 'take after their father, and bear absolutely no resemblance to their uncle.'

★   ★   ★

'I hadn't been expecting the topic of grandchildren to pop up tonight, had you?' I questioned on the taxi journey back to David's flat. 'Is she panicking about securing an heir . . . like royalty?' I giggled, burrowing my face into the shoulder of David's cashmere coat, the one I had just bought him for Christmas.

'Beats me,' said David, shrugging the shoulder I was resting on. 'I've given up trying to guess my mother's motives. I'm just pleased she didn't do or say anything to upset you, or make you uncomfortable, that's all. I don't want you running for the hills after meeting her.'

'*I'm sure David didn't even see how bad she made me feel. How unworthy and insignificant,*' Ally had confided to me. Oh, he saw, Ally. He saw it all.

'Just wait till she meets my own mother,' I said, yawning widely. 'It'll be like looking into a mirror.'

David pretended to shiver and drew his arm around me, cinching me closer against him. 'I suppose that's something we ought to have discussed by now.' His voice was soft and low, so that the taxi driver couldn't hear.

'What?'

'Babies. You *do* want children one day, don't you?' I closed my eyes, realising we had accidentally wandered into one of the most important conversations of our relationship. 'Obviously not yet,' David continued. 'I know we both have our careers, and that you want to set up your own business too. But one day . . . ' He left the question dangling in the air, like a precious star that had slipped from the sky.

'Aren't you worried that we'd be terrible parents? We've hardly had the best role models to follow.'

David pulled me against him. 'And that is precisely why you and I are going to be absolutely brilliant parents. All we have to do is think about our own upbringing . . . and then do the exact opposite.'

I smiled into the darkness of the taxi, feeling the prospect of a future family waiting for me in the years ahead, like a glittering reward.

'I *do* want children,' I confirmed happily. 'I want it all. Marriage, a career, and then a perfect little replica of you to make everything complete. But I do have one condition, and I'm afraid this one is a deal breaker.'

'And that is?' I could hear the small vein of worry behind his question.

'That your brother categorically and emphatically *has* to be their godfather.'

'Agreed,' said David with a happy grin, tightening his hold around me.

Ally

The small Relatives' Room seemed suddenly crowded with the ghosts of the past I had unwittingly summoned. Wordlessly I got to my feet and slipped out into the ward. The unit was softly lit apart from the nurses' station and the two occupied rooms at either end of the linoleum-covered corridor. For a single second I felt as though I was standing on the Equator, being tugged by the polarity of opposing poles. My reawakened memories pulled me to the room on my right, but my heart, my soul and everything that I held dear in my life pulled me to the left. That was the way I turned.

Nothing appeared to have changed within Joe's room. There still seemed to be an awful lot of people around him, and none of them seemed to be any closer to bringing him back to me. I stood in the shadows of the corridor, and watched through the glass, my heart yearning to be in there with him, my brain terrified of what I might learn if I were.

I had fallen in love with David quickly and dramatically, as though the very ground I was standing on had crumbled beneath me, leaving me to tumble in free-fall into an abyss. With Joe it had been so much more gradual, sliding inch by inch towards him, so subtly at first that I hadn't even realised it was happening, until it was too late to have stopped the inexorable journey. Not that I had ever wanted to.

Ally — Eight Years Earlier

The first sight I ever had of Joe was of his backside; I've really never got tired of reminding him of that. The first time he ever met me, I threw up two minutes later. He loves telling that one too.

I had stumbled into the kitchen of my family home, feeling absolutely terrible. My dad had had a gastric bug over Christmas, and Mum had come down with it a week later. I thought I had managed to dodge the bullet, but I'd woken that morning feeling dreadful, so I guessed not. The last thing I had wanted or expected to find, as I blearily entered the kitchen, was a workman preparing to rip out our old units and replace them with new hand-crafted ones.

I'd forgotten my mum had warned me that someone was coming round the following morning to begin the work. So, when I walked into the kitchen, wearing a skimpy strappy top and old faded PJ bottoms, I did a cartoon-like double-take when the first thing I saw was a neatly taut, denim-covered behind. Happily the sight was devoid of any trace of 'builder's bum', because no one needs to see that, with or without a stomach bug. In fact there was nothing about the man, who instantly got to his feet as I entered the room, that could possibly make a person feel nauseous. Far from it. He was tall, and had a warm wide smile, set in a more than passably attractive face. His short-cut sandy-coloured hair was flecked with tiny pieces of plaster, making him look as though he'd been

144

caught in the confetti fallout of a nearby wedding. He seemed giant-like in proportions in our small kitchen, but I think that was probably due to his thick-soled work-boots and the fact that I was barefoot. He was muscular and broad shouldered, like a rugby player. A rugby player with a large chisel in his hands.

'Good morning,' he greeted, with an easy smile, putting down the tool and extending his hand to me. 'I'm sorry if I woke you. Your mum said you were still asleep. I was trying to be as quiet as possible.'

My eyes went to the kitchen clock and I saw it was well after nine. I'd slept badly last night, every night if truth be told, since David and I broke up. Insomnia was just one of many lingering reminders of my failed relationship.

'I'm Joe, by the way. Joe Taylor,' he said, still holding out his hand in the kind of polite greeting you somehow don't expect from a surprisingly good-looking tradesman you have just found in your kitchen.

Feeling a little slow and stupid I put my hand in his, instantly aware of the coarsened texture of the skin of his palm. It felt nothing at all like David's hand. I shook my head in annoyance. I *had* to stop doing that.

I opened my mouth to complete my side of the customary exchange. 'I'm . . . I'm . . . going to be sick!' I completed, removing my hand so it could cover my mouth as I ran from him at speed towards the downstairs cloakroom. I only just made it in time, throwing myself to my knees before the toilet, without even bothering to shut

145

the door behind me. Several horrible moments later, I was done. I rocked back on my knees, and ran my hand across my mouth, which felt disgusting. What I needed more than anything was a drink of water. And suddenly there one was, appearing like magic over my right shoulder.

'Here, drink this.' I took the glass gratefully and raised it to my lips. 'Don't take too much at once,' he advised, 'or it might not stay down.' I had no desire for a repeat performance, so I followed his advice carefully. It was mortifying enough to throw up in front of a complete stranger; I certainly didn't want to do it twice.

The water was reviving, and after a few mouthfuls I set the glass aside. His hand was outstretched, waiting for me, and it should have been weird to use it to help me to my feet, but I did. And it didn't feel weird at all.

'I am so sorry about that,' I apologised, a blush of embarrassment flooding my face with the colour that my bout of nausea had washed away.

'Don't worry about it,' he dismissed with a half smile. 'It's a common reaction people have when meeting me. I've kind of got used to it.' I laughed, instantly liking him. 'How do you feel now?'

'Better. Much better,' I confirmed. 'But I think I must be coming down with the same thing my parents have both had, so you'd better keep your distance.'

He shrugged, but made no move to step away from me. If I'd thought he looked tall and broad in the kitchen, then I felt totally dwarfed by him in the close proximity of the tiny downstairs cloakroom.

'I've got a pretty hardy constitution. I think I can risk it,' he said, cupping my elbow as he led me gently from the room, as though he was the householder, and I was the outsider. That too should have felt uncomfortable and off-putting, but again it didn't.

Back in the kitchen once more, he pulled out one of the pine chairs from the table. 'Why don't you sit down for a moment.' I sat. 'So, as I was saying,' he continued, as though nothing had happened, 'my name is Joe. I'm going to be here for the next few weeks, working on the kitchen.' I nodded, still feeling embarrassed about what had just happened. I hated anyone seeing me like that.

'I take it you are Alexandra Felicity Nelson.' My eyebrows rose at the use of my full name. He grinned and nodded in the direction of the adjacent dining room. 'I saw your wall of fame.'

I gave a small cringe of apology. The entire wall beside my piano was covered with framed certificates and diplomas from my many music exams, as well as photographs taken at every single recital or performance I had ever been in. To say that my parents were proud of my achievements was an understatement.

'Ally,' I corrected. 'Just Ally.'

'Well, Just Ally, is there anything I can get you? A cup of tea? A slice of toast?'

I shook my head. My stomach was more settled, but I had no desire to test just how far I could push it. My dad hadn't been able to eat a thing for days over Christmas.

'Well, I won't need to disconnect the power

today, so you can always change your mind later. If you don't feel up to fixing anything yourself, I'm happy to do it for you.' He really was incredibly nice, and perhaps that was why I felt the sting as my eyes began to fill with tears. It didn't take much to push me over the edge these days. A sad advert on TV, a sloppy Rom Com DVD I'd watched the other night with Max, the empty place at the Christmas table where once my grandmother had sat. All had the power to reduce me to tears. It was like David had let a new emotional Ally out of hibernation when we were together, and now that we weren't, I was really struggling to get her back in her box.

We stared at each other for a moment, both a little unsure of how to proceed. Perhaps some of my discomfort was due to the fact that I was suddenly aware of just how inappropriate my revealing strappy vest was for chatting to a stranger. I brought my legs up onto the seat, hiding my breasts from view. Not that I could accuse him of looking anywhere except my face when he spoke. But still.

'I should probably get out of your way,' I suggested, making no move to get off my chair.

'You're fine where you are. Don't go rushing off if you still don't feel right.'

I didn't feel right. Far from it. But I didn't think that was going to change for a long time to come.

'Is this what you do, kitchens and stuff?' I asked artlessly, waving my arm at the stack of beautifully carved cabinet doors resting against the wall.

He smiled at my choice of words. 'More stuff than kitchens, at the moment. All types of joinery, really. At least for now.'

'That sounds intriguing. Have you a grand plan for the future?'

'Hasn't everyone?' he replied easily.

I tried to keep my smile in place, but I could feel it starting to slip. 'Hmm. I guess so.'

This time it was his turn to pause before speaking. 'You don't sound so sure.'

'My plans are kind of . . . fluid . . . at the moment. I should have gone back to university a couple of weeks ago, but, well . . . things have happened, so I think I might be hanging around here for a while.' This was really unlike me, sharing so much with a stranger, but there was something about him that made it easy to reveal more than I intended. I had only known him for twenty minutes, and already I could sense he was a good listener.

'Can you do that?'

'People drop out all the time.'

He tried, and failed, not to look shocked. It was a similar expression to the one I'd already seen on the faces of Mum, Dad and Max. I just hadn't expected to see it on the guy who was fitting our kitchen, that's all.

'Anyway, it's not dropping out. Not really. I have my dissertation to write, and most of our lectures are finished, and I can catch up with the on-line notes for those that aren't.' I stopped abruptly, realising I was still trying to justify my decision, probably more to myself than him. He was just making polite conversation. I'm sure he didn't care one way or the other about the spectacular mess I had made of my life.

He bent to pick up a tool by his feet, and turned it over in his hands for several seconds before speaking. 'Your mum did mention something. About a break-up.'

My head flew up in shock. I couldn't believe Mum had told him something so personal. What next? Were the butcher and the postman about to pop round offering me tea and sympathy?

He correctly read the expression on my face. 'Don't be angry with her. She was just looking out for you. Being a good mum. I could tell she was really concerned about you. And she was worried that your ex might show up here while she was at work. That's why she mentioned it, so I could keep an eye out for you.'

'Well, thank you. But that really won't be necessary,' I said, my voice so tight it was an effort to squeeze out the words.

'She didn't ask me to interfere. And of course, I wouldn't,' he assured me. 'It's obviously none of my business.'

I nodded, my eyes stinging from tears I really didn't want to shed in front of him. 'No. It isn't. But that's not what I meant. It won't be necessary for you, Mum or anyone else to look out for him, because he's not going to come here. Not now. Not ever.'

'I see,' said Joe turning his attention back to the cabinet he'd been working on when I first walked into the room. I thought the subject was — thankfully — over and done with, until he turned to look back at me over one broad shoulder. 'Then he's an idiot, if you don't mind me saying.'

'For not coming after me?'

He shook his head slowly. 'For letting you go in the first place.'

Ally

A flurry of movement caught my eye as the medical team began to file from the room, deep in discussion. I looked up anxiously, searching for the face of the doctor who had accompanied me to the ward, but he was no longer among them. It was a nurse who came to stand beside me, gently touching me on the arm. 'Mrs Taylor?'

I didn't look at her. My attention was still fixed on the departing doctors. 'Where are they going? Has something else happened?' I asked desperately.

The hand still resting on my arm patted me gently. 'No. The shifts are changing shortly, that's all. They need to make sure the medical team taking over your husband's care are up to speed.'

I stared after the retreating medics, wanting to scream at them to come back and not even consider going home to their warm cosy lives, their wives, their families and their perfect unbroken worlds until they had finished the job they had begun. Until Joe was made well again. Was that an unreasonable request? It didn't seem so to me. How many doctors would be on duty for the rest of the night? Would their time be split between the care of both patients on the ward: the man I loved now and the man I had loved then?

'Would you like to sit with your husband while they do the handover? It's going to take ten to fifteen minutes. You could have a little time alone.' I nodded gratefully, blinking in the bright lights as I followed her into Joe's room.

'Hey, I'm back,' I said to his silent motionless body. The nurse bustled around the room, clearing away items that had been left discarded, sliding shut drawers and cupboards and restoring order to the room. She glanced with a practised eye at Joe's chart and then spent several moments carefully studying the various displays on the multitude of machines my husband was hooked up to.

She positioned a chair beside the bed and gently pushed me down onto it. 'Is anyone here with you?' she asked kindly. 'A family member, a friend?' I thought of the woman I had just left behind in the Relatives' Room and shook my head.

'No. No one. I hadn't wanted to phone anyone until I had something positive to tell them. My husband's parents are old and I didn't want to worry them unnecessarily.'

The nurse squeezed my shoulder, and I could see she was weighing up whether or not it was her place to say what was on her mind. 'Perhaps it might be a good idea to give them a call, and let them know what's happened,' she suggested gently. I felt something — which I suspected was my heart — plummet within me. 'And it would be good for you to have someone to lean on, too, a friend perhaps.'

She left the room in slow hushed steps, assuring me that she would be just outside if I should need her. But the person I really needed was the one right there in the room with me, if only he'd wake up.

I held his hand tightly in mine, hoping to magically or medically transfer whatever he needed to recover through our interwoven fingers. I wanted so very much to believe he was clasping my hand in return, but in reality I knew that only one of us was maintaining our grip. I kissed the too-pale fingers, and the work-roughened calloused surface of his palm. 'Come back to me,' I whispered into the skin that no longer smelled of Joe.

Ally — Eight Years Earlier

It's hard to say when my friendship with Joe began to gently nudge the pain of losing David to one side. It happened in such tiny degrees, that at first it wasn't even discernible — at least not to me. It was only looking back that I saw it come together and begin to blossom, as though our relationship had been captured in time-lapse photography.

At night, I still cried silently into my pillow, missing David in a way that was so visceral, it literally felt as though he had been bodily torn from me. Yet in the morning light, the weakness that had me reaching for my phone at three a.m.

was gone. And as I descended the stairs, to the sound of Joe's tuneful whistling against a backdrop of his saw drawing through wood, those feelings were as hard to hold on to as a half-remembered dream.

I learned a lot about Joe Taylor in the six weeks that he took to fit our kitchen. One of the things I *didn't* learn until a great deal later, was that there was no way it should have taken even half as long as that to complete the job.

'I like Joe, don't get me wrong, and the standard of his work is terrific,' my father had said over dinner one night, about three weeks after the kitchen renovations had begun. 'But it's just as well we agreed a price for the job up front, because if I had to pay him by the hour, I'd be bankrupt before he was done.'

I dropped my head to hide the pink flush I could feel warming my cheeks, as I dragged my spoon through the spaghetti sauce on my plate. I knew I was at least partly responsible for the slow completion of the project. I spent far too much time each day in the kitchen, idly chatting with Joe, and as a result neither my dissertation nor the cabinets were progressing as quickly as they should. Joe was just so easy to talk to, and despite his being six years older than me, we had so much in common. There was also a refreshing maturity in being with someone whose idea of a good night out wasn't defined by how many tequila shots you could consume before the evening even began. And Joe was funny, really funny, with a quick-witted ready humour, that always took me by surprise. It made me sad to

154

realise how little laughter there had been between David and me by the end. It was as though our constant bickering had eroded it all away, smile by smile, and laugh by laugh, and neither of us had even noticed it going.

I think that was when I knew that despite everything, I was going to be alright again, that I was going to get through this and come out whole on the other side — when I realised I still remembered how to laugh. And I had Joe to thank for that.

'Do you have another kitchen to fit when you finish up here?' I asked one day, looking around at the bank of new units which now lined our walls. To my layman's eye his work here was almost done. I felt a strange pang at the thought that he would soon be gone, which was weird, but with Max away at college I could feel the loneliness waiting in the shadows like a hidden stalker.

'Not exactly, but I've still got a fair bit to do here before I'm done.'

I suppose the surprise must have registered on my face, because he looked a little uncomfortable as he said, 'Well, it's mainly just finishing off stuff. But I'm a bit of a perfectionist.' He said it as though it was almost something to be ashamed of.

'Me too,' I confessed. 'If I get just one note wrong, I have to go right back to the start of the piece and play it again.'

'I know,' he said with a small grin.

'Sorry,' I apologised. 'I guess you must be kind of fed up with Beethoven's Sonatas by now.'

'Not at all,' he contradicted. 'You're broadening my horizons.' We shared a mutual smile, and I instantly recalled the day when I'd looked up from my piano and seen him leaning against the doorframe watching me play with an expression on his face that had stayed with me long after he had climbed into his van and driven away that night.

I'd commandeered one end of the dining-room table with my laptop, notebooks and a dozen text books, yet I spent far more time than I should in the kitchen, carefully stepping over Joe's tools and lengths of wood to make us both endless cups of tea and coffee. After a couple of days I invited him to join me at the pine kitchen table for lunch, rather than eating in the solitude of his van's cab, and the pattern of our days had been set.

One morning I walked into the kitchen and found Joe busily absorbed in sketching out a design on a large sheet of paper at the table. I passed behind him, and tried not to notice the familiar clean fresh fragrance of the shower gel or shampoo that he always used. But my nose betrayed me, for it had already squirrelled the aroma away in the vaults of my memory, in a file clearly labelled 'Joe'.

I looked over his shoulder at the sketch. It was of a kitchen, far larger than ours. I watched the swift strokes of his pencil adding small details to the drawing, lifting it with subtle shading into a miniature piece of art rather than just a diagram. Even to my untrained eye, I could see he had a real talent.

'Is that your next project? Whose kitchen is that, it looks really nice.'

Joe straightened and laid down the pencil, turning to me with his slow easy smile. 'It's a long-term ongoing job actually, because the client keeps running out of money.'

'That's tough on you.'

'Not really. I'm the client.'

My eyes flitted from his face back to the pencil sketch before him. 'You are? But I thought you lived in a shared rental with friends?'

'I do. Or rather, I did,' Joe explained. 'I bought this place a year ago, totally derelict, and I've been doing it up room by room, until it was habitable enough to move into. The kitchen is the next stage.'

I leaned down a little closer, to better study the drawing, and a swathe of my long dark hair fell forward, brushing against his cheek. I apologised hurriedly, and tossed it back over my shoulder. 'It's a great sized room. Can you actually cook, or is that all for show?' I asked, pointing to the impressive old-fashioned range he had drawn nestled into the recess of a large fireplace.

'I do alright,' he said. 'I have three or four dishes I can pull off without poisoning anyone. I'll have to invite you round for a meal when it's done, so you can judge for yourself.'

For some reason his innocent invitation — which I was certain he'd only made out of politeness — made me feel oddly jittery, so I dipped my head once more, not caring if my hair fell forward, welcoming the concealment. 'You

157

know what you should do? You should build an island in the centre of the room,' I suggested, running my fingernail over the large vacant space in the middle of the drawing. 'I think they look amazing in big kitchens — they really work well.'

He didn't reply, and I wondered if he thought it was rather cheeky of me to be telling him what he should do with his own kitchen. After all, he was the expert here, not me. 'Sorry. It's nothing to do with me. Your design looks great just as it is,' I back-pedalled.

He looked at me, and it was hard to properly read the expression on his face through the strands of my hair hanging between us. Wordlessly he picked up his pencil, and in just a dozen or so strokes an island unit suddenly appeared in the picture.

He straightened in his seat and looked at me, a thoughtful expression in his eyes. 'Something like that?'

I nodded, suddenly overcome with a peculiar sensation, which for some strange reason was making my heart beat a little faster. 'Yes, that looks perfect.'

Ally

The nurse was apologetic when she knocked discreetly on the door before entering the room ten minutes later. 'I'm sorry, but the doctors need to run some more tests, so I'm going to have to ask you to step outside again.' It was too soon, far too soon. I hadn't had the chance yet to

158

tell Joe that I would have to call his parents. And there were other things I hadn't told him: one of which was that the woman I'd hoped never to see again was sharing the waiting-room with me, and the man *he* hoped I'd never see again was right down the corridor, fighting his very own battle to survive. I got shakily to my feet feeling guilty, as though I was hiding secrets.

'You'll come and get me, as soon as I can come back?' I asked the nurse urgently, as she shepherded me through the door. We both looked up at the sound of approaching footsteps as a cluster of white-coated figures headed our way.

'The very minute they're done,' she promised.

★　★　★

'I'm sorry, Ally. I don't think I understand what you're saying. You're telling me Joe fell on some ice?'

The mobile line was clear enough, and I knew that wasn't the reason why my mother-in-law hadn't grasped the situation. It was, after all, well outside of the boundaries of normal.

'No Kaye, he fell *through* some ice. On a frozen pond.'

'How? Why? What was he doing there?'

'I don't know. The police couldn't tell me.' I heard her gasp and knew immediately I'd said the wrong thing.

'The police? Who called the police? Was there a crime? Was Joe attacked and thrown onto the ice?'

I took a breath and tried to steady my voice.

Joe's mother was a natural panicker. Every winter cold was the flu, every headache a lurking brain tumour, every unexplained pain the forerunner of something incurable. Each black fear and prediction she had made over the years had thankfully proved to be groundless. But now, on this night, she had her first genuine reason to worry about her only son, and I had no way of reassuring her.

'No one else was involved,' I replied with careful patience, before realising that I had no idea if that was even true. I was still none the wiser myself. 'The police came to the house to tell me.'

'Oh no. Then it has to be bad. Really bad.' I knew I should be trying to calm her down, to lessen her anxiety, it was what Joe would want me to do, but it was virtually impossible when her words were exactly echoing my own fears and terror. 'Let me just tell Frank,' she said and there was a loud clatter which I knew meant that she had simply dropped the phone to the floor and gone in search of her husband. I was doing this very badly, and if I wasn't careful I would end up being solely responsible for giving both of them a stroke or a heart attack, or both.

'Ally. Which hospital are you at?' My father-in-law's voice was overly brusque, which I knew was his way of hiding his emotion. He'd spoken in just those tones the very first time I had placed Jake in his arms as a baby, with the words 'And here is your grandson.'

'We're at St Elizabeth's, but — ' I began.

'Right. Well, we'll . . . um . . . well if we leave

right now, we should get there in five hours or so.'

I felt a hard knot of anxiety rise in my throat like bile, turning my voice into a squawk of dismay. 'Frank, no. You can't drive here in this blizzard. It's far too dangerous.' I hesitated and then stepped clean over the daughter-in-law boundary by adding, 'And besides, it's not safe, you've not driven in years. It's a terrible idea.'

I was being harsh, but only because I knew Joe would be apoplectic if he had any idea of what his father was considering. He'd been insisting for ages that they should sell their old car. '*If it's not there, he won't be tempted to jump into it one day, if there's some sort of emergency,*' he had said, never for a moment realising how prophetic his words would be, nor that *he* might be the very emergency that he was worrying about.

Eventually I managed to persuade my in-laws to abandon the idea of driving themselves to the hospital, by assuring them I would arrange for someone to collect them and bring them to their son. I broke the phone connection and leaned back against the exterior wall, looking out bleakly over the hospital car park. All of the cars now wore thick white fluffy blankets of snow, several centimetres deep. No one should be on the road in these conditions, and especially not anyone who was past pensionable age, so that ruled out my own parents or my kindly next-door neighbours. I had no idea how to find a taxi that would be willing to undertake the journey, and the pressure of yet another thing to

161

worry about threatened to buckle me.

I don't know why it took me so long to work out who to ask for help. He was the one person who would know what to do, who wouldn't panic, who had my back and who loved Joe almost as much as I did. The ringtone sounded different, but then transatlantic ones always do.

'Max Fellows,' he trilled in my ear, his voice now bearing even more of a New York twang than the last time we had spoken. He had a lazy ear that picked up accents easily, it was probably the only idle part of his entire body.

'Maxi, it's me. Ally. Something awful has happened.'

Every emotion I'd been careful not to reveal in my conversation with Kaye and Frank broke through the poorly erected dam I had shored in place. It took several false starts before I was capable of responding to Max's rapidly fired '*What's wrong?*' Stumbling over my words I eventually managed to explain what had happened to Joe. It was almost impossible to get to the end of each sentence without crying.

'Who's there with you at the hospital?' Max asked, his concern — as ever — directed at me. 'And who's looking after my godson?'

'Jake's at home, with our neighbours. He's . . .' I had to draw in a really long breath to finish what I was trying to say, 'He's waiting for me to bring his daddy home. And Maxi, I'm so scared that's not going to happen; I don't know if Joe's going to come out of this.'

'Of course he will,' Max asserted firmly, and I wanted more than anything to believe him, but

162

memories of the looks on the doctors' faces and in the eyes of the nurse told me something else. 'Don't you give up on that man,' Max sounded almost angry with me, and perhaps that was just what I needed. 'Joe is strong and healthy. And more to the point he would walk through fire and flames to be with you and Jakey. He won't leave you alone. He couldn't.' Max's own voice shook a little as he pressed on. 'So, are you by yourself at the hospital?'

A small humphing sound whistled through my lips. 'If only,' I said, unable to suppress the running stitch of hysteria threading through my words. 'David and Charlotte are here too.'

The line cracked for several moments against my ear before Max's voice cut through the interference. 'Sorry Ally, the line broke up. For a moment I thought you said David and Charlotte were there.'

'I did. They are.'

'You called your ex and his wife to sit with you?' Max's voice had risen a good two octaves in incredulity.

My responding laugh was cyanide bitter. 'No. But by some billion-to-one coincidence David's also a patient here. Charlotte and I are sharing the waiting-room.'

'Fuck me.'

I heard muttering in the background and knew that Max must be hurriedly summarising the situation to Justin, his partner.

'Give us a second, sweetie,' Max requested. I closed my eyes on the snowstorm and the car park and imagined my old friend sitting in one of

163

his oddly shaped designer chairs, looking out of the large floor-to-ceiling window in his loft apartment. All of New York would be laid out hundreds of feet below him; cars and buses would be trundling along the grid-patterned streets like miniature pieces in a toytown set. I could almost imagine the early afternoon sun slanting in through the glass, bisecting the gleaming wooden floor in glowing chevrons.

'Okay,' said Max, his voice relocating me back across the dividing ocean to the snow-covered hospital car park. 'One problem at a time. Give me the address of Joe's parents. There's a car service we use in the UK, who won't say no if we call them up, whatever the weather.' That was the benefit of having a successful friend; he knew how to make things happen. Since moving to America Max's career in fashion design had soared like a rocket, but his partner Justin was already way ahead of him. Together they were a formidable combination. I'd never asked Max for help before — even though it had been offered several times. But tonight, for Joe, I'd have dealt with the devil himself, struck just about any bargain imaginable, to fix things.

I dug into my bag, found my address book and rapidly dictated the details to Max. As we spoke, I could already hear Justin in the background phoning the limousine company. One tiny straw was lifted from the burden on my back.

'Okay. That's your in-laws taken care of. Don't worry about phoning them, I'll call them with the details in a few minutes when we hang up.' Tears of gratitude stung my eyes. 'Now are you going to be okay until about eleven o'clock tomorrow morning?'

My brow furrowed, not following his meaning, although afterwards I realised that he'd probably made his decision during the first minute of our phone call.

'What's happening at eleven?'

'That's when I should be with you. There's a flight out of JFK late this afternoon which I should be able to make.'

'You're coming here? To London? For me?' More stupid tears, but there was just no way of stopping them now.

His voice, with the unfamiliar American undertone, sounded suddenly gruff. 'Of course not for *you*. I'm coming to give that great big gorgeous husband of yours a piece of my mind for scaring us all like this.' His voice lowered and softened, flowing through my chilled limbs and warming me. 'Just hang tough until I get there, sweetie. Stay strong. I'm on my way and remember that I love you.' Raw emotion thrummed through his voice. 'All *three* of you,' he added. And without saying another word, he hung up.

I stayed in the car park until I had gained a little more control over my chaotic emotions. It was such a huge thing to do, to drop everything, abandon whatever else was going on in his life and fly across the Atlantic to be by my side. I knew how very lucky I was to have someone who would do that for me. For us. My thoughts were full of Max as I slowly began to retrace my steps back into the hospital building, absently noting

165

that the falling snow had already obliterated all signs of my passage. I raised my eyes to the skies, imagining Jake with his cute button nose pressed against the window, excitedly watching the world change into a white wonderland, while all I could do was worry about its effect on the roads, skies and runways, the things that were bringing the people I loved to this place.

Max and Joe had hit it off from the very beginning, which had been a totally unexpected and wonderful surprise. On paper they were worlds apart: the witty, fast-talking, trend-driven fashion designer, who'd fallen on his smart leather-booted feet right into the bustling hustle of Manhattan, and the softly spoken, naturally reserved craftsman, with the hidden sense of humour, who wore comfortable faded jeans, loved being outdoors, country music . . . and me. And that was what they both had in common, Max had said, after that very first meeting. *'That's our common denominator, that's what's going to make us friends, and keep us friends for ever. Because we both love you to death.'* I shivered suddenly, as though a whole flock of geese had just trampled over my grave, remembering those had been his very words, 'love you to death'.

Of course another reason why Max had whole-heartedly embraced my relationship with Joe was because he *wasn't* David, because *their* first encounter had been nothing short of an explosive disaster, which had ignited the first major argument in my new relationship.

166

Ally

The day had begun badly. For a start I'd forgotten to set the alarm on my phone before falling asleep the night before. I had woken in a heart-lurching panic as the house vibrated to the slamming of our front door, which fell just short of registering on the Richter scale. It was the first time I was grateful that the warped frame required superhuman effort to close it, otherwise Max would have been left waiting for me at the station for hours instead of just minutes.

I picked up my phone to check the time, swore at the display on the screen and jumped free of the messy tangle of my bed. I didn't even have time for a shower, I lamented, racing to the bathroom and mercifully finding it empty. I quickly brushed my teeth and splashed cold water onto my sleep-puffy face, and reached blindly for the first thing my hand came to in the wardrobe.

Less than seven minutes after waking from a deep sleep, I too was slamming the front door, and racing at a pavement-pounding run towards the station, where at that very moment Max's train would be pulling in. We'd had this weekend planned since Christmas, when it had occurred to us that we were both halfway through our respective courses and yet had still never visited each other's student homes.

'Finally I'll get to meet your charming prince,' Max had teased on the phone when we'd been tying up the final arrangements.

'If you call him that to his face, I will seriously

167

have to kill you,' I warned, wriggling more comfortably into the armchair, where I'd settled down for our chat. 'Actually David's not going to be around until Sunday, he's got some rowing society event he has to attend. Still, that gives us the whole day for me to show you round the town and give you the big campus tour.' I was already getting stupidly excited at the prospect of seeing Max for the first time in months.

'Sure you'll still recognise me?' he had teased.

'I'll just look for the best-looking guy at the station.'

'Me too,' he said lightly.

I paused for a second, not sure how to acknowledge his throwaway comment. I'd known Max was gay even before I knew what gay meant, even before I knew what straight meant, come to that. But this was the first time that he had ever said anything, given even a smallest hint, about that part of his life. To be perfectly honest, nothing about him could be less important to me. To me he was just Max, my dearest and closest friend in all the world. Everything else was totally irrelevant.

On our first day of primary school we had walked hand in hand through the school gates, our friendship already long established. Nothing that had occurred in the intervening years had put so much as a dent in it. Perhaps the closeness of our bond had shut others out, or perhaps we were always destined to be happiest not being part of a large group.

Max hadn't been a typical football-loving, pushing and shoving little boy, and I had been a studious, quiet little girl, who really only opened up when seated before a piano keyboard, or later with a trumpet in my hand. Our friendship had been a perfect fit then, and it still was now.

It started to rain when I was still only halfway to the station: big, heavy, pounding raindrops, the kind that send you from damp to drenched in a matter of minutes. I squelched as I ran on in my canvas trainers, already regretting that I had only pulled on a thin hoodie over my t-shirt and hadn't stopped to find my waterproof jacket. I was fifteen minutes late and dripping from head to toe as I burst into the train station and scanned the concourse. Max was standing to one side, his phone in hand.

'There you are,' he cried, slipping the mobile away, 'I was just phoning you.'

I paused before replying, bending at the waist to combat the searing stitch in my side. 'Overslept,' I wheezed, raising my head and feeling an unpleasant trickle of water running off my hair and down the back of my top.

'You probably shouldn't have stopped for a fully clothed bath before leaving the house then,' he observed wryly.

I raised one arm from its resting place against my thighs and pointed beyond the entrance to the station. I'd always thought my lung capacity was pretty good — it has to be when you play a brass instrument — but I was still horribly winded from my sprint. 'Raining,' I gasped.

Max raised one eyebrow. 'Your sentence construction seems to have suffered a little since our last meeting. Is that what love does to you?'

'I didn't say I was in love,' I replied, my breathing still laboured.

Max raised his other eyebrow to join the first. 'I know,' he said, pulling me against him for a hug and wrinkling his nose as my soggy clothing instantly saturated him. 'But I bet you are.'

Still holding me close to his side Max picked up his bag and we headed for the exit. The rain showed no signs of abating, in fact, if anything it was falling even harder.

'We could wait it out,' I suggested, looking up at the marble-grey skies, which were heavy with clouds. 'Or we could get a taxi,' I added, nodding my head towards the line of vehicles queued up at the nearby rank.

'Well, it's easy to tell which one of us has a rich boyfriend,' Max joked, squeezing my shoulder to make sure I knew he was just teasing. 'We're students, Ally, we don't jump into taxis; we catch the bus, we hitch lifts from dodgy strangers . . . or we walk.'

'We'll get wet.'

'You're *already* wet. And now I'm not far behind you. Let's make a run for it.'

He caught the slightly alarmed look on my face at the word 'run' and amended his suggestion. 'Let's make a slow squelchy walk for it.'

They say there's a point you reach when you simply can't get any wetter. I think I might have to dispute that theory. We had the pavements pretty much to ourselves, all other pedestrians having sensibly taken shelter in shop doorways or under awnings.

'Loving your city,' declared Max, as a lorry

rounded a sharp bend and sent a huge surge of water through the air towards us.

'This was *your* idea,' I reminded him, picking up the pace and shaking the hair that was plastered to my face out of my eyes.

Max grabbed my hand then, a mischievous light flickering in his eyes. 'Come on, where's your sense of fun,' he urged and then jumped like an exuberant child off the high kerb straight into the deep muddy puddle at its edge. The swell of water drenched us both. His eyes were twinkling as he wordlessly dared me. *Oh what the hell.*

'You're nuts,' I declared as I jumped down beside him. Laughing like the children we had suddenly stepped back in time to become, we both looked up to see a huddle of onlookers crammed into a shop doorway shaking their heads slowly at us. We shared an old and treasured look and then headed off, splashing determinedly through every puddle we passed until we reached my house.

It wasn't quite so funny when we stood shivering on the doorstep as I fumbled to get my key in the lock.

'I don't know why I listen to you,' chided Max as we dripped over the threshold and into the hall. We kicked off our shoes, and left them leaching water onto the coconut doormat.

'I need a shower,' I declared, peeling my hoodie off my back, as though I was shedding a skin and dropping it on the floor. 'I'll be quick and then you can jump in after me.'

Max nodded gratefully. 'Point me in the

171

direction of your kitchen and I'll make us both some tea.'

That was one of the great things about Max, I thought as I raced up the stairs to the bathroom. He wasn't the sort of friend who would expect you to wait on him. He had an easy chameleon nature that allowed him to fit in effortlessly wherever he went. I'd never really understood before what people meant when they said someone was comfortable in their own skin. But I did now.

The shower was deliciously reviving and if I hadn't been aware that Max was sitting uncomfortably waiting for his own turn, I would have spent far longer under the steaming jets, slathering foaming gel over my limbs, which were glowing pink from the heat. I wrapped my hair in a towel and plucked my short terry robe off the hook on the back of the bathroom door.

Max and I slipped past each other in the bathroom doorway, like precisioned synchronised swimmers. 'I left your cup of tea in the messiest bedroom I found. I guessed it was yours.' I stuck my tongue out at him and headed for my room, passing Elena on the landing.

'I really like your friend Max. He's so funny, he had me in stitches downstairs,' she said with a smile, shrugging into her coat and heading for the stairs. I returned her smile, feeling her compliment glow warmly within me. Everyone loved Max, always had, always would. David would too, I was sure of it.

Ignoring the chaos of my unmade bed, I pulled a comb through my hair and plugged in my hairdryer. By the time Max had emerged from the bathroom my hair was dry, but I was no closer towards getting dressed.

He rapped on the door. 'You decent?'

'Yes, come on in,' I called, looking down to make sure the towelling edges of my robe were covering my nakedness. I did a weird little double-take as Max entered my room wearing just a towel knotted at his waist.

'Wow. Someone's been spending some serious time at the gym,' I said, trying to do a wolf whistle, which failed spectacularly. You'd think, being a musician, I'd have been better at it.

'You noticed,' said Max, preening a little and checking out his reflection in my full-length mirror, where his recently acquired six-pack was easily visible. 'Does it look good?'

'Your abs are fine, it's the size of your head that worries me,' I answered, lobbing a tissue box at him. He ducked at just the moment when the whole house once again shook as the front door was slammed. Elena on her way out, I thought.

'Throw things at me, would you,' said Max adopting a mock threatening tone as he headed across the space between us. 'I might just have to put you over my knee and punish you, for that.'

'Yeah, good luck with that,' I said, giggling at the thought as I easily pushed him back, my hands splayed on his shoulders which were still damp from the shower. And it was at just that moment, when we were — admittedly — caught in a rather compromising tableau, that my bedroom door opened and David entered the room.

'Ally, Elena said it was okay to come up — ' he began and then his words just fell away as he saw his girlfriend, wearing very little at all, mock wrestling with a strange man who was wearing even less.

I froze and then turned towards the door, my hands still resting on Max's body. David's eyes raked the room and suddenly I saw what he saw: the unmade bed, the almost naked man, being held by his girlfriend, her skin pink and flushed.

'David,' I cried, striving for a greeting, but sounding more horrified than hospitable. 'I wasn't expecting to see you today.'

'I believe I can see that,' he replied, his voice taut like piano wire.

My eyes flew to Max and my hands fell from him as though he was burning me. 'This isn't what you think,' I began, trying to inject a degree of light-heartedness into my voice and failing miserably.

'Actually Ally, I really don't know what to think. Why don't you explain it to me. Try words of one syllable, because I'm having a bit of difficulty right now working out what's going on here.'

His words were cold, but beneath them I could hear the hurt of betrayal. I shook my head as though I was trying to fight my way out of a really bad dream.

'David, this is *Max*. My friend from home.'

David's eyes flicked over my old friend and there was a look in them that warned me that this whole situation could so easily escalate into something even worse unless I defused it — fast.

'Max?' David queried, his face contorting in a

frown. 'But Max is a *girl*.'

'You told him I was a girl?' queried Max. 'That was a little harsh. *Girly*, maybe. But definitely not a girl.' I knew he was only trying to infuse some humour into the proceedings, but I didn't think it was going to help.

'I don't understand,' David said, shaking his head as though that might make sense of the picture before him. 'You said your old friend *Maxi* was coming to stay; it's the only friend from home that you've ever spoken about.'

'That would be me,' declared Max.

'As in *Maxine*,' David emphasised. 'I assumed Maxi was a girl.'

'You know what they say when you assume. It makes an ass out of — '

'Not now,' I hissed at Max who dutifully clamped his mouth shut.

'Notwithstanding the gender, I don't think you made it clear how . . . *close* . . . the two of you were. Or what was going on here before I showed up.' He looked pointedly at the bed.

'Nothing was 'going on',' I countered, and I could hear anger tightening my voice. Max clearly recognised it, but David seemed oblivious that his suspicious accusations were about to light a touch paper to the fuse. 'The bed is unmade, because I overslept. We got drenched in the rain on our way back from the station, so we both had showers as soon as we got in.'

I saw the uncertainty flickering in David's eyes, even while something else pushed its way into the forefront of his mind.

'Look mate, this really is completely innocent.

175

Ally is telling you the absolute truth. We're just friends. Let's start over here, shall we? I'm Max,' he said, holding out his hand, which in hindsight was a bad move as the towel he was gripping around his waist slipped as he extended his arm to David.

I raised my hand to shield my eyes.

'For Christ's sake!' exclaimed David, as Max fumbled clumsily to grab hold of the towel.

'Oops,' he said in his most charming voice, but David was in no mood to be charmed. Instead he turned back to me, suspicion still there on his face.

'Just out of interest, where exactly was *Maxi* planning to sleep during this weekend visit? Does this close friendship extend to you two sharing a bed together?'

'Ewww,' muttered Max.

'No. Of course not. He was going to sleep on my floor, on the airbed in a sleeping bag.' I nodded to one corner of the room, where those items were sitting in readiness. For the first time I saw David's certainty waver.

'Still, this isn't exactly normal behaviour between friends, is it?' David questioned. 'Friends of the opposite sex, I mean. You say it's all 'innocent', and I want to believe you, Ally, but you're both virtually naked here. What am I supposed to think?'

'You're supposed to trust me,' I said sorrowfully. 'You're supposed to know — better than anyone — that I would never, *have never*, done anything like that.'

There was a small softening in David's

176

expression. 'In your eyes, Ally, I'm sure it is all completely above board,' David conceded. 'But I know what guys are like. They say they're just friends with a girl but — you know what — it's always something more.'

'It's not with Max and me,' I assured him.

'Really?'

'Yes. Absolutely.' I glanced up at Max and caught the sympathy in his eyes and something else. He reached out and took hold of my hand, which did nothing at all to dissolve the doubt on David's face. Very slowly he turned to my boyfriend.

'Not that I feel the need to justify myself to you, but I am not going to stand here and let you talk like that to someone I love.' David's mouth tightened into an angry line. 'I am not, never have been and never will be at all interested in Ally in the same way that you are.'

'No Max, you don't have to — '

David looked on and even though it should have been patently obvious what Max was telling him, he still didn't seem to get it.

'I'm gay, you dick head,' he said.

That was the moment when I knew they were never going to be friends.

5

Ally

The hospital foyer was much busier than it had been earlier. More patients had arrived and were scattered in small clusters, like survivors from a battle. Some held blood-stained bandages to their wounds, several were cradling an arm or a wrist, a few had their feet propped up on the seats beside them. I guessed the slippery pavements had claimed a fresh batch of victims.

I kept my head down as I headed back to the lifts, but before I reached them I heard my name being called out above the soft hubbub of the wounded.

'Mrs Taylor.'

My head spun in the direction of the summons and I saw a tall shape in a dark uniform detach himself from a group of people seated in the far corner of the room. The voice belonged to the policeman who had come to my house, the bringer of bad news, and suddenly I knew why the expression which urged you not to '*shoot the messenger*' had been born. My footsteps faltered as he beckoned me to join him. I'd already spent far too long outside on the phone and the urge to return to the ICU, to be close to Joe, compelled me like a spell.

Maybe it was the authority of the uniform he wore, but I changed course and headed towards

178

him and the group of people he had been talking to. His eyes were kind as they watched me approach.

'How are you doing, Mrs Taylor? I understand there's been no change yet in your husband's condition?'

I shook my head fiercely. *Don't be kind to me,* I thought desperately. Be professional, be curt, arrest someone, give someone a ticket, just don't be kind to me. But I guess telepathy isn't something they teach them at the police academy, because he continued. 'I'm so very sorry to hear there's been no improvement yet. But don't give up hope. You'd be surprised at the miracles we hear about every single day in this job.'

I gave a small watery smile. I knew he meant well, but I'd stopped believing a long time ago that bad things didn't happen to good people.

'We've been piecing together what happened to Mr Taylor this afternoon, and I thought it might help you to learn what your husband did. On the seats behind me are the Webb family, they've been waiting here for several hours hoping they'd be able to speak with you.' He must have read the confusion and uncertainty on my face. 'You're going to want to hear what they have to say,' he added softly.

I looked beyond him at the family who were staring at me with sad eyes and a whole spectrum of different emotions, ranging from sympathy to gratitude and finally guilt. I didn't know who they were, or what their connection was to Joe, but if the policeman was right, these

179

strangers held the missing key that would unlock the mystery of why my husband was fighting for his life in an intensive care ward instead of sitting in our front room with our son and me.

The woman got to her feet, her young daughter hanging desperately on to the hem of her jumper. The woman's eyes were awash with compassion as they met mine. 'Mrs Taylor, my name is Fiona and this is my husband Paul and these are our children Marty, Ellie and Josh.' I had pretty much forgotten all of their names even before she had finished speaking. 'And we just wanted to say that we owe your husband the kind of debt no one can ever repay.' I looked over at the policeman, hoping he could clarify the woman's mysterious statement, but he just nodded gently, urging me to listen on. 'Your husband was walking through the park this afternoon — '

My fault, I thought. *I had the car. I should never have taken the car.*

'And he came to the rescue of our oldest son, Marty, who had fallen through the ice on the frozen pond.'

'And Todd,' chirped in the little girl, Ella? Ellie? 'He rescued Todd too.' Her mother silenced her with a gentle 'Hush, sweetheart.'

She looked back at me and her eyes were diamond-bright with tears of gratitude. 'Our dog had fallen through the ice and Marty was trying to get him out when he got into difficulties and the ice beneath him cracked.' As did her voice as she spoke.

A strange feeling stirred deep within me. Part

of it was anger and the other part was pride. A child in danger. Of course Joe would have gone to save him. Without hesitation, without thought, without any sense of the risks he was taking. I loved and hated him in that single moment for his bravery.

'My kids say he didn't hesitate, not even for a second,' she continued, glancing down at her children for confirmation. Three wide-eyed faces nodded back at her. 'He went straight onto the ice himself and managed to get Marty out. The kids were so scared, but he was calm and kind and kept reassuring them everything was alright, that they were going to be okay. Then he pulled Marty out of the water and got him back to safety.'

I nodded, my vision of the woman suddenly twisted and distorted behind the tears her story had produced. What she said was so very Joe. He *was* calming and reassuring. I thought of his hand gripping mine in the depths of labour, his eyes focused on my pain-contorted face, telling me over and over again that he was there, he was with me, together we could do this.

The eldest child — the one who I guessed was Marty — had burrowed his face in his father's jacket, but the quilting did little to muffle his sobs. 'It's all my fault. If I hadn't tried to rescue Todd, then Mr Taylor wouldn't have had to rescue me. He's sick now because of me.'

His father patted the back of his head and I knew Joe would not want me to let him carry this burden. Walking stiffly, like someone much older than my years, I crouched down before the child and gently touched his shoulder.

'Marty. Marty.' At first I thought he wasn't going to look at me, but then slowly he lifted his head from his father's side to meet my eyes. His own were deep pools of blame. 'Marty, please don't be sad, and don't blame yourself. Joe would have come to get you off that ice even if you'd have been screaming at him to stay away. He's a daddy too, you see,' I heard the boy's father draw in his breath sharply at my words, 'and the most important thing in the world to him is keeping our little boy safe, and I know, I just *know* that when he saw you in trouble, he would have done everything he could to help you.'

'He did. He was so brave. He's like a real life superhero.'

I smiled sadly. 'Yes, Marty. That's just what he is.'

The little girl standing beside her mother was tugging even more urgently on the hem of her mum's jumper, in a way that was probably going to render the garment completely unwearable after today.

'And Todd,' she said quietly. 'He was a superhero because he went back onto the ice a second time to rescue Todd too.'

Fiona Webb looked stricken with guilt. 'The children adore that dog,' she said, putting her arm around her young daughter's shoulders and drawing her to her side as she spoke. 'After Marty was safe, the children were still frantic about the dog . . . ' The woman sounded beyond apologetic as the picture of what must have happened next became clear. 'I think maybe Mr Taylor — '

'Joe,' I amended.

' . . . Joe must have realised one of them might still try to go after it . . . so he did instead.' Her words made sense, but even without the presence of the children, Joe wouldn't have been able to stand by and watch an animal suffer. This was the man who picked up birds with broken wings and took them in a shoebox to the RSPCA; who bought humane mouse traps and drove the captured rodents miles away to open fields to release them. There's no way he would allow a dog to drown in front of the children. I got slowly to my feet, my heart aching. The young girl suddenly left her mother's side and threw her thin little arms around my legs. 'Mr Taylor is the bravest, kindest man in the whole world,' she said.

'He is,' I confirmed sadly. 'He really is.'

★　★　★

I tried to keep the thought that Joe had saved Marty, risked everything, his life, his future, our future, all because of Marty, in the forefront of my mind. Don't get me wrong, I love animals, I really do, and we'd talked many times about getting a dog or a cat for Jake to grow up with. But I couldn't let myself think of the pay-off Joe had gambled with. The dog had lived . . . I was truly glad of that, really I was. But still . . . for a dog? Really?

There was a strange, glowing aura of light

183

shining through the glass porthole in the door to the Relatives' Room. As I slowly released the handle and walked in I saw it was coming from an open laptop which was on the seat beside Charlotte. I don't think Charlotte was initially even aware that I'd entered the room, because she was absorbed in what appeared to be a fairly intense telephone conversation. I felt my shoulders tightening in annoyance at her cavalier use of a mobile phone. How typical of her not to care. But as I glanced back into the corridor, fast disappearing from sight by the closing door, I could hear no warning klaxons sounding, so perhaps the use of a mobile didn't actually cause everything in a hospital to shut down. I slowly lowered myself onto one of the chairs, which happened to give me a clear view of the webpage Charlotte must have been reading before her phone call.

My eye was initially caught by the familiar NHS logo on one corner and then, when I saw the heading, it would have been impossible to look away. *Viral Cardiomyopathy*. I thought I'd heard of the condition before and although I could remember very little about it, I knew it was serious. Potentially even more serious than a heart attack. So she'd lied to me before. Well, it wasn't the first time. I craned forward in my seat, trying to read the scattered sections of text that Charlotte had highlighted in yellow. I've got pretty good night vision — you need it when reading musical scores in dimly lit auditoriums and theatres. So with a little squinting I managed to distinguish several words and phrases from

184

the internet page, and was then instantly sorry that I'd done so. *'Attacks the heart'*, *'Permanent damage'*, *'Severe and life-threatening heart failure'*. I must have made some small sound, because Charlotte pivoted sharply in her seat, saw the direction of my gaze and slammed down the lid on her laptop.

'Sorry Veronica, what were you saying?'

Despite all the years that had passed, I was almost ashamed at the way my insides curled and tightened as I realised Charlotte was talking to the woman who was her mother-in-law. The woman who had done practically everything within her power to make sure she was never mine. I started to rise from my chair and pointed at the door, not wanting her to think I was deliberately eavesdropping on what I'm sure was a very difficult conversation. I could hardly imagine Veronica had mellowed much in the intervening years. Surprisingly Charlotte shook her head, indicating there was no need to leave. So I didn't.

I tried not to listen, but it was virtually impossible not to do so, and besides there was part of me that was curious to know how she had tamed the tigress enough to be allowed entry into that preciously guarded family.

'No, Veronica. I completely agree. Yes, you're right. Absolutely. Yes, definitely.' So that was how it was done, was it? Total compliance. No wonder Veronica and I had never got along. But then, there *had* only been that one meeting.

★ ★ ★

185

'Unbelievable,' muttered Charlotte, staring with numbed incredulity at the mobile in her hand for a long moment after the call was completed.

I looked up and saw her shaking her head at the small device, as though some lingering trace or essence of the woman she had just been talking to was capable of seeping from within it.

'My mother-in-law is like an unstoppable force of nature.'

'I remember,' I said bitterly, the taste of the past still capable of stinging like lemon juice in a cut. For a moment Charlotte looked startled, as though she hadn't realised she'd spoken her thoughts out loud . . . and to me, of all people.

'Oh, sorry. I forgot, you know her . . . of course you do.'

'Not really,' I replied, uncomfortable at the mention of anything that tied me to her husband. 'Certainly not well.'

'I don't think *anyone* knows Veronica well,' Charlotte said in a revealing moment. She dropped the mobile back into her designer bag, with a humourless laugh. 'She's on her way right now to persuade the captain of her cruise ship to divert to the nearest port so she can fly back home.'

'Well . . . if anyone can do it . . . '

'Yes, I know . . . it's her.'

For just a second Charlotte's eyes met mine and there was a moment of shared understanding. We both jerked back from it, as though from a live current.

'I need to stretch my legs,' Charlotte declared, jumping suddenly to her feet. She strode to the door, her gait jerky. Agitation followed her like a visible shadow; she couldn't outwalk or outrun it, but perhaps she didn't know that yet. She paused with her hand on the doorknob, torn and uncomfortable by the need to ask even the smallest of favours from me.

'If they come looking for me . . . the doctors . . . will you tell them I'll just be five minutes or so?'

I nodded my agreement. The least we actually said to each other, the better. Charlotte clearly thought so too, because she left the Relatives' Room without another word.

Charlotte

'One coffee to go, please,' I said, watching as the steaming liquid jetted like a black waterfall into the waiting cup. I could feel a jarring, jangling sensation thrumming deep within every part of me, making caffeine possibly the very last thing I needed right now. It would be all too easy to blame my frayed nerve endings entirely on David's mother, because God knows, she could get under someone's skin more effectively than anyone I'd ever met — including *my own* mother — which was quite an achievement. But this time Veronica wasn't solely to blame for the pulse rate that wouldn't settle, nor the acid indigestion which felt as though it was corrosively burning me up from the inside out.

This was what fear, laced with total and unbridled panic felt like. This was the mother anxiously watching the clock when her child was late home; this was the relative waiting when the plane went down; or the earthquake shook the town, or the tornado struck. This was the helplessness you felt when the life of someone you loved was in hands other than your own. This is what made you broker that deal with God, and made you promise you'd never ask for anything else, ever again. God and I hadn't exactly been on speaking terms recently, but here in the quiet deserted hospital cafeteria I asked, no *pleaded* with Him to make everything right for David. I could let everything else go — if I had to — but not David, never him. I'd strike any bargain that I could to save him, just as he'd saved me, twice from danger and then every single day since we'd been together.

I delved into my wallet for a handful of coins to pay for my drink, and then hesitated before reaching for a note instead. 'Actually, could you make that *two* coffees, please.'

I didn't know if Ally would accept anything from me. Had the fast-flowing current of water beneath the bridge washed away the bad blood between us? Or was it still lurking beneath the surface: a billowing red cloud of animosity that had drowned the fledging friendship we had once known?

Charlotte — Six Years Earlier

The coffee was strong and hot, exactly the way I liked it, but I couldn't enjoy it. Nor the view of the city slowly coming awake through the glass wall of windows in David's dockside flat. I sat at the white marble breakfast bar, staring with unseeing eyes as vibrant orange streaks splashed through the grey early morning sky, like a canvas where the artist had suddenly changed his mind. I watched the scene change from night to day. Change. It was an inevitable part of life. You couldn't stop it, or fight it. People changed all the time, friendships came and went (I certainly had reason to know that), and relationships changed, evolved and moved on. But what about feelings — did they ever really change? I wanted so much to believe that they do. I wanted to be as sure as it was possible to be, that the love my fiancé felt for his former girlfriend was gone, that no lingering trace remained. I wanted her bleached from his mind, his heart and his soul, and for a time I thought this had happened. But had I just been fooling myself?

'There you are,' said David, emerging from the bedroom, looking immaculate and handsome in a charcoal grey suit and dazzling white shirt. My breath caught in my throat as he slid his arms around my waist and burrowed through my long blonde hair, until his lips found the side of my neck.

'Hmm . . . you smell good. Or maybe it's the coffee,' he said teasingly, reaching out to pour himself a cup. I smiled, but it felt forced.

'Are you feeling alright? You seem a little quiet.'

He said her name. 'I'm fine,' I assured. 'Just a little tired. I didn't sleep very well.'

His brilliant blue eyes clouded in concern as they closely studied my face. 'You *were* restless last night. The sheets on your side of the bed look like they've been caught in a tornado.'

'I think *you* might have been responsible for that,' I said, my voice becoming a little husky. Like an arc of electricity, the memory of the passion we had shared crackled between us.

'I think we both were,' he corrected.

He said her name.

I should say something, I should tell him. He'd been dreaming. I'd known that from the fluttering movement of his eyelids, and the small murmuring sounds from deep in his throat. He lay upon the tangled sheets, illuminated in a beam of milky white moonlight lasering through the window. Even in sleep he was handsome: his dishevelled dark hair called out for me to touch it; the shadow bristling his chin beckoned my cheek to graze it; the soft curve of his sleeping mouth whispered to my lips. I couldn't resist. Propped on one elbow, I slowly lowered my face and gently kissed his sleeping mouth. His lips curled at the touch of mine, and parted slightly. He was still asleep, of that I am certain.

'Ally.'

He said her name.

He said her name.

I froze, incapable of movement or speech, even breathing was an effort. And then, just to be certain that my misery was complete, he said it again. 'Ally.'

I lay back on the pillow, biting my lower lip so that my tears made no sound. Our wedding was less than six weeks away. I'd had my final dress fitting, menus were finalised, the flowers were ordered, the venue had been paid. Everything was in place. We were ready, finally blissfully ready, for the next exciting adventure in our lives to begin.

And then, wherever his dream had taken him, whatever he was seeing behind those closed lids. *He said her name.*

Ally

It was inevitable that just moments after Charlotte left, the door to the small darkened room would be edged open. A nurse I hadn't seen before stuck her head through the opening.

'Mrs Williams?'

No, but I got pretty close. 'She's just stepped out for a minute. I'm Mrs Taylor. Do you have an update yet on my husband, Joe?'

The nurse shook her head regretfully. 'Sorry. I'm afraid not. It's Mrs Williams the doctors would like to talk to.' She looked anxiously down the length of the corridor. 'Do you know which way she went?' There was concern in her eyes, which I didn't want to acknowledge. I heard the words forming before I could stop them.

'Is something wrong with David? Er, I mean Mr Williams. Has something happened?'

'Are you close family? A relative?'

I almost was didn't count as an appropriate response, and our complicated interwoven back stories were of no interest or relevance to anyone except us.

'No, I'm not.'

191

'I'm sorry, but we aren't able to discuss the condition of patients with friends.'

Not one of those either, I thought. The nurse paused, clearly uncomfortable. 'I'll pop back in a few minutes when Mrs Williams returns.'

I paced a little as I waited. When that didn't work I stared unseeingly through the window, watching small flakes of snow hitting the pane like kamikaze pilots and dissolving like fallen tears down the glass. I kept glancing anxiously at the door, waiting for Charlotte to return. I didn't want to be holding on to the burden of worrying about anything or anyone except Joe. This weight was his wife's to shoulder, not mine, but somehow memories of David and what he had once meant to me were forcing their way back up the well down which I'd thrown them. I didn't want to feel these thoughts, remember these emotions, the ones that might just, even after all these years, have the power to undo me.

I jumped when Charlotte's shadow fell across the door, startled even though I had been expecting her. Equally startling were the two cups of coffee she was carrying. She held one out to me, awkwardly, as the door clicked shut behind her.

'I'm sorry. I couldn't remember how you take it. It's . . . it's been a while.'

I looked at her outstretched hand, no olive branch, just a Styrofoam cup that trembled slightly as if she was uncertain of my reaction. It wasn't an apology; we were many years too late for that. But we were going through something that was drawing us back together, re-stitching the seams we had ripped apart. On this one terrible life-changing night, we had been tossed together like survivors in a lifeboat, and had no one to turn to except each other.

Ally — Eight Years Earlier

The crazy thing was, the first time I met Charlotte I *really* liked her. Instantly. It was practically the friendship equivalent of love at first sight. We connected in a way I had never done with another girl, either at school or university. There was something about her that was so appealing; she was funny, quick and self-deprecating. It was the first time, *ever*, I had found anyone other than Max who I felt could be a true and lasting friend, not just a drive-by acquaintance. It was only a long time later that I realised one of the reasons I'd been so drawn to Charlotte was that she was — in almost every way — a female version of David. Opposites attract, that's what people say, isn't it? And for a very long time, David and I proved that old maxim to be true. But sometimes like is drawn to like just as powerfully. David and Charlotte proved that.

The first time we met she had been struggling up the path to David's new rental property, her entire upper body obscured behind an enormous cardboard box. All I could see was a pair of slim legs covered in faded denim jeans and sparkly jewelled flip-flops which revealed her perfectly painted toenails.

'Hi there,' she said, her voice muffled as her mouth was pressed against the side of the box. 'Please tell me this is number sixty-three and I haven't just walked up the drive of my new next-door neighbour.'

I laughed and went quickly down the front steps towards her. 'Here, let me help you with that,' I offered, taking the weight of one side of the box. 'And yes, this is number sixty-three. Are you moving in?'

It was a pretty stupid question, but she didn't call me on it.

'Yes, I am,' she said and peered around one corner of the box to see me. 'Hi. I'm Charlotte Butler.' She grinned. 'I'd shake your hand, but then a box full of Ikea's finest crockery is going to go crashing to the ground at our feet. Are you moving in too?'

I shook my head, but I don't think she could see me behind the box of kitchenware. 'No. But my boyfriend is. I'm just helping him.'

'Ah,' she said on a comprehending sigh, as we carefully negotiated the step and shuffled backwards into the hall. 'Which way now?'

'The kitchen's to the right,' I said, groping behind me for the door handle to let us into that room. It wasn't until we had deposited her box onto the large, slightly scratched pine table, that I saw all of her for the first time. I had thought she was pretty when I had glimpsed her outside the house on the path, but I was wrong. She was way beyond that. She was gorgeous. She was tall and slim with model-perfect features, and her long blonde hair was pulled back in a ponytail which was meant to look casual, but was so immaculate she could have walked down a red carpet and not looked out of place. Her t-shirt was plain black, its capped sleeves showing off a deep golden tan that I very much doubted she'd acquired over the rainy UK summer. It stopped short of the waistband of her jeans and left a gap of several centimetres, just enough to show that the tan was an all-over affair.

'Phew, that's better,' she said with a grin. 'I don't know why I have so much kitchen stuff, because I never cook anything anyway. Sorry, what did you say your name was?'

I realised then, that I hadn't even told her. 'Alexandra. Well, Ally to all my friends.'

'Then I hope that I will definitely be calling you Ally,' she said with easy charm. 'I am well down on my friend quota at the moment — I may have to advertise for some! So which one of my housemates — who I haven't met yet — are you going out with: Andrew, Pete, David or . . . oh no, I've forgotten the other one.'

'Mike is the one you're missing. And I'm with David,' I replied, aware that my smile became softer and my eyes warmer as I said his name. 'So you haven't met *any* of them yet?'

'No,' she said, going around the kitchen and opening drawers and cupboard doors and peering inside. Finally she found a couple of empty ones. 'I was on the university's overseas exchange last year, so I've been studying in California for the last twelve months.' That explained the tan. 'It was great, but I've kind of lost touch with the people I knew in first year, and I hadn't got a place to live. Then a friend of Pete's told me that they needed one more for this place. So I took it.'

'Without seeing the house first or meeting them?' It sounded such a rash decision to have made so lightly, and one I wouldn't have contemplated in a million years.

Charlotte just shrugged. 'Hell yeah, why not. They're just a group of guys, how hard is it going to be to get along with them?'

As it turned out, particularly for one member of her new household, not that hard at all. But I was a long, long way from knowing that yet.

I helped Charlotte unload the rest of her belongings from her car. I think that's when I first suspected her background was far more like the rest of David's friends than mine. Her car was new, and the suitcases buried beneath a layer of boxes and files bore a famous designer's insignia. Not your typical student after all, I realised, remembering how I had transported the final load of my clothes in a black bin bag. But at least I hadn't had to struggle to do it single-handedly, as my new friend was having to do. My parents had dutifully driven up to assist me every single time I'd moved: from first year's hall of residence, to my second-year property and finally to the house I was sharing for this, my final year.

It just seemed natural to help her unpack when we had finally brought all of her belongings into the house and up to her room. It was the one directly opposite David's, a nice bright sunny double which looked out onto a small and neatly tended back garden. The house was far from being a typical student rental, and that was well reflected in the price I knew David was paying for it. It was almost double my own rent — and I'd thought *that* was expensive. But David had just shrugged when I commented on it, and I knew that here again was yet another small difference between us. I was always going to be the type of person to look at a price tag and then decide whether or not to buy, and he would always do it the other way around.

'This is really nice,' I said, looking around the room with the newly laid carpet, large double bed and vast wall of wardrobes. The room was large enough to have a desk and a deep bookcase in one corner and still not look cramped.

David had hired a van and gone with the other guys to collect the items they had put in storage over the summer, and as I had nothing to do until he returned, I stayed chatting to Charlotte as she unpacked. I even made the bed for her, while she hung her very un-student-budget clothing away in the wardrobe. Everything I unpacked or opened was new. From the thick, pillow-like duvet to the Egyptian cotton high-thread-count sheets. 'That's my mother's contribution to my house move,' she commented, and although it was said as a joke, I thought I could hear a trace of bitterness in her words. 'Every item lovingly handpicked . . . by a personal shopper.'

I didn't know how to reply to that, and fortunately I didn't have to, because just then I heard the sound of the front door opening in the hall below as the rest of the occupants of the house returned. I ran down the stairs to greet them, and it was almost comical watching Pete, Mike and Andrew crane their necks to see past me to the beautiful blonde girl lightly descending the steps behind me.

I opened my mouth to introduce her, but she beat me to it.

'Hello there,' she said, and then surprised them all by going up and kissing each one of them on the cheek in greeting. Was that how they did things in California, or was that just her? 'It's great to meet you all. I'm Charlotte.'

Pete, Mike and Andrew shared a look which was pantomime obvious. 'I think we may have just won the housemate lottery,' declared Mike solemnly, before identifying themselves with matching grins.

A moment later a small rattling noise sounded from beyond the front door as a key was inserted into the lock and David entered the hall.

'Aha, so you must be David,' Charlotte declared, her voice warm and teasing. 'The final man I'm going to be living with for the next year.' And with that, despite the fact that I was standing right there, she reached up and laid her hands on his shoulders to kiss his surprised, although clearly not disappointed, face. And that was the moment I first began to lose him.

★   ★   ★

Someone once told me that relationships break up in one of two ways: either little by little, like water gradually eroding away and disintegrating a rock, or in a huge explosion like an erupting comet. For David and me, it wasn't either/or — it was both.

Charlotte — Eight Years Earlier

There's an old song I remember, where they talk about meeting the man of your dreams . . . and then meeting the woman who married him. Well, that was what happened to me the day I moved into 63, Warwick Road — but kind of in reverse. I found a friend — or a potential one, anyway, and then met her boyfriend, who turned out to be the man of *my* dreams, a position he had held unchallenged for five years. And the worst thing of all, was that he didn't even remember me.

I knew him instantly as I stood in the hallway of my new home, surrounded by my housemates. The other three all seemed pleasant enough, and I was prepared to overlook the slightly lustful look on Mike's face as he did that uncomfortable top-to-toe appraisal thing men do, as though you've suddenly been struck blind or have no problem with being assessed like a bit of meat on a hook. I had no intention of getting romantically involved with any of the three guys I had just met; life could get complicated enough without forming relationships with people you shared with. And then the door opened, I turned towards it and there he was, looking even better than I remembered. I could feel the shock draining the blood from my face, and to conceal my fairly blatant reaction I leant up rapidly to kiss his cheek, buying me a few more precious seconds to compose myself. But damn it . . . he even *smelled* just the way I remembered. I suddenly recalled one sad afternoon a few months after we'd met, when I'd trawled through every single male fragrance in a department store, trying — and failing — to find the exact brand of cologne he had worn.

Of course, when I stepped out of David's rather startled embrace I could see the changes that the last five years had brought. He was broader in the shoulders, maybe even a little taller. His hair was shorter now than it had been back then, although for most of the time it had been concealed beneath a dark woollen beanie. The most startling difference was on his face, where the softness of boyhood had been honed and chiselled into the features of the man he had become. But his eyes . . . his eyes were the same ones I had seen over and over again in my dreams. Oh God, I felt sick, actually physically *I-bet-I-am-going-to-throw-up-in-a-minute* sick. In order to escape, I made some silly comment about wanting to make them a cup of tea to say 'hello' and darted into the kitchen, leaving the four men and Ally standing in a bemused cluster in the hall. I leant back against the kitchen door as though trying to barricade myself in against the onslaught of memories that were tumbling almost as viciously as the avalanche which had precipitated our meeting. I buried my face in my hands, and felt the burn of my flushed cheeks beneath my palms. How was this possible? What weird and sadistic stroke of fate was responsible for bringing me back into the life of the person who I'd last seen halfway up a Swiss mountain? I shut my eyes and remembered my final glimpse of him through the closing ambulance doors, his face still shadowed with concern as they drove me away.

I felt the pressure of the kitchen door opening behind me, and leapt away from it. Ally slipped through the crack.

'I thought I'd give you a hand with that tea, seeing as you probably don't know where everything is kept,' she said with a kind smile.

'What? Oh, yes, the tea,' I added hastily, my eyes darting around the kitchen looking for the kettle.

'Are you feeling okay?' Ally asked, her head tipped quizzically to one side as she studied my face. I found myself looking back at her every bit as intently, as though somewhere within the pretty features, the large oval eyes and the soft pink lips I would find the answer to why David was with her. There was so much I wanted to ask her about him and their relationship. I struggled to think back over the last few hours. Had she mentioned how long they'd been together, how they'd met, or whether their relationship was serious? No, of course she hadn't. Why would she share any of those intimate and private details with someone she'd only just met?

I had to be extremely careful here, I realised. I had to make sure I did or said nothing at all that would arouse her suspicions. And giving her the Spanish Inquisition about her love life was certainly not the way to go.

Oblivious to my inner turmoil, Ally and I made tea together, or rather *she* made the tea and I stood by uselessly watching as her long nimble musician fingers ripped cellophane from packets and spooned sugar into mugs. My contribution was to pull a tin of luxury chocolate biscuits from the box of provisions someone had packed for me.

The lounge was better furnished than most student rentals, but there still weren't enough seats for all of us. Mike jumped off the settee in a huge show of good manners to offer me his place. I bet the novelty of that wears off soon, I thought, as I smiled my thanks and slid onto the still-warm cushion. David was occupying an oversized armchair on the opposite side of the room, and when Ally had lowered the tray of drinks onto the table he reached for her hand and pulled her gently down onto his lap. I tried to sip my tea, but something the size of a golf ball appeared to be lodged in my throat. The boys were talking animatedly about some club they were keen to try out that night, and I nodded slightly distractedly when they asked if I wanted to join them, all the while unable to tear my eyes away from David's hand which was absently tracing small circles against the curve of Ally's waist. She looked up and smiled warmly at me, and I felt like a traitor when I returned it. I allowed my eyes to travel to David, whose arms moved to link around her slender waist, pulling her more securely against him. How could he not recognise me? True I had been younger, just seventeen, on the day of the avalanche, but physically I hadn't changed that much, had I? We had spent seven long, cold hours huddled together on the side of the mountain, waiting for help to reach us. The arms which were now wound around his pretty dark-haired girlfriend had cradled me against him. The fingers caressing her skin had gently wiped the tears from my eyes and brushed the long blonde hair from my brow when he'd carefully lifted off my ski helmet. As though he could sense the intensity of my scrutiny, David's unforgettably blue eyes locked on mine. There was nothing in them, no recognition, no memory that once our faces had been so close together, I had felt the brush of his impossibly long dark lashes tickling my cheek every time he blinked. His eyes were unfathomable cobalt pools as he broke our contact and turned his attention back to Ally, who had just finished recounting something — that I had totally missed — to the rest of the group. I guess it must have been funny, because everyone laughed, so I did too. David pulled her closer towards him and kissed her lightly on the curve of her mouth. My lips stung, and it wasn't just the large mouthful of hot tea that caused that, it was because I too knew the feeling of that mouth on mine. He was hers now, this was no casual thing, that much was obvious. But damn it, those lips had been on mine long before they had known hers. And somehow I was going to have to finally learn how to forget that . . . or find somewhere else to live.

It had been a schoolgirl crush; deep-down, of course I'd always known that. It was something I should have let go of a long time ago. It was nothing; a moment, a single day, its life span shorter than that of an exotic butterfly, born and dying all within twenty-four hours. No wonder he didn't remember me. But still, unless he rescued injured seventeen-year-old girls from snow-covered slopes every day of the week, you'd have thought that something of the incident would have stayed with him. Just the smallest lingering recollection? Apparently not.

I have no idea what drivelling nonsense I responded with when they quizzed me, like a team of interrogators, about my year in California. I guess I didn't say anything too outrageous or ridiculous. I *do* remember one of the boys asking me if I had a boyfriend, and I'd allowed my eyes to flicker in David's direction to see if he looked in the slightest bit interested in my reply. His face was an impassive blank canvas.

'No one special. Besides, I've only been back in the UK a few weeks, I'm going to need time to wean myself off the American jocks before I start looking around.' I forced myself to laugh along with the rest of them at my small attempt at humour.

'You and David should get together,' said Andrew, his mouth half-full of chocolate digestive. I felt my fingers tighten around the handle of my mug, with enough force that I was

204

in danger of breaking it clean off. 'He's just got back from a summer in the good old U S of A,' Andrew continued, foraging in the tin for another gold-wrapped biscuit as he spoke. 'You two probably have loads in common.'

More than you know, I thought, before replying offhandedly, 'Hmm maybe.'

Another quick glance at David, who didn't even appear to be following the group conversation any longer, his attention totally on the girl curled within his arms.

That first week was a gruelling test of endurance. It was like an exam that I was determined to pass. I *would* get through this, I would not let a childish teenage fantasy dictate the life I lived now. Unfortunately, as the university term hadn't yet begun, no one had lectures to attend, nor a home of their own to go back to, I found myself thinking with irritation, when Ally showed no sign of returning to her own house. She was never far from David's side, nor he hers, making it practically impossible to catch him alone, not that I had even the smallest of clues as to what I would say to him if I did.

Thankfully things got a little easier with each passing day. At nights I allowed myself to be dragged out by my remaining housemates to what they assured me were the best drinking holes and clubbing hotspots in town. At least it spared me from having to watch David and Ally hand-in-hand quietly climbing the stairs to his room each night. And by the time I returned home, considerably less tipsy than my companions, I was too exhausted to fixate on the oblong shaft of light scything out from beneath David's door, or worse, straining my ears for the sound of squeaking bed springs in the silent house. I had spent so many nights going to sleep with my own fantasy version of David, it was going to take some time to adjust to the fact that the real-life version was literally just across the corridor from me. In the arms of another woman.

★　★　★

The house was surprisingly quiet as I prepared breakfast for myself later in the week. I ate my cereal standing propped up against the kitchen worktop, feeling the chill of the cold marble surface against the small of my back, where the skimpy vest top of my pyjamas didn't quite reach the bottoms. I put my bowl into the sink, which was already overflowing with the breakfast crockery paraphernalia of my housemates. Lectures were now well underway, so I guess everyone had been in too much of a hurry to load the dishwasher. I realised with a touch of guilt that I didn't even know which cupboard housed that appliance, and that it had probably been Ally who'd taken over that particular chore for the last few days. For some reason that made me angry, as though she had won yet another round in a contest she didn't even know she was competing in. I found the dishwasher — *really guys, it wasn't that hard* — and began to rinse the accumulated plates before loading them into the machine. I turned the tap on full and a cold

206

jet of water hit a plate, spraying me from collarbone to midriff. 'Terrific,' I muttered, peeling the saturated vest from my skin. It clung determinedly to my breasts and despite the discomfort I gave a twisted smile, knowing how much Mike would have enjoyed the impromptu spring break contest.

I was still fiddling around with my top when the kitchen door soundlessly swung open and David entered the room. His eyes took in everything, including the skimpy garment which outlined the fullness of my breasts, their nipples embarrassingly prominent, thanks to the temperature of the water.

'Interesting look,' he observed, his tone giving absolutely nothing away, but he opened a drawer and tossed a small fluffy hand towel my way. 'Here.'

I swabbed ineffectually at the top while he filled the kettle and reached for a mug from the rack.

'Coffee?'

I nodded in reply, suddenly shy at being alone with him, and that had absolutely nothing at all to do with the state of my clothing. 'Is Ally still upstairs?' I asked, and then cursed myself for bringing her instantly into the only private moment we had shared since I'd moved in.

'No. She had a nine o'clock seminar. She won't be around here so much now term's started. She does a lot of music society stuff, and spends an inordinate amount of time in the library.' He smiled crookedly and my heart tripped a little, because it was just as I remembered it. 'She's determined to get a First, and she will too. I've never known anyone work so damn hard for anything.'

'Good for her,' I said, and surprisingly I meant it. I liked his girlfriend, or what I knew of her, which admittedly wasn't much. What I *didn't* like about her was that she *was* his girlfriend, or that anyone was, come to that. 'I think I'm going to struggle to get back into the work ethic. It was a more relaxed vibe out in California,' I confessed.

David passed me my coffee and I was very careful to make sure my hand never touched his in the exchange. I had the cup raised to my lips when he asked softly, 'So how come the year in America? I thought you said that when you got to university you were just going to stay put for the entire three years.'

Coffee burnt my tongue and the roof of my mouth, but I wouldn't realise that until much later. I looked at him over the hazy steam rising from the mug, my eyes wide with shocked surprise.

'You remember?' My voice was a hushed whisper, as though we were talking in church. 'You know who I am? You remember me?'

He shook his head gently as though he couldn't believe I had asked that question. 'Of course I remember you, Charlie girl. You're not the sort of person who is easily forgotten.'

I opened my mouth, and then closed it again, temporarily lost for a reply. His eyes watched me carefully. Not only did he know who I was, he also remembered the things I had told him during the hours we were marooned. He had even remembered the stupid nickname he had given me. My eyes went to his and then of their own volition dropped down to his lips. I wondered what else he remembered.

'I didn't want to say anything in front of the other guys . . . I didn't want to make things awkward for you.'

I nodded carefully. 'I get that. Thanks.'

He shifted his weight suddenly, and dropped his eyes to the contents of his coffee mug, as though the script of what he wanted to say next was written on its ceramic interior. 'I also didn't think it was necessary to say anything to Ally about us having met before . . . ' His voice trailed away, but there was a question within it. He was asking me if it was okay to keep our previous encounter a secret. I closed my eyes for a moment, teetering on the edge of a decision, much as I had teetered on the precipice as the hurtling wall of snow came tumbling down the mountainside behind me.

'Obviously, if you're in any way uncomfortable about that . . . well, then I'll explain it to everyone. It just seemed as though it might be simpler if we kept what happened that day, back there on the mountainside. It *was* a long time ago.'

I tried hard not to show that I understood perfectly what he was saying here. I read the sub-text as though it was highlighted in neon marker pen. He had no need to worry, I was far from being the innocent dewy-eyed girl who he had rushed to help five years earlier. He'd moved on, and didn't want to jeopardise his present relationship by revealing the surprising and unexpected attraction that had grown like an exquisite crystal out of the snow surrounding us on the mountain, and had then melted away almost as rapidly when we left it behind.

'Sure,' I said, trying to feign a nonchalant little shrug. 'Consider it forgotten.'

A small spasm crossed his face, and for the life of me I didn't know why. I was agreeing to his request, wasn't I? Yet if I didn't know better I'd have thought he looked almost disappointed at my easy capitulation.

For someone who wanted the whole incident to remain unspoken, he seemed strangely reluctant to let it go. 'So, your ankle healed up okay? You don't seem to have a limp or anything.' I extended my bare foot and rotated it for his inspection.

'It was a clean break. It healed well,' I informed him, and then realised my words could equally apply to our own transitory relationship. It had certainly been a clean break, no denying that. But unfortunately I don't think I had healed from it nearly as well as he had done.

'Do you still ski?'

'Yes. There's no reason not to. It was just one of those bizarre freak occurrences that you can't predict or control.' Once again, my words could easily be referring to so much more than just the avalanche.

'So, we're good here, are we?' David asked, suddenly sounding far less certain and assured than he had done before. It was almost as though proximity to me was drawing the nineteen-year-old back out of the man once more.

'Absolutely,' I affirmed and then he went and ruined everything by reaching out his hand and lightly touching the bare skin on my upper arm, and a million nerve endings screamed out in reaction. I could lie to his friends, his girlfriend, even to *him* if I had to, but there was one person who recognised that the past still had the power to snatch us back and reignite feelings that should have died a long time ago. Me.

Charlotte — Thirteen Years Earlier

I suppose the accident was my fault. Not the avalanche itself, of course; that had been caused by the heavy overnight snowfall, the change in wind direction and the heat of the sun. But the fact that I was caught up in it couldn't be blamed on anyone else but me. With hindsight and the passage of time I was at least able to acknowledge that. Put an angry and frustrated teenager in a ski resort for ten days and force her to act as a buffer as she watches the gradual disintegration of her parents' marriage, and it all gets a little easier to understand. Throw in a handful of recklessness, a large dose of overconfidence and a casually overheard conversation about an exhilarating off-piste ski run, and the recipe for disaster is almost complete.

The group of boys who entered the ski and boot room directly ahead of me couldn't have been more than a couple of years older than I

211

was, although every one of them towered above me, making me feel suddenly much younger than my seventeen years. In the small cosily heated room it was impossible not to overhear their conversation as I located my skis and comfortably dry boots. From what I could make out, they were planning to abandon the 'tame' tourist-heavy runs for something a little more challenging that morning. I'm not sure when the idea of tagging along with them occurred to me, or why. No, scratch that, I knew why. I'd been testing and pushing against every rule and restraint that had been imposed on me for quite a while; it was only a matter of time before I did something downright foolish. I had scribbled a brief note and slipped it beneath my parents' door, before leaving the hotel for the slopes. My mother was probably still asleep, and my father . . . well, if the shouted recriminations of the previous night were correct, he too could still be in bed. Just not with my mother, that's all.

I spoke hesitantly, my voice barely louder than a whisper, to a young lad with bright ginger hair as we queued for the cable car which would take us up the mountain. 'Would it be okay if I tagged along behind you guys when we get up there?' I nodded my head to indicate the summit, which the cable car was jerkily dancing us towards. The boy turned his bright blue eyes on me, and the reluctance in them was easy to read.

'Er, I'm not sure . . . it's a pretty challenging descent. How good are you?'

'Excellent,' I said with false bravado. 'Practically professional.'

He snorted, and his eyes crinkled at the edges when he grinned, making me realise he was probably a little closer to my own age than his companions.

'I'm good enough,' I said, happy to back-pedal a little. 'I've skied all my life.'

'Black runs?' he questioned. I nodded. 'Me too,' he replied, 'But I *still* had to argue with my older brother all through breakfast before he grudgingly agreed to let me join him and his friends. Bloody brothers,' he finished with a long-suffering sigh. I gave a sympathetic nod as though I understood how annoying siblings could be, but of course I had absolutely no idea. 'I'm Rob, by the way,' my new acquaintance said, suddenly ripping off a glove and offering me his hand.

'Charlotte,' I replied, pulling off my own bright pink ski mitt to place my hand in his.

When the cable car came to a jerky stop the passengers jostled out in a jewelled sea of brightly coloured quilted jackets. My red-haired companion hovered a little awkwardly beside me, his eyes on a group of about eight young men standing some distance away to the right of the main pathway. They were laughing and chatting loudly as they bent to fasten skis onto boots.

'That's my lot over there,' he said, lowering his voice, although there was no danger of any of them being able to overhear us. 'Why don't you just hang back for a bit and then follow our tracks. Perhaps I'll see you at the bottom?'

I smiled and nodded, and tried to pretend I

didn't see the hopeful look in his eyes. He seemed nice enough, but I wasn't interested in yet another five-minute relationship. That was half the trouble, wasn't it? Absolutely everything in my life had a short expiration date — even my family, it now seemed.

'Enjoy the ride,' he said, pushing away from me to join the rest of his party. 'I bet it's going to be a real thriller.'

His words were a great deal more prophetic than he could ever have imagined.

As the last of the passengers from our cable car skied away in the direction of the marked run, I heard the voice of caution and good sense speaking firmly in the back of my mind, instructing me to follow them. I ignored it.

I spent longer adjusting my skis and goggles than I needed to, allowing Rob's group to get a decent head start. I didn't want them to think I was crashing their party, nor did I want any nosy, bossy older brother sending me away like a naughty schoolgirl. It was a free mountain. They couldn't prevent me from following their chosen route, could they? I counted to two hundred before digging my ski poles into the crust of white snow and setting off.

It was one of those wonderfully crisp blue-skied days that makes skiing seem like the best activity in the whole world. The snow from the night before was thick and powdery underfoot as I followed the tracks etched in its surface like signposts beckoning me onward. I hesitated for a moment when I came to a fence where the gate had been forced open, creating a small white mountain at its base, a tiny replica of the one I was about to ski down. Was I really going to do this, I thought, frowning at the steep descent which began to fall away almost immediately on the other side of the wooden barrier. I looked down and saw that most of Rob's group had already begun to ski down the slope. They were already a long way ahead of me. The sun dazzled my eyes as I brought my hand up like a visor and watched them zigzag through the deep unblemished snow, scoring it like an artist etching lines on a canvas. I glanced back in the direction I had just come, the one that led to the marked run. *Go . . . don't go?* I teetered for a minute before gritting my teeth, pulling my ski goggles down from my helmet and heading for the backcountry route.

The first forty-five seconds of my downward journey were unremarkable enough. The last forty-five were totally unforgettable. The route I was following was challenging, but not so much that I couldn't still appreciate the raw breathtaking beauty of the snowy descent. I wove around rocky outcrops which punctured the blanket of white like sharp grey teeth waiting to bite. The path narrowed and my hands instinctively tightened their grip on my ski poles as I exerted every last ounce of concentration. Beside me to the left the slope fell away sharply, and from the corner of my eye I saw a dense copse of fir trees far below, their branches thick and heavy with snowfall. I remember thinking that they looked so far away and small they seemed almost unreal, toy-like, more closely resembling those tiny decorations you see adorning Christmas cakes, than actual trees.

Just seconds later the baking analogy took a much less appealing turn when I saw the snow beneath my skis begin to shift and change in format. *It looks like sifted icing sugar,* I remember thinking, not realising the significance of what I was seeing. Then the sound began, it was like a thundering rumble of a freight train rapidly hurtling down the mountain behind me. I could hear its roar, even above the sound of blood pounding in my ears and that of my own suddenly increased heartbeat. I risked a brief glance over one shoulder and instantly regretted it. The top of the mountain, so majestic and still just moments earlier, had come to life, like a slumbering white behemoth. An enormous snow cornice had broken away and was sliding and rippling with ever-growing momentum down the slope behind me, swallowing the snow in its path and belching it back out in a huge white wall of approaching danger. I crouched lower and tried to increase my speed, still not realising that to outrun it was an impossibility.

The air around me became heavy and laden with snowy particles, all racing to try to get to the bottom of the slope ahead of me. I knew it would only be a matter of seconds before the monster chasing behind me took the lead. Then through the haze of snow I saw a dark blue flash materialise from out of nowhere, or so it seemed. The shape crossed my path about ten metres ahead of me. It was another skier, man or woman it was impossible to tell, but like me they were about to be swallowed up by one of nature's most deadly and hungry predators. The skier ahead of me glanced behind them, and I saw then that it was a man; a split second later he turned away from the approaching avalanche and back to me. Everything seemed to slow down as adrenaline kicked in and I saw the skier in blue nod his head towards the drop-off to the left, even as he angled his own skis in that direction. He nodded again, as though urgently asking me a question. He was telling me to jump. To leap over the edge, down God-knows-how-many metres to the snow-packed ground below, to escape the avalanche. Something even colder than the icy terrain I was hurtling over gripped my heart. I skied, but I didn't jump. I never had, and today certainly didn't seem like a good time to start. He nodded one last time, even more imperatively, swerved slightly in one final change of direction and then flew off the edge of the slope. For a second he appeared to hover in mid-air, like a large blue hummingbird surrounded by skis and poles, and then he plummeted out of sight.

The sound behind me was now deafening and my skis no longer felt as though they were *gliding* over snow, but more as though they were tripping and stumbling upon it. Unless I was willing to risk being buried beneath tons of snow and debris, I had run out of options. I swerved so abruptly that I almost lost my balance and fell, but at the last moment managed to stay upright. The precipice was approaching at speed. I had no idea what lay below: trees, rocks, the broken and battered body of the other skier? No sane and sentient person would even consider jumping. I jumped.

I felt the snow disappear from under me and suddenly there was air beneath my skis. My own speed and momentum meant that my trajectory wasn't straight downward, but instead — for just a few exhilarating moments — I was airborne, virtually free-falling like a skydiver. Then physics or gravity or some other damn scientific ruling intervened and I was going down, in an uncontrolled and desperate tangle of poles and flailing arms. I could see the ground approaching, thankfully devoid of rocks, but directly ahead of me were the trees that suddenly didn't look small, innocuous, or anything at all like cake decorations. Which was really unfortunate, because I was practically certain there was no way to avoid crashing straight into them.

I almost landed on my skis. I don't know how, sheer luck I guess. I hit the snow with a *whump* which jarred every single one of my internal organs with such force that I felt sure a few of them were probably repositioned by the impact. Miraculously I appeared to have missed colliding into the densest section of the thicket of trees, but there was still one last fir ahead of me. If it had grown just half a metre or so to the left a few hundred years ago, or if I'd jumped just one second later that day, I might have made it. I tried to veer away, but I hadn't regained my balance from my landing, and in my panic I lost control as my skis crossed and I cartwheeled into the air before crashing into the snow. Pain — like

I had never experienced in my life — exploded within me as my left ski clipped an exposed root of the tree as I hurtled past.

A kaleidoscope of colours filled my head. Red: blood pulsing, the bright vivid red of pain. I could feel it everywhere, but mostly in my left leg. Then there was blue: flashing beside me, leaning down over me, dark blue, the colour of a ski suit — not mine, I was in pink. The last colour was white. White everywhere: over me, under me, pressed against my goggles, inside my mouth and nostrils as I came to a halt, face down in the snow.

'Don't move!' Those were his first ever words to me. Later I'd always felt there should have been something more memorable or less prosaic to that first introduction than just that shouted command. Still, it did the trick. I stopped trying to struggle to move and let my head flop back down on its frozen cold pillow. I exhaled sharply, blowing the snow from my nose and spitting it from my mouth. It came out tinged with pink, like an exotic piece of marbling. Except there was nothing at all exotic about internal bleeding.

He knelt beside me, but all I could see of him was the blue waterproof material of his ski pants. His voice was surprisingly calm and steady. 'Where are you hurt?'

'Everywhere,' I gasped, my lips grazing the snow beneath my face as I spoke. 'Has it gone? Is it over?' Raw panic had turned my voice into the screeching cry of a terrified bird.

'It is. It's finished.' I strained my ears, but the cacophony of nature had fallen silent. 'We were lucky,' he continued. 'If we hadn't jumped when we did . . . '

Face down in the snow, with my left leg feeling as though it was being consumed in a fiery furnace, I couldn't say I felt particularly lucky.

'What if it starts again? What if there's an aftershock?'

'That's earthquakes,' he replied, his voice measured and placating. 'I think we've got enough to worry about for the moment; let's not invent new reasons to panic.' He shifted his weight and bent down a little closer towards me, but still I couldn't see his face. 'Now, where does it hurt most?'

'My left leg . . . ' I replied, my voice wobbling as shock flooded through my veins, washing away the last dregs of adrenaline, ' . . . it really hurts.'

'I'm just going to check you for any other injuries, okay?' My helmeted head gave a small, terrified bob. I felt his hands upon me then, gentle as they carefully ran down my spine, and then travelled the length of each arm from shoulder to wrist.

'Are you . . . are you a doctor?' I asked as he continued what appeared to me to be an extremely thorough examination. My voice was a hopeful whisper, echoing hoarsely in the snowy valley.

'No,' he said, shifting from my field of vision as he shuffled downwards and ran his hands from the top of my thigh down to the ankle of my right leg. Thankfully he stayed far away from its counterpart. 'But I *did* get a first-aid badge when I was in the Boy Scouts,' he added.

It was a little too soon for levity, given the circumstances, especially when the reassurance that I was in safe hands had just dissolved away like a spring thaw. Not that I needed a qualified medic to tell me what I already knew.

'My leg's broken, isn't it?'

'It might just be your ankle,' he replied, as though that might somehow cheer me up. 'It *is* kind of at a funny angle.'

That's never what you want to hear. 'Let me see,' I said, struggling to raise my body from the bed of snow. His strong hands came out and gently pressed on my shoulders, pinioning me down. 'You shouldn't move. You could make it worse.'

'*Akela* tell you that, did he?'

'Are you *always* this feisty, or is it just on avalanche days?'

There was something about him that was quite engaging, and in any other situation I'm sure I would really appreciate his brand of humour. Just not today.

'No, it's usually only after I fly a hundred metres or so through the air, and then collide with a tree that does it. Now are you going to help me turn over, or are you just going to sit there and watch me struggle to do it myself?'

He gave a deep sigh, and I knew he didn't quite know how to deal with my determined streak. That was okay. Very few people did.

'It was nowhere near that distance,' he corrected, moving to stand beside me. I felt his hands burrowing in the snow beneath me, creating two little troughs. 'I'm going to lift you up, and carry you over to those trees back there.'

'Okay,' I said, suddenly subdued.

'It's going to hurt like crazy.'

'Understood,' my voice was little more than a whisper.

'I still think this is a terrible idea.'

'Duly noted. I won't sue you or the Boys' Brigade for malpractice.'

'You're funny,' he said, and although I couldn't see his face, I thought he might be smiling. 'Okay, on the count of three. One . . . two . . . '

He lifted me on two, the bastard. But it probably didn't matter. I had already passed out from the pain by the time he had got to his feet.

★ ★ ★

I'm not sure how long I was unconscious. Long enough for him to have climbed up to the top of the precipice and driven both of our crossed skis into the snow to act as a marker. I came to with a long moan of pain.

'Told you it was a bad idea,' were his opening words. He was crouched down beside me, still panting from the exertion of having climbed the slope. Slowly I turned my head towards him. Very little of his face was visible. The navy woollen beanie was pulled down low and the snow goggles — which presumably he'd worn for the climb up the slope — were still in place, so all I could really see was his mouth and chin, with a hint of dark stubble shadowing upon it. 'How's your leg?'

'Still broken.'

He smiled, and the whole lower half of his face was instantly transformed. His teeth were dentist-advert white and perfectly straight. Good genes or expensive orthodontia, I wasn't sure which.

He had propped me up against the broadest of the tree trunks and had carefully extended my legs flat out in front of me. I looked down at my two limbs encased in the bright pink snow-suit. Already the ankle of the left leg was beginning to swell, bulging the fabric outwards and making my snow boot cut painfully into the flesh.

'I think it's just my ankle,' I conceded. 'Should we take the boot off?'

'Definitely not. In fact, we shouldn't even think of moving you again until they get here.'

'They who? Your friends?'

He shook his head, 'No. The ski patrol. We're staying right here until they find us.'

'But . . . but that could take ages. Wouldn't it be better if you carried on down the slope and went for help?'

He lowered himself onto the ground beside me. 'Firstly, you don't leave a casualty alone after an accident,' he said, pushing the goggles from his face and pulling off his woollen hat to run his fingers through his thick shock of black hair. 'And secondly,' he continued, turning to face me, 'There's no path left to ski down.'

The breath caught in my throat, and I never did figure out if it was his words or the sheer perfection of how he looked that caused it. He had the type of face you seldom saw in real life;

it was normally smiling back at you from the pages of a glossy magazine, or filling a twenty-metre-wide cinema screen. His eyes were the most amazingly clear blue, like sunlight shining on an ocean, or polished sapphires in a jewelled crown. I felt like I'd seen them somewhere before . . . perhaps in an advert for tinted contacts?

'I . . . I don't understand what you're telling me. Explain.'

He lifted one of my pink-mitted hands and held it between both of his. Any comment which required hand-holding to deliver it couldn't be good. 'The trail has gone. It's all rocks, tree stumps and deep drifts. Even if I *could* leave you, I don't think I could ski down it, and I don't know any other way to get out of here.'

His words hung in the air between us, like deadly icicles, as the seriousness of our situation finally began to dawn on me.

'But how will they know to come looking for us?'

He smiled gently at my slightly idiotic comment. I guess my powers of reasoning weren't exactly firing on all cylinders. 'Because the guys I was with will have alerted them. If they followed the trail we took yesterday, they should all have got safely to the bottom before the avalanche came down.'

'And if they didn't?'

A look of genuine concern darkened his face, and clouded the blue of his eyes. 'I can't let myself think of that.' He turned from me then, and stared unseeingly across the snowy expanse of the clearing. 'My younger brother was among them. He was one of the last skiers to set off.'

Inside my head something clicked, and the pieces of the puzzle revolved, rotated and then fell neatly into place. No wonder his blue eyes had seemed familiar. 'You're Rob's bossy older brother, aren't you?'

'Not the name I usually go by,' he said, his attractive mouth twisting in a half smile. 'Usually people just call me David. And you are . . . ?'

'Confused,' I said. 'Rob told me to hang back before following your group. He was the last person to set off towards the trail. So how come they left you behind?'

David squinted slightly as a dazzling beam of bright sunlight caught him directly in the face, illuminating a look I couldn't easily identify.

'I wasn't *left behind*. I stayed.'

'Why?' I asked, already afraid I knew the answer. Yes, there it was in his eyes. 'For *me*? You stayed behind for *me*?' He gave a small shrug as though it was no big deal, which we both knew was one big fat lie. 'You got caught in an avalanche . . . you could have died on that slope, for *me*?' David looked altogether uncomfortable as I pieced together what had happened. 'Your brother told you I couldn't handle the trail, didn't he?'

David tried to look nonchalant, and failed totally. 'Rob was just . . . *concerned* . . . that's all. So I hung back to check you were okay.'

'And nearly got killed in the process.'

'No one died here,' he said, trying to steer the conversation back onto a more light-hearted footing. 'Or even came close. Jeez, you *do* like to exaggerate, don't you?'

* * *

It took them seven hours to find us and stretcher me off the mountain. It took only half of that time for me to fall for David. Not that I ever considered for a single moment telling him how I felt. *Obviously*. But even through the fear, trauma and panic of waiting to be rescued, the attraction between us was undeniable. Something happened that day on the mountain. Something neither of us could have planned for or predicted . . . or have prevented.

* * *

'So, Mystery Girl, you never told me your name. Are you a holidaying Snow Bunny or a humble Chalet Girl?'

'I'm here on vacation with my parents, actually. And my name is Charlotte.'

'So *Charlie Girl*,' he teased, a twinkle in his eyes at his humorous play on words. 'Where are you from? Where's home?'

'Everywhere . . . nowhere,' I said, with a sigh. 'In the last eight years I've lived in six different countries and been the 'new girl' in the international school in each of them. My father's job takes him all around the world, and where he goes, we go. But maybe not for much longer.' I snapped my lips on the admission, knowing I shouldn't be sharing such personal family details with someone I had only just met, but somehow I felt sure he could be trusted.

I waited for him to troll out the expected response, about how great it must be to have seen so much of the world. But he surprised me. 'That must have been hard on you,' he said, accurately piercing through the tough outer carapace I wore as protection. 'And lonely.'

'It *is* hard to maintain lasting friendships when you're constantly on the move,' I admitted, pretending I couldn't see the look of sympathy in his eyes.

It was a long day. We talked for most of it. I slept a little, which was a blissful escape from the pain. But there were some moments I knew would stay with me for ever. Like when he lifted the ski helmet from my head, and his fingers lingered for just a moment too long as he smoothed down the statically charged long blonde strands of hair, brushing them from my face with a gentleness that woke an unknown sensation within me. Or when I'd complained of the cold and he'd unzipped his jacket and pulled me against the warmth of his body, wrapping the sides of the thick quilted material around me like a cloak. We'd stayed like that for hours, my heart beating in tandem with his, his expelled breath gently fanning my face.

It felt as though we had both been trapped within a perfect miniature snow globe, where nothing we did or said could be touched by the outside world. And when the combination of pain and fear made me tearful, it had felt completely natural for him to reach down and gently tilt my chin up towards him, His wind-chilled lips lowered and fastened on mine, but his tongue was warm, as his experienced mouth taught me that — despite what I thought — I had never, ever been properly kissed before. He kissed me like a man, and my easily given and broken seventeen-year-old heart never forgot that.

We never acknowledged what was happening, but something fiery and alive was born that day in the ice and snow. Something so powerful that I felt no relief, just regret, when finally two red-jacketed figures skied into the clearing, pulling the toboggan stretcher that would carry me off the mountain down to the waiting ambulance below.

6

Charlotte

Ally had her back to me, staring out of the window when I re-entered the Relatives' Room. She turned, startled, and for a second it was hard to believe that almost a decade had passed since we'd first met. The years had been kind to her, and silhouetted against the black pane of glass, in her skin-tight jeans and fitted jumper, she could easily have still passed for the fresh-faced, enthusiastic music student who haunted my past, my present and my future. Even her figure hadn't changed, despite the fact I knew she and her husband had at least one child.

Something bitter and bile-like rose in my throat, and for just a second I felt myself staggering on the edge of that familiar abyss. I bit hard on my lower lip, and pulled myself back, yet still I noticed the tremor in my hand as I held out one of the Styrofoam cups towards her.

'I'm sorry. I couldn't remember how you take it. It's . . . it's been a while,' I said hesitantly.

Very slowly, her hand came up and relieved me of the cup. 'Thank you,' she said, looking distinctly uncomfortable. I thought it was because she didn't want to be beholden to me for anything, not even a cup of caffeine and hot water, but it wasn't that.

'The doctors want to talk to you. A nurse came looking for you a little while ago.'

I felt the blood drain from my face — you hear about that all the time in books, but it was the first time I'd ever experienced it. My cheeks felt suddenly cold and then my neck. It was there in my hands too, an inching creeping chill that ran through my fingers despite the fact they were wrapped around a steaming cup of coffee. Within me, I knew blood was racing to preserve internal organs, coursing at speed through capillaries and arteries to reach my heart. In a way that David's was suddenly incapable of doing.

I sat down heavily on one of the uncomfortable chairs. 'Did they say . . . ? Is David . . . ? Has something happened?' No clarification or translation of those garbled half sentences was required, at least not by Ally. On this one night we were able linguists, who spoke exactly the same language.

'No. I don't think it was that.' She saw my panic, or heard the small sound I couldn't prevent from escaping. 'It *wasn't* that,' she amended. 'They just needed to talk to you.'

I got to my feet swaying slightly, and hoped there was still enough blood pumping to my legs to get me out of the door.

'Look, just stay here. *I'll* go and find the nurse for you,' offered Ally.

'No,' I said, 'I'll go.' It was as instinctive in me as breathing, the need to separate her from anything to do with David. As it turned out, neither of us had to leave the room. We both jumped as the door opened and a nurse I didn't

230

recognise walked in, followed by two doctors.

'Oh good, you're back,' said the nurse with relief. I glanced briefly in her direction without registering anything at all about her. She was just a metre from me, and I wouldn't have been able to identify her again if my life depended on it. My attention was fixed wholly on the two doctors, both of whom were also unfamiliar. My heart sank a little. I wanted continuity; I wanted one heroic doctor, stoically staying at David's bedside until he was well again. I wanted a physician with the Hippocratic oath tattooed on his soul, not an ever-changing carousel of medics who jumped in and out of the fight.

'Mrs Williams,' began one of the white-coated men, 'could we have a word?' He gestured towards the door. I had a horrible certainty that outside this room there waited only terrible news.

'Tell me what's happened. It's bad, isn't it?'

'We'd like to update you on your husband's condition. Would you come with us, please.' His smile was like a waxwork's: the right shape, in the right place, but there was no humanity behind it.

'No,' I said, startling everyone in the room with my refusal. The doctors exchanged a meaningful look, while the nurse suddenly found the toes of her sensible black shoes absolutely riveting.

I swallowed, trying to stop the panic from rising up in my throat and choking me. 'Whatever it is you have to tell me, you can tell me now. Here.'

One of the doctors took a small step forward

and laid his hand gently on my forearm. He must have been able to feel the thrum of nervous tension vibrating through me, beneath his palm. 'I know this is very difficult for you — ' He broke off, and his eyes flashed towards Ally, who was standing, statue-still, at the edge of the room. 'Perhaps it might be better if we spoke in private?'

'Charlotte, it's okay. I'll step out,' Ally said, and I don't know what sounded more weird, my name on her tongue or the odd tremor in her voice.

'It doesn't matter,' I said, watching Ally's steps falter as she came to a stop near me. I turned to the doctors, anxious to get the Band-Aid pulled off the wound as fast as possible. 'Just tell me.'

The doctor nodded slowly before speaking. 'We are growing increasingly concerned about your husband's condition. Despite our best efforts he is still showing very little sign of improvement, which we would have hoped to see by now. So far he doesn't appear to be responding to any measures we have employed. His condition remains grave.'

Okay, I take it back, I thought, feeling like a small child who just wants to put her hands over her ears to shut out the truth. *I don't want to hear any of this after all.*

'Ideally he should be transferred to a specialist cardiac unit, but at the moment, given his current status, we feel it would be extremely unwise to move him.'

With every word the doctor was pushing me closer and closer to the edge of despair. I knew he was still standing there before me, I could hear him talking, but the words were muffled and seemed to be coming from far away, as though I was drowning beneath a raging torrent. I couldn't breathe, I couldn't think. My hand moved convulsively, flapping as though looking for a lifeline. And then found it. Ally's fingers gripped mine so tightly I could feel the bite of her wedding band cutting into my palm.

'What happens now? What can you do for him?' That should *so* have been my question, but it came from her instead.

'Obviously Mr Williams is being monitored continually, but the next twelve hours are going to be critical. In the meantime we have sent out an urgent call for a Cardiothoracic Surgeon and we will keep you updated as to when they get here. Unfortunately,' his eyes went to the window and the raging snowstorm beyond, 'we aren't being helped by the severe adverse weather conditions. The snow.'

I followed his line of vision. Small drifts were beginning to build up at each corner of the outer window sill. The roads had been bad earlier, and if the storm continued like this they would only get worse. The irony of it all wasn't lost on me. Snow had brought David into my life, and now — if it prevented specialist medical care from reaching him in time — snow could take him away from me.

'I want to see him.'

'Of course. We'll take you to him now. You'll find him very drowsy, due to the medication, but he's still awake.'

The doctor looked down at Ally's hand, still firmly gripping mine. 'I'm afraid we can only allow one visitor at a time at his bedside.'

Ally's hand dropped away like a rag doll's. 'Of course . . . yes . . . obviously.'

During the short walk to David's room I tried to conjure up an expression to paste over my trembling lips, so he wouldn't be able to read how terrified I was feeling.

'Charlotte.' I spun around, just a few paces short of David's open door. 'Your bag,' said Ally, holding out the leather tote that I had unthinkingly left on the floor of the Relatives' Room.

'Thank you,' I said, taking the bag and slipping it over my shoulder. I saw Ally's eyes travel beyond me. I saw them go to David, watched as a muscle tightened in her throat, and followed the passage of a single glistening tear drop as it gathered and then slipped slowly from her long sooty lashes. She turned on her heel, so abruptly that her hair swirled around her head like a matador's cape, and went back up the corridor at a pace just short of a run.

Ally

I hurried to Joe's room, like a poison victim in need of an antidote. I found it the minute I slipped through the open doorway. Even here, in these dreadful circumstances he had the power to soothe and calm me. He was the signpost in the dark when I was totally lost, the candle in the

234

window, lighting my way home. I longed for him to open his warm caramel-coloured eyes, and wrap his strong arms around me. Only those eyes were now taped shut to protect them from drying, and his arms lay like branches of a felled tree, needles in veins, with tubes and wires hooked up to machinery.

The solitary nurse holding vigil in Joe's room turned at the sound of my arrival. She smiled kindly. 'I was just coming to get you, Mrs Taylor. You can sit with him now for a while, if you'd like.'

I nodded, my throat too tight with emotion to thank her, and then stopped midway between standing and sitting in the chair beside his bed, as the nurse continued. 'See Joe, I told you she'd be here in a minute. I told you not to worry.'

'Has he woken up?' I asked in an explosion of hope. 'Has he been asking for me?' I might possibly never forget the expression of sympathy on her face as the nurse looked at me, and then softly crushed my burgeoning relief to smithereens beneath her sensible work shoes.

'Well, not exactly. *I'm* the one doing all the talking.' She touched Joe's shoulder gently, and suddenly I was very glad that she was the person on duty in his room. 'But he's a good listener, and he's been patiently letting me prattle on for long enough. I'm sure he's more than ready to hear a voice he *really* cares about. Isn't that so, Joe?'

'He can hear us?' I asked, my eyes going from the nurse to the immobile face of my husband. There was no sign at all of acknowledgement, no indication that our words were reaching him. He still looked so far away.

'Well, we believe that hearing is the last of the senses to go, and there are literally hundreds of reports of people who recall having heard things from the depths of a coma.' She squeezed my shoulder encouragingly. 'It's got to be worth a try.'

I nodded, and attempted a grateful smile, but my wobbling lower lip made that impossible. The nurse, breaking I am sure at least a thousand rules of protocol, put her arm around my shoulders. 'Just hearing your voice might help him find his way back.' She passed the box of tissues from Joe's nightstand, knowing instinctively her words would make me need them.

'But what should I talk about?' I asked.

'Well, if it was me,' said the nurse gently, 'if it was *my* husband,' I saw a brief flare of thankfulness on her face that it was not, 'then I'd remind him of the special moments we've shared over the years, the important times . . . our very best memories.' There was an unexpected mistiness in her eyes as she spoke. 'Remind him of those, because if *I* was lost, trying to find my way back to the people I love, then those are the words I would want to hear.'

'Me too,' I agreed quietly.

Ally — Eight Years Earlier

I often think that Joe and I did everything backwards. I moved in with him, and *then* we fell

236

in love; I had Jake, and *then* we got married. In those early weeks, after my parents' kitchen was finally installed, I didn't even realise how much I missed having him around to talk to on a daily basis, how much of a gap he had left behind, until suddenly he wasn't there any more. Mind you, it was hard to miss him that much, because scarcely a week went by without him calling around to 'fix' something that had been bothering him about the kitchen. He changed all the cupboard handles — twice — after informing us they'd been recalled as faulty by the manufacturer. He came back to refit what looked to us to be a perfectly affixed trim on the worktops. He also spent some considerable time confessing that he still 'wasn't happy' with several of the wall cabinets.

After one visit, my father thoughtfully closed the front door and returned to the kitchen, giving my mum a meaningful look. 'While I'm delighted Joe's such a conscientious craftsman, I can't help thinking that his hopes of running his own business are never going to get off the ground, if he devotes this much after-care to each of his jobs.'

I looked up from the detailed tutor notes I had received by email that morning, as my mother replied with a gentle laugh. 'Somehow I don't think the drawer runners were the only thing that pulled Joe back today.'

I frowned, absently waving my pen through the air as though it was a conductor's baton. 'What do you mean?'

Her smile widened, and from the open door of

the fridge I heard my father quietly chuckle. I swivelled in my chair and saw his shoulders were shaking gently.

'What? What are you both going on about?' My mum's pale blue eyes were silently eloquent. 'Me?' I asked, my voice much more of a squeak than I'd intended. 'You think *that's* why he keeps coming back? That he's coming to see *me?*'

A timeless smile curved my mother's lips, making her suddenly look decades younger, and incredibly pretty. It was the face my father had first fallen in love with. 'Isn't it obvious, Ally? Why else would he keep calling round?' she asked.

'Er . . . how about to make sure you're happy with the kitchen you just spent a fortune on?' I said, for some reason beginning to panic that I had somehow disastrously misread my new friendship. I liked Joe, *really* liked him. But not in that way. Not in the way my parents were thinking. Joe was a new friend, perhaps one day he'd prove to be a loyal and good one. But as for anything else . . . well, forget it. My parents should know better than to hint at it being anything else. Especially now.

I wasn't healed yet. I wasn't even close. Memories of David weren't going to be planed away like wood shavings by this charming, attractive carpenter who had just happened into my life. Maybe, if things had been different . . . ? I gave myself a mental shake. Things were the way they were. I knew it, and my parents knew it. Or at least I thought they did.

The wounds might be starting to heal, but the

scars were going to take a whole lot longer to fade away. And until they did, I was in no position to even consider starting a new relationship with anyone. I bent my head, staring at the typed notes which had inexplicably blurred together into squiggly black tadpoles wriggling across the page, and waited for them to turn back into letters.

★ ★ ★

Three weeks later I was standing in the High Street, staring into a shop window when I saw the reflection of a familiar van pull into one of the parking bays behind me. In the plate glass of the window Joe looked even taller and broader than I remembered. It was, I realised, the first time I had ever seen him outside of the confines of our home.

I had less than a moment to check my own image in the glass as he locked his vehicle and began to walk in my direction. It was an uncommonly warm day at the end of March, and I'd come out dressed only in a long fluffy soft-knit jumper, that clung to my curves a little more revealingly than I'd have liked, worn over black leggings tucked into my new sheepskin boots.

I don't know why I didn't turn around to greet him. I don't know why I kept studying the shop window with such intensity, you'd have been forgiven for thinking I was planning a smash and grab on the place. Actually, that's a lie. I knew precisely why I didn't turn around. But when he called my name, I had no choice. I turned, my smile of greeting fluttering a little at the edges, like a flag in the breeze.

'Ally. What a nice surprise. How are you?'

I hadn't seen him for several weeks, not since the visit when my parents had made me question our friendship, so perhaps that was why my heart began to beat a little faster as he stood before me on the pavement. His eyes dropped for just a moment, and although it wasn't an invasive appraisal, it still made me slightly anxious. Although to be fair, my own eyes had done pretty much the same thing, noting the black jeans and the dove-grey casual shirt. They weren't what he usually wore to work, and I would know, and as it was approaching lunchtime I wondered if perhaps he was on his way to meet someone. Maybe he had a date? A feeling I had no business owning squirmed within me at the thought, and I realised with surprise that I was suddenly incredibly nervous.

'I'm very well, thank you.'

'You look good . . . I mean, you look well . . .' he said, sounding unusually flustered. The fact that he too was nervous was as puzzling as it was interesting.

'So what prised you away from your piano and laptop today? Have you finished your dissertation already?'

I loved the way he had taken such an interest in my university degree, even though it was a totally different path from the one he had chosen to follow. 'Now, wouldn't that be great?' I said, smiling widely. 'No, I haven't, but then it's not due until the end of May — the dissertation, that is.' I was stumbling awkwardly over even the simplest of sentences and I truly had no idea why. Thankfully he changed the subject and turned to look at the window display I'd been studying so intently when he pulled up.

'So, what are you thinking of buying, or are you just window shopping?'

'I think most of this is slightly outside of my student price bracket,' I joked, nodding towards the cards in the estate agent window, displaying some of the most expensive properties our town boasted. 'Actually, it was the rentals I was looking at,' I confided, pointing towards the display on the far side of the window.

'Really?' Joe asked, turning away from the window to look at me. There was genuine surprise on his face. 'You're moving out of your parents' home? Now?' I bristled a little at what I thought he meant. 'Before you've finished your degree?'

I relaxed and felt the tension slide off me, as he stood with his head angled quizzically, waiting for my reply. 'I don't think there's ever an easy time to finally fly out of the nest,' I replied, repeating the same words I'd said to my parents only days earlier. Thankfully Joe didn't look distraught or burst into tears, as my concerned parents had done. But I couldn't entirely blame them for their reactions. It was natural for them to want to protect me, when life had thrown me up against the buffers. But that didn't mean I was acting irrationally, or that I hadn't properly thought things through. Because that was pretty much all I *had* done for the last few months. I was officially all 'thought out'.

'I think many people find it hard after uni to move back home,' I admitted. 'You're used to living your own life, coming and going as you please, making your own decisions, and then suddenly that's all gone and you're back home again, as if the last three years had never been.' Except that wasn't the case in my own situation. I wasn't the same person I'd been before I'd packed up all my belongings and thrown myself into student life. And a lot of that was due to David, but even more of it was due to me.

'I suppose it *must* be hard,' Joe conceded.

There was a long moment of silence, and I really hoped he wasn't going to ask me any more questions, because I scarcely knew myself exactly why now — of all times — this felt like the right moment to strike out for my independence. I just knew that it did.

A change of subject was much needed, and I found it in the first thing that came to mind. 'You're looking unusually smart today,' I commented, before realising how rude that sounded.

'You mean as opposed to my usual vagrant layabout look?'

My already flushed cheeks went a couple of shades pinker.

'Actually, I've just been to a meeting with my local, friendly, bank manager.'

'How did that go?' I asked, and then bit my lip at this further impertinence. What was wrong with me today? I seemed to have lost all ability to filter my thoughts before they came tumbling out of my mouth. I should watch that — it could end up getting me into an awful lot of trouble.

'Well, he is definitely a bank manager, and he definitely lives nearby. So two out of three isn't bad.'

I made a non-committal sound of sympathy, feeling uncomfortable that I had accidentally probed into his private financial matters.

'Actually, I have an idea about something. Are you doing anything right now? Is there somewhere you need to be?'

'Nooo,' I replied, drawing the word out hesitantly, unsure of why he was asking.

'Would you come with me? There's something I'd like to show you.'

'If it's your etchings, then I've seen them already,' I quipped.

He laughed out loud at that, causing several passers-by to turn their heads. 'No. It's actually more interesting than that. I'll even throw in lunch,' he added as a further temptation.

I should probably have paused longer than I did before agreeing. I'm sure it made me look far too needy for company, but I said 'yes' with the kind of stupid alacrity that gets kidnap victims featured on milk cartons all over America.

★　★　★

Joe's van smelled of wood and teak oil, and he apologised profusely for the tools, boxes of screws, and rags he hurriedly had to clear from the floor of the passenger side before I could sit down.

'So where are we going?' I asked as he pulled

out into the busy lunchtime traffic.

'You'll see,' Joe said mysteriously, before returning his attention to the road. Our conversations had always been full of easy chat and banter, but during the brief journey I kept mentally double-checking and editing everything I said before I allowed it to be aired, anxious I wasn't giving off the wrong signals. If Mum had been right, and Joe's interest was more than just platonic, this was going to be really awkward.

I always think there's something intimate and revealing about what people leave in their cars. The metal boxes we hide inside and keep securely locked can give away as many secrets as a safe deposit box. I looked around Joe's van, but there were no discarded fast-food wrappers, mangled drink cans, or screwed-up parking fines to fill in the missing pieces of how he lived. Aside from the tools he had moved, and a neatly clipped bundle of receipts, there was nothing that gave him away at all. Embarrassingly, I think he might have guessed what I was doing from the frequent sidelong glances he took as he drove. I squirmed a little in my seat, as though I'd been caught snooping.

Looking for an easy distraction, I reached for the dashboard where the silver edge of a CD protruded from the player 'May I?' I asked, my finger poised on the disc.

He gave a small shrug. 'I don't think we share the same musical tastes, but go ahead,' he said.

I pushed the CD in place, and moments later the car filled with the sounds of a banjo-plucking intro to a country music song. I waited until the end of the track before teasing him lightly. 'How come you never said you were 'a little bit country'?'

'It's my guilty secret.' He laughed, knowing there was no malice in my words. 'I'll turn it off,' he said reaching his hand towards the eject button.

'No. Let it play,' I said, extending my own hand to prevent him. Somehow, with his eyes fixed on the road, our fingers ended up clashing and colliding in a tangle of digits and that's when something I hadn't been expecting at all happened. It felt as though my hand had passed through a naked flame, and then been plunged into a large bucket of ice. I think I might even have gasped softly as I drew back my arm, laying my hand carefully in my lap, like a bird with a damaged wing.

I was totally confused by my unexpected reaction and had no way of knowing if Joe had been aware of that strange sensation. Perhaps he had, because he certainly jerked sharply on the wheel as he pulled us into a parking space that looked way too small for his van, but which he managed to squeeze into with practised ease. He nodded towards the bakery in the small parade of shops. 'I'll just go and get us some lunch,' he said, his hand already on the door latch.

'Let me give you some money,' I said, reaching for my purse. He put his hand out and stilled my arm. I looked down at his broad fingers on my forearm and waited for the weird electrical thrill to come again. Nothing. Perhaps I had imagined it, after all.

'I think I can spring for this one,' he said with a smile. 'I'm not quite bankrupt yet.'

I looked flustered, hoping I hadn't embarrassed him by the offer. But Joe was too comfortable in his own skin for that to happen, I realised.

'But I'll let you pay when we go to a fancy restaurant,' he joked, shutting the car door and heading off to buy a couple of the delicious baguettes that the bakery was well known for.

The smell of warm bread, nestling on my lap, made my stomach growl embarrassingly as we drove on. 'Sorry,' I apologised, suddenly absolutely ravenous. Luckily we were almost at our destination. We had reached a section of town I didn't know very well and I stared with interest out of the windscreen as we pulled into a narrow street lined with elegant Victorian properties. It was totally different from the road where my family lived, and I peered out of the side window as we passed many impressively renovated three-storey homes. We drove almost to the end of the road, before Joe pulled up outside a less than immaculate property. The front wall was crumbling and in need of repair, and the iron gate was hanging a little crookedly from its fixings. The house itself looked in need of a little TLC — and a couple of gallons of paint wouldn't go amiss either.

I climbed out of the van and stood on the pavement looking up at the house which I knew had to be Joe's. 'Come inside,' he said, holding the rusted metal gate aside, so I wouldn't brush against it.

I think the kindest thing I could say about the

house was that one day, when enough money and time had been spent on it, it was going to be beautiful. You could see it already, here and there. The original tiles on the hall floor gleamed with a waxed sheen, and the grout had been painstakingly replaced, but all the internal doors and the totally-out-of-place modern banister were bizarrely painted bright blue.

'It was a rental for quite a long time,' Joe explained, ushering me down the hallway towards the kitchen. 'It still bears the scars.'

I laughed, familiar enough with just how bad student rentals could be.

I stopped in my tracks as I entered the kitchen. It was very much a work in progress, but I instantly recognised it from the drawing Joe had sketched out when he was at our house. The cupboards were just carcasses, there was only one tiny area which had a worktop fitted, and there appeared to be several things missing — important things, like an oven or a fridge. But one thing that wasn't missing was the island unit, which was already half built and positioned exactly where I had suggested putting it. For some silly reason I was strangely touched.

'It looks good. All of it,' I confirmed, looking around at the semi-completed kitchen. There was an awful lot still to do, and if he worked at the same rate he had done at our place, he wouldn't be eating a home-cooked meal for a long time to come.

Joe drew out a couple of tall stools for us to sit on, and I was thankful he had his back to me, retrieving some plates, as I struggled to climb up.

It was a less-than-graceful manoeuvre, and I was glad not to have a witness.

He waited until we'd finished eating before asking, 'Would you like the grand tour now?'

'Absolutely,' I said, placing my hand in his, which he had gallantly held out to help me down from the stool.

I followed him from room to room. Some looked like they were just this side of being condemned, while others looked like they could have been lifted from the pages of a beautiful homes magazine. There didn't seem to be a logic to his renovation schedule, but he'd finished the sitting room and one of the bathrooms. He led me up to the top storey of the building, and reached for the handle on a door that had been lovingly restored to its natural oak finish. 'And this is the master bedroom,' he said, his voice sounding a little strange, as he allowed the door to swing open. The room had polished oak floors and a large cast-iron double bed in its centre, with crisp white linen and thick downy pillows. I stood hesitantly on the threshold, uncomfortable about stepping across it to enter his private domain. I saw a small bundle of discarded clothing he had left in a heap on a velvet chaise positioned beneath the window. I recognised a couple of his favoured t-shirts from the pile of laundry, and began to feel a little warm.

'Very nice,' I commented, still not venturing into the room. I could see our reflections in a tall free-standing mirror positioned in a corner. I was holding on to the edge of the doorframe like a first-time sky-diver who has suddenly thought better of the whole idea. Joe was beside me, an encouraging look on his face.

'So, do you like it?' he asked, as though my opinion was terribly important. He was acting really weirdly, and I had no idea why. 'Will you be comfortable here? Is the room big enough for you? Is the bed okay?'

I felt the muscles of my face all decide to freeze at once, so only my eyes were moving. Left to right they went, from him to the bed and back again. I wasn't scared. Well, maybe just a little bit. If this was Joe's idea of seduction, no wonder he was single.

'There's an en suite through there,' he said pointing at a pair of oak double doors on the far wall. 'Would you like to see it?'

'No thanks, I'm good,' I said, my voice a small squawk.

'The shower is big enough for two,' he added as though that might make me change my mind. What did he think, that we were going to rip our clothes off and have a quick splash around? I wondered if this was how women ended up being held prisoner in cellars for decades. For the first time I questioned if my dad had bothered taking up any references before they'd commissioned Joe to do our kitchen.

I risked a glance over my shoulder at the double flight of stairs I would have to descend before I reached the front door.

'I thought fifty pounds a week would be reasonable. How does that sound?'

I smiled weakly, and wondered if that was what he was asking for my ransom, or if that was what he was going to pay me for my services.

'Until I've got the rest of the place done up, I don't think I could reasonably ask for more than that in rent, do you?'

★ ★ ★

It took him at least ten minutes to stop laughing, and when he did, his eyes were still watering with humour. 'You really thought I was kidnapping you?'

'I didn't know *what* to think,' I said, sounding a little huffy. Okay, so it had been a tiny bit amusing, but he was going too far now. I had a horrible feeling this might be something I would never live down. 'And to be fair, you never mentioned that you were showing me the house as a potential lodger.'

'So what on earth did you think I was doing when I took you up to my bedroom and started talking about the bed?' I didn't answer, but the flush that went from my cheeks clear up to the roots of my hair did it for me. 'Oh. I see,' Joe said, his face sobering as he absorbed just how badly I had misinterpreted his intentions. Then he lost it all over again and burst out laughing. 'I'm sorry, Ally. I thought I'd said something on the drive over.'

'Well you didn't.'

'Sorry about that. But now we've cleared things up, what do you say?'

'I'm going to feel bad turfing you out of the master bedroom in your own house,' I said guiltily.

'I'm quite happy to use the double on the floor below, it's nearly done and I don't need the en suite. Unless, of course, you fancy sharing after all?' he asked, his eyes twinkling mischievously.

'Ha ha. Very funny.' I looked around the sitting room, with its open fireplace and comfortable reproduction furniture where we had ended up. 'It's a lovely house, Joe, and I would be happy to be your lodger, if you really think it will work out. That I won't be in your way.'

'I work late most nights, so that will give you plenty of time to study and practise your music in peace. And the walls are thick enough here that you don't have to worry about disturbing the neighbours.'

'Thanks,' I said with a laugh. 'Is that a reflection on my musical skills?'

He smiled warmly. 'Not at all.'

His mobile rang then, and he went into the kitchen to take the call. I got to my feet in his absence, idly doing a circuit of the room that would soon be not just his, but mine too.

His solution was logical, and eminently afford-able, but I still knew I would meet with resistance from my family at my decision to move away right now. But Joe's suggestion would benefit us both, he needed the extra income from my rent, and I couldn't think of a better use for the money my grandmother had left me, than using it to start standing on my own two feet. I would still be close enough to my family that they'd be there when I needed them (and I *would* need them, I knew that only too well), but just far enough away to give me my independence.

My hand trailed over Joe's expensive-looking music system which looked a little out of place in the period decor of the room. Beside the gleaming chrome unit was a small stack of CDs. Unashamedly snooping this time, I flicked through the boxes, smiling as every single one depicted someone in a checked shirt, or riding a horse, or sitting on a post and rail fence. I strongly suspected he might be a tad more than just 'a little bit country'. But there was one box that was different from all the rest. It felt lighter as I picked it up, and I knew instantly why. I pressed the small silver button on the machine and the flap slowly slid open, revealing the CD still inside. It was the one he'd been listening to last. I ran my finger lightly over the title. Beethoven's Sonata No. 5. It was the piano piece I had been practising for my final performance assessment. The piece he must have literally heard a hundred times while he was working at our house. I nudged the CD door to a close, as though I'd stumbled over a secret he hadn't wanted to share.

Charlotte

I'd seen David look many shades of terrible before. I'd seen him ashen white at his Aunt Helen's funeral. I'd seen him sea-sick grey on a small fishing boat in Corfu, on our first holiday there. I'd even seen him a curious shade of green, when I'd given us both food poisoning by undercooking a turkey one Christmas. But I'd never, ever seen him look as bad as he did lying on that hospital bed, hooked up with wires and tubes to monitors that bleeped alarmingly when he moved. He was white, bone white, with dark grey smudgy circles ringing his eyes. The change in him in just a few short hours was terrifying. If I had doubted the veracity of the doctors, the proof that they were right was lying there right in front of me.

I thought at first he was asleep when I crept quietly into his room, but his eyes fluttered open as I slipped into the chair someone had thoughtfully placed for me at his bedside.

'Hey, you,' he said, his voice a breathy parody of its normal tone. 'You still here, then?'

I pulled the chair a little closer to the bed and reached for his hand.

'Yeah. One of the nurses says this really cute doctor comes on duty later. Thought I'd hang around till then.'

His blue-grey lips curved into something that was meant to be a smile.

'How are you feeling?' I whispered, leaning over and kissing him gently. His lips felt cold, although the room was blisteringly hot, like a greenhouse in a heat wave.

'Kind of woozy. Don't know what kind of shit they've got me on, but it would go down really well in the clubs.'

I darted a glance at the nurse standing at the foot of his bed, hoping she realised he was just joking, or high on meds. Her eyes never smiled, they were too full of sympathy.

'I've been having these really weird dreams.

And then just now I thought I heard . . . ' his voice trailed away.

'Heard what?'

'Nothing. Just rambling,' he finished. His eyes went to mine and there was such a look of sadness in them that it suddenly hurt to breathe. 'I'm so sorry, Charlotte, for doing this to you.'

'Sorry for what? This isn't *your* fault. You didn't do this on purpose.'

'No, but I know how freaked out you get about hospitals, and now I'm putting you through all this.'

'I told you, I'm just here for the hunky doctors,' I replied sassily, except I ruined it by choking on a small sob at the end.

'Come here,' he urged, his voice a shallow gasp. He moved his arm, creating a small space for my head. I didn't know if it was allowed, I didn't know if they'd tell me off, or if I'd set one of the barrage of machines behind him into a frenzy, and I didn't give a damn. I leaned forward as far as I could, and rested my head in the hollow of his shoulder.

We stayed like that for a long time, the only sound in the room was the hum of the equipment and the quiet swish of the nurses' soft-soled shoes as they bustled around the room, doing all they could to keep the man I loved alive.

'So, I'm guessing by the expression on your face when you walked in here that I look pretty bad.'

'I wouldn't say that. I've seen you look far worse.'

'Oh yeah, like when?'

For a moment I was lost for a reply, and then the perfect one came to me.

'When we had that Hallowe'en party in Warwick Road, and you dressed up as Beetlejuice.'

He frowned for a second, fighting the medication to pluck the memory from some forgotten recess in his mind. 'Ah yes. That was quite a night, as I remember.'

I gave a long sigh, grateful he hadn't forgotten the night that had been so pivotal in our relationship. For it was the night when everything had first begun to change.

Charlotte — Eight Years Earlier

The party had been Pete's idea. 'It'll be great. It can double up as a belated housewarming bash.'

'Very belated,' David commented dryly. 'We moved in over two months ago.'

Pete flapped his hand to bat away such a trifling detail. 'We could have skeletons in the loo, and spiders everywhere, and those pumpkins with candles inside.' He was like a hyped-up ten-year-old who'd consumed way too much sugar. 'Come on, Charlotte, back me up here. They must have gone in for all that kind of shit when you were in California last year.'

I shrugged. 'I guess so. It's a big thing over there. For the *kids*,' I teased, throwing a small cushion at his head.

He caught it deftly with one hand. 'That's us. A bunch of big kids. So it's settled then?'

That was why, on a Saturday morning three weeks later, I was climbing a very rickety ladder we'd found in the garage, to begin transforming our fairly clean house into a haunted hovel. Positioned on the top rung of the set of steps was a box of decorations, consisting of numerous plastic spiders and metres of polyester fake cobwebs.

'If we wanted it to look like that, we needn't have bothered hiring a cleaner,' observed David, walking past and casting a dubious look at the mildew-coated stepladder I was about to climb.

'He is *so* not in the party mood,' commented Mike, giving me a broad wink as I began to undo the roll of cobwebbing. 'Have another fight with Ally, did you?'

My hands stilled on the roll of white billowy gossamer, as my eyes darted to David. His shoulders had flexed at Mike's words, as though a sharply pointed arrow had found its way home, but aside from throwing his housemate a look that was more scary than any Hallowe'en mask I'd seen, he said nothing. I was desperate to know what Mike had been referring to, but it looked as though David had no intention of being drawn on the subject.

I thought back over the last three or four weeks, trying to remember if I'd seen or heard any hint of discord between them, and then felt guilty for realising I was disappointed when the answer came back as 'no'. Not that Ally had been around much lately, but her schedule was more hectic than the rest of ours, and her work ethic considerably higher. Her absence had allowed me more opportunity to spend time in David's company, which was a dual-edged sword, because the more I got to know him — on an ordinary day-to-day basis — the more I liked him. I had *so* wanted to grind my stupid seventeen-year-old's fantasy of him to smithereens underfoot, but all that had happened was that with every passing week I liked him *more* instead of less. Thankfully, he continued to remain blissfully unaware of my pathetic little crush.

'You're going to need to hang those things right up in the corner,' observed Mike, from the comfort of his armchair.

I looked up at the cornice that was still several feet above my head, even though I was almost at the top of the steps. I held on to the top rail and grimaced slightly at the slimy feel of the slippery wet wood under my fingers.

'Careful,' said Mike, levering himself out of the chair. 'You don't want to fall and break an ankle.'

'Been there. Done that,' I said, wondering if David, who appeared to have totally tuned out what was going on in the room behind him, was listening.

'Let me hang on to you while you reach up,' offered Mike, as I wobbled alarmingly, trying to find my balance before reaching up with the decorations.

'Sit down,' said David, moving with surprising speed across the room and cutting Mike off before he could reach me. 'I'm taller than you, and stronger. I've got it.'

'I told you before, arm-wrestling is *not* a test of strength,' retorted Mike, not bothering to disguise the irritation in his tone. But it had to be said that Mike was a good four inches shorter than David. He could hardly argue with that.

David placed two firm hands on either side of my waist, instantly centring me. 'Okay?' he questioned, and I gave a sharp nod in reply, suddenly not sure I could trust my voice. I stretched up towards the ceiling, and David's hands which had been spanning my hip bones through my t-shirt were suddenly on my bare skin as the fabric rode upwards. I think Mike was still muttering something about an arm-wrestling re-match, but I could scarcely hear him above the dull thud of my heart. David's fingers were firm against my body, gripping tightly enough to ensure I didn't slip and fall and break my neck. He wasn't to know that the skin beneath his hands was burning like fire under his touch. I gulped audibly as he repositioned his hold to get a better grip on me.

'Don't worry, I've got you,' said David, totally misinterpreting the source of my panic. The warmth of his breath gently fanned a small patch of exposed skin at the base of my spine, which was on a level with his mouth. I leant higher, anxious for this to be over with, yet simultaneously wishing it could go on for ever. I was vaguely aware of Mike getting up to put the kettle on, and although he was still in the room, suddenly it felt as though David and I were completely alone. His hands had moved to my ribcage, so I knew he must have been able to feel the change in my breathing from the rapid hitching movements of my diaphragm. I was frantically jabbing drawing pins into the plaster, securing the last wisps of polyester in place, when I detected an almost imperceptible change in his hold. The hands supporting me had loosened their grip, and the pads of his fingertips were pressing gently on my sun-bronzed torso, as though forensically marking the fact that he'd been there. I gasped and dared to look down, to find David's eyes were trained on my face, and there was a look in them that was impossible to read.

'Hey, that looks great,' Mike observed, returning to his seat with a cup of coffee. 'Really mysterious.'

'Isn't it?' said David, his hands leaving my body to grip mine in support as I clambered back down the steps a great deal faster than was probably wise.

★ ★ ★

Hours later, when I was slipping into my fancy-dress outfit for the party, I still hadn't been able to shake off what had happened when I was on the ladder. Or even work out if it had happened at all. Nothing like it had occurred before over the last two months, and given how committed David and Ally were, it seemed far more likely that the whole thing might just have been the product of my over-active imagination.

I stepped in front of the full-length mirror to examine my outfit. I'd gone for a Bram Stoker inspired look, choosing a sheer floaty white gown for a funeral shroud, and hoping it was fairly obvious that I was supposed to be a newly created vampire. I carefully pinned my long blonde hair into a loose knot on the top of my head, exposing the two small red puncture marks I had painted on my neck. My face was dusted with pale powder, a few shades lighter than my usual cosmetics, and across my lids I'd blended several different shades of dark grey and inky black. I'd kept my lips unpainted, making them look truly bloodless. I was pleased with the overall effect; I looked decidedly deceased. Except, that is, for the pulse pounding visibly at my throat, and the rise and fall of my breasts, which swelled against the flimsy fabric that only just succeeded in covering them.

There was a knock on the door and my name was called. The pulse rate increased and my exposed cleavage surged up like the cresting wave on a tide I walked over to the door.

'Wow, you look incredible,' said David. His eyes were pleasingly directed solely on my face and neck; I felt sure Mike's would have focused somewhat lower.

David was wearing an extremely eye-catching and instantly recognisable black and white striped suit.

'Oh, are you not going in costume?' I asked innocently.

'No. I'm — ha, ha. Very funny. I need some help.'

'What do you want me to do? Say your name three times?'

'You're killing me,' he said with a twisted smile. 'Can you give me a hand with my make-up? And believe me, that is not something I ever thought I'd hear myself say.' He held out a small bag, which had probably come with his fancy-dress costume. I took it from him and looked inside: white base, black for the eyes and some green to look like moss, nothing too challenging there.

'Yes, I can . . . ' I began, a little hesitantly. 'But don't you want to ask Ally instead?'

'I would have done. But she texted earlier to say she's got held up and won't be here until later, and I haven't got a clue how to do it. Without make-up, I'm just an idiot in a dodgy striped suit.'

I smiled and held my bedroom door open a little wider. 'Come on in then.'

What he asked of me was every bit as much of a challenge as I'd feared it would be. It was all well and good telling myself to keep my distance, remember the boundaries, just keep things on a friendly footing, but having him sitting on the edge of my bed, his legs apart to allow me closer access to his face, was just this side of torture. I pushed the hair back from his forehead before I began, and it felt just the same as I remembered, thick and springy beneath my hand. I wondered if he had any memory at all of me sinking my fingers into it while we kissed in the snow. Somehow I didn't think so.

Very carefully I smoothed the white base

across his skin, knowing my fingers were trembling as they worked, and hoping that he couldn't feel it. His eyes were on my face the entire time, and it was actually a relief when he had to close them as I painted on the panda-like black circles. David was too astute, too observant, and I knew how very easily he could slip beneath my flimsy guard.

I stepped a little closer, my knees bumping against the edge of the mattress, as I began to apply the speckles of green shading to the edge of his mouth. There was so little distance between us, I could feel his every exhalation gently fanning the exposed valley between my breasts. I felt the moment his respiration changed, and could pinpoint exactly when each breath began to come just a little bit quicker than the one before. I knew then that he wasn't immune to my proximity. My heart was tripping and jumping erratically as I continued to dab patches of colour against his lips.

'Charlotte — ' he began.

'Don't speak,' I instructed.

He was silent for no more than a second or two. 'Charlotte, I need to — ' Once again I cut him off, knowing that I must.

'Seriously, David. Don't speak. Not now. Not ever.'

His brilliant blue eyes burned into mine. *Why?* they asked.

You know why, my own replied.

But —

I shook my head sadly. *Please don't. We mustn't talk about this ever again.*

He nodded, and there was a lingering sadness in his look. The conversation was closed, and neither of us had uttered a single word.

Ten minutes later I stepped back to allow him to study his reflection in the mirror. He gave a satisfied nod. I too was pretty pleased with my handiwork, and even more so with my self-control. I didn't know how far things might have spiralled away from us if we'd let them, but I felt proud that we'd both realised we could never allow that to happen. We walked together to my bedroom door, David saying something about retrieving his wig, while I was heading downstairs to check the guys had got the music sorted. We opened the door and then froze side-by-side within its frame, as we came face-to-face with Ally at the top of the stairs. She was carrying her coat, an excessive amount of carrier bags, and her trumpet case, which seemed to travel wherever she did. Several of the bags slipped from her fingers, making a series of tiny percussion sounds as they landed on the carpet. Her shock and surprise at seeing us emerge together from my room was apparent, although somewhat overshadowed by her bizarre costume. On her head she wore a black plastic witch's hat, the type they sell in supermarkets, her pretty face half-obscured by the long straggly strands of green nylon hair attached to the brim. Her eyes were largely hidden from view beneath a crazy set of plastic glasses, attached to a large hooked nose, complete with a disgusting fake wart.

I couldn't help myself. She looked so funny, that I just couldn't stop the highly inappropriate snort of laughter from getting away from me. It was, quite possibly, the very worst thing I could have done, given the circumstances. Ally reached up and ripped the glasses from her face, throwing them angrily down to the ground where they landed among the fallen bags. She said nothing, not one word, just stared at us both for what seemed like an eternity, making up her own story of what she thought she was seeing.

'Ally, no — ' began David, stepping away from me and towards her. *Always towards her*, I thought. He reached out a hand, but she batted it away, her eyes still darting between us both.

'Charlotte was just helping with my costume,' he explained.

'*Really?*' she countered, her voice cyanide-bitter as she bent to retrieve her bags, the long green wig not quite managing to hide the hurt expression on her face.

'Don't be ridiculous,' David countered, trying to pluck the bags from her unyielding fingers. 'I needed someone to do the face paint. And you said you were going to be late.'

Ooh no, I thought, inwardly wincing at his mistake. *Don't make it sound like this was her fault.*

'Yeah well. I made an excuse and got out of the last hour of rehearsal. I thought I'd surprise you.' She turned and flashed a quick glance in my direction. 'I guess *I* was the one who got the surprise, though.'

It was a good exit line, I had to give her that. She turned sharply, and wrenched open the door to David's room and disappeared into its darkened interior. David fixed me with one last helpless look before he followed, shutting the door firmly behind him. His words were an indistinguishable low rumble through the door, but Ally's stinging reply travelled clearly into the hall. 'This is *nothing* like that time with Max, and you know it.'

★ ★ ★

The Hallowe'en party had been a complete disaster. Even without that awkward and embarrassing misunderstanding with David and Ally in the hallway, the night was a total write-off. Not that I could blame the party for the killer hangover I'd had the next day. That was all my own doing.

I hadn't lingered long on the staircase after David and Ally had disappeared into his room. Even so, the sound of their raised voices was easily heard through the thin walls. I hurried into the lounge, where Pete was busy filling a bucket full of water with several bags of shiny red apples. He looked up at my arrival, and grinned widely, dislodging his plastic fangs. Muffled shouts from above came through the ceiling and Pete and I both looked upwards, as though the script for their argument was written on the plaster.

'*Again?*' Pete questioned, before turning his attention back to the apple-bobbing preparations. 'I wonder what it's about *this* time.'

I shrugged. I had no intention of telling him — or anyone else for that matter — that on this occasion I knew exactly what our housemate and his girlfriend were in disagreement about. Me.

'There, that ought to do it,' Pete declared, positioning the bucket on a thickly folded towel.

I bent down and examined the metal pail. 'Isn't that the one Mike threw up in last week?'

Pete looked at me a little sheepishly. 'I recommend giving the apple bobbing a miss,' he advised.

★ ★ ★

The house was packed, and I recognised almost no one in the heaving throng. David and Ally had eventually come downstairs, and from a safe distance across a crowded room, it appeared that they'd settled their differences, or called a truce. Either way, I thought it wise to keep my distance from both of them, and allow the red-hot dust to settle a little more.

The kitchen was a sea of bottles, and the floor a horrible sticky mess of spilled beer and other substances, which probably didn't bear closer inspection.

'Vodka eyeball?' asked Mike, carrying a tray of shot glasses where small gruesome sweets wobbled and bounced inside jelly shots. I grabbed one, and allowed it to slither into my mouth. I could feel Mike's eyes on me appreciatively as I ran my tongue lightly over my lips. You had to admire his persistence. And while I had every intention of drinking far more than I probably should that evening, there wasn't enough jelly or vodka in the world that could make me *that* stupid. Nevertheless, at his urging, I took another couple of small glasses 'for the road'.

The music was loud and pounding, and with the front and back doors thrown open for ventilation, I could only hope that one of the guys had remembered to warn the neighbours we were having a party. Or better still, invite them. I peered through the hazy residue from the dry ice machine, that Pete had insisted we hire for the party, but could see neither of our elderly neighbours among the crush of people. I giggled to myself at the thought.

'What's so funny, beautiful?' I looked up at the tall stranger with long straggly blond hair, who was standing with a group of his friends near the doorway. I think I knew straight away that they'd probably crashed the party. For a start, they all looked a little too old to be students, and from their overheard comments, I suspected that educationally they may have peaked at primary school.

I gave an inward shudder, hearing echoes of my mother in my patronising comment. Perhaps what happened next was because I was over-compensating for that wayward thought, or perhaps I was always destined to do something foolish that night. I just don't know. Because when the blond guy reached for my hand and dragged me towards the centre of the floor, saying, 'Come on, dance with me,' I didn't do what any sane person in the world would have done, and tell him 'no'.

He held me uncomfortably close, so tightly

that the zipper from his leather jacket actually left indents on my breasts which were crushed up against him. I should have pulled away from him after that first dance. I should have recoiled from the mingled smell of spirits and nicotine on his breath. I didn't even know his name, and he certainly didn't bother asking mine. I felt his hand sliding up and down my back, each sweep taking him lower and lower until he was virtually grabbing my bum.

'Skinny little thing, aren't you?' he said, which I could only assume was his idea of a chat-up line. 'Although not everywhere,' he finished with a leer, peering down the front of my dress.

Okay, that's enough now, I thought. But just as I was about to step out of his arms, I glanced to my left and saw David watching me carefully from the edge of the room. I'm not sure where Ally was, which was probably just as well, because there was a look on her boyfriend's face as he watched me that was blistering enough to reignite their earlier argument.

I'd like to think it was the alcohol that made me so stupid and reckless. If not, I was going to have to admit to some pretty serious character flaws. Without stopping to think about my actions, I lifted my head towards my rough-around-the-edges dance partner. He didn't give me any opportunity to rescind the unspoken invitation. His mouth came down on mine as though he was trying to devour me, all hot lips and invading tongue. *Are you watching this?* cried my dumb alcohol-fuelled brain. *Do you see how over you I am?*

Eventually, even my desire to show David that there was nothing at all between him and me, couldn't keep me with my mouth against this stranger's for one second longer. I pulled back sharply, only just stopping myself from wiping the unpleasant coating of his saliva from my lips with the back of my hand. I glanced over to where David had been standing, but there was no one there. He probably hadn't even seen my small childish display.

'Come back here,' growled the blond guy in the biker jacket, taking a large swig from his beer bottle, clearly in order to lubricate himself for round two. Only there wasn't going to be one.

I resisted his pull as he tried to draw me back against him. 'No, I don't think so,' I said firmly, suddenly feeling all-the-way sober, and more than a little ashamed of the way I was behaving.

'Really?' he slurred, swaying slightly on his feet. 'Well I say, yes.' He reached for me, but I side-stepped and he stumbled clumsily before rounding on me. 'You know what you are,' he said, spitting angrily into my face. I guess he was determined to share his saliva with me, one way or another. 'You're a fucking tease.'

I didn't dignify him with a response. I just turned on my heel and wove my way, as fast as I could, through the crowd to the kitchen.

'Everything alright?' asked Andrew, who had observed the tail end of the nasty little episode.

I grimaced. 'Just some jerks from town,' I replied. 'I don't think they were invited.'

'I'll keep an eye on them,' he assured.

I stopped only long enough to grab a can of

soft drink from the counter in the kitchen and went straight out into the back garden. It was cold, my dress was as thin as a negligée and apparently an open invitation that I was fair game, but nothing was going to induce me to go back into the house until I'd calmed down.

I was still sitting on the uncomfortable wooden bench when I heard the tinkling of breaking glass coming from within the house, followed by noisy shouting. I lifted my head like a woodland creature sensing danger. More angry shouts and the sound of something heavy crashing to the ground. I got to my feet, pleased to find that the cold night air had cleared the rest of the alcohol from my head. A shape flew out the back door and it took me a moment or two to realise it was Pete. He ran the short distance across the lawn to where I stood.

'Charlotte, do you know where David is?'

I came back instantly on the defensive. 'No. Why ask me? I haven't spoken to him all evening.'

Notwithstanding whatever drama was playing out inside the house, Pete still took a beat to regard me curiously. Heavy footsteps thundered up the gravel path, as Mike joined us in the darkness. 'I can't find David anywhere,' Pete reported.

'Don't bother trying. He and Ally left a while ago. They've gone back to her place for the night.' I felt something I couldn't properly define clutch me, somewhere in the region of where my heart had once lived.

'Why are you looking for him?' I asked my two

housemates, who were already turning back towards the house.

'We just wanted a bit of extra muscle power, that's all. There's a group of gate-crashers who are getting pretty out of hand. I think it's time we showed them where the door is.'

★ ★ ★

The following morning I stood and surveyed the lounge. Two of the dining-table chairs were broken, as was a pane of glass in an internal door. The bucket had been tipped over, and water was puddled across the wooden floor, decorated here and there with trampled Red Delicious apples. There were drink rings on practically every piece of furniture, which might or might not come out with polish, and several cigarette burns on the sofa cushions, which were definitely there to stay.

'There goes our security deposit,' I said sadly to Pete, who was dragging a large black plastic sack full of bottles towards the wheelie-bin.

'Hell of a party, though,' he declared. 'Quite a night.'

Charlotte

'Yes,' I said to David, whose eyes had fluttered to a close, showing a worrying network of blue veins on their lids, that I swear hadn't been visible before. 'The Hallowe'en party was certainly quite a night,' I agreed, echoing his own words.

I leaned towards him and gently kissed his cheek. 'Why don't you try and get some sleep now?' I curled my fingers through his, so that even in his dreams he would know I was still with him. 'I'll be right here when you wake up,' I promised.

His smile, like everything else about him, looked weak and diluted, but he closed his eyes, as instructed.

Ally

I shut the door of the Relatives' Room firmly behind me, as though I could keep out the memories that had followed me like a band of phantoms down the hospital corridor. I really hadn't been expecting that gut-wrenching, visceral reaction to seeing David looking so sick. I was shocked that he still had the power to affect me like that, after all this time. And angry. I didn't want anything to detract from my concern over my own husband's condition. It was probably totally irrational, but I was afraid that if fate, God, or even the team of hospital doctors, sensed any division in my loyalties, Joe would be the one to pay the price. If only *one* man could survive this night, it *had* to be Joe.

It had become so ingrained to never allow my thoughts to stray back to David and me, that I was really struggling to slam the door on them, now they'd found a crack to creep through. And it wasn't the *bad* memories I was afraid of, I could handle those. I could remember all too well our break-up, how everything we'd felt for each other had imploded like a dying star, leaving us with nothing but a gaping black hole where our feelings had once lived. What scared me most, was that it was suddenly getting much harder to remember why I *hated* David, and a whole lot easier to recall why I'd loved him in the first place.

I took a deep steadying breath and allowed my mind to go back eight years.

Ally — Eight Years Earlier

The Hallowe'en party wasn't the start of it, although for a long time I believed that it had been the catalyst. But later, I realised all the clues had been there for a great deal longer; I'd just been too blind to see them.

With hindsight, the things that I'd thought were charming at the time appeared a great deal less so. As the calendar pages took us further into autumn, it became harder to force a smile each time I arrived at David's, to find Charlotte and the guys immersed in a cut-throat PlayStation game, or watching some bloodthirsty DVD on television. Charlotte had moved from place to place her entire life, and had mastered the art of blending in down to perfection. She was like an exotic chameleon, fitting in with David's friendship group, in a way I'd never been able to do. But, as much as I marvelled at her ability, at the end of the day, what can you say about a chameleon, except that it's just an A-List lizard?

I'm not sure when vague disquiet about her growing closeness to David changed to actual suspicion. It wasn't any one thing, but a whole load of little ones. Almost from the very beginning I'd found it weirdly uncomfortable seeing her toiletries sitting beside his on the bathroom shelf, as though they rightfully belonged together. Her soap touching his; her bright pink razor resting upon his on the edge of the basin; their toothbrush bristles touching in the glass on the shelf.

'I'm *sorry?* You're jealous of Charlotte's *toothbrush?*' Max's voice was positively dripping sarcasm.

'No. Not really. Not at all . . . well, just that it's there in the bathroom, I guess.'

'You'd rather she *didn't* clean her teeth?'

'Don't be ridiculous,' I said into my phone, realising my old friend would probably store up every one of my stupid comments, and lob them back at me in years to come.

'Because, that would certainly stop David being interested in her,' Max declared, warming to his theme. 'No one fancies a girl with halitosis. Perhaps you should nick her tooth-brush, soap and razor? Smelly, hairy, with stinky breath. That ought to do it.'

'You're not being at all helpful, Max,' I said mulishly.

'Er, could that be because you're not talking much sense here, my lovely?'

'And, F-Y-I, I never said David was *interested* in her — not in that way. I don't know where you picked that one up.'

'I think it was probably you, with your impure thoughts about her Bic razor,' Max said with a chuckle.

Despite myself I laughed, and then sighed. 'It's just she's . . . she's . . . she's *everywhere*.'

'Well, I hate to be the one to break it to you, hon, but she *does* live there.'

'I know that.'

'I thought you said one of the other guys in the house was into her, anyway?'

I gave a small disappointed hum. 'He is, but she's never going to go there.'

'And neither will David. He's crazy about you, remember?'

'I know. It's just that we've been squabbling about such stupid stuff recently.'

'Ally, you and David are *always* squabbling. It's your thing.'

Max was right. The frequent verbal sparring had always been there, and win, lose or draw, it had always been resolved in each other's arms, or better yet, beneath the duvet. Sometimes I thought we were both guilty of instigating the spats, simply because the resolutions were *so* worth it. But over the last few months I'd noticed a slightly sharper edge to our disagreements. Perhaps much of that was down to me, I owned. I was putting an awful lot of pressure on myself with less than two terms left until Finals. Plus I'd taken on more responsibility with the music society, which was leaving David and me with even less time together than before. And I'd been so damned tired recently.

'And you just know,' I continued, 'that good

275

old 'Charlie Girl' is going to be the friend waiting in the wings with a sympathetic ear, whenever I'm not around.'

'Well in fairness, Ally, you can hardly object to him having a close mate of the opposite sex. After all, you have *me*.'

'You're different, Max,' I said.

'Mortally wounded here. Just because I bat for the other side — '

'Not because of that,' I interrupted, secretly delighted he was now so comfortably 'out' around me that he'd even discussed a few dates he'd been on. 'The difference is, you and I have *history*. We've known each other for ever. Charlotte has known David for precisely five minutes. How can they possibly claim any sort of connection? They're practically strangers.'

But for strangers, I had to admit they certainly appeared to get on very well together. She was clearly much closer to him than any of the other guys in the house. Something David denied — almost a little too ardently — I thought, whenever I'd mentioned it.

'Charlotte's just one of the blokes. She gets on with everyone in the house,' David had countered.

We were lying in his bed on a Saturday morning, and for once we had the house to ourselves. 'It's just that she seems to get on *especially well* with you.'

David turned from me then, to put his mug of tea back on the bedside table. 'You're just being silly. Charlotte doesn't have many other friends, so it stands to reason that she's going to hang

276

around with us more than anyone else. And neither of our courses have much contact time, so she and I have been virtually thrown into one another's company at home.'

Wisely, I'd held my tongue, and made no further comment, sensing how easily this one could tip over the borderline into an argument. But even as I'd willingly gone into his outstretched arms, and he'd pulled my naked body on top of his, I couldn't dismiss the small niggling worry that had burrowed like a bur into my subconscious.

7

Ally

I was jarred out of the past by the ringing of my phone. I pulled it from my pocket, and saw the word *Home* on the screen. I put the device to my ear, concern for my child, throwing hospital rules on mobiles right out the window.

'Hello?'

My neighbour's friendly voice came instantly back, saying all the right things. 'We're all perfectly fine here, Ally. No need to panic.' How did she *do* that? How did she know I was so far into disaster-mode, every little thing was now a potential catastrophe-in-the-making? 'Jake just wanted to talk to you before going to bed.' Her voice lowered to little more than a whisper. 'He got a bit upset a while ago, and I think it would help if he could just say goodnight to you.'

'Of course. Can you put him on, Alice?'

'Will do. He's right here. How are you holding up, Ally? Any change yet at your end?'

I closed my eyes and instantly an image of Joe in his hospital room hologrammed itself onto my retina. 'Not yet. But I'm staying hopeful,' I replied, trying to inject my voice with more confidence than I actually felt.

'Absolutely, sweetheart. It's all any of us can do. Here's Jakey now.'

'Hello big man, how are you doing? You're up awfully late.'

'Hey Mummy, how's Daddy? Is he there with you? Can I talk to him?'

Just hearing his young voice was almost my undoing. The love that tied him to us, wound itself like an unbreakable chain around my throat, choking the words off, as I tried to answer him. I swallowed noisily. Jake was seven, but he wasn't stupid. If he heard me crying, he'd work out how serious things were.

'Daddy's in his room at the moment, honey. He's still sleeping.'

'But it's not his bedtime yet,' Jake challenged, and then his voice dropped as he shared his secret with me. 'I don't think Alice and Stan know about proper bedtimes, Mummy, because they've let me stay up much later than you do.'

I smiled, and I hope that came over in my voice, rather than the silent tears that were running down my face as I spoke to the smallest person in my life, who owned the biggest piece of my heart. 'Well, just for tonight, it doesn't matter. But you really should be heading off to bed now.'

'Can you wake Daddy up before I go, so I can tell him goodnight?'

My hand went to my throat as though to physically stop the sob from ripping its way free. 'I think Daddy still needs to rest some more, Chicken. I tell you what, as soon as he wakes up, I'll tell him you called. How about that?'

'Okay,' he replied, but I could hear the wobble in his voice. A mother knows; even miles apart, down a crackling phone line; she just does.

'What is it, Jakey? What's wrong?'

'I want Daddy here, and you too. I like Alice and Stan, but they're doing it all *wrong*.'

I felt an overwhelming helplessness, hearing the urgent need in my child's voice tugging me towards him, while the other end of that same rope was anchored around my sick husband's bed. Impossible choices: I needed to be with both of them, and they both needed me.

'Tell me, sweetie.'

Jake's voice dropped to an exaggerated stage whisper, which I knew Alice would be able to hear. 'Stan put the toothpaste on my brush, but after I'd cleaned my teeth . . . he didn't check them. Not the way Daddy does.'

It was one of the many tiny rituals Joe and Jake shared. Joe had always taken the lead parent role at bedtime. I didn't think even *I* could fill his shoes, and certainly our well-meaning neighbour didn't stand a chance. My hands were fisted, the nails biting into my palms as I sought to remember Joe's words.

'Okay, open wide. Let's see how you've done.' Somewhere in my house I knew my seven-year-old was opening his mouth to the phone. 'Yep. All good. No cavities in there. Well done, my man.'

Jake was quiet for a moment. 'You're not quite as good as Daddy at that,' he declared solemnly. 'And you didn't high-five me.'

'Sorry, sweetheart. I promise I'll do it better next time . . . until Daddy can take over again.'

My answer satisfied him enough to allow him

to go to bed and fall asleep, with hopes of a better tomorrow. I really envied him that.

* * *

Too restless to remain in the Relatives' Room, which was starting to feel more and more like a prison cell, I wandered back down the corridor in the direction of Joe's room. The glass-walled cubicle was so crowded with doctors, it was virtually impossible to see the bed, much less Joe. I craned my neck, searching for the kindly nurse who had allowed me access earlier. I found her in the far corner of the room, and waited hopefully, my weight shifting from foot to foot, until she caught my eye. She read the question on my face and regretfully shook her head. I couldn't go in yet.

I had to admit, Joe seemed to be claiming the lion share of medical attention on the ward tonight. I pushed through the double swing doors that led to the hallway, unable to decide if that was a good or a bad thing. They were impossible-to-fathom equations. Did more doctors equal a sicker patient? Did the ratio of medics multiply the probability of a good outcome? I lowered myself onto the top step of the linoleum-covered stairs, and sighed. You didn't need to be a mathematician to work out that the odds weren't good.

In true ostrich fashion, I buried my head against my knees, trying to think of nothing except how refreshing it was to feel a cool draught rising up from the stairwell, after the stifling heat of the ward. But a cooling breeze wasn't the only thing floating up from below. The first few notes were barely audible, but perhaps my ear was more attuned to the strain of music than most people's. Melodies mingling with the aroma of antiseptic, suddenly made me think of the classical CD I'd insisted we play in the delivery room, on the night I'd had Jake. I'd been so determined that the first thing the baby should hear when it arrived in the world was music. But in reality, nothing could be heard above my noisy tears of happiness and relief, or Joe's marvelled exclamation of, 'It's a boy!'

Like a siren call, the music pulled me to my feet. I descended half a dozen steps and then stopped, listening to the sweet sound of a choir singing Christmas carols in a ward far below me. I wasn't aware that I was gripping the handrail so tightly, until I looked down and saw the contours of the knuckle bones outlined in sharp relief. *Silent Night*. Of all the carols they could be playing, what were the chances of it being that one? On this night, when serendipity was weaving the threads of our lives into a living tapestry, I wondered why I was even surprised.

Ally — Eight Years Earlier

I picked up the bundle of music scores, and began to rapidly flick through them one more time.

'Ally, relax,' urged David, from his position on the other side of my small dining table.

'I can't,' I replied. 'I just need to check the running order one more time.'

His hand came across the glass-topped table and settled over mine. 'You've checked it four times already. You've done all that you can do. You've spent the last six weeks working on this. The concert is going to be fine. If you carry on this way, you're going to make yourself sick. You've hardly touched your meal,' he observed, nodding his head towards the plate with the two pork chops that I hadn't been able to face. In fact, just the sight of them sitting in their cold gravy, with tiny speckles of fat floating on the surface, was making me feel actually physically sick.

I picked up our plates and dumped them on the draining board. 'I know you think I'm being daft, but organising this concert is a *huge* responsibility. I have to get it right.' With less than twenty-four hours to go, I was already a nervous wreck. 'Honestly, if I'd known how much work I was going to have to put in, I'd never have agreed to do it.'

'Yes, you would,' David contradicted, coming up behind me at the sink and winding his arms around my waist. 'You wouldn't have turned them down when they asked.'

'Maybe not,' I admitted truthfully. 'But we've hardly had a single evening together since I took it on.'

David shrugged as though that wasn't important. I wasn't so sure. Since the Hallowe'en party night we had both been walking a precarious tightrope, both trying way too hard not to rock a

283

boat that had already hit an iceberg. We just hadn't acknowledged it yet.

I sighed, and leaned back against the rock-steady length of him and closed my eyes, realising I was so overwhelmingly exhausted I could have fallen asleep right there. I was going to have to dig deep to find the energy to get through tomorrow night. There were flyers all over campus advertising the midnight Christmas Orchestral Extravaganza, and every time I saw one I felt a shiver of apprehension run down my spine. Perhaps David *shouldn't* stay over, I thought, because if I didn't get a decent night's rest, there was a good chance I'd have nodded off on stage before the opening bars of the first carol.

'I just need to make some final changes to the strings on *Silent Night*, then I'm done,' I assured David, as I scraped my leftovers into the bin. I felt a small unpleasant heaving sensation in the pit of my stomach, as the smell of congealed pork wafted up from the pedal-bin. I slammed the plastic lid down. God, I could *not* get sick before tomorrow night. I just couldn't.

'So, are you still planning to meet me backstage before the start of the concert?' I asked. 'Because you *could* come along earlier and listen to the run-through.'

David tried to disguise the look in his eyes before I saw and named it. Too late. I'd clocked it, and it was the same one I'd have worn if you'd asked me to sit through a Test Match. 'I think maybe one concert a night is enough for me,' he said, pulling me slowly into his arms.

284

'I suppose I should be grateful you're coming at all,' I said, inwardly cringing at the peevish note in my voice. This is what stress does to you, I thought. And it wasn't the first time I'd snapped at him recently.

'Of course I'm coming. It's your big night. I hope you've reserved a centre-stage front-row seat for your tone-deaf boyfriend?'

'I certainly have, although I think it's finally dawning on me that I'm never going to make a music lover out of you, am I?' I added, a little disappointedly.

David leaned back with a familiar twinkle in his eye. 'We'll just have to settle on me being a different kind of lover,' he teased, bending his head to kiss me in a way that made my knees forget how to hold me up.

I tightened my arms around his neck. 'Encore,' I murmured. And he obliged.

* * *

The sound check went well, the choir rehearsal had gone perfectly, and the recital hall looked great, with a Christmas tree positioned to one side of the stage, twinkling with ice-white lights. So why couldn't I shake the overwhelming sense of apprehension that was hovering over my head, like my own personal storm cloud? I had checked and double-checked everything off my mental list of potential disasters that could occur that night. Yet still, as the first audience members began to file into the hall, I could feel my unease beginning to grow and multiply, as it took on a life of its own. I peered through a crack in the Green Room door, and my eyes scanned the auditorium. David was late, and I was trying really hard not to feel irritated by that. He still had time to get here, but he was cutting it awfully fine. Although billed as a 'midnight' concert, it was actually scheduled to begin at eleven p.m., and I wondered if he'd been persuaded to go to the pub with the guys and had somehow lost track of time.

I pulled my phone from my bag and checked — yet again — to see if there was a message from him. I hesitated for a moment, trying to decide whether there was enough time to call him before we went on stage. But before I had the chance, one of the choir hurried up to me with a question about their solo, then the percussionist accosted me in a panic because she couldn't find the sleigh bells anywhere, and before I knew it, there was no time to do anything except pick up my trumpet and get ready to lead the processional file of performers out of the Green Room. I did just manage to fire off one quick text before I dropped my phone back into my empty trumpet case. 'Where are you?' It looked a bit terse, so I softened it with three kisses and jabbed Send.

'We're on,' said the saxophonist, who was listening at the door for our introduction. I smoothed down my plain black shirt and pencil skirt, and took my place at the head of the line of musicians.

'Good luck, everyone,' I said. I glanced back — just once — at my trumpet case, hoping to hear the ringing of my phone, letting me know my boyfriend was on his way.

David's vacant seat was the only empty one in the entire auditorium. Fortunately, as I was conducting for the entire performance (in between joining in for some of the brass sections) I had my back to it, and didn't have to see it as a constant visual reminder that David had let me down. Even so, I could feel it stinging me like a small wound, at the base of my spine, as we segued between traditional instrumentals to favourite carols. Every time I turned back to the assembled concert hall, to acknowledge their applause, or introduce the next item, I kept hoping that at some time since I'd last looked, his seat would now be filled. That he'd be sitting there, smiling proudly at how well it was all going, or mouthing a silent apology to me for being late. But for the entire first half of the concert, his seat remained empty.

The audience were still clapping and cheering enthusiastically as we left the stage for a short interval. Many members of the orchestra and choir went to join friends and family members, most heading towards the trestle tables to one side of the hall, where mulled wine and hot mince pies were being sold. I resisted the fragrant pull of the warm spicy drink and headed straight back to where I had parked my belongings. My hand dived to my phone, expecting to see missed calls, voicemails or texts to explain David's non-appearance. There was nothing. Not one word. For the first time since the concert began, I stopped feeling annoyed and started to get worried. He had *known* how important this night was to me, how hard I'd been working towards making it a success. He should have been here over an hour ago. So what could have happened to delay him?

His phone rang until voicemail took over and answered for him. 'Hi David, it's Ally. Is everything okay? Where are you? Call me as soon as you get this.' I paused for a moment, before adding, 'I'm getting a bit worried now.' I disconnected the call, but kept my phone gripped tightly within the palm of my hand for the entire duration of the interval, willing it to ring as I anxiously waited for his reply. None came.

I can't say that David's absence affected the success of the concert. But it certainly ruined it for me. Even the combined applause from my fellow musicians and the cheering audience as I took my solo bow, couldn't quite dissipate the feeling of panic that had been steadily growing throughout the evening.

The final piece of the evening had been *Silent Night*, and I conducted the choir and musicians with eyes that sparkled brightly with tears of nostalgia. The carol had always been my favourite; it was the first one my grandmother had taught me to play on the piano, and every time I performed it I always felt a little bit closer to her. I'd wanted so much to share this moment with David. I'd wanted to look across at him as the final notes faded away and see the love and pride on his face. I wanted him, just for a moment, to slip inside my world and see why music meant so much to me. Only he wasn't there.

There is always heaps to do at the end of a concert. It's an unglamorous moment when the audience finally departs, someone flicks on the glaringly bright house-lights and you have to change from musician to roadie, as music stands, amplifiers and all the other paraphernalia of a concert has to be packed away securely into storage rooms. I kept half an eye trained to the door as I worked, still expecting — or hoping — to see David dash in, apologies tumbling out of his mouth. I even found myself contemplating how long it would take me to forgive him if he'd simply *forgotten* to come to the show. I whipped metres of amplifier lead around the spools, tugging sharply on each rotation and trying to squash the warring feelings within me that were vying for supremacy: anger and alarm.

Eventually the last of the equipment was stowed away, and apart from a few stragglers, most of the orchestra had left. David had been planning on coming home with me after the concert, and I didn't know if I should still wait around for him to show up, or go to my place and see if he was waiting for me there. Why the hell wasn't he answering his phone? Had he been in some sort of accident? While I was on stage, blasting out *Ding-Dong Merrily on High* on my trumpet, had he been lying in a gutter at the side of the road, having been struck by some stupid drunk driver? Once the visual had been planted in my mind, it was almost impossible to uproot.

'Sorry love, I need to lock up now.'

289

I jumped as the caretaker opened the double doors of the auditorium. 'Oh, okay,' I said, scrambling to my feet and picking up my trumpet case. I guess that decided it for me. I'd go to my house first and if David wasn't there, I'd move on to his.

My home was in darkness, and as both Elena and Ling were away for the weekend, there was no chance that David was waiting for me inside. Nevertheless, I still called out *'Hello. Anyone home?'* as I undid the door latch and dumped my trumpet in the hall. I probably would have jumped through the roof if there had been an answering reply. God knows, I was already jittery enough after my walk home. I never used to worry about walking alone at night, but since David and I had been together, he'd been adamant that it was an unnecessary risk to take, and had insisted on always walking me home, even if he wasn't staying over. I think some of his apprehension must have rubbed off on me over the last year, because I had felt decidedly uneasy as I speed walked through the quiet streets. It was after one o'clock in the morning, and the streets were deserted and eerie, with low lying patches of murky fog lingering like ghost clouds along my route.

I decided not to tempt fate too many times in one night, and called a local cab company, whose card I found pinned to our kitchen noticeboard. Less than ten minutes later I was sitting in the back of a taxi, which smelt vaguely of antiseptic and strong mints, and giving the driver David's address.

As we got closer to our destination and rounded the final bend which led to David's street, I leaned forward in my seat, preparing to direct the driver to the house. But there was no need. David's home was lit up like a Christmas tree. Lights blazed from every single window and spilled out of the front door, which was wide open. For just a second it reminded me of the Hallowe'en party, but whatever was going on inside those walls tonight, it certainly wasn't a party.

There was a police car parked at the kerb, its blue lights eerily illuminating the front garden. Parked behind it was a first-response paramedic vehicle.

'Hello. Something's happening here,' commented the driver, the monotony of his shift suddenly elevated by this new excitement. 'Wonder what that's all about. Now, which house are we heading for?'

I said nothing. My throat was too constricted in fear. The driver glanced into his rear-view mirror and saw my face. His own sobered instantly. 'Is that where you're going?'

I nodded, my eyes wide and unblinking as I began to fumble with the catch of my seat belt. The cab pulled in behind the emergency vehicles and I thrust a note into the driver's hand and leaped out. My feet almost slipped beneath me several times on the rime covering the pavement as I raced towards the open front door. I barrelled through it, calling out as I ran, 'David. David are you here?'

A shouted response came from the direction

of the lounge and I threw open the door with such force that the handle left a small imprint in the plaster wall. I came to a halt so abruptly that I rocked on my feet as I tried to take in the scene before me. The lounge was crowded with people, and my eyes frantically raked the room, processing the faces of strangers as well as those who belonged there, until I found the one I was looking for. David was sitting on the couch; his arms were tightly wound around someone who definitely didn't belong in them.

'David!' I cried, his name a combined exclamation, question and gasp of relief. He turned towards me and the world rocked and swayed once more. He was gently attempting to disentangle Charlotte's arms, which were locked tightly around him, as he got to his feet, his eyes on mine the whole time. Well, one of them was, the other was swollen half-shut and already an ugly purple-coloured bruise discoloured his cheekbone. His lip was split too, not badly, just enough to make the sound of my name sound slightly slurred.

'What happened to you? Were you in an accident?' I asked, my thoughts still on drunken drivers ploughing into pedestrians in the dark. Then I realised that theory made no sense. For the first time I looked at Charlotte, and saw beyond the fact that she was hanging on to my boyfriend as though her life depended on it. I saw the dishevelled hair and the tear-swollen eyes, and as my gaze dropped lower, I noticed for the first time the raw and bloody grazes on her knuckles.

I looked over to where Andrew, Mike and Pete were standing to one side of the room, their faces grey, like shocked gargoyles. Andrew and Pete met my eyes with a look of sympathy. Mike's remained riveted on Charlotte, fury emanating from him in almost palpable waves.

'Will someone please tell me what's happened here?'

'Charlotte was attacked tonight.'

Charlotte — Eight Years Earlier

The stupid thing was: I *never* went to the supermarket alone; I never went without my car; and I never went late at night. But on that one fateful evening, I did all *three* of those things.

In an uncharacteristic fit of diligence, I'd spent the entire evening working in the university library. I had an assessment deadline looming and had done nowhere near enough work to pass it. The library had been warm and cosy, and surprisingly conducive to study. *Who knew?* I worked on, as the tables and benches around me gradually began to empty, until there were only a handful of students working quietly in glowing pools of light from the desk lamps.

It was only the persistent growl of my stomach that pulled me away from my studies. I glanced at the wall clock, and was surprised to see it was after ten p.m. Little wonder that the library was practically deserted. It was Friday night, a few weeks before Christmas break, and most students were probably out in one of the many clubs or bars in town, indulging in some early seasonal celebrations. I clicked the lid shut on my laptop and slid it into my bag along with several text books.

I'd actually rather enjoyed my period of academic industry, which was troubling on several levels, because it made me wonder how much more I could achieve if I actually pushed myself. But also, it made me question whether I was, in some small way, trying to be more like Ally. I'd never been the type of girl who'd contemplate changing just to get a man to like her, and the idea that I might be doing so now, even subconsciously, was somewhat disturbing.

A surprisingly cold wind, as vicious as a pecking crow, nipped sharply at my exposed skin, as I stepped out of the warm cocoon of the library. I yanked the zipper on my short leather jacket all the way up to my neck, but even with my scarf wound several times beneath my chin, it was still bitterly cold. I stamped my feet on the pavement, regretting the high-heeled fashion boots, which might look great with my skinny jeans but did little to keep my feet warm. I was cold, tired and hungry, and not in the mood to hike all the way back across campus to reach my bus stop.

What I really wanted was to be curled up on the settee at home, with a plateful of something far too full of carbs to be good for me. Too late I remembered there was nothing in the fridge except for a stale loaf of bread, some mouldy cheese and a whole load of beer. That was one of the problems with living in a house of men:

shopping was never very high on anyone's list of priorities.

There *was* a twenty-four-hour supermarket not far from campus, but going there would put me on the 'wrong' side of town, in every meaning of the phrase. Making a snap decision, I turned around on the path leading to the bus stop and headed instead down a narrow footpath which led off campus. I'd only been to this store once before, and that had been in broad daylight, but I was pretty certain I could remember the way to the small industrial estate by the railway lines, where it was located. It wasn't far.

That was my first mistake.

I walked quickly, head down against the wind, the heels of my boots clattering like tiny percussion instruments on the paving slabs. I crossed a footbridge over the train tracks and it was almost as though I'd passed through border control from one country to another. This was the area of town that boasted the cheapest — and shabbiest — student accommodation, the dodgiest pubs and the highest crime rate. Despite the orange orbs of light from the street lamps, glowing like giant struck matches in the darkness, I didn't feel comfortable crossing the exposed expanse of the practically deserted car park. I didn't relax until I saw the familiar blue-and-white lit fascia of a well-known supermarket chain, in the far corner of the industrial estate.

There is something eerie about being in a supermarket late at night. Perhaps it's the lack of mums pushing trolleys with noisy toddlers sitting in them, or the scarcity of staff milling around filling shelves. Whatever the reason, the supermarket felt weird bereft of meandering customers and employees. Only one of the tills was currently manned, and as I walked past the small queue of shoppers waiting to pay for their goods, a young man with a closely shaven head and an ear full of piercings joined the back of the line. Something about him was vaguely familiar, but I couldn't place where I'd seen him before. I passed behind him, my nose wrinkling slightly at the smell of alcohol which hung around him like an invisible fog. He called out something to an unseen companion in one of the nearby aisles, and then belched unpleasantly. He seemed to find this ridiculously funny.

I was halfway up the frozen goods aisle when I realised where I knew him from. My footsteps faltered, and I stopped in front of one of the cabinets and looked back towards the tills. Yes, I was positive. He'd been one of the group who'd gate-crashed our party and caused all the damage. The group the guys had eventually thrown out. As I stood watching, his companion emerged from the direction of the alcohol section, carrying two hefty twelve-packs of beer.

Him, I knew instantly. I needed no time for the penny to drop, or for any other type of prompt to place him. The last time I'd seen him, he'd been trying to stick his tongue down my throat, and I don't think his invasion plans had ended there. Neither of them had noticed me, and there was absolutely no reason why they would, or even *recognise* me, come to that. After all, I *had* been dressed and made-up like a vampire the last time our paths had crossed. Nevertheless, a small warning voice started whispering in my head, a voice I refused to listen to.

That was my second mistake.

I should have gone right then, when they hadn't yet seen me. I could easily have slipped unseen from the store and they'd have been none the wiser that I was ever there, and the night would have ended in a completely different way. But it's easy to be wise in hindsight, isn't it?

Like a small animal transfixed by a cobra, I kept looking in his direction. His first glance was just passing, cursorily checking me out, like he probably did to every single female who crossed his path. Something about me must have tripped the '*she'll do*' switch in his brain, because he looked back with greater interest. I turned quickly, heading up the aisle, but it was too late. I'd already seen the dawning recognition in his eyes. He'd remembered exactly who I was.

It's virtually impossible to elude someone in a neon-lit supermarket; all I could hope for was that he wasn't interested enough to pursue me. I ping-ponged up and down a few aisles, like a silver ball in a bagatelle machine, before my luck ran out. I'd just convinced myself that I had massively overreacted, and that he'd probably paid for his beers and gone, when he stepped out in front of me. He leaned an arm against a concrete pillar, effectively blocking my way.

I decided ignorance might be my best course

of action. If nothing else, it would put us on a more level playing field. 'Excuse me,' I said, not making eye contact. He didn't budge. I tried again. 'Sorry, do you mind if I get past, please.'

'Well, here's the thing, gorgeous. I think I *do* mind, actually. How have you been, beautiful? You *do* remember me, don't you?'

Playtime was over. I raised my head slowly, pleased that I sounded so calm as I finally met his eyes. 'Yes, I do.'

He reached out a hand as though he was intending to touch my face, but I stepped back and brought the metal shopping basket I was holding between us, to form a barrier.

'Ooh, you weren't so standoffish last time we met,' he protested, taking a step towards me, so that the basket butted against his ribcage. 'Still I'm glad you remember me, because I certainly haven't forgotten *you*. In fact I've been having some pretty vivid dreams about you.' He breached the basket barrier by grabbing hold of it and pushing it to one side. 'Want to hear about them?' he asked on a leer.

'Not particularly,' I replied, taking a step to one side. The aisle was too wide for him to totally obstruct it, but I really wasn't expecting him to reach out and grab my wrist as I went to leave.

'Hey, where are you off to in such a hurry? You and I never got to finish our little date, did we?'

I looked up at him coolly, glad the scarf round my throat effectively hid the pulse I could feel pounding at its base. 'Yes we did. We're all done.'

'I don't think so,' he contradicted. 'You can't

just go thrusting those titties at me one minute and then acting like you think you're somehow better than me the next.'

There was so much wrong with his perception of what had happened on the night of the party, it was hard to know which bit to correct first. 'I wasn't thrusting or offering you anything. You crashed our party without an invitation. We had one dance and then you were asked to leave.' I conveniently managed to feign amnesia about the kiss, which I hadn't exactly repelled. Well, at least not initially.

His eyes narrowed nastily, and for the first time I wondered if I might actually be in trouble here. 'You little — '

Fortunately I never got to hear his opinion of my character, because just then his pierced friend came up, staggering under the weight of the two packs of beer. 'Where the fuck did you get to?' he challenged his companion. 'You left me at the bleedin' checkout, but you've got all the bloody money.' He turned then, as though he had only just noticed that they weren't alone. I guess observational powers didn't rank high on his particular skill set. 'Who's this?'

'It's the posh bird from the Hallowe'en party. The one who got us chucked out. Remember?'

I considered pointing out that actually they'd done that all by themselves, but it really wasn't a dialogue I wanted to get into. His friend shook his head vaguely, either dismissing me, or truly unable to remember anything that had happened any longer than five minutes ago.

'She and I were just getting reacquainted

here,' the straggly blond told his friend.

'No, we weren't,' I corrected firmly, seizing the moment to squeeze past them both. 'We're all done.'

I strode away, adrenaline propelling me onwards. I could hear them muttering behind me, and although I couldn't make out precisely what they were saying, I *did* hear the pierced one tell his friend, 'For Christ's sake, let it go. She doesn't want to know. Forget it.'

It was good advice. It's just a shame he didn't take it.

But that one was *his* mistake, not mine.

★ ★ ★

I re-wrote what happened next many times over the years. In most edits I didn't scurry like a terrified rabbit out of the supermarket into the dark night. In many versions, I chose to report the man to the duty manager in the store. In some, I called a cab to take me home. In a few, I miraculously gained a black belt in karate, and kicked his ass in the car park, in a truly spectacular fashion.

The reality was somewhat different.

It's hard to say when I first realised I was being followed. I was nervous crossing the deserted car park, but I'm pretty certain no one was pursuing me then. When I set out on the path beside the train track, there was still no one behind me. As much as I hated to admit it, the encounter with the blond guy in the supermarket had left me rattled. I was fairly good at deflecting unwanted male attention, but there was something bitter and angry motivating his interest in me. This pursuit wasn't about attraction or desire; it was more a need for retribution.

Despite the height of my heels, I walked speedily to the footbridge. My breath billowed from my mouth like empty speech bubbles in a cartoon, and my chest rose and fell beneath my jacket, although that could just as easily have been from nerves as exertion. Knowing that beyond the bridge I still faced a ten-minute walk before I'd be back on campus ensured my pace never slackened.

I tucked my chin firmly into the folds of my scarf and began to climb the metal treads of the footbridge. Taking this route alone and in the dark had been a stupid and reckless decision, I could see that now. I'd always been amazed at how irresponsible some people were about personal safety. I thought I was more sensible than that; I thought I had a better in-built sense of self-preservation. I thought wrong.

I was halfway up the staircase when I heard the echo of a sound ricocheting through the darkness. It came from the direction of the path I had just travelled. I froze. From my elevated position I had an excellent view of the path. If anyone was approaching the bridge, I should be able to see them clearly in the street lamps' orange pools of light.

I stared into the darkness for a full minute, but it felt more like ten. I was positive I hadn't imagined the sound, but where was the person who'd made it? I felt adrenaline coursing through my veins in readiness. If it came down to a question of fight or flight, I knew which one I was going to choose. Despite the fact that every tread on the metal staircase was covered with slick patches of black ice, I miraculously managed to avoid each invisible hazard, as I ran up one side of the bridge and down the other.

I leapt from the last step and hurried down the path, stopping only when the street lamps did. How had I failed to notice this stretch of path was unlit on my journey in? The only illumination now came from a cloud-covered moon and a sprinkling of stars, scattered like diamonds across the black velvet sky.

I was moving cautiously forward when a new sound carried through the night. A dull metallic sound. The kind of sound made when something heavy (heavy like a boot) connects with a metal step. My phone was in my hand and my fingers were flying over the screen before I had time to consider my actions. Later, I questioned why it was *his* number I had dialled, and not 999? In all honesty, I simply didn't know. The instinctive need to reach out to him in a moment of crisis surprised even me.

David answered on the first ring, and just hearing his voice calmed me a little, but my own still shook as I whispered hurriedly into my phone.

'What do you mean, 'someone's *following* you'? Who? Can you see them now? Where the hell are you, anyway?'

I peered into the darkness. 'No, I can't see anyone at the moment. But it's pretty dark here.

Perhaps there's no one there, after all,' I finished lamely, starting to feel foolish that I'd created a huge melodrama about nothing. Then I heard another metallic clang through the darkness. 'Someone might be on the bridge,' I whispered.

'Charlotte, you're making no sense. What bridge? Where the hell are you? I thought you went to the library this evening.'

'I did. But now I'm on that path by the railway line, near the footbridge.'

'What the hell are you doing there?' There was no mistaking the anger in his tone. '*I* wouldn't even walk there alone at night.'

Great, thanks for that, David. Very helpful, I thought.

'Where are your car keys?' David asked urgently.

He clearly hadn't been paying attention. 'I don't have my car with me. It's at home.'

'I know that. I'm looking at it out the window right now. Where are your keys? I'm coming to get you.'

'No. You don't have to do that. You've got plans for tonight,' I added, suddenly remembering he'd been going to some big musical event with Ally. 'David, really, I just got myself a bit spooked, that's all. You don't have to come. That wasn't why I called you.' *Wasn't it?* A voice protested in my head. Isn't that *precisely* why he was the one you chose to call, instead of Mike, Andrew or Pete?

'Charlotte, either you tell me where your keys are kept, or I'm phoning the police myself.'

'No. Don't do that,' I begged hurriedly.

303

'Keys,' he said tersely.

I may have hesitated for a second, possibly two. 'On the desk in my room.'

'Hold tight,' he promised, and I felt his words sliding over me, like a protective suit of armour. 'I'm on my way.'

* * *

It was cold on the path, the temperature was dropping rapidly and nothing I was wearing was particularly effective at keeping out the bitter bite of the wind. I paced up and down in a small rectangle as I waited for David, like something in a cage. With every passing minute I began to feel more foolish. Clearly no one had been following me after all. I wasn't usually such a drama queen, but I'd massively overreacted, and even worse I'd dragged David into my paranoid delusion too. He was going to be rightfully furious when he charged in here to rescue me, only to find the danger had only been in my imagination.

I waited for ten minutes, before it occurred to me that I should have continued walking down the dark path towards campus. Too rattled to think clearly, I'd just been wasting time. David was sure to be there by now and just knowing he was close by comforted me. That probably explains why, when I felt a hand come to rest on my shoulder, my first feeling was one of overwhelming relief. I sighed and felt the tension slipping away with my exhaled breath. 'Thank you so much for meeting me,' I said with a smile as I turned to face him.

'My pleasure,' he purred, his hand tightening as his fingers dug into the hollow beneath my collar bone. 'Thanks for waiting for me. I thought you would.'

'What?' I cried, my mind still grappling with the realisation that the man standing before me wasn't David. 'Get off me,' I said, shaking my shoulder to throw off his hand, but his grip was manacled on to me, like talons into prey.

'I'm not *on* you,' he said, and I heard the slur in his voice, even before I smelled the beer on his breath. 'Yet.'

There was no mistaking the meaning of his words, and fear and bile rose up in my throat in an unpleasant cocktail. I put my hands on his chest and shoved with all my strength, but he was surprisingly strong. His free arm came around my back and thrust me up against the hard wall of his body, effectively imprisoning both my arms between us.

'Stop playing games,' he said, his face lowering. 'You know you want this just as much as I do.' I struggled in his hold, like a lunatic in a straitjacket, but I just couldn't get away from him.

'Let me go!' I shouted into his face, which was inching closer towards mine. 'I'm waiting for my boyfriend,' I lied, my voice trembling. 'He'll be here any minute now.'

'I'm already here,' he said in a throaty growl as his mouth captured mine. I kept my lips tightly clamped together, gritting my teeth so hard I probably ground off several layers of enamel.

Even so, he managed to prise open my jaws. His tongue was like a thick twisting snake filling my mouth, poisonously lashing against mine, so forcefully that I gagged in reaction. I fervently hoped I was about to throw up, all over the pair of us.

He took his mouth off mine, and I gasped in the cold night air as though I were drowning. His eyes were small glittering slits and I could see a feral red haze burning within them. He was beyond the point of listening to reason, if ever that moment had existed. The hand that gripped my shoulder so hard he'd already left five fingerprint bruises, now slid down the front of my jacket and fastened on to my right breast. His fingers bit through the leather and squeezed my flesh painfully. His breathing increased until he was practically panting with lust. 'Been dreaming of these,' he muttered, squeezing so hard it brought tears of pain to my eyes. His hand went to the zipper of my jacket and when he began to slide it down, I pulled back sharply and broke his hold on me.

'I said: Get. The. Fuck. Off. Me!' I yelled, emptying the air from my lungs with my warning. Although he no longer had hold of me, his hand still gripped a handful of leather jacket, and although I pulled with all my strength, he wasn't letting go. I bucked away from him, but he hung on in a deadly tug of war.

'My boyfriend is going to destroy you,' I threatened, battering on his arm, trying to make him release me.

He pulled a mock frightened expression, and

spoke in a high girlish tone. 'Ooh I'm so scared. Big old boyfriend is on his way.' He snapped back to his own voice. 'Stop jerking me around. There *is* no boyfriend. Unless, of course, you mean me?' He tried to pull me back against him, but finally some long-ago-learned self-defence tactic surfaced from wherever it had been stored. I twisted in his arms so that my back was to him. I could feel the bulge in his pants pressing up against me as I brought up one leg and rammed it downwards, with as much force as I could muster. The heel of my boot connected with the arch of his foot. He swore, and then grunted as I twisted the stiletto, as though I was grinding an insect into obliteration. It was a pretty good analogy.

'You bitch,' he muttered, his voice guttural. He shoved me with such force that I fell to the ground. In a panic I struggled to get back to my feet, knowing I had to run. Now. But I was too slow. He was standing over me, and what he intended to do next was written all over his face.

I scrambled backwards on my bottom, my feet pin-wheeling for purchase on the slippery path. He dropped to his knees, smiling. Unbelievably, he still thought this was funny. I closed my eyes, dreading what was coming. I only opened them when I heard the sound of something heavy falling to the ground accompanied by a grunt. The blond man was getting to his feet, but David swung a kick which connected with the back of his legs, felling him again. David turned away from the man on the ground and hurried towards me.

'Charlie, are you okay?' he asked, reaching his hand out to me. I placed mine within it as he began to pull me to my feet. 'Did he hurt you?' he asked, his voice almost unrecognisable.

I opened my mouth to reply, but my words changed into a cry of warning as a dark shape swept down upon us. I didn't see the swing of the blond man's punch, but I heard the sickening sound as the bones of his knuckles connected with David's face. David's hand released me, and I tumbled back onto the ground once again as the two men faced each other like feuding animals.

'I should kill you,' David said, his voice so low the words were virtually a growl.

'I'd like to see you try,' taunted his opponent. He brushed the long greasy blond hair from his forehead, and I was happy to see a bloody gash on it.

'You should run. Right now,' warned David.

'And you should keep that little bitch on a tighter leash,' the man countered. 'She was all over me like a rash.'

David made a sound I really don't think I've ever heard a human make before, and then launched himself at my attacker. Arms were flailing, and feet were flying in blind kicks as they grappled together. Physically they were equally matched, and the fight could have gone either way. But David was powered by something beyond rage, and I could see he was gaining the upper hand. His fist connected with the man's face, with enough force to send him reeling backwards, but not enough to stop him. But perhaps he was winded, because he bent low over his boots, as though recovering from a stitch.

I don't know what might have happened next if the clouds obscuring the moon hadn't shifted slightly, allowing just enough light to shine down for me to spot the knife he had pulled from within his boot.

'David, look out!' I cried, as the man leaped up, brandishing the blade in small sweeping arcs through the air. His pathetic attempts to emulate a samurai would have been laughable, if it hadn't all been so very terrifying. David took his eyes away from the crazed man just long enough to look my way.

'Charlotte, run!' he ordered. I scrabbled back to my feet, but didn't do as he'd commanded. 'Get out of here,' David barked, stepping to one side, effectively luring the man with the knife further away from me. I could hear a whooshing sound each time the knife cleaved threateningly through the air, each swipe taking him closer and closer to David.

'For Christ's sake, Charlotte, go!' yelled David. But I didn't leave, and it's not just that I've never been very good at following orders. Even if there'd been an entire gang of knife-wielding hooligans, I would still have held my ground. Nothing on earth would have persuaded me to abandon him.

Without thinking, I picked up my bag from where it had fallen, gripped the handles with all my strength, and like a hammer thrower at the Olympics, swung the bag with my laptop and text books in it directly at the face of the man with a knife. I heard a sickening breaking sound, as bag connected with assailant. I think the sound was plastic casing rather than bone. Even so, my aim had been good, and the weight of the bag hurtling towards him had done the rest. The knife fell from his hand with a noisy clatter and David kicked it into the undergrowth flanking the path. The blond stared malevolently at us both, his hand cradling one side of his face. For a second I didn't realise it was almost over. But he did. Even the dumbest of animals knows when it's time to retreat. With one last hate-filled look, he turned and ran.

I fell into David's arms and the tears, that would know no stopping for several hours to come, began to fall.

Ally — Eight Years Earlier

'Oh my God, David, what were you thinking?' David leaned across and rapidly shut the door of the kitchen, the room he'd led us both towards after finally managing to extricate himself from Charlotte's hold.

'Sshh,' he urged, pulling me into his arms. But I was still trembling in reaction to the news, and far too overwrought to fall into them.

'Seriously, how could you have been so reckless? He had a *knife*,' I emphasised, my tone putting the word into emboldened capital letters. 'You could have been stabbed.' My voice dropped lower, still in shock. 'You could have *died*.'

He tugged me towards him, and this time I went. 'Didn't you even stop to consider the danger, before you leapt into the middle of it?'

His breath fanned the top of my head as he cradled me against him. 'To be perfectly honest, no. I didn't stop to think. But, even if I had, I'd have done exactly the same thing. The guy was off his head, on drink or drugs, I don't know which. But I do know he was out to hurt someone tonight.'

'Precisely,' I said, into the fabric of his shirt. 'And it so easily could have been *you*.'

'But if I *hadn't* got involved, then it would definitely have been Charlotte,' he reasoned. I sighed, knowing I should be proud of his heroism, but all I could think of was how very differently this night could have ended. 'You tell me, Ally, what else was I supposed to do when she phoned?'

Slowly, very slowly, his words penetrated through a maelstrom of mixed emotions. I arched back in his arms, the better to see his face. 'I'm sorry, I don't understand. Phoned? Where from? I thought she'd been attacked outside the house, and that you'd rushed out to help her?'

For the first time David looked uncomfortable, and I felt him physically bristle at my words. 'No. Charlotte was down by the railway bridge. She called when she realised she was being followed.'

I took a long pause before replying, as I processed and assimilated this new information, rearranging things in my mind as the picture I

311

thought I was seeing changed into something entirely different.

'I would have thought,' I began carefully, 'that most people, when being chased by a person with a knife, would call the police . . . not someone they share a house with.'

David looked uneasy. 'Well, to be fair, Charlotte didn't *know* he had a knife at that time. In fact, she wasn't even sure — '

'That is not the bloody point,' I snapped. 'You're not her bodyguard. You're not a vigilante. She could have got you killed. Have you even *seen* your face?'

He shook his head, and I could tell that only one of us seemed to be concerned about his safety, and it didn't appear to be him.

'I'm sorry that you're upset about this.' *Upset wasn't even in the ballpark.* 'But I'm *glad* I didn't stop and think it through. You *do* realise what that bastard was probably about to do, don't you?'

Of course I did, and I wouldn't have wished that on anyone — not even my worst enemy — and Charlotte was still a very long way from claiming that particular title. But something about David, and the latent fury in his voice as he spoke, worried me more than anything else. His rage and protectiveness were coming from depths I had never known existed within him.

'I guess this explains why you weren't there tonight,' I said with a resigned sigh.

David's brow furrowed, and I felt a stab of pain, sharper than any knife, as I realised he had no idea what I was talking about. I saw the moment when the memory of where he was *supposed* to have been that evening returned. I followed his facial expression as it went from confused to contrite.

'Oh God, Ally. I'm so sorry. The concert. It was tonight, wasn't it? It went right out of my head.'

His words ground even more salt into the wound he had unknowingly inflicted. I tried to keep it from my voice, but I think we both heard it. 'So it would seem. I phoned and texted you — quite a few times — when you didn't show up.' I hated what I could hear in my voice, but it was coming from somewhere deep within me, and I just couldn't hold it back.

'My phone must have got damaged during the fight. I'm so sorry. By the time we'd called the police, and then the paramedics had insisted on looking us both over . . . well, everything else just went. I completely forgot about you.' Of all the things you hope never to hear your boyfriend say, that had to be right up there in the top ten. 'How did it go?' he asked.

I shook my head, refusing to allow the conversation to veer back towards normality. I was still too hurt and angry. 'I'll tell you about it tomorrow. Look, can we just go back to my place now? It's late and we're both exhausted. Have the police finished with you?'

His arms slid from my body and his hands reached for mine. I should have known from the awkward expression on his face that I wasn't going to like what he was about to say.

'Well, I kind of promised Charlotte I'd stay

313

here tonight. She's still pretty shaken up.'

The words were on my tongue before I could stop them. 'Yeah, well, you kind of promised *me* you'd be at the concert tonight and walk me back home, but . . . ' I shrugged and left the rest of my sentence hanging in the air between us.

David looked genuinely surprised at the bitterness in my voice. 'Look, we can still be together tonight, we'll just stay here instead. Charlotte's worried this guy might turn up again. He knows where we live, and he looks like the type to bear a grudge.'

'All the more reason for you *not* to be here,' I countered. 'Also, in case no one has noticed, there are three perfectly capable men who also live here. God, Mike would probably sleep on the floor outside Charlotte's door, given half the chance. She doesn't need you here too.'

'Well, I promised I would be,' David said, sounding irritated for the first time.

'So you're choosing her over me. Is that it?'

The hand holding mine fell away. 'Of course not. Don't make it about that, because it's not. Don't go there, Ally.'

But I couldn't stop. To be perfectly truthful, I'm not sure if I even wanted to. This had been coming for a long time. 'We're already *there*, David, in case you hadn't noticed. I'm going to ask you this only one more time. Will you please come home with me, *your girlfriend*,' I added, just in case he needed reminding who exactly held that title, 'or is there something else going on here, besides your need to play action hero through the night?'

314

'That isn't fair, Ally.'

'Nothing about tonight has been fair,' I lobbed back. 'But what happened earlier can't be changed. It's what you do now that's important. Are you coming with me, or staying with her?'

'It's not that simple.'

'It's *exactly* that simple.'

Thirty-three seconds passed before he answered me. I know, because I was counting how long it took for everything to fall apart.

'I *have* to stay,' he said firmly, and I suddenly realised we'd arrived at the place we'd been travelling inexorably towards for quite a long time. I felt the loss of him like a real and physical ache, even though he was standing right there in front of me.

'Ally, don't do this. You're being unreasonable.'

He was right. I was. But now we'd driven to the edge of the cliff, I could see no way of reversing back from the precipice. We stared at each other miserably, both too headstrong and determined to give way. It was a blueprint of many of our arguments. Only we'd never clashed over something this serious before. Our relationship had become a runaway train, hurtling towards imminent derailment. And although we both knew we were about to be declared its casualties, there wasn't a damn thing we could do to stop it.

The police car was gone, but I was grateful to see that, for some reason, the taxi driver had chosen to remain, parked in front of the house. It was almost as though he'd known I was going to be in need of a lift home. Funny, because up until a few moments earlier, I certainly hadn't.

'I'll call you tomorrow,' David said as he followed me down the path.

'I think perhaps we need some time apart,' I said, my voice beginning to crack. Was I really going through with this?

'This is ridiculous,' David muttered. 'I'll call you in the morning, when you've calmed down.'

He did. Many times. I didn't pick up. Perhaps he even went round to my house. I'd like to think he hadn't let me go quite so easily. But I wasn't there. After a long and sleepless night I had made my decision. My lectures were finished, and the work I had to do for the remainder of the term could be accomplished just as easily from home.

Like a wounded animal in need of sanctuary, I packed up my belongings and caught the first train of the day back to my home town. I kept hoping that David would follow me. That somehow, whatever there was between us was strong enough to survive this. If we'd been in a film, he'd have been there at the station, running along the platform as the train pulled out. Or he'd be parked on the drive of my family home, leaping out tired and dishevelled from sleeping in his car, when my taxi pulled up.

But he did none of those things. I walked away from him, from us. And he just let me go.

8

Ally — Eight Years Earlier

'Okay, try them now,' Max said, stepping off the set of steps he had climbed to hook up the fairy lights on our tree. I flicked the switch and several hundred twinkling LED lights dazzled us both. I tried to summon up the feeling of pure joy this moment usually elicited, but I came up empty. Max moved to my side, put an arm around my shoulder and gave it a friendly squeeze.

'It's gonna get better, you know.'

'You've been saying that for the last ten days. You're a lousy psychic. You also said he'd call, or turn up. You said he wouldn't let this be the end.' There was a reproachful accusation in my voice, as though I genuinely blamed my old friend for making me false promises.

'I really thought he would,' Maxi admitted, putting both his arms around me and hugging me tightly. 'I thought you two were the real deal. And for what it's worth, I *still* don't think anything was going on with him and Charlotte.'

I gave a shrug, able to acknowledge with better perspective now, that I might have been wrong about that one. 'There were still things that weren't right between us, even if you lift Charlotte right out of the equation; things we were never going to be able to change.'

'Such as?' Max prompted.

'Such as the fact we argue like cat and dog; we want totally different things from life; we come from polar opposite backgrounds; his mother thinks I'm a gold-digger . . . and he can't sing.'

'Hmm. Yep, that one's always the kiss of death to any relationship,' Max declared, nodding wisely.

I shoved him gently with the flat of my hand. 'Don't make me laugh. None of this is funny,' I ended sadly.

'I know,' Max said, gently kissing my forehead. 'But it's all going to work out. You'll see. Everything happens for a reason.'

'That's another prediction I'm not sure I believe. It's going to take nothing short of a miracle for David and me to get back together.'

'A Christmas miracle!' Max exclaimed, clapping his hands in over-exaggerated glee and then looking at me from beneath his long floppy fringe to make sure I knew he was joking. I managed to conjure up a smile for my old friend. The last couple of weeks would have been unbearable without him around, I didn't even want to think about how much I was going to miss him when he took up the internship he'd been offered in New York the following summer.

'Just see how you feel when the holidays are over. Use the time you're apart to think it all through, and in the New Year, perhaps everything will be completely different.'

As it turned out, Max had a far greater knack for making predictions than either of us realised.

★ ★ ★

I was late, but the softly falling snow meant that I didn't dare drive any faster, so there was nothing I could do about it. I squinted and hunched further forward in the driver's seat of my mum's car, trying to concentrate on the road ahead and not the mesmerising onslaught of snow, which was as dazzling and disorientating as driving straight into the tail end of a comet.

I should have set out hours earlier, or taken the train, but my decision to attend the Snowflake Ball had been so last-minute, my only option had been to drive. I was probably going to have missed the meal, but that wasn't a problem, because even the thought of food made my stomach churn in protest. A feeling of anxiety kept cresting inside me like a breaking wave, because I had absolutely no idea how David was going to react when I walked into the marquee that night. After a year of feeling I knew exactly what he was thinking at any given moment, it was unsettling to find myself lost in the unfamiliar terrain of somewhere we'd never been before in our relationship, with no compass or map to guide my way.

This evening was always destined to be memorable for us, for it marked the anniversary of when we'd first met. But when David had surprised me with tickets for the ball two months earlier, neither of us could have predicted just how unforgettable this night would be. For a start, who would have known we'd be arriving separately; that we wouldn't have spoken to each other in over three weeks, or — in the words of a well-known TV series — that we'd be 'on a break'.

'Are you sure you don't want me to come with you?' Max had gamely offered, when I had finally decided there was a certain serendipity in returning on the night of the ball. 'Even Cinderella took a few old rodents along for moral support, you know.'

I had squeezed his hand gratefully, but had shaken my head. 'Thank you for the offer, Max, I love you for it, but I think this is something I have to do by myself.'

It had been far easier to be brave back at my house, especially with Max bolstering my confidence by whistling in admiration as I twirled before him in the red satin floor-length dress David had bought for my birthday.

'I can't accept this, it must have cost a fortune,' I'd said, as my fingers busily peeled back the layers of tissue paper from the oblong box with the embossed gold lettering. Hidden beneath the crinkling white paper was a dress I had first seen in the window of the most exclusive boutique in town. I had no idea how much he'd spent on it, because it wasn't the type of shop where they put the prices in the window. Enough said.

'This *was* the one you were looking at, wasn't it?'

'Yes, it was,' I admitted, gently lifting the dress out of the box, 'but I still can't accept it. It's too much.'

David had shrugged away my objections, as though they were trifling and inconsequential. 'Well, they won't take it back, and it's going to look stupid on me, so I guess you're stuck with it.'

I had held the dress against my body, loving the rich texture of the fabric against my skin, even while I was trying, as graciously as I could, to decline the gift.

'Look, if it worries you so much, why don't we call it a combined birthday and early Christmas present?' David had suggested.

'What, for like the next ten years?' I joked.

He had smiled slowly at me then, in the way that could still make my heart forget the rhythm of its own song.

'Why not,' he said, his brilliant blue eyes twinkling as they met mine. 'We're going to be together for all of them.'

I swallowed, and felt my cheeks grow warm and my pulse quicken at his casual and easy acceptance that our future paths were interwoven. He sounded so sure. So certain.

I broke free of the memory as I smoothed down the satin of the fabric over my stomach. Max circled me slowly, as though I was a thoroughbred horse he was considering buying. 'Gorgeous dress,' he declared, all fashion student. 'And gorgeous girl in it,' he completed, all best-friend-for-life.

As I pulled onto the university campus it was hard to keep that small confidence boost pinned in place. I followed the arrowhead signs and parked the car in the designated area and walked briskly over to the marquee entrance, shivering beneath the thin wrap I had thrown across my bare shoulders.

For a moment it felt as though I had actually stepped back in time. The same sparkling white

LED lights were threaded through the same branches of the trees, and up ahead I could see a familiar arch of twinkling fairy lights beckoning me towards the marquee entrance. I closed my eyes and saw the empty pathway suddenly peopled by ghostly silhouettes in party clothes, retracing the footsteps they had taken twelve months earlier. I swear I could even hear the echo of the shouted ribald comment after David had saved me from falling on the ice. *'Not got another girl falling at your feet?'* The irony, that despite every good intention or obstacle in our path, I had done exactly that, was not lost on me.

★ ★ ★

I waved my ticket under the eye of the solitary security guard on the door, who was busily involved on his phone with something far more diverting than door duties. He barely glanced at it before nodding, sweeping his arm in a flourishing gesture, and waving me into the marquee. I checked my wrap in the cloak area and took a quick glance in a nearby mirror. The cold night air had brought an attractive blush to my cheeks, and my hair gleamed with an unaccustomed shine my conditioner rarely managed to achieve. I pulled myself up a little straighter, took a deep grounding breath, and prepared to enter the main marquee.

The feeling of déjà vu hit me even more powerfully here than it had done on the pathway. I guess the organisers of the event had found a formula that worked, and they'd stuck with it. Here once again were the ice sculptures — leaping dolphins this time rather than penguins — and just like last year, a canopy of colourful balloons bobbed in captivity behind a ceiling net, waiting for their release. I looked around the room, taking it all in. Last year I'd been one of the performers, and it definitely felt different to be a legitimate guest.

The meal had long since been served and cleared away, and even the Moonlighters must have finished their set, for the students were mostly out of their seats, milling around the marquee, moving from table to table and catching up with friends. Shrieks of laughter coming from the direction of the chocolate fountain made me turn around. Cheered on by the rest of their party, two boys appeared to be in competition to see who could stuff the most marshmallows into their mouths. I suddenly felt too old to be there. I'd never really embraced that element of student life, and I wasn't at all sorry that I would soon be leaving it behind.

Someone swore and apologised all in one breath, as they bumped into me. I turned around to an accompaniment of beer bottles clinking and jostling together on a tray, because I'd recognised his voice. 'Hi, Mike.'

David's housemate swayed a little, and the bottles did another *Do-si-do*, before miraculously remaining upright, despite the alarming kilter of the tray. I reached out and straightened it, but Mike scarcely seemed to notice. Several emotions rippled across his face, none of them stayed in place long enough for me to name.

'Ally,' he said at last. 'I didn't know you were coming tonight.'

'I had a ticket,' I said, waving the embossed card that was still in my hand. He looked down at it with a great deal more concentration than the man on the door had done.

'Of course, David bought them, didn't he?' I nodded, totally unprepared for the inexplicable lance of pain I felt at the sound of his name. 'Did *David* know you were coming tonight?' Mike questioned, enunciating each word so carefully, I wondered how many trays of drink he had already transported across the marquee to his table.

'No, he didn't,' I answered truthfully. 'To be honest, I didn't decide myself until quite late this afternoon.'

Mike nodded, as though that explained everything. Perhaps it did for him, but I still had a thousand unanswered questions. 'He *is* here tonight, isn't he?' I asked.

'Who?'

I tried not to sigh with impatience. This was like pulling teeth. But I'd seen Mike the worse for wear enough times to know that the way his eyes kept darting nervously around the room wasn't just down to the amount of beers he'd consumed.

'David. Is David here?' I asked, aware that my heart had started to pound uncomfortably within my chest.

'Yeah, he is. Somewhere,' Mike replied vaguely. He paused for a long moment. He might have been considering what to say next, or simply just trying to remember where on earth his table was. He *was* pretty wasted. 'I think the last time I saw him he was heading for the silent disco,' Mike said at last, and there was something about the tone of his voice that made the small hairs on the back of my neck prickle in alarm.

I thought he might accompany me to the annexe off the main marquee where the silent disco was set up, but when I'd taken a dozen or so steps, I turned around and saw he was still standing exactly where I'd left him, the tray of drinks at a forty-five-degree angle, and a worried expression on his face.

I didn't see them to begin with. The room was largely in darkness, lit only by the pulsating multicoloured lights from the DJ's podium. Overhead a rotating spotlight beamed flashes of strobe lighting onto the headphone-wearing crowd. My eyes travelled the room, watching the dancers in the disorientating light as they silently moved to their chosen music. There's something quite spooky in watching a room full of people energetically dancing to something you can't hear. Some of the crowd were singing random snatches of whatever they were listening to. It was like the very worst of karaoke, and I couldn't recognise a single tune. But, to be fair, I wasn't exactly concentrating on music at that moment.

I don't know what drew my eye to the darkened corner of the annexe. Perhaps a prism from the overhead glitter-ball had caught it, or was there something more powerful that caused me to slowly turn my head towards the small recess beside an exit? I don't remember crossing the dance floor. Either the gyrating students had parted before me like a biblical sea, or I'd simply mown a few of them down in my path. I wasn't looking where I was going, because my eyes were fixed only on the darkened corner, where my boyfriend stood with his arms wound around the one person I had always feared I would find there.

They were completely absorbed with each other and never saw me approach. Charlotte said something and laughed, and then pointed up at the large cutting of mistletoe suspended above their heads.

Don't do it. Don't do it. Don't make me have to see this. But perhaps seeing it was exactly what I needed, to finally accept that our temporary separation had just become permanent.

David's mouth lowered to hers, and she arched her body into him as her hands left his shoulders and her fingers threaded through his thick, dark hair. Something inside me died. I felt its passing, like a ghost. I didn't say a word. I didn't have to. The same intuition that had allowed me to find him in the dark alerted him that I was there. His eyes were on me, even while she still had claim to his mouth. I saw the horror in them as he levered himself from her. He opened his mouth, but no words came out. There was nothing he could say, no excuse he could conjure that could undo this moment. At least he had the grace to realise that.

'Ally,' he said eventually and even his voice sounded different, as though the taste of her had tainted it. 'I'm sorry. I never . . . This isn't what you think it is. What are you doing here?'

'Don't,' I said, lifting a trembling hand as though it could hold back the lies and excuses. 'I don't want to hear it.' David's face was stricken with sorrow and guilt. I could hardly bear to look at either of them. 'I don't want to hear that you didn't know what you were doing, that you're as drunk as the rest of your friends, or that it meant absolutely nothing to you.' I saw Charlotte wince at that one. 'I don't care if all of that is true, or none of it is. It doesn't matter. Not any more.'

'Ally,' David began, taking a step forward and reaching out for me.

I don't know how I would have reacted to his touch, but I never got the chance to find out, because Charlotte laid a stalling hand on his forearm and stopped him. Suddenly, from nowhere, a fiery cauldron of rage erupted within me. If I had stopped to think for even a millisecond, then what happened next could have been averted. I abhor violence. It scares me. And that made what I did next even more terrifying. It was over in a split second, but I saw it all in slow motion: I saw my hand arcing through the air, the palm flat, the fingers slightly splayed. I saw the look of horror on Charlotte's face as she read my intention. I saw the four red lines marking her perfect cheek as my hand fell away. Then everything speeded up.

Charlotte gasped in shock, and so did I. Only then did David move, swiftly positioning himself between us in protection. Hers or mine? I wondered bitterly. Mortified by what I had just done, I looked at David and saw his eyes were two hard glittering sapphires, frozen in ice. They bored into me with an expression I knew I would never be able to erase, before he turned to her. 'Are you alright?' The concern in his voice tore the skin from me, leaving me raw and injured. And alone.

'I'm fine,' she said, her hand cradling her cheek.

'What the hell were you thinking of?' yelled David, turning back to face me.

'Funny. I was about to ask you the same question.'

David looked uncomfortable, and then frowned as he looked over my shoulder at the dance floor. I glanced behind me, noting with embarrassment that our altercation had attracted the attention of quite a few onlookers. I saw headphones being eased off, as the mini-drama unfolding before them drew them away from the disco.

I heard the vague tinny strains of music still playing from discarded headphones, as David spoke. 'What are you even doing here?' he asked. 'You made it pretty clear the other week that you didn't want to see me again. So why the big entrance tonight, Ally? Three weeks of silence and then you just turn up like this. What was I supposed to do, fall into your arms?'

Anger and pain twisted and folded the speech I had mentally prepared, so that it became not a white flag, but a venomous dart. 'No,' I refuted. 'But you weren't meant to fall into *hers* either.' I nodded in the direction of Charlotte who was watching us both very carefully, but saying nothing.

'That's not how it was — ' he began, and then broke off and ran his hand distractedly through his hair. 'You know what, think whatever you like. You're going to anyway.'

I looked at him as though he was a total stranger, in much the same way as he was looking at me. Where was the man I was so sure I'd been in love with? How had this all gone so horribly wrong? We stared at one another, two gladiators with no strength left to go in for the kill.

'I think you'd better go,' David said eventually, inclining his head towards the exit. 'We both need time to cool off.' He glanced over at Charlotte. 'And I'm way too angry about what you've done to talk to you tonight.'

I too looked across at Charlotte, meaningfully. 'Likewise.'

I turned to leave, everything I had wanted to say to him had dissolved away, as though it had been written in invisible ink. I reached the pinned back canvas flap leading to the cold December night and turned to face him one last time. 'I'm not coming back, David.'

Perhaps he thought I was just looking for a dramatic exit line. He had no idea that I was deadly serious. 'I'm not asking you to,' he replied, his words scything me to the ground in one deadly blow.

He didn't realise it then, or perhaps he did, and just didn't care. Maybe he'd *never* really cared enough. But my words weren't an empty threat. I wouldn't be returning in January. I couldn't stay here and watch Charlotte deconstruct everything that had once been mine and make it hers. I looked at him one last time, as though it was important I engraved this moment into my memory.

'Goodbye David,' was all I said, as I slipped through the exit into the night, and out of his life.

Charlotte

Hospitals are different in the middle of the night. For relatives, that is, not patients. Anyone who is unlucky enough to have sat up through the small hours at the bedside of someone they love will know what I mean by that. For a start, the night seems endless. During daylight hours the wards are buzzing with activity. Doctors, nurses, cleaners, technicians and administration staff make it seem as though you are resident in the middle of a very busy city, in rush hour. That all goes away at night. Stripped to its bare bones, the hospital seems remote and deserted, like an island where a few unlucky castaways have been washed to shore, hopelessly waiting for rescue. Or in this case, for morning.

Despite the urgings of the nurses, I didn't want to sleep. Sleep was for normal nights, for our real life. Sleep was for our over-sized bed, with the marshmallow-thick duvet and the down and feather cushions that had cost a fortune, but had been so worth it. It felt disloyal to allow myself to slip away for even a few minutes into oblivion, and leave the horrors of the day behind. So I sat by David's bedside, in the hard plastic chair that didn't fit a single contour of my anatomy, and rested my head on the mattress beside his hand. But my eyes felt hot and gritty, and eventually, despite my best of intentions, they closed.

The nurse's hand on my shoulder woke me.

'Is something wrong?' My eyes went to David, who was still deeply sedated in faux sleep from a cocktail of medication. It was a stupid question really. Everything was already far beyond wrong. What I should have asked was: *Has it all just got even worse?*

'No. There's been no change. But it's not your husband I'm worried about. It's you. You need to rest properly. You need to lie down.'

I shook my head, wanting to dismiss her concerns. Don't worry about me, I wanted to say. My heart's not the one that's in trouble here, it's his. I'm the tough one. Ask anyone. *'Charlotte Williams? I've heard she's quite formidable to work for? Very successful, though. Built up quite a reputation in her industry. I don't suppose she and David will ever have kids. Well, would you give up their kind of lifestyle to have a family?'*

I'd overheard all of those comments and more besides. And they were all wrong, so wrong. That wasn't me at all, just a façade that I'd worn for so long I'd forgotten how to take it off, how to unglue it. There was only one person who saw beneath it. He was the one who would rub my

331

shoulders until the stress of the day finally seeped out of my knotted muscles. He was the one who would take me in his arms in the hospital parking lot, after I'd sat dry-eyed and silent in the consultant's office while they spoke of exploring 'other options'. He was the one who would hold me until the shoulder of his suit jacket was damp from my tears. His were the hands that would gently unfurl my fingers to remove the crushed fertility leaflet from my fist.

He was the strong one. He was the one with the good heart. Only, not that good at all, as it turned out.

'I don't want to leave him,' I whispered to the nurse.

She patted my back. 'You won't be leaving, you'll be just down the corridor. If he wakes, we'll fetch you, you have my word.'

I got to my feet, wobbly with exhaustion, and noticed the pillow and the two blankets in her arms. 'Even if you only manage an hour or so, it will help,' she said kindly. 'You're going to need your strength for tomorrow.' She nodded towards David. 'He needs you well and strong, not dead on your feet.' Her voice brooked no argument. She passed me the bed linen as she gently propelled me towards the door.

'Just for a little while then,' I conceded. The nurse nodded, clearly pleased. My legs felt stiff and uncoordinated as I walked back down the corridor to the Relatives' Room, like a displaced refugee, clutching the bedding to my chest.

In the end, all I achieved was seventy-five minutes before the emergency alarm woke me.

Ally

The emergency siren screeched through the silence of the ward, instantly throwing me out of the fitful sleep I'd fallen into. My legs tangled in the blanket that someone (*who? one of the nurses?*) must have thrown over me as I slept. The vertebrae in my back screamed in protest as I leapt off the hard PVC-covered chairs that I'd pushed together for a makeshift bed. On the other side of the room I saw Charlotte, also scrabbling to her feet. She hadn't been in here when I'd fallen asleep; she'd been with David.

Through the porthole window I could see a red flashing light blinking on the wall beside the nurses' station. It bathed the room in an eerie blood-like glow. The alarm in the corridor galvanised us, and after a momentary shared look of panic we both ran to the door. Neither of us stopped to collect our footwear, kicking aside my black leather boots and her red-soled stilettos as we raced for the corridor.

The siren was much louder here. It filled my head, my ears and my heart with dread. It was the stalling engine of the jet plane, the call to man the lifeboats, the announcement to evacuate the building. It was someone's life hanging in the balance. Charlotte and I hesitated for a millisecond in the doorway, like lemmings with a change of heart. Then she looked to the right and I looked left.

'Crash trolley!' yelled a voice from somewhere I couldn't see.

'Coming through,' came the shouted reply.

I heard the sound of wheels and the slapping of feet as a nurse emerged in front of us pushing the drawer unit containing the equipment needed to bring someone back. But who? The nurse thundered past, so close she almost ran over our bare feet in her hurry to reach his room. She was heading right. Charlotte fell into her slipstream and ran behind her. After a moment of hesitation I followed, throwing a grateful look over my shoulder as I ran. The two nurses in Joe's room stood watching their colleagues swarm to the emergency, before turning back to their own patient.

The crash cart was driven through the doorway at such speed it was a miracle that it didn't collide with the frame or any of the waiting medics at David's bedside. We barrelled through the entrance behind it. I could hear snatches of barked-out instructions, none of which sounded intelligible, but thankfully everyone in the room seemed to know what they were doing. Everyone apart from Charlotte and me, that is. One of the nurses was kneeling on the bed, her arms locked as she performed CPR. David's chest rose and fell, as though he were running, but the movement wasn't of his making, it was hers. The pillows supporting him had been thrown into the far corner of the room, and David's head was literally bouncing off the mattress at the nurse's efforts to bring him back. Yet he gave no sign of being aware of it. A continuous beep and a straight line on the monitor positioned by his bed, told us that he wasn't.

'David!' Charlotte's cry was almost inhuman. It was an animal in torment, a soul being ripped from its body, a woman witnessing the death of the man she loves. She tried to push her way through the rugby scrum obstacle of doctors and nurses, all the time screaming his name.

'Charlotte, no!' I cried, but she was deaf to all sounds. Nothing and no one would stop her from reaching him, especially not me.

'Get them out of here,' ordered an extremely harried-looking doctor, glaring angrily at one of the nurses. With a strength it didn't look like she possessed, the nurse placed her arm across Charlotte's torso and literally dragged her away from the bed. Charlotte struggled to get free, but the nurse must have doubled as a bouncer in a nightclub, because she knew exactly what she was doing. Charlotte's arms were outstretched towards her immobile husband as she was pulled from his bedside. Panting from her efforts, the nurse eventually manoeuvred Charlotte back into the corridor. From behind her I could hear commands I recognised. Anyone who has ever watched a medical show on TV would do.

'Charging.' 'Clear.' There was a loud bleeping sound, followed by a heavy thump, as though a large sack of grain had been thrown from a hay loft.

'Nothing. Resuming CPR.'

'Again.'

'Charging.'

The nurse had positioned herself in the doorway, providing a living, breathing wall Charlotte would have to break through if she

335

wanted to re-enter the room, but the fight had left her. She placed her hands on the glass and pressed her face against it as she watched the team at work.

'You have to stay out here,' the nurse explained unnecessarily. 'You have to give them room to work.' She looked from Charlotte to me. Charlotte showed no sign of having heard her, so I nodded our agreement.

'I understand. But please . . . ' the nurse looked at me, waiting for the end of my sentence, ' . . . please . . . tell them not to stop doing what they're doing. Tell them not to give up.'

It was a promise she couldn't make and I had no right to ask it, on a dozen different levels. Charlotte lifted her face from the glass to look at me. Her breath had left a cloudy circle imprint behind, and through the middle of it, trickling slowly down the pane, were tears. She turned back to the room, just as someone within it pulled on a cord, and venetian blinds rattled down like shutters from ceiling to skirting, concealing the raging tug-of-war as the doctors attempted to pull David back into this world and out from the next.

Satisfied that we weren't about to go barging through the door behind her, the nurse returned to David's room, leaving the corridor empty except for the two of us. Despite the overheated hospital ward, Charlotte was shivering violently. Shudders ran through her body, as though the storm outside had somehow found a way to permeate the walls of the building and was seeping inside her.

She collapsed into a nearby chair, wrapping her arms around her, like she was trying to prevent something from escaping, or getting in.

'I'm going to lose him,' she said, her voice small and defeated.

'You don't know that. You can't.'

Her eyes met mine and then flashed to the closed door of David's hospital room, daring me to contradict her.

'David's strong. He'll fight back.'

I took the seat beside her, moving it slightly so that I could see the activity from within Joe's room.

She followed the direction of my gaze. 'You should be with your husband. With Joe.'

'In a minute,' I said quietly. 'Unless you'd prefer to wait alone?'

I could hear the passage of each passing second on the large-faced clock fixed to the wall before she answered. 'I'd like you to stay.'

Five small words. They weren't enough to tear down the wall between us. But they were a start.

Charlotte

Seventeen minutes. That's how long it took before they brought him back. I died alongside him many times over before the door finally opened and one of the doctors stood in its opening, nodding slowly, and giving a weary smile. Death hadn't wanted to let David go, and it had been a battle, I could see that.

'He's not out of the woods yet . . . but we've

337

got him back . . . ' His lips pursed at the end of the sentence, but I already knew the words he had decided not to add. *For now*.

'Can I come in? Can I see him?'

'Just give us a few minutes, then you can, but only for a moment.'

I nodded, wanting to thank him, to thank everyone, but he'd already disappeared back into David's room. 'Thank God,' breathed Ally, and I could hear the genuine relief in her voice and God help me, the feeling was back for a moment, the one that had stalked me for years.

I turned with the suppleness of a geriatric to look at her. There was nothing on her face to suggest the past had stayed with her as vividly as it had with me. I opened my mouth to tell her that I'd changed my mind; that she didn't need to wait with me any longer; that she should go to her own husband now. But that wasn't what came out at all, and I don't know which one of us was more shocked.

'David never cheated on you, you know.'

It was clearly the last thing she had expected me to say. Everything seemed to freeze around us, the noise from the ward, the howl of the storm outside, all of it fell away as we looked at each other, alone in the eye of the hurricane we'd created all those years earlier. Ally blinked, her eyes staying shut for a fraction too long; her throat moved, but no words came from it.

'I know what you think, Ally, what you've *always* thought. But you were wrong.'

When she eventually spoke, there was no bitterness in her voice, just a tired resignation.

'None of that matters any more. None of it is relevant. Especially not tonight.'

'You're wrong. Tonight it matters more than anything.'

'I don't agree.'

'You don't have to. You just have to listen. You can hate me all you like afterwards . . . but don't hate him, don't hate David. He doesn't deserve that, he never did.'

Charlotte — Eight Years Earlier

'What do you mean, they broke up? When did that happen?'

The boiling water I was pouring reached the rim of my mug and slowly trickled over the top and onto the work surface.

'Charlotte!' cried Pete.

I put the kettle down, my hand trembling slightly.

'Stand back. Let me do that,' said Pete, swooping in with a sponge cloth and enough sheets of kitchen roll to entomb a passing Egyptian. I watched him swabbing up my mess, before tipping out the tea and making me a fresh mug. This was pretty much how it had been 24/7 since the night of the attack. I think they were all a little bit envious of David, who'd charged in like Bruce Willis on a mission and rescued me. To compensate, my other three housemates seemed determined to provide me with the kind of protection service even members of the royal family would envy. I would have to say something soon, get them to ease off a bit, especially as the police had now arrested the guy.

But right now my mind was on other things. 'So when did this happen?' I asked, lowering myself onto one of the kitchen chairs. 'How come no one told me?'

'You've kind of had other things on your mind,' said Pete. He was right. It felt like I'd spent the last week living in a surreal world, where I'd fallen out of my normal life and dropped straight into the middle of a TV crime drama. I'd never even been *inside* a police station before, but over the last seven days it had started to feel like my second home.

'So what happened between David and Ally?' I questioned, trying to keep a neutrality I wasn't feeling in my voice. 'Was it his decision, or hers? And why hasn't he said anything about it to me?'

'He probably didn't want to worry you,' suggested Pete, throwing a couple of slices of bread into the toaster. I really hoped they weren't for me, because I had suddenly lost my appetite.

'Why would it worry me?' I asked, trying to sound indifferent, and failing miserably.

Pete shrugged and began pulling jars out of the cupboard, so I wasn't able to read the expression on his face as he replied. 'Because it all seems to have kicked off on the night of your attack. I think Ally was mad at him for getting involved, and then one thing must have led to another and then . . . ' his voice trailed away.

'And then what?' I asked, passing him the jar of peanut butter that he was clearly searching for.

'Dunno,' Pete replied, his answer lost in the sticky dollop of Sun-Pat's finest which he'd loaded onto his toast. 'He says he doesn't want to talk about it.'

'He'll talk to me,' I vowed quietly.

* * *

Except, he wouldn't. I had to wait until much later that day to finally get David on his own. It had been particularly tricky managing to evade Mike, who took his body-guarding duties even more seriously than the other two.

'There's nothing to say,' David replied, and there was a tight-lipped look on his face that should have told me not to probe any further. But there was no way *that* was going to happen.

'Pete said you and Ally rowed.'

'We *always* rowed,' said David wearily. 'Hadn't you noticed?'

Deaf, dumb and blind people would have been aware that their relationship was volatile and vocal, but they'd also have been able to see that it was passionate, exciting and loving. And having spent far more time than was good for me watching them closely, I knew that better than anyone.

'But then you always made up.'

'Not this time.'

'Why not?'

David sighed, and ran his hand helplessly through his hair, making him look achingly vulnerable. It made me want to fold him in my arms; it made me want to hold him close and tell him everything was going to be alright. It made

341

me want to kiss him.

I put myself on the other side of the room in case I actually did any of those things. But there was still one question I had to ask.

'Pete said he thought that you might have rowed about . . . ' my voice became hesitant and unsure, ' . . . about me?'

David's head came up and he stared at me with a look I simply couldn't interpret. 'You? Why on earth would we have argued about you?'

★ ★ ★

'I can't believe I'm doing this,' I muttered under my breath as I walked up the narrow pathway. I should be jumping up and down and punching the air in victory now that David was single once more. But instead I was standing in front of Ally's front door, mentally rehearsing the speech I'd been honing all day. The one that was meant to persuade her to go back to her boyfriend.

I'm sure one of my mother's analysts could have made a life's study out of me and my screwed-up feelings of responsibility. I wanted David for myself. I had since the very first day that I'd met him. But not by default. Not like this. I wanted him to look at me, and want me, *choose* me. And not as his second choice. If he'd made the decision to leave Ally all by himself, that would have been different, but I knew that — intentionally or otherwise — I was partly responsible for the fact that David now looked more miserable than I'd ever seen him look before. And I was determined to be the bigger person here and try to fix that.

I heard the rattle of the security chain behind the door, and stood a little straighter and held my breath. I didn't recognise the girl who opened the door. But she seemed to know who I was. Her almond-shaped eyes narrowed in her beautiful face and my mind scrambled a barrage of memory cells in search of her name.

'Hello. It's Ling, isn't it?' Her eyes narrowed even further. If she does that any more she won't be able to see me at all, I thought, a nervous giggle threatening to escape.

Ally's housemate nodded tersely. 'What do you want?' she questioned sharply. 'I'm just on my way out.'

I looked down at her feet in their pink fluffy slipper socks and the baggy jogging bottoms she was wearing. Somehow I didn't think she was telling the truth. 'I won't keep you. Would you mind telling Ally that Charlotte is here?' I asked, calling on every ounce of the politeness that had been drummed into me, in order to keep my voice pleasant.

'I can't do that.'

Can't or won't? 'This won't take long. I just want a quick word with her. I'm a friend.' The look Ally's housemate gave me told me that we both knew that wasn't entirely true. Well, not any more.

'I can't tell her, because she's not here. I already explained that to David. What is it with you lot?'

She had thrown me off my prepared speech by revealing that, far from being indifferent, David had actually been here before me. I felt my confidence beginning to waver.

'Ally. Is. Not. Here. She. Has. Gone. Home,' Ling said, enunciating each word, as though I was a very annoying foreigner.

'Oh. Okay, thank you, I — ' but I was already talking to the door knocker. Ling had gone.

★ ★ ★

We all tried to persuade him, but David was adamant, he was *not* going to go to the Snowflake Ball. He was as stubborn and intractable as a block of concrete. There was no moving him when his mind was set. In fact, the only person I'd ever met who could be that obstinate was Ally. It was little wonder that they'd reached a frozen impasse where neither of them could play their way out of the stalemate they'd created.

Not my problem, I thought, spraying a spritz of perfume at my throat and in the hollow of my cleavage. Let it go. I studied my reflection in the mirror, blinking as the silver sequins covering the gown flared like a thousand tiny flash bulbs as I turned under the light to examine my dress from all angles. It was a little over-the-top for a student ball, more of a red-carpet sort of a gown. Bought from a designer collection seen on a catwalk, my mother still had no idea that I'd rather have had something ten times cheaper, which we'd actually shopped for together. I shook my head, refusing to allow myself to be dragged down tonight by the things in life I *didn't* have.

The guys were dressed and ready, with two rounds of tequila shots already under their belts when I joined them. They whistled appreciatively when I walked into the room, and I made some silly comment about how well they'd all scrubbed up, as I took the tiny glass Mike held out to me.

'When's the taxi coming?' I queried.

'Any minute now,' said Pete, checking his watch.

'Has anyone seen David? Does he know we're leaving soon?' I asked, trying to sound nonchalant and indifferent. Mike gave me a strange little look, so I guessed that was a fail.

'He's in his room. I heard music playing, but he's not going to change his mind. Not now.'

I shrugged and slipped my arms into my coat which Andrew was holding out for me. Who needs a boyfriend, I thought. I was the lucky Cinderella who got to go to the ball with *three* Prince Charmings. How many girls could say that?

'Taxi's here,' said Pete, pulling back the curtains and spotting the vehicle idling at the kerbside. We tumbled into the hallway in a jostling huddle and had already opened the front door when the soft pound of footsteps made us turn around. David was lightly descending the stairs, dressed in an immaculate dinner suit. The crisp white of his evening shirt made the tan of his skin look even warmer, and his vivid blue eyes sparkled as bright as cobalt.

'Changed my mind,' he said succinctly.

There was a chorus of noisy cheers, and a bit

of back-slapping, but I was quieter, meeting David's eyes with a warm smile. He smiled back.

* * *

It was a good night. Term was over and everyone was in the mood to celebrate.

'I think it actually looks even *better* than last year, don't you?' Pete asked artlessly, as we took our places at the circular snowy-linen-covered table. I intercepted a warning glance from Andrew, and realised they must have agreed between them not to refer to the previous year's ball. It was quite sweet in a way, their clumsy efforts at trying to shield David from his own memories. But I could have told them they were wasting their time.

I'd seen the way he had scanned the marquee as soon as we entered it, looking for a tall dark-haired brunette who was — almost certainly — a couple of hundred miles away from here. I also saw the way he carefully ensured he chose a seat with a direct view of the stage, and heard his casual enquiry to one of the organisers about when Moonlighters would be playing.

'She's not going to be here, mate. You know that. She doesn't even *play* with that band anyway,' Andrew told David unnecessarily. 'She was just stepping in last year.'

'Depping,' said David quietly. 'They call it depping.'

* * *

I'd like to think that alcohol wasn't entirely responsible for what happened that night, although it would be stupid to deny it played its part. We seemed to empty the six bottles of wine on our table just a little bit faster than those around us. We ordered more, then moved on to champagne. I think some of it was pre-Christmas exuberance, and some was an understandable reaction to the undeniably fraught events of the last three weeks. My attack, and the fall-out from it had affected us all, and I don't think we could be blamed for wanting to kick back and enjoy the night. But there were, undoubtedly, other things for which we couldn't claim to be blameless.

I was aware of Mike's eyes on me as I pulled my chair a little closer to David's, to hear what he was saying above the noise of the music. Or that was what I told myself, anyway. David was showing no visible signs of intoxication, which is more than I could claim. When Pete picked up the half-full bottle of champagne to refill our glasses, I placed my hand firmly over the top of the flute.

'No more for me,' I said.

'Tipsy Person,' teased Andrew, laughing uproariously at his own humour in a way that only the inebriated can do. Everyone laughed. Everyone except David. Something about Andrew's words had speared him like a tiny dart. I saw it in the twist of his mouth and the cloud that covered his eyes. He got quickly to his feet, as though to outrun whatever emotion had just tried to snag him.

'Fancy checking out the silent disco?' he asked, holding his hand out to me.

We wove our way across the floor, well, I wove more than David did, if I'm being perfectly honest. I kept hold of his hand, partly because it helped me to navigate in a straight line, and partly because . . . just because.

'Maybe we should go outside for some air,' David suggested gently, watching my concentrated efforts to perform something I thought I'd mastered a good twenty-one years earlier — walking.

'I'm sure it's these heels,' I said, blaming my four-inch stilettos, which I'd always been able to walk in perfectly well before. David laughed softly, and was still doing so when a dinner-suited first year staggered back from the chocolate fountain, his mouth dripping melted confectionery like a vampire at a slaying. The guy swayed for a moment, much to the amusement of his companions, and then cannoned straight into me.

'Hey, watch where you're going,' David warned, glaring angrily at the younger man, as I tumbled into his side. I let out a small yelp of pain as my ankle twisted sharply and I felt it buckle beneath me. I would have fallen to the floor in a glittering inelegant heap of sequins had it not been for David's strong arm, which shot out at lightning speed, catching me around the waist.

'Idiot,' muttered David, staring at the student who had already launched himself back towards the fountain. 'Are you alright?' His head was bent low towards mine, and he was still holding me cinched tightly against him.

I tentatively put some weight on my foot and winced. 'Shit. Bugger it. Ouch.'

'I take it that's a no,' said David, his eyes betraying a concern that belied his light-hearted comment.

'It's my ankle,' I said, throwing a death-ray stare at the group of students rough-housing around the chocolate fountain. 'The one I broke skiing. It's always been a bit iffy since then. It's my weak spot.'

'And there I was thinking there was *nothing* weak about you,' David teased. 'Only now we've found your Achilles ankle.' He might have gone on like that for a little longer, but he sobered when he saw me flinch as I gingerly took a step forward.

'That looks really painful,' he said, and even above the noise of the ball, I could hear the worried note to his voice. His eye scanned the marquee. 'I think there was a St John's Ambulance tent outside. Why don't we let them check you out?'

'I don't think it's *that* bad,' I said, anxious not to let the evening end with a trip to A&E. 'I just need to rest it for a bit.'

David looked far from happy with my refusal, but tightened his grip on my waist and guided us through the crowd towards the silent disco, which was considerably closer than our table. I hobbled beside him, until we came to a halt at the darkened annexe packed with students vigorously gyrating to soundless music. There was nowhere to sit; nowhere I wouldn't be barged into by the posse of rhythmically challenged dancers, so I gestured towards a small recess I had spotted near the exit.

'We could stand over there for a minute,' I suggested.

The ground beneath the canvas flooring was uneven underfoot, and even with David's support my walk was an ungainly lollop.

'Someone should take a look at this,' David said, dropping to his knee, his hand carefully encircling my ankle, which was throbbing painfully and already beginning to swell. His fingers were like flames on my skin, scorching and branding, blazing a fire trail of memories back to our first meeting.

A group of girls walking past clutched at each other's arms and stopped, openly staring at us. The penny dropped with an almost deafening clang.

'Get up, you idiot,' I hissed, wrenching my foot free and ignoring the lance of pain that travelled all the way up my leg. 'They think you're about to propose.'

He laughed, turned to the girls and shook his head regretfully and they walked off, clearly disappointed. I clutched on to him, shaking with laughter and wobbling on one leg, until his arms fastened around me in support once more. I should have told him to release me, that I was in no danger of falling. But the truth was I wanted no release from him, neither physical nor emotional. And as for falling . . . well, wasn't that already far too late?

From within the disco, the circling spotlight that appeared to be searching for escaped prisoners among the dancers, panned through the darkness towards us, and settled on an area above our heads. We both looked up. Suddenly I knew what this tiny alcove had been intended for, because suspended from the ceiling on a length of red silken ribbon, was a large sprig of mistletoe.

I laughed nervously.

'Oh,' said David. 'I see.'

I tried to think of something light or amusing to say, something to take away the tentative question in his eyes as he looked at me. It was a bad time to have temporarily lost the faculty of speech.

'Do you think we should?' David asked, inclining his head upwards to the provocative piece of foliage dangling above us.

'Probably not,' I managed to say, in a voice that didn't even sound like mine. I thought there might have been a tiny glimmer of disappointment in his eyes, which disappeared when I added, 'Unless it's bad luck not to . . . '

I felt his arms tighten a little around me, no longer holding me up just because of my injury. We were going to do this. We really were, and there was a very real danger I would pass out before his mouth touched mine, because it was suddenly getting really hard to breathe.

David's head lowered as though in slow motion, and my lips were already parted, waiting. His kiss was a kaleidoscope, twisting the present and merging it with the past in a prism of glittering lights that took me back to the side of a snowy mountain and our first kiss. Retracing the path they had taken five years earlier, my hands left his shoulders and my fingers threaded into his hair, trying to anchor me to something that wasn't mine and that would slip away from me in moments.

And that's exactly what happened. But not in the way I had expected. David's mouth, so gentle and tender on mine, suddenly froze. They call it being petrified when you are turned to stone. I think that's what we both were, in every meaning of the word, when we looked up and saw Ally watching us from the shadows.

I'd lost David long before his arms fell away from me and he turned to face her. Ally looked beautiful, I remember thinking, beautiful and tragic, like a heroine in a book. So what did that make me — the nasty villain determined to ruin the happy ending? Ally was trembling, I could see that even from this distance, from shock or rage, I didn't know. Either way I could feel the guilt crashing down on my head, like a ton weight in a cartoon. She was hurling out insults, like tiny balls of barbed wire, and most of them were hitting their target. I knew this argument. I'd heard it so many times before, on the lips of my parents. That's what made it so much worse. I knew better than this; *I* was better than this.

'Ally,' David cried, reaching out to her.

I don't know what I thought I would achieve, but I only knew I had to try, so I too took a step towards her, forgetting my injured ankle. I stumbled and grabbed hold of David's arm to keep myself from falling. In hindsight, it would have been far less painful to have crashed to the floor.

I could see what was about to happen. I could see it, I just couldn't believe it. It was as shocking as witnessing an angel wielding a machine gun. I saw Ally's hand flying through the air, a tiny flat-palmed Exocet missile that was securely locked on target. I was too stunned to swerve, duck or even block her, so she landed a pretty impressive slap across my blood-drained cheek.

Everything speeded up the second her hand connected, and the blood that had been absent flooded back to my flesh with a vengeance. I cradled my cheek. She'd slapped me. She had actually slapped me. I thought that would be the biggest shock of the night. But there was an even greater one: David's reaction.

He was incensed, suffused with a fury I had never seen in him before. He moved between us, positioning me safely behind him, creating a human shield with his body. He turned and asked me something; perhaps he was checking if I was alright. I have absolutely no idea if I answered him.

Their fight was short, and ugly. I'd heard them argue many times before, but never like that. I wanted to be a thousand miles from there, and yet a horrible compulsion rooted me to the spot, ensuring I didn't miss a single word as the man I loved tore into the woman *he* loved, and she cut out his heart right in front of me. And I couldn't do a damn thing to stop her.

9

Charlotte

'He mourned you, you know. Like you'd died.' I gave a bitter laugh as I bit down more firmly on the cyanide capsule I'd avoided for years. 'I think he'd have gotten over you more easily if you actually *had*.'

Ally's face turned chalky white. I knew why. It felt wrong and dangerous to talk of death in these corridors. It was close enough already, we didn't need to invite it to pull up a chair and join us.

'David grieved. It wasn't just a break-up — at least not for him. It was genuine grief, we could all see it.' I paused, wondering if I had the strength to carry on. Apparently I did. 'Sometimes I think he's still grieving in a way. Even now.'

'I . . . I . . . ' Ally looked from David's closed door, back up the corridor to the room where her own sick husband lay, before finally turning back to me. 'Why are you telling me this? Why now? Tonight? It all happened so long ago. We've all moved on.'

'Have we? Sometimes I'm not so sure. Maybe the slates haven't been wiped as clean as you think. Maybe there are still secrets hiding in dark corners. Perhaps it's time they came out.'

Ally shook her head fiercely and looked again

towards her husband's room, as though she could draw strength from him, even from this distance. There was a vulnerability to her, like a deer who knows the hunter's cross hairs are positioned right over its heart.

'He looked for you everywhere, you know.'

Ally swivelled back to face me. Her eyes were bright with tears and there was a brittleness in her voice as though each word had been snapped off. 'Well, he didn't look very far, did he? I hadn't left the country, I was home with my parents. I wasn't hard to find.'

'I think it was easier for him to look for you in the places he knew he *wouldn't* find you,' I said, acknowledging something I had believed for a long time. I was suddenly tired, bone-achingly tired, and I didn't want to be doing this, I didn't want to be opening this door, but somehow I couldn't stop myself.

'It was worse on campus. It was like he had an inner radar. He'd be talking and laughing, yet you'd see his eyes follow any girl with long dark hair.' My laugh sounded hollow as though the humour within me had withered and died. 'He also attended a lot of concerts in those final months, for someone who wasn't that interested in music.'

'Graduation day was the worst, though. But then I think we *all* thought you'd be back for that.'

I closed my eyes, and was suddenly back in the darkened auditorium. It was a sweltering hot day, and we were all melting beneath the heavy weight of our graduation robes. Each faculty had an allocated seating area, and from where he sat David couldn't see the Music students. I was two rows behind him. Close enough to see him pick up the programme and run his finger under her name of graduating students. When they started calling up Ally's classmates, I saw him stiffen, his eyes fixed on the short flight of stairs leading to the stage where they were filing up, waiting for three years of hard work to be exchanged for a red-ribboned scroll. But they'd gone straight from the Ms to the Os. Although written in the programme, no microphoned voice called Alexandra Nelson to the stage.

'I graduated in absentia,' Ally said quietly.

I nodded. 'I didn't see David for almost a year after graduation.' I saw genuine surprise on Ally's face. 'We were never together at university. Not even after you left.' I could have stopped there. There was no need to bare my entire soul to her. But I wanted no more secrets here. 'But that was *his* decision, not mine.'

Ally's green eyes held mine for a long moment, before she nodded. And I could tell I wasn't telling her anything she didn't already know. Her suspicions had never been entirely groundless.

We both jumped at the sound of the door opening behind us.

'Mrs Williams?' I leapt to my feet as though on springs. 'Just five minutes, now,' the doctor warned.

I was at the door, ready to duck beneath his white-coated arm, or barrel him out of my way if he didn't clear a path and let me through. Ally's voice was so quiet, that I'm surprised I even heard it. My name on her lips still sounded alien to me. 'Charlotte, I'm . . . I'm glad you told me this. Even after all these years, it couldn't have been easy.'

I didn't need to tell her that it hadn't been. The truth was written all over my face. I turned to go, but she wasn't quite done yet. 'Charlotte,' Ally reddened slightly, and she raised her hand to her face. 'I'm sorry for . . . ' her voice faltered; she lost the words to complete her apology and instead ran her fingers across the smooth plane of her skin, from cheekbone down to jaw line.

I never thought I would hear her say that. Even more astounding, I never thought I'd hear myself say, 'Forget it.'

And yet I did.

Ally

Joe's room was a haven of quiet after the frenetic activity in David's. The nurse attending to him turned and smiled as I entered. She was yet another new face.

'Come for a wee visit, have you?' she asked, in a soft Scottish burr, as though wandering the hospital like a refugee in the middle of the night was quite normal. I suppose to her it was.

'Has there been any change? Any sign of him coming round?' I asked, taking my place beside Joe's bed.

The nurse shook her head regretfully, and

then busied herself in the furthest corner of the room, to give us as much privacy as the glass-walled cubicle allowed.

'I'm back,' I whispered, bending to kiss Joe's cold, still cheek. The ends of my hair dangled across his face. It should have tickled or irritated him, but he didn't so much as twitch. I reached for his hand, threading my fingers between his. 'Max is on his way,' I said conversationally, as though we were chatting over dinner and it was our farmhouse kitchen table between us, instead of a rock-hard hospital mattress. 'Jake will be so excited to see him again. And so will I. It'll be good to see an old face.' I didn't add that I'd already had my fill of spectres from my past for one night. There would be plenty of time to tell Joe all about that when he woke up.

I glanced over at the nurse, who was doing her very best to look as though she wasn't listening to our conversation. But I couldn't shake the horrible feeling that she was the *only* one listening. I searched for some sign that my words were reaching Joe, but there was nothing. I laid my head down on the woven blanket beside his hand, inhaling that indefinable 'hospital smell' on the fabric. It took me back to another night, in another hospital. Except that time *I* had been the one in the bed, and Joe was the one beside me. I smiled into the waffle thread of the blanket. It was the only time I had ever seen my strong and capable husband afraid of anything.

Ally — Seven Years Earlier

I was bent double, gasping in pain, when I heard Joe's key in the front door.

I raised my head as he walked into the sitting room. From the mirror hanging over the fireplace I knew my face was drained of colour, and there was a thin slick of perspiration on my brow. One look at me, hanging on to the back of the sofa and struggling to stand up straight, and Joe's complexion quickly matched mine for colour.

I put his first ridiculous comment down to sheer panic.

'Oh my God Ally, what's wrong?'

I waited until the pain had swept out like a tide, glorying for a moment in its absence. Then I rubbed my hand against the low nagging pain in the small of my back, which told him what he needed to know. Although as my belly was easily the size of a small weather balloon, I was surprised he needed even that hint.

'It's time? It's time?' So much for all of his assurances that he was crisis-proof, I thought. 'But it can't be time. It's too soon. Are you sure it isn't something you ate?'

'Not unless I've eaten a baby,' I said. For once, my brave attempt at humour, which I thought was quite witty given the circumstances, failed to amuse him.

'But it's too early. You're only thirty-six weeks,' Joe said. He frowned, talking more to himself than to me. 'Although that's nothing to worry about. Everything is viable by now. The lungs should be good. But still, the baby might be a little on the small side.'

I could feel the beginnings of a new contraction, but I still had time to sound amazed. 'How on earth do you know all that stuff? Do you moonlight as a midwife?'

Joe looked a little embarrassed as he replied. 'Well, you've been leaving baby books lying around the house for months. I thought you wanted me to read them.'

'No. I'm just untidy,' I gasped, feeling the pain digging fingernails as sharp as talons into my abdomen. Instinctively I threw out a hand, and Joe's large, work-roughened one caught it. He held on to me as though I was in danger, hanging from a cliff face as he slowly pulled me away from the pain and back to safety. I was surprised at the comfort I found in just the strength of his hold.

'Have you called the hospital?' Joe asked, when he was certain I was capable of talking again.

'No, because I'm not having this baby yet. Not tonight and not without my mum. I'm not deviating from my birth plan.'

To his credit, Joe seemed to be recovering from his initial moment of panic and spoke soothingly, as though I was a toddler about to throw a major tantrum in a public place. 'Ally, I know you've planned on your mum being your birth partner, but as she's six hundred miles away in Scotland, I think you might have to be a little flexible on that one.'

'But I don't want anyone else with me. You

360

know that,' I added accusingly.

'Yes I do,' Joe replied equably. 'And to be fair, if everything had gone to plan your parents would be back from their trip and we wouldn't be having this conversation. But *you* were the one who insisted they didn't cancel their holiday, weren't you?'

It was the closest Joe was prepared to go to a reproach. But I couldn't, in all conscience, have allowed my parents to put off a trip they'd really been looking forward to, a trip they'd booked long before they knew I was pregnant. Once the baby was born, Mum was going to stay with us for as long as I needed her, so it didn't seem fair to ask them to cancel their coach trip around the Scottish lochs.

'I'm seriously not having this baby without Mum,' I said mulishly, my voice wobbling with fear and my lower lip joining in for good measure.

'Okay, that's fine,' Joe said reasonably. 'But just on the very small off-chance that your parents *aren't* able to get back here on a supersonic jet, or in Doctor Who's TARDIS, don't you think it might be a good idea if we get you to the hospital? Just in case?'

I gripped his hand, as another contraction began to sneak up. I saw Joe glance at his wrist-watch and knew he was timing them. He really *had* been reading those books, I thought, straightening up with a slightly twisted smile. 'Don't fancy delivering a baby in your front room?'

'Not if I can help it.'

361

I nodded. There was no point in taking it out on Joe. It wasn't *his* fault the baby had decided to put in an early appearance. 'Sorry,' I apologised.

'What for?'

'For being snappy and unreasonable.'

He gave me a small smile. 'You weren't.'

I smiled back. 'Not yet. But I can guarantee I'm going to be. Didn't you know? It's in all the books.'

Joe looked somewhere between resigned and terrified. 'Just tell me where your case is and let's go,' he urged.

★ ★ ★

It was only a twenty-minute drive to the hospital, but by the time we'd swung onto the sprawling site, my sassy attitude had already dissolved beneath the waves of pain that were flooding in far quicker than I'd been expecting. I'd read the same books Joe had, plus my mother's experience as a nurse had prepared me — or so I thought — for a lengthy drawn-out first labour. But this wasn't a slow tide easing into shore, it was more like a tsunami that threatened to engulf me.

'Just breathe, Ally,' instructed Joe, his eyes on me instead of the road ahead.

I had to wait for the pain to abate a little before gasping in reply, 'I *am* breathing.' Although I had to admit, I was doing it as smoothly as an asthmatic marathon runner. Why had no one warned me about this? I felt

362

overwhelmed, scared and hugely ill-prepared. And it didn't matter that I was a capable young woman who was about to become a mother herself, because all I wanted right then was my own mum beside me.

'It's going to be alright,' Joe promised, taking his hand from the wheel and gripping mine.

'No, it's not,' I said tearfully. 'Nothing is alright. Nothing. It's all happening too quickly, and Mum isn't going to be with me.'

He took his eyes from the road again, making me grateful that there was so little traffic around, because I really don't think he was concentrating on his driving at all. 'No, she won't be,' Joe agreed sadly. The hand still holding mine squeezed it gently. 'But I will.'

That wasn't in my plan. Nor his. But with those three words Joe threw me a lifeline, and I grabbed on to it. 'Promise?'

'Promise.'

Joe pulled into a parking space, wrenched on the van's handbrake and jumped out of the vehicle with the speed of a stuntman. 'I'm going to find a midwife to help us,' he said through the open door of the vehicle.

'I think I'm okay to walk,' I started to say, but the final word turned into a banshee's wail. I looked up at Joe with horrified eyes. 'Oh God. I want to push,' I gasped, finally realising there was every chance I was about to become one of those women who simply don't make it inside the hospital on time.

'*Don't* push,' Joe implored before disappearing at an impressive sprint towards the glowing lights of the maternity unit. He was back in less than a minute, virtually dragging two midwives with him, one of whom was propelling a wheelchair so fast it was practically flying over the potholes in the tarmac.

All three of them raced around to the passenger side of the van. The midwives took over, managing the situation with an artful blend of calmness and urgency. 'I think she's in transition,' came Joe's voice from somewhere behind them, sounding more than a little panicked. 'And she wants to push.'

'I'm in a transit, not transition,' I panted back in denial. 'And I'm *not* giving birth in the car park, I'm really not,' I said, as though I had any choice in the matter.

The two women exchanged a knowing look. 'Don't worry. No one is giving birth out here tonight, my love,' the elder midwife assured me. 'Although you certainly wouldn't be the first person who had. But we've still got time to get you up to the delivery unit.' I don't know whose sigh of relief was greater, Joe's or mine, but they were both cut short as the midwife added, 'As long as we hurry.'

I don't remember much about the speed flight in the wheelchair through the car park, or whether we even stopped at Reception to book in. I remember a short ride in a lift, and seeing Joe's worried face reflected in the burnished steel of its walls, before the doors slid open and we were in the brightly lit corridor of the delivery unit.

I realised time was of the essence as we

hurtled down the passageway, with the midwife calling out as she ran, 'I need a free room. Now.'

Luckily there was one, and as we swung into it I suddenly realised our party of four had diminished to just three. Joe stood at the doorway, still holding my small case which he'd remembered to bring from the van.

'Don't just stand there. Come on in,' urged the midwife, already moving to the sink to scrub her hands, while her colleague wheeled in a trolley laden with all sorts of things I really didn't want to know about, but was rather afraid that very soon I would.

'Actually, I'm not . . . it's just that she hadn't planned . . . I don't think this is . . . '

The midwife turned to me, with a look of exasperation. 'Do you want him in or out?'

I looked at Joe, my eyes pleading and frightened. 'In,' I whispered.

Everything seemed to stop for a moment. Even the onslaught of contractions faded into the background, as Joe's face softened with an expression I don't think I'd ever seen on it before. He took a decisive step across the threshold and towards the bed.

'In it is,' he declared, reaching for my hand.

★　★　★

It wasn't the measured and controlled birth that I had planned. My mum wasn't there to witness the arrival of her first grandchild. In fact, we never even got word to her at all until after Jake was born. But it wasn't quite as rushed as the midwives had first feared. There was time for Joe to set up the CD player I'd packed in my case, and ensure the soothing strains of my favourite Debussy concerto were playing quietly in the background. There was also time for Joe to rub tiny slivers of ice over my dry lips, mop my forehead with a cooling cloth, and lose several layers of skin on his palm, as my nails dug deep into his flesh as everyone chorused at me to 'push'. I remember them asking Joe if he wanted to see the baby crowning, and the weird look on his face when he politely declined. Then everything merges into a flurry of blurred memories, which culminate in a pretty impressive first cry as Jake entered the world, and moments later was handed to a euphoric-looking Joe.

I will never forget the expression on his face as he looked down at the small, undeniably prune-like, scrap of a human being cradled in a blue blanket in the crook of his arm, before moving with such caution you would think he was defusing a bomb, to place the baby into my waiting arms.

There were tears in his eyes as he looked down on us both. I know I didn't imagine that. It was the first time I had ever seen him cry. The second time came much later, on our wedding day.

'You are incredible,' Joe said, his voice awed as he watched me fall in love with this tiny human being who would change my whole future. 'Amazing, astounding and incredible. I will never, ever, forget this moment. Not for the rest of my life.' His voice was hushed as though he was speaking in church, or in the company of angels as he gently reached out to caress my head, his fingers weaving through the long strands of my hair.

Ally

My eyes were closed and I realised I must have fallen asleep. I could still feel the scratchy hospital blanket beneath my cheek. And I could still feel the memory of Joe's fingers sliding through my hair. My scalp tingled at the phantom touch, as his fingertips gently grazed the sensitive skin of my ear. It felt so heart-breakingly real.

'Ally,' his voice was a hoarse croak, but it pulled me out of the depths of slumber and shot me to my feet as though my chair was electrified.

'Joe!' his name was almost unintelligible on my lips, swallowed by a noisy gulp and a loud sob. 'You're awake. You're back. Oh thank God.'

I gripped hold of the hand that had been caressing my hair, latching on to it with all my strength to anchor him to me. I felt him return my grip, but I couldn't see him properly any more because I was crying so much. I rubbed the back of my hand brutally across my eyes to clear my vision.

Joe was still horribly pale, his eyes were blinking rapidly in the over-bright room and on their lids were tiny traces of the tape he had torn from them. But he was awake, he was alive, and the joy of the moment couldn't be eclipsed by anything. He was back and it was the miracle I'd been silently praying for.

I whipped my head around for the nurse, but wouldn't you know it, she must have stepped out for a moment, for we were alone in the room.

'Oh Joe, I can't believe it. I've been so terrified. You looked so sick.'

'Oh baby, don't cry,' he urged in a croak that was almost his normal voice.

'I thought I was going to lose you,' I said, running my free hand over every inch of his face as though I needed tactile verification of the miracle.

Joe shook his head slowly, his lips finding the sensitive hollow of my palm and kissing it. 'You'll never lose me. I'm not going anywhere. I promised you that a long time ago.'

I nodded at the memory. It was what he'd told me on the night he'd proposed, dropping to his knee and taking my hand and placing it over his pounding heart as he told me how much he loved me, and that if I said 'yes' I would make him the happiest man in the world.

And of course I'd said yes, and Jake cooing in his crib behind us had added his own agreement.

'I should get the doctors,' I said, looking over my shoulder to see if there was anyone in the corridor who could summon them.

'In a moment,' Joe said, his eyes fastening on my face as though drinking in the sight of me.

'I want them to check you're alright.'

His hand came up to cradle my face, dragging with it the tubes attached to his arm. 'I just want this moment. I just want you.'

That made me cry again. 'Joe, you have me. You'll always have me. Although I swear if you ever frighten me like this again, I might just kill you myself.'

He laughed, but there was no strength in the sound. 'There was a boy. How is he? Is he alright?'

My tears were raining fast, even as I was smiling down at him. A human rainbow of emotions colouring me in; it was everything I loved about him. 'He's fine. You saved him, you were a real hero. I saw them downstairs earlier on. You saved their whole family,' I told him quietly, keeping to myself the thought that his bravery had almost destroyed our own. 'You could so easily have died in that water, Joe.'

'Water? Oh, yes the sea, I remember.'

'No. The lake in the park. It was frozen and you went through.'

Joe looked at me strangely as though I was surely mistaken, before the memory floated back into his consciousness. 'Oh yes. I remember now.'

A single finger of fear tapped me lightly on the shoulder as though it was trying to get my attention, but I ignored it. 'I should go and phone Jake. I should let him know you're alright.'

Joe looked confused. 'He's too little to disturb in the middle of the night.' Joe's face softened, as it always did whenever we discussed Jake. 'How is our baby boy?'

I frowned, and somewhere deep inside me a

tiny alarm bell began to ring. 'Big enough to give up Simba to keep you safe,' I said, nodding at the plush toy still positioned by the footboard of the bed. Joe studied the soft toy, a new frown creasing his forehead, as though he'd been given a puzzle he wasn't equipped to solve.

'Look, let me get someone in here to examine you. They should be shining a tiny flashlight in your eyes and checking you know what day of the week it is.'

'In a minute,' Joe repeated. 'I just want to hold you in my arms for a moment, then you can summon as many doctors as you like.' He held out his arms and I flew into them, ducking beneath an IV tube to nestle against his body. I could feel his heart beating beneath my head, it was thundering fast, as though he'd run a race to come back to me. I wondered if the sound of my voice, reminding him of our past, had shown him the way home.

'Before I fell asleep I was reminding you about the night Jake was born. Did you hear that?'

Joe's hand came up and rested on the back of my head, stroking gently. 'I don't think there's any chance of me ever forgetting a single thing about that night. How could I?' I smiled into the solid wall of his chest. 'I remember telling you how much I loved you, right there in front of the doctor who delivered the baby,' Joe said.

Like an animal sensing the presence of danger, I tried to raise my head, but Joe's gently caressing hand wouldn't let me. Something was wrong. Very wrong. Joe was mistaken, he'd never said that — at least not on that night. And Jake's birth had been attended by the two women midwives who had rushed to the van with him, not a doctor. He was remembering everything wrong, and a new chill ran down my back.

Very gently I disentangled myself from Joe's hold and reached for the emergency call button and pressed it. I half expected to hear a distant buzz or ringing sound, but there was nothing, just an eerie silence. My finger remained on the button and I pressed continually as though sending a Morse code message: *There's something wrong with my husband.*

'What else do you remember about that night?' I questioned carefully, hoping he couldn't read the concern in my eyes. Where were the doctors? Where was the nurse that was supposed to be continually by his side?

'Everything,' said Joe, although behind his smile I could see he had caught the anxiety I was failing to conceal. 'I remember going out into the waiting-room, with Jake in my arms.'

I was shaking my head slowly from side to side. That had never happened.

'I remember how everyone leapt to their feet when I walked in. Your parents were crying, they were so happy.'

'My parents were in Scotland,' I breathed, so softly that I don't think Joe heard me.

'And my mum and dad just couldn't stop smiling. I've never seen them look so happy. They even brought Todd with them, do you remember?'

'Todd? Who is Todd?' My voice was a ghost, full of fear.

'My dog, of course,' Joe replied, although the certainty in his voice wavered as he saw my face. 'My dog . . . he went through the ice . . . is he alright?'

I jumped off the bed. 'I have to get someone,' I said, already rushing from the room. I threw one last terrified look at the man who had come back to me, and was now slipping away once more. The hallway was empty. Someone should already have come hurrying when I'd pressed the call button, and I had no idea why they hadn't.

'I need some help here,' I cried out in the empty corridor. 'I need a doctor. Now!' I didn't care if I was overreacting, I thought, as I ran towards the nurses' station. They could tell me off for making a fuss *after* they'd examined Joe. I reached the desk, which was lit with a small downward-angled desk lamp. There was a cup of tea still steaming beside it, but no one there to drink it. I ran behind the desk and pounded on the door where I had seen the nurses congregate earlier. Were they having some sort of meeting? Why hadn't they answered the emergency call, or come when I screamed for help?

I didn't bother waiting for a reply and flung open the door. The room was empty.

I could hear the hitch of panic tagging on to every breath as I ran back into the corridor. There was only one place everyone could be. Because there was only one other patient on the unit that night. Everyone had to be in David's room.

It felt as though I was running through thick syrup as I sprinted down the hallway, my bare feet making small slapping sounds on the linoleum. I glanced at the Relatives' Room as I raced past, but it was empty. Of course, Charlotte would be at David's bedside. I screeched to a halt outside his room. The ceiling to floor blinds were still pulled down. I didn't even bother knocking this time. I burst through the door and straight into a nightmare. The room was empty. Not just of people, but of everything. The walls were bare, there was no bed, no medical equipment, nothing. It was all gone.

I stood in the middle of the floor, and heard the door slam shut behind me. I raced back to it, but as hard as I tried I couldn't open it. It was locked.

'Joe,' I screamed, desperate to alert him that I was still there, that I hadn't abandoned him. Hot tears were coursing down my face. 'Joe! Joe! Joe!'

★ ★ ★

A hand was on my shoulder, gently shaking me. I could feel the scratchy hospital blanket beneath my cheek, only it was wet, completely sodden with the tears I had silently been crying in my dream.

'Is she alright?' asked a voice I recognised, weighed down with a degree of concern that I didn't recognise in it at all.

'Aye, she was just having a wee nightmare, that's all.'

I didn't want to raise my head. I didn't want to look up. And I didn't want to look at Joe, because I knew what I'd see there, and I didn't think my heart was strong enough to take it. But I looked. Of course I did. I had to. His eyes were once more taped shut, his arms were motionless at his sides and the only sound was the soft hiss of the machinery breathing for him, because he still couldn't do that for himself.

Charlotte

I hesitated for a moment, unsure of how solid the bridges we'd been building were beneath us. Were they strong enough to hold me? I took a tentative step forward and rested my hand lightly on her shoulder. It said *I'm here*; it said *I know what you're going through*; it said, *Keep strong.* Ally turned her head; her eyes were over-bright with tears, which spilled as she blinked.

'I came to find you,' I said unnecessarily. Ally nodded, understanding there was so much more behind those five words than either of us was capable of expressing properly.

'How's David?'

I gave a small, lost shrug. 'I don't know. I don't think *they* know. They're expecting the cardiologist any time now.' I bit my lip, before continuing. 'I don't think that can be a good sign. They don't drag those guys out in the middle of the night for nothing.'

Ally's face was a perfect mirror reflection of my own fears.

'So, this is Joe,' I said, striving to make my voice sound as though this wasn't the most bizarre way of meeting the man who Ally had turned to, after she'd finished with mine. He actually looked very nice — well, as much as you can tell from someone who is completely unconscious. He looked strong and capable, and I imagined he had one of those faces that turned unexpectedly and amazingly good-looking the moment he smiled. There were grooves running like fantails from the corners of his closed eyes. This man did a lot of smiling. He was happy, they both were, and something inside me broke free and took flight, and it felt good and somehow sort of right. It felt that there was a reason we were all here tonight in this place. There was healing to be done, and I didn't mean by the doctors or nurses, but by us. And it was happening right now. I wondered if Ally could feel it too.

The aura in Joe's room was different to David's. I wasn't really a spiritual sort of person, but the yin and yang symmetry couldn't be denied. In David's room the battle was full-on and aggressive. Joe was in the same fight, that much was obvious by the gravity of his condition, it was just being staged much more quietly, that's all.

My eye travelled the room and settled on the one thing that looked totally out of place within it. There was a small cuddly toy lion propped up in the blanket valley between Joe's feet. I saw Ally stiffen slightly as she caught me looking at it.

'Lucky mascot?' I hazarded.

Ally looked uncertain, although I had no idea

why. 'It's . . . it's not his.'

I nodded. 'Does it belong to your child?'

Ally's emerald green eyes widened in surprise, and I realised then that she probably didn't think I knew she and Joe had children. I'd always wondered if she'd recognised me that day. I guess she hadn't.

Charlotte — Four Years Earlier

The winter sun was low, and despite pulling the sun visor down, I still had to reach for my sunglasses in the glovebox. I was smiling as I slid them in place, in fact I'd pretty much been smiling for the last forty-five minutes, ever since I'd walked away from the restaurant. I'd virtually had to squash a childish desire to skip in my high heels over to my parked car, which certainly wouldn't have been the right impression to make, had the clients still been watching me. But I could probably be forgiven, because it's not every day you clinch the biggest deal you've ever brokered, right out from under the noses of the rest of the competition. It was the sort of deal that elevated you out of the baby pool and let you swim with the big boys.

I glanced down at the caramel-coloured leather briefcase on the passenger seat, and patted it with satisfaction, my fingers grazing over the discreet C.W. embossed in the corner. It had been a gift from David, to bring me luck, he had said. And it had certainly done that, although the signed contract within it wasn't my victory alone. Tomorrow I would celebrate with the small team of employees who had worked without complaint long into the evenings with me to make this happen. And tonight . . . I let my hand skim over the bottle of champagne laying beside the briefcase . . . tonight I would celebrate with my husband.

David had been behind me all the way, encouraging and supporting me. Telling me I could achieve anything I wanted in life, all I had to do was believe. I felt my good mood begin to slip slightly as a critical voice (which incidentally sounded disturbingly like my mother's) whispered in my mind that sometimes just believing wasn't always enough. I shook my head, feeling the swish of my newly styled blonde hair swing and fall back into place, as I blocked that thought from slithering in like a serpent. No more of that. Not today.

I didn't know the town I was driving through, but I trusted the sat nav to get me home in enough time to be waiting with two chilled glasses of vintage champagne when David walked through the door. Perhaps I would wear that dress he liked so much, I remember thinking, as I followed the automated voice when it instructed me to take the next turning. Or perhaps I wouldn't wear anything at all . . . I was still smiling at the thought when the traffic lights at the pedestrian crossing ahead of me changed from green to amber. My foot pressed slowly down on the brake, my mind still on the evening ahead. I noticed the scene around me peripherally, the way you do when you're driving. There was a funfair set up in a large park on the left-hand side of the road, and there were three figures at the crossing opposite its entrance, waiting for the signal to change. I could see two adults, both clasping the hand of a small child who was three or maybe four years of age — like most people without children, I wasn't that good at judging age. I remember the child was holding a balloon on a stick, grasped within their hand, and I even recall noting the familiar logo of a high-street bank etched on the bobbing balloon.

It's the sort of memory that should be instantly logged and then dismissed by your subconscious, and I have no idea why this didn't happen. It was almost as though some inner part of me already knew that I should be paying closer attention. The day was bright, but cold, and the child was well wrapped up in a thick quilted coat, with the hood pulled up to cover its head. The child's mother wore no such coat, and it was her hair I saw first. It was blowing behind her, like the long chestnut mane of a thoroughbred. I remember thinking it was suddenly uncomfortably warm inside my per-fectly air-conditioned car. It wasn't her, of course it wasn't. Lots of women had hair that shade, that length. And anyway I hadn't seen her for four years and she could have cut it, or dyed it, or anything. It was just a passing resemblance, that's all.

I saw her bend down to say something to the child, then the man looked at her and she laughed, turning towards him . . . and me. She looked the same — and entirely different — as she had done the last time I had seen her. Ally had always been beautiful, even though she truly had never seemed to realise it. But now, smiling up at the man beside her, who I could only assume was her husband, and holding tightly on to the hand of the small child between them, she looked radiant and complete.

Everything that was missing from my own life was there on her face. She wore it casually and carelessly, not realising she had possession of all that I dreamed about. She hadn't stolen it from me. What she had was her own, but I wanted it. Well, not *that* child or *that* man, but I wanted what she now had. I wanted it with David.

I heard the beep of the signal alerting them that it was safe to cross. I could feel my right foot trembling on the brake pedal, as I stared at the trio as they stepped from the kerb. The man turned my way, and raised his hand in thanks. My own hands gripped the steering wheel with such intensity, I left tiny fingernail indents on the leather trim. They walked in jaunty strides, lifting the child off its feet and swinging him in a series of bouncing leaps across the striped zebra beneath them. They were almost at the other side of the road, almost gone, when the woman turned back towards my car and lifted her arm to add her thanks to her husband's.

The smile I remembered so well froze a little and a small frown furrowed her brow. Was she just dazzled by the sun, or had she seen it was me? I pressed myself further back against the thick padding of the driver's seat, trying to sink from view. She was ten metres or more from me, the sun was in her eyes and I was behind a tinted windscreen and wearing sunglasses. The chances of her having recognised me were so slight they were hardly worth considering.

I had almost convinced myself that Ally had no idea of the identity of the driver in the shiny blue car at the crossing. Except, as they mounted the pavement, and the child between them tugged them impatiently towards the funfair, I saw her in my rear-view mirror, staring after my car as I drove away.

Ally — Four Years Earlier

It couldn't have been her. Of course it wasn't her. The hair was wrong for a start. *And of course, it was totally unlikely that she'd had a haircut in the last four years*, taunted a voice in my head. She and David didn't live anywhere near here. *And you know that, how?* The car didn't look like something she'd choose to drive. *You do realise you're grasping at straws here?*

'Ally? What do you think?'

I came back to the present with a jolt, to my husband patiently waiting for me to tear my eyes away from the now empty road, and my small son, who was trying his three-year-old best to pull my arm out of its socket in his eagerness to reach the funfair entrance.

'Sorry. What did you say?'

380

Joe smiled as he reached into his back pocket and pulled out his wallet. 'I said, how about we go out for dinner after the fair? All three of us. We ought to celebrate.'

I felt something inside me melt at the expression on his face, which in its own way was almost as excited as the one our son Jake was wearing. Just for a very different reason. He hadn't been sure how things would go at the bank that morning, but I'd never been in any doubt. It was a good business plan; he'd worked hard on it. It deserved to succeed.

'That loan isn't going to last us very long if we blow it all on fancy dinners.'

'I think Jake would probably prefer burger and fries to filet mignon, to be fair,' Joe teased, pulling the bright red hood back and ruffling our little boy's thick, dark hair affectionately. 'What do you say, kiddo, shall we have a rest from Mummy's cooking tonight?'

'Yes please, Daddy,' enthused my son, in a way that wasn't entirely complimentary to my culinary skills, but it didn't matter. Nothing mattered today. Today was a special day, and I wasn't going to let some silly random sighting of someone who probably wasn't even *her* upset me. Charlotte had no power to hurt me, not any more. Thanks to Joe and the life we'd built together, I was finally fireproof. But that didn't stop the terrifying thought from intruding: Just what would I have done if it *had* been her, and she'd stopped the car and got out?

Charlotte

'Does it belong to your child?'

Ally took a surprisingly long time to answer, and before replying she curled her fingers into the fur of the cuddly toy, as though just touching it earthed her in some way. 'Yes. Yes, it does. It's our son's.'

The nightmare — whatever it had been about — had clearly rattled her far more than she'd let on. Everything about her seemed suddenly nervous and jittery, as though the threads holding her together had slowly begun to shred, filament by filament. It made me think of a string of small lustrous pearls slowly falling like white rain from a broken strand.

'Do you and David . . . ' Ally's voice faltered, as though some intuition had warned her my answer could hurt someone. But who, her or me? 'Do you have children?' she finished.

It was almost as though she knew. But how could she? Even our closest friends had no idea. I never spoke of it. I wanted no one's sympathy or compassion. I hid my infertility as though it were a guilty secret. But there were clues, if you looked closely enough. I overcompensated. A lot. The largest bouquet in the maternity ward? That was the one I'd sent. My name was on the gift tag of the ridiculously oversized teddy, or the expensive designer baby outfit. I was careful to let no one but David see how a little piece of me died each time someone we knew said: '*We have some really exciting news . . .* '

Ally had fed me my cue. My answer was

practised and convincing, I must have said it fifty times or more. But when I opened my mouth, the excuses about careers, travel, timing and lifestyle all stuck in my throat, like an obstruction I might choke on.

'Actually, we . . . we can't have children. Or rather *I* can't.' If anyone had told me that I would reveal this for the first time, to the woman my husband had loved before me, on the night when there was a very real danger I could lose him for ever, I would have called them crazy. I was practically placing a dagger in my enemy's hand and asking them to slice me with it.

Ally stared at me for a very, very long time before saying quietly, 'I'm sorry to hear that, Charlotte. Really, I am.' I didn't doubt for a minute that she was sincere, I could see it in her eyes. She reached for Joe's motionless hand and wove her fingers through his. 'You know, they've told me it might help bring him back if I talk about our happiest memories, remind him of all the good times, and practically every single one of those involves Jake.'

I nodded, as though I understood, but I had only an outsider's knowledge of what she was talking about. I knew as much as anyone could glean from peering through a crack in the curtains of a play for which they'd failed the audition.

'Jake. That's a nice name,' I commented.

And that was the moment when it happened. Ally leaped to her feet so abruptly, her chair would have crashed to the floor if I hadn't reached out to catch it. She didn't even seem to notice. Her eyes were bright but a little unfocused, and although she was staring in my direction, I got the impression she was looking right through me.

'I have to go out . . . somewhere. Have you seen my bag?'

I glanced around the room, my eye meeting the curious gaze of the nurse on duty. She gave a small shrug, but her expression said it wasn't her place to dissuade her patient's wife from leaving the hospital. Well, I didn't think it was exactly mine either.

'Ally, it's the middle of the night. Where could you possibly need to go at this hour?'

'Just out,' Ally replied mysteriously. Clearly she had no intention of sharing her secret with me. Which was hardly surprising, seeing as a couple of hours ago we hadn't even been on speaking terms.

Ally had dropped to a crouch and was looking beneath Joe's bed, presumably for her missing handbag.

'You probably left it in the Relatives' Room,' I suggested, remembering our frantic dash from there when the alarm had sounded for David. Ally gave a sharp nod of agreement, and I could practically see a plan evolving behind her eyes, and whatever it involved I could tell there would be no deterring her from it. None of my business, I told myself. Nevertheless when she headed for the door, I followed. She went straight to the place where her coat was bundled on the seat, thrusting her arms crazily into its sleeves, like a lunatic leaping into a straitjacket.

The analogy was no exaggeration, because there was a kind of mania to the way she was acting. I didn't think she would listen to me, but it was worth one last try.

'Ally, where are you going? You can't just leave the hospital. Joe needs you.' It was true, and should have been my trump card, but Ally just shook her head in denial.

'It's for *Joe* that I'm going,' she said, from a kneeling position on the floor, as she continued to hunt for her missing bag. 'Ah, here it is,' she declared, plucking the black tote out from its hiding place with a vigorous yank on its straps.

Her hand swooped inside it, like a heron catching fish. 'Did you happen to notice if there were any twenty-four-hour shops near here? A supermarket maybe?'

I was shaking my head slowly, wondering if I should either forcibly restrain her from going, or offer to accompany her. I didn't think I'd have much success with either option. 'I'm not sure. There might have been a mini-mart or something on the corner of the road opposite,' I said doubtfully. 'Sorry. I don't remember.' The taxi journey to reach David already seeming like it had happened weeks or even months ago, instead of just hours.

'Yes, I think you might be right,' Ally declared stuffing her feet into her boots. 'If any of the doctors need me, can you tell them I won't be long?'

'So you're coming back?'

'*Of course* I'm coming back,' she replied, as though I was insane. Which I thought was pretty rich, seeing as *I* wasn't the one about to go haring off into the night like a mad woman.

As she spoke, Ally continued to rummage frantically within the depths of her bag, her hands capturing and then discarding its contents. 'Damn. Where is it? Where's it gone? Where's my purse? It's not here.'

She looked across at me as though I knew the answer. If she accused me of swiping it, I was just going to walk out. 'Are you sure you had it when you got here?'

'Of course I had it. I always keep it right here,' she declared, thrusting the bag towards me so I could see the empty side pocket where apparently her purse should be.

'Well, when did you last have it?' I asked reasonably.

Ally was too stressed to be reasonable. 'I don't know. This afternoon, at Jake's school . . . no, wait. I might have taken it out when I thought there were carol singers at the door. Only it wasn't carollers, it was the police, coming to tell me about Joe's accident.'

The fever in her face died at the memory. 'I must have left it in the hall.' She looked so bereft I didn't even stop to think about whether it was wise to be encouraging her on whatever mission she was so hell-bent on completing. I reached for my own handbag, slid open the zip and extracted my wallet. I flipped it open and pulled out a twenty-pound note.

'Oh no, I couldn't,' said Ally, her eyes fixed on the note I was holding out towards her.

'Is that enough? Do you need more?'

Ally stopped protesting that she had another option and reached for the money. 'This is fine. I'll pay you — '

I waved my hand dismissively. 'Just go and get whatever you need so desperately and then get your butt back up here.' I looked in the direction of first David's room and then Joe's. 'I can't keep an eye on both of them for long, you know.'

10

Ally

I jabbed repeatedly at the call button of the lift, until I was rewarded with a single ping announcing its arrival. There was no one in the carriage as the doors slid open, but that was hardly surprising, given the lateness of the hour. The entire hospital was in sleep mode, and as I followed signs for the main concourse and the exit, I passed no one in the corridors.

There were several shops in the hospital foyer, all in darkness, and I didn't doubt for a moment that one of them sold the item I was dashing out into the cold December night to buy. I'm sure it was sitting there on a shelf, all I had to do was wait until morning for someone to come along and roll up the metal security barrier. I *could* wait . . . but I had no intention of doing so.

I looked out at the fiercely swirling snowstorm buffeting against the automatic glass doors, before burrowing a little deeper into the raised collar of my coat and striding towards them. The doors hissed apart and belched me out into the December night on a small pocket of warm air, which the wind instantly swallowed. Snowflake flurries whipped my face, stinging my flushed cheeks like a swarm of insects.

My black coat had turned completely white by the time I finally stepped through the hospital gates and onto the public highway. The road was empty, but thankfully lit well enough by the amber glow of the street lamps. I looked left and right, seeing nothing beyond the swirling white particles except shuttered shop fronts and darkened windows. It suddenly occurred to me that perhaps wandering around deserted streets in an unfamiliar area at this hour wasn't exactly a wise decision. I was certain that Joe — who never got angry with me about anything — would be furious if he knew the risk I was taking. Good. I couldn't wait for him to tell me off, yell at me even (although it was hard to imagine my easy-going husband doing that). He should know that nothing except sheer desperation could have prised me away from his bedside tonight.

Remind him of the good times. That's what the nurse had said. And I'd tried that, but it didn't seem to be working. There were a thousand good times to remember in our past, but maybe looking backward didn't have the power to pull him away from the place where he was lost. Perhaps what he needed was the prospect of something wonderful *ahead of us.* Something in our future. It was too early, I knew that. I hadn't intended to think about doing this until just before Christmas. I'd even pictured the moment: it would be Christmas Eve, Jake would be asleep (finally), and it would be just the two of us, making another new favourite memory. Joe would be leaving smudgy boot prints on the hearth, while I finished arranging presents beneath the twinkling lights of our tree.

Each year we exchanged a single gift on Christmas Eve before going to bed, and although some people might think it a little strange, I already knew *exactly* what I hoped to wrap within a nest of tissue paper and give to him this year.

The shop was just where Charlotte had said it would be. The neon signage flickered through the darkness, and drew me towards it like a magnet. Surprisingly, considering the hour, I wasn't the only shopper in the bright fluorescent-lit supermarket. I passed several people in the aisles carrying fully laden shopping baskets, browsing in front of freezer cabinets or dithering by the displays of fruit and vegetables. I spent no time wondering who on earth did their grocery shopping while the rest of the world was asleep, but headed straight for the toiletry section at the rear of the shop.

I found what I was looking for straight away. There were several to choose from, some more sophisticated than others. They had clearly come on a long way since I'd last had need to buy one. Quite out of character, I didn't even bother considering their individual pros and cons, or even which was the most economical, but plucked up the packet that was digital (because I like technology) and promised it was 99% accurate (because I like to be certain).

I passed the assistant Charlotte's twenty-pound note, and shifted my weight impatiently from foot to foot as she proceeded to conduct just about every test imaginable to check it was genuine. The woman was either anally thorough, or an ex-employee of the Bank of England. My hands were balled into tight fists of frustration as she held the note to the light, tilting it this way and that to check its authenticity. I guess it must have been a quiet night for the shop staff after all.

Eventually satisfied that I wasn't doubling up as a counterfeiter in my spare time, my purchase was handed to me in a white paper bag. I actually don't remember my journey back to the hospital. I know I was half running through the falling snow (which was a little dangerous, considering the icy pavements), but I don't remember crossing the road, or even if I looked before doing so (which was even more dangerous).

I summoned the lift, but got off on the floor below the one where Joe lay. I was looking for a Ladies' room somewhere far less populated with staff than the Intensive Care Unit, and from the dimly lit wards leading off from the bank of lifts on this quiet floor, it looked as though I'd found it.

I headed for the sign with the blocky silhouette of a woman, pushed open the door and flicked on the light. Aware I was acting more than a little bit paranoid about being interrupted, I didn't dare take the long narrow box out of its bag until I had slid home the bolt on the cubicle door. I lowered the lid on the toilet and sat down to read the sheet of instructions, as thoroughly as though I was sitting an exam on them the following day. I think part of me was screaming out to just get on with it and pee on the damn stick, while another part was too scared of what I would see there after I had.

At about the point when I could virtually recite the instructions without looking, I got to my feet and pulled the pregnancy test from its box and prepared myself, once again, for the longest three minutes of my life.

Charlotte

It wasn't my fault that Ally had run off into the night like a woman possessed. I couldn't have stopped her, even if I'd tried. But that didn't prevent me from feeling the guilt of an enabler. I was used to feeling a lot of things about Alexandra Nelson (now Taylor), but concern wasn't one of them. Nevertheless, after she'd practically run off the ward, clutching the money I'd given her, I went to the far corner of the room and stood by the only window that had a view of the road outside the hospital, and waited.

It was snowing so heavily I wasn't even sure I would see her at all when she emerged from the hospital grounds, but I did. At least I think it was her. I leant close enough to the glass for the chill of the pane to feel uncomfortable against the skin of my face. Yes, it was definitely her. She was standing on the pavement, and she looked so small and vulnerable out there all alone in the snow, that I had to fight the urge to pull on my own coat and go after her. Which was totally ridiculous, because if I did that there would be no one here for either of our husbands.

I kept standing by the window until Ally had disappeared from sight. I glanced at my watch,

392

noting the time . . . just in case . . . I had no idea what I was worrying about, but I couldn't shake the feeling of anxiety that was bristling like an irritant against my skin. It was cold standing there in the corner, beside the draughty window, and eventually I turned away from the blackened pane of glass.

It's strange how things work out. How everything happens for a reason. I never really stopped to think about things that way before, but afterwards it all seemed so glaringly obvious, that I wondered why I had ever doubted it. If Ally hadn't believed her bag had been lost, she probably wouldn't have pulled it out with such force that something within it would have tumbled out. If her purse hadn't been missing, I never would have given her the money. If I hadn't given her the money I wouldn't have felt responsible for her heading out into the night. If that responsibility hadn't led me to stand beside that precise window, then I never would have noticed the oblong leather purse half hidden behind the legs of the chair. And if I hadn't found Ally's purse, then absolutely everything would have been different.

I bent to retrieve the leather wallet, intending only to pick it up and keep it safe until Ally returned. I certainly had no intention of opening it, or of prying within it. But the catch was loose, or something bigger and more powerful than any of us was at work that night, because the clasp fell open and the purse opened like a book in my hands. On one side, trapped behind two plastic windows was Ally's pink driving licence, and a bank card. All perfectly normal and exactly what you'd expect to find there.

On the other side, behind another plastic window, was something that most definitely should not have been there at all, and just the sight of it drained the blood from my face and made my legs so weak I seriously doubted their ability to hold me up. I sank slowly onto a seat, my eyes transfixed on the photograph that didn't belong in Ally's purse at all . . . because it should have been in mine.

My fingers were trembling as they reached out to touch that familiar face trapped behind the plastic protection. I felt his brilliant blue eyes boring into mine from the wallet, as my fingertips grazed tenderly over the dark hair of his head. I closed my eyes, knowing the feel and texture of it as well as I knew my own. I could feel the sting of tears that blurred my vision making the face I have loved for so long swim and shimmer before me.

Why? How was this possible? How could I not have known this? He looked just the way I had always known he would. I'd seen him a hundred times in my mind, but I never thought, I had never even considered, that the first time I ever saw a photograph of David's child it would be in Ally's purse instead of my own.

Ally — Eight Years Earlier

I hadn't wanted to give Max a lift into town. My mission was definitely something I wanted to do

394

alone. But he said he needed to pick up a couple of things before returning to college after the Christmas break, and I simply couldn't think of a decent enough excuse to stop him from coming with me.

'So can I cadge a lift?' Max asked, seeing my hesitation. 'I promise not to backseat drive,' he said with a grin. Max hated the way I drove, and I hated the way he constantly told me so.

'Erm, yeah, sure,' I replied, hoping he would put my reluctance for company down to my post-break-up misery, which I was still wearing like a rattlesnake skin, that I couldn't quite manage to shrug out of.

Luckily, Max headed towards the opposite end of the High Street to the shop I wanted to visit. The chemist's was crowded, and several people looked up as the bell above the door clanged when I walked in. My steps faltered, and I scanned the random shoppers for faces I recognised. Thankfully there were none. I picked up one of the plastic baskets by the door and began to wander up and down the aisles. I shuffled self-consciously past the displays of toiletries and electrical gifts left over from Christmas, imagining the real purpose of my visit was printed in scarlet lettering on my forehead for all the other shoppers to see. I walked past the stand displaying what I'd come to buy several times before I found the courage to stop. By the time I did, my basket was filled with a cellophane-wrapped box of my mother's favourite perfume, some shampoo, a bag of cotton wool balls, and a bright red nail varnish.

None of which I had intended to buy.

I was running out of time and if I didn't hurry, Max was likely to come looking for me, which was the very last thing I wanted. I was acting like a nervous teenage boy about to buy his first pack of condoms. The thought made me smile wryly. It would have been a preferable purchase to the one I was about to make, although not entirely unconnected.

I was just handing my debit card to the shop assistant when Max's voice whispered in my ear. I jolted and gave a gasping wheeze of surprise.

'Hey, relax, it's only me,' he said, with a laugh. 'Why so jumpy?'

I think my eyes glazed for a second, before I lied to my friend. 'Oh, no reason.'

The assistant passed the white pharmacy paper bag across the counter to me, and I could see the top edge of the box I'd just bought below the rim of the bag. I practically snatched the carrier from her hand and scrunched the top edges together, effectively hiding my purchases from sight.

We walked back to my car, with Max irritatingly wanting to look at the sale displays in all the shop windows, while all I wanted to do was get back home. The bag beneath my arm felt as though I was carrying a ticking bomb through the High Street. A bomb capable of exploding not just my world, but that of many other people, to smithereens.

Max said nothing on the fifteen-minute journey home. He waited until I had pulled onto our drive, engaged the handbrake and switched off the car's engine. I turned to him, expecting he would open the passenger door and get out, but he didn't move.

'So, how late are you?'

'I . . . I . . . what are you talking about?'

He turned to me then, with a look of disappointment. 'Really, Ally? You want to play that game?'

I shook my head sadly, all the time aware that a feeling of relief was already beginning to course through me. 'How did you — ?'

'Let's just say that MI5 aren't going to be knocking at your door any time soon. You'd make a terrible spy.' I looked at him, trying to see if there was even a trace of judgement on his face. But there was none, and I should have known there never would be. 'Besides, you were a bit slow snatching the bag away. I saw the box.'

'You never said anything.'

'While you were driving? You've got to be joking. You take your life in your hands when you get into a car with you at the best of times, without throwing something like this into the conversation.' Somehow he always knew just how to make me smile. It was the very best part of being his friend. 'So, you never answered my question. How far along?'

'Well, I might not be 'along' at all. It could all just be down to stress,' I admitted.

'What!' exclaimed my old friend, throwing open his door. 'Here I am, practically knitting some bootees, and it might all be for nothing.'

I was properly laughing as I leaned over to the back seat and plucked up the carrier bag that would be able to tell my future far more accurately than my friend could do.

Max scooted around the front of the car and put his arm around me. 'So when are we going to do the test?'

'We?'

'Absolutely,' he confirmed, pulling me closer to his side. 'Whatever happens, Al, you're not facing this alone. Now come on, let's go and pee on a stick.'

★   ★   ★

Each one of those three minutes felt more like an hour. At Max's insistence we had gone to his house to do the test. 'You don't want your parents to come home while you're waiting for the results,' he reasoned.

'I guess not. Although it's been twenty years or so since they actually came into the loo with me.' I couldn't believe how much better I felt knowing that Max now shared the secret that had been burning inside me for the last week. My grandmother had always said 'a problem shared is a problem halved' and I don't think I had ever fully appreciated what she meant by that, until now.

While I disappeared into the bathroom with the rectangular box, Max used the time to do some quick research on his laptop. I returned with the small stick, and placed it carefully on his chest of drawers to await the results.

'It says here that you can get false readings on some of these kits,' he said. He shook his head at the screen. 'Well, that's no good. We need to know for sure, one way or the other.' He snapped shut the lid of his laptop and went over to stare at the stick. 'Nothing happening yet,' he reported.

I was sitting on the edge of his bed, head down, my attention riveted on the weave of the denim in my jeans.

'Maybe we should have put it in the light, or somewhere warm?' he suggested.

'I don't think that makes any difference,' I said, my voice resigned.

'God. This waiting sucks, doesn't it?' Max declared, looking at his watch. 'Thirty seconds gone. Is that all?'

'You're really into this, aren't you?' I said, looking up at him, bent low over the white indicator stick, and peering at the tiny plastic window.

He straightened and looked at me with just a tinge of sadness. 'Given the way things are, this is probably going to be the only time in my life I'm ever in this situation. It's the closest I'm likely to get to finding out what it's like to discover you're going to be a daddy.'

I couldn't help myself. I burst into huge gulping sobs, and he rushed across the room to my side and scooped me into his arms. He let me cry into his shoulder, patting my back and smoothing down my hair at the back of my neck in gentling strokes.

'Shh, shh. Please don't cry. You don't even know what the result is yet.'

I sniffed, but said nothing. Because I knew. I'd

done no other test; I hadn't seen a single doctor or nurse, but I knew that within me something was changing. There was life in me.

'Oh. Time's up!' cried Max, easing me gently off his lap and racing across the room. Apart from the quiet ticking of an old-fashioned alarm clock, his bedroom was silent, as he bent over the dresser. Very slowly, my old and dearest friend straightened up and turned to me. Never before, in all the years I had known him, had I seen that expression on his face.

'There are two blue lines,' he said, his voice subdued.

Of course there were.

Ally

I didn't turn around to look at the test, which I had placed on the back of the cistern behind me. Instead I read the various inscriptions carved into the wood of the toilet door, as though they were a riveting bestseller. By the time one-hundred-and-eighty seconds had passed, I could tell you who everyone who had visited the cubicle before me was madly in love with.

I got to my feet and reached for the test stick. My feelings were the exact opposite to what they'd been eight years earlier. Then, I had been praying for the test to be negative; *this* time I was desperate to see just one word in the small grey window. Pregnant.

I thought at first that I'd simply mis-timed the test; that it was the small flashing hour-glass still displayed in the corner of the screen. But when I lifted the stick and examined it more closely, I saw the hour-glass had been replaced by a tiny diagram of a book.

'What?' I cried aloud in the small tiled room. 'You've got to be kidding me. A book?' I peered closer. It was *definitely* a book. I snatched up the instruction sheet, which I clearly hadn't studied nearly well enough, because I had no idea what this meant. It took only seconds to find my answer. *'An error has occurred during testing.'* Error? What sort of error? How was it even remotely possible that I had done it wrong? It was hardly rocket science. I leaned back heavily against the cubicle door, the instruction sheet crumpled in my hand. *'You should test again using a new test.'* I glared down at the failed device that had snatched away the lifeline I had wanted to throw to Joe.

'I don't have another test,' I told it angrily, feeling hot tears of frustration burning in my eyes. 'Nor the time or money to go and get one.'

★ ★ ★

I walked up the remaining flight of stairs to the ICU, feeling deflated. Charlotte had her back to me when I entered the Relatives' Room, so I had no warning of the firestorm I was about to walk into, until she slowly turned around, my missing purse in her hand.

I was overwrought and tired, and I think that's what made me slow to realise the implications of what was about to happen. My lips were parted, ready to ask her where she had found it, or to thank her, I'm not sure which. But she gave me no chance to speak first.

'Were you *ever* going to tell him? Or me?'

'I . . . what are you talking about?' I asked stupidly, although I could already feel the thud of my heart pounding in my chest, as though it wanted to be somewhere far away from this room. I didn't blame it, because so did the rest of me.

'*This*, Ally. I'm talking about *this*,' Charlotte declared dramatically, separating the two halves of my purse and turning it towards me, as though I might possibly need reminding that there was a photograph in there of my son, whose resemblance to his biological father was just this side of uncanny. 'Your son Jake is David's, isn't he?'

I think for a single ridiculous millisecond I thought of denying it, but how could I? The proof was irrefutable. I nodded slowly, as the demons I had been running from for the last eight years finally caught up with me. In my head I could hear the voices of my parents, Max, even of Joe too, silently saying, 'We *told you this would happen.*'

'When . . . ? How . . . ? Why didn't you . . . ?' Charlotte seemed to have lost the ability to construct a fully-formed sentence, and I could hardly blame her. I watched the emotions running across her perfect face. Anger, pain and then something else, as one last dreadful thought occurred to her. 'David. Does he *know* about this? Has he known all along?'

I shook my head vehemently. 'No. Of course not. He knows nothing about it.'

There was relief in her eyes, but it didn't stay there long, the anger pushed it away.

'How could you do this? How could you keep this from him? He has a child. Your son is his flesh and blood, and yet you've kept it from him all these years. Do you have any idea what a difference this would have made?'

Now it was my turn to be angry. 'How can you, of all people, ask me that? I know precisely how different everything would have been if I had told David of this.' My chest was rising and falling with anger, and both of our voices were raised in a room where people usually spoke only in hushed whispers. 'If David had known about this, you wouldn't be his wife now . . . and I wouldn't be Joe's,' I concluded sadly.

Charlotte looked as though she was going to deny my words. They were new and unfamiliar to her, but to me they were a long-chanted refrain. 'We both know the kind of man David is. He would *never* have turned away from what he thought was the right thing to do. If I had told him that I was pregnant, he would have come back to me.' I said it without false modesty or pride. It wasn't a testimony to the love we had once shared that made me certain I was speaking the truth; it was a deeper knowledge of the man.

Charlotte looked at me for a very long time, and I could tell that she wanted more than anything to say I was wrong, that David would have let me go, that he would have been prepared to parent and support his son from a distance. But we both knew him better than that.

'After what happened at the Snowflake Ball, I knew there was no going back,' I said, feeling something like relief to finally have the seal broken on the secret I had hidden for so long. 'There was no second chance for David and me; we were too broken. Our relationship was over, and even if neither of you realised it then, your own was already beginning.'

There was acknowledgement in Charlotte's eyes, and something else which made me wonder just how close they had been, even when David had still been mine. She seemed to physically shrug that memory aside, as she continued like an interrogator determined to learn the truth. 'But you knew, on that night, you *knew* you were having his baby?'

I shook my head in denial. 'No, not then. Not for many weeks later.'

Charlotte sank slowly onto one of the chairs, as though the weight of the revelations flying around the room had pressed her down in submission. 'Does Joe know that Jake isn't his?'

I think of everything that Charlotte had said, that was the one thing that shocked me the most. '*Of course* he does. I could never lie to him about that.' I winced at the hypocrisy in my words, and knew I deserved Charlotte's stinging retort.

'Just to David, then,' she said bitterly, as though the words were poison on her tongue. Her face changed then, and she looked so sad that part of me actually wanted to go to her. 'Do you know how much he wants a child? Have you any idea at all how devastating it is not being able to give him one?'

There was nothing I could say, and even if I thought of something, I doubt I would have been able to get it past the lump of guilt that was lodged in my throat. I closed my eyes and heard the echoes of a long past conversation.

★ ★ ★

'Ally, you have to tell him,' Max had insisted.

'No, I don't.'

My head was lowered and Max had had to hunker down on the ground before me, forcing me to look at him. 'Ally, this is wrong. You know it is. David has a right to know. He'll want to do the right thing.'

I lifted my head at that, my face awash with tears. 'Don't you think I know that? But it won't be right, not for him or for me. Nor,' I said, realising at last that there was another individual in this equation. 'Nor for the baby.'

Max shook his head, and I could tell he was torn between supporting me, and telling me I was making the most ridiculous and selfish decision of my life.

'Don't you see, this is precisely what his mother was certain I would try to do: that I'd try to trap him in some way. She had me pegged as a gold-digger from the first moment she saw me.'

'What the fuck does it matter what his mother thinks? We know that's not true. For Christ's sake, David will know it's not true. He knows

405

you. He loves you.'

'Loved,' I said sadly, correcting the tense. 'We loved each other, but now . . . now he has someone else, and whether you think I'm right or wrong, I'm going to do this by myself.'

'You're wrong,' said Max firmly, and there was something in his voice that made me look deep into his eyes. I saw there were tears in them, and I loved him at that moment more than I ever had before. 'You're not alone.' He gripped my hands tightly within his. 'And you never will be.'

Charlotte

'Mrs Williams?'

I jumped at the summons. I hadn't even heard the door open, much less notice the nurse standing in its frame, saying my name. The nurse eyed Ally and me with visible caution. It was hardly surprising, I'm sure our raised voices had carried out into the corridor. 'Mr Beardsworth the cardiologist has just arrived. He's with your husband now. If you'd like to come with me, I'm sure he'll want to speak to you when he's finished his examination.'

For one stupid and insane moment I wanted to say to her, 'Actually, I'm in the middle of something here. Can I get back to you when I'm done?' Obviously I said nothing of the sort, but I shot Ally a meaningful look, which I was pretty certain she could interpret. It said: We're not done yet. This is far from over.

I was still shaking with reaction as the nurse led me down the corridor to a small, unoccupied office. I felt like an archaeologist who'd discovered something so dreadful, all I wanted to do was throw the soil back over it and pretend I had never found it at all.

David had a child. All these years when we had been hoping and trying for a baby . . . and he was already a father. He just never knew it. How could Ally have done something so unforgivable? And how was David going to react to the news? Was he even strong enough to be told? I guess I would know the answer to that one after the consultant had finished his examination.

Charlotte — Four Years Earlier

'I think we should see another consultant.'

David paused for a moment before passing me the fresh glass of wine he had just poured out. 'We've already seen three,' he said carefully, taking a seat beside me on our white leather sofa, the one that would never see small sticky imprints of jam-covered fingers on its pristine surface. He reached for my hand and held it in his, as though the sting of his words could be lessened by our physical contact. 'Maybe it's time we finally accepted what each of them has told us.'

I shook my head, like the defiant child I would never be able to conceive myself. 'There was something I saw the other day on the internet — '

'Charlotte, no. Enough. You have to stop this.' David's cobalt-blue eyes were full of concern. 'You're not going to find some miracle answer on Google, something the doctors have overlooked. I think we both need to accept that things aren't going to happen that way for us, and start exploring some of our other options.'

'You mean *adoption?*' I said the word as though it was something to be ashamed of, as though it represented failure. I couldn't help it, but that was how I felt.

'That's one way we could go,' David said, gently taking the wine glass from my hand and placing it on the coffee table (the one with the corners far too sharp for a toddler). He pulled me into his arms, laying my head on his chest, directly above his heart. I could feel the throb of its steady rhythm through the silky cotton of his shirt. 'There are so many babies all over the world; babies who need a home; babies who need parents to love them.'

'I know that. But if we go down that road, it's going to mean we've finally given up on having one of our own, and I just don't know if I'm ready to do that yet. I don't know if I *ever* will be,' I admitted shakily. David's sigh ruffled and disturbed my hair, but he said nothing as I continued. 'It's just that I can see them so clearly, in my mind. I've seen them for so long.'

'Who?'

'The children we're never going to have,' I answered sadly.

He let me cry for only a minute or two, before tenderly lifting my chin from his chest, bringing our faces just inches apart.

'We don't need to *make* a baby to have a family. I know you think that having a biological replica is important, but really it isn't. At least not to me. I don't need to see a little person with your hair and mouth, my nose and eyes, your bony elbows and my hairy legs.'

I blinked back my tears. 'That's one singularly ugly baby you've just described,' I said solemnly.

His eyes were warm and smiling at me. 'Indeed it is, Mrs Williams. And frankly I don't think we can afford to take that risk.' He was trying to tease me out of the black hole I had crawled into, I knew that. But beneath his light-hearted words, he sounded serious. 'It's not the genetic blueprint that makes you a parent, that's just an accident of biology.'

'And you really don't care that you could have had that '*accident of biology*' if you'd been with . . . ' My courage deserted me at the last moment ' . . . someone else?'

'I don't want or need anyone else. Just you.'

I closed my eyes when he kissed me, but somehow never quite managed to shut out the image of the dark-haired, crystal-blue-eyed children we'd never have.

Ally

'You have my permission to say *I told you so*,' I told my comatose husband, who currently couldn't say anything at all. The nurse in his room, with a discretion I was immensely grateful

409

for, never even glanced around as I spoke to her solitary patient.

'You warned me, you all did. But I just kept hoping that somehow it would never happen.' I gave a small bitter laugh. 'I should have realised how futile that was, shouldn't I? There's something like invisible barbed wire that keeps tying us all together. You think it's gone, you think you're free of it, but if you run too far the other way . . . well, it just cuts you down.'

I pulled my chair closer to the bed and ran my hand down Joe's arm. Could he feel that? Somewhere in the darkness did my touch have the power to reach him? 'She'll tell him, of course she will.' I closed my eyes on all the pain that lay ahead, for all of us. 'I suppose I can't blame her for that. They're close, I can see that, and she won't keep secrets from him.' A smile softened my face and I looked down on him with love. 'Just the same way that I couldn't from you.'

Ally — Eight Years Earlier

'So what did Joe say?' asked Max. The phone line was surprisingly clear from America, leaving me with no possibility of saying 'Sorry, you're breaking up. I can't hear you.' 'Ally, you have told him now, haven't you?'

'Not exactly. Not in so many words.'

Max's voice was tinged with disbelief and amusement. 'How many words does it take to tell him you're going to be bringing a squalling

410

infant into the house?'

I sighed. 'I know. I should never have left it this long. I probably should have told him before I moved in.'

'Oh, do you reckon?' asked Max, his voice heavy with feigned sarcasm. 'Sounds like something I should have suggested at the time. Oh, hang on a minute . . . I did! Seriously though, Al, what are you going to do if he asks you to move out?'

'Go back to Mum and Dad's, I suppose,' I said, my voice sad and resigned.

'I just don't understand why you've put it off for so long.'

'Because I didn't want things to get weird between us. I didn't want it to change. Everything's been going so well lately. I can study in the day, give music lessons in the afternoons and practise as late as I like in the evening. Joe's so easy-going about everything. And we get on so well, it's like we've known each other for years.' Ironically, I sounded a little sad as I said in conclusion, 'I laugh a lot these days, too.'

'I'm starting to feel a little jealous, here,' joked Max. 'It's good to hear you sounding so happy and positive, and I'm *glad* you've got someone to talk to now I've gone. For the record, I think Joe seems like a really great guy and a good friend. But d'you know something, friends, *real* friends, tell each other stuff, especially if they live in the same house.'

'Uh-huh.' I knew exactly where Max was going with this.

'Yes, they do. Important stuff, you know like . . . we're out of milk . . . have you paid the electricity bill . . . did I happen to mention I'm having a baby later this year? Little things like that.'

I laughed, but beneath it I could see that Max had a valid point. It was time (long past time, really) to let Joe know that I hadn't been entirely honest with him.

★ ★ ★

I picked my moment carefully. I waited until I was pretty sure he had only a few minutes to spare. That way if he was hugely angry, he would have to leave for work and hopefully cool off in the interim. Our mornings had fallen into a comfortable pattern of sharing the kitchen while we each made our own breakfast. We wove in and out of each other's paths like choreographed ballet dancers.

I kept eyeing the clock, waiting until he had just five minutes and half a cup of tea left, before nervously clearing my throat. I was really regretting my nibbled mouthfuls of toast, because I could feel them lodged in my throat like particles of grit. I washed them down with a huge mouthful of orange juice, and replaced the glass with a little more force than necessary on the worktop.

'Joe, can we have a quick word about something before you leave?'

He glanced towards the wall clock. I could have told him not to bother — we had four minutes and twenty-five seconds. There was time to do this — just.

'Sure,' Joe said agreeably. He gave me his slightly crooked engaging smile. 'What's up?'

'Well, it's kind of hard to know where to begin.' There was a warmth on his face as he waited patiently for me to potentially ruin our cosy and comfortable living arrangement. 'It's just that there's something I should have told you a long time ago . . . before I moved in, actually. And I will understand — totally — if you want me to leave . . . because well . . . this is . . . well, it's not what you signed up for. So, please don't worry about — '

'Is this about the baby you're having?'

I blinked at him, like an owl. A very surprised and stunned owl.

'Well, is it?' he coaxed.

'How did you . . . ? Who told you . . . ? When did you . . . ?'

Joe was shaking his head gently at each of my fractured questions. 'No one told me. I figured it out myself, some time ago.'

I glanced down at my flat stomach. I was still in my size ten jeans, although admittedly the waistband was starting to feel a little tight these days. But I still didn't think I looked pregnant. 'When did you know?'

'Before you moved in here,' he said quietly, his eyes kind.

'You knew back then? But why didn't you say anything at the time? Why didn't you even ask me about it?'

Joe gave an easy shrug, and I knew his

413

question could so easily be flipped over to ask: *Why didn't you tell me?* I could feel the warmth of a blush begin to burn my cheeks. I dropped my eyes, focusing my attention on the faded denim of his cotton shirt, noting the way it only just managed to stretch across the breadth of his shoulders; how he'd rolled up the sleeves at the wrists to make it easier to move; how one button near the bottom looked as though it was in danger of falling off. I was ready to answer any question you might care to ask me about his shirt. Just not about my pregnancy or my failed relationship with David.

'I figured it wasn't really any of my business.'

I should have known he wouldn't pry. But I still felt bad that I'd hidden the truth from him. 'I'm really sorry for not saying anything. I can be out by the weekend. And, obviously, I'll pay you rent until the end of the month.' My head was lowered and I was staring at the terracotta floor tiling, so I didn't realise how close he had come until I saw his heavy work-boots directly in front of me. I looked up slowly, and he waited for my gaze to finally reach his face.

'Why exactly are you leaving?'

I looked at him with more than a little confusion. 'Because I'm going to have a baby.'

'Yes, I know that. Why does that mean you have to move out?'

I was now way past confused, I was totally mystified. And then I suddenly realised that he probably hadn't grasped my full intentions. 'Joe, I'm not giving this baby up. I'm keeping him . . . or her.'

Joe simply nodded. 'That's what I thought.'

'A baby is going to disrupt everything. For a start there's going to be baby stuff all over the place.'

'It's a big house.'

'They wake in the middle of the night. A lot.'

'I'm a heavy sleeper.'

'They moan when they're hungry.'

'Well, I do that too.'

'They smell . . . sometimes.'

'Ditto.'

I shook my head. He was making this way too easy for me. Far easier than I deserved. 'They make a lot of noise.' It was my final argument.

'Ally, you play the piano and the trumpet. You make a lot of noise. How much worse can a baby be? I can handle the noise.'

I should have laughed then, because there was humour here. Instead I burst into tears. He didn't put his arms around me, or try to comfort me. But he did tear off a couple of squares of kitchen towel and pass them to me. I mopped my eyes as best I could, and was almost smiling when I looked gratefully into his face. 'Hormones,' I apologised. 'I should warn you, I may cry . . . a lot.'

'Do you know, for someone who is trying to talk me into this, you seem to be going a very strange way about it.'

'I just wanted you to know what you were letting yourself in for if I stay.'

Joe nodded solemnly. 'Okay. I have duly noted everything you have said. Consider me warned.' He did reach for me then, laying a hand on my shoulder and patting me, as though I were a fretful child. 'But you don't have to leave.' He hesitated for a moment. 'I don't *want* you to leave.' For a second there was something in his eyes, which disappeared even before I could properly identify it. There was a brief moment of awkwardness, one of the first, I think, there had ever been between us, before he glanced at the clock. We had overrun my anticipated time by quite a long way.

'I have to go. We can talk some more this evening, but I have no problem at all with keeping things just the way they are.'

He was almost out of the kitchen and heading for the hallway before I asked my last and most curious question. 'Joe, if no one told you, and I don't look pregnant yet, then how did you know?'

He stopped at the doorway and turned around. 'It wasn't any one thing. You were sick in the mornings when we first met, then your decision not to return to university, and finally the urge to move out of your parents' home. They all pretty much decided me I was right. Then, of course, there was the final clue.'

'Clue? What clue?'

It was the first time I had ever seen him blush. 'Er, well . . . your boobs . . . they got bigger,' he mumbled, before hurriedly heading for the front door.

I stared down at my (admittedly inflated) chest, and was still laughing long after I heard his van start up in the street beyond the kitchen window.

11

Charlotte

'I don't understand.'

Mr Beardsworth looked tired. I guess it didn't matter how many years you'd been a doctor, being dragged from your bed in the middle of the night probably never got any easier. Even harder was having to deliver to relatives the kind of news he'd just given to me. There was sympathy and quiet patience on his face, as he allowed me to absorb the information. But I was nowhere close to acceptance of the terrible diagnosis. I was still looking for a way out.

'But surely there *has* to be some other option? What about a bypass, or fitting a pacemaker or something?' I was desperately throwing random medical terms at him, without any idea of what either procedure actually involved. I imagined the cardiologist saw a lot of that, because to his credit he didn't point out I might possibly need more than ten years of watching *Grey's Anatomy* to make that kind of decision.

'If we were dealing with heart disease, or severe angina, then a bypass might be a solution. But in your husband's case, the heart *itself* is too badly damaged. Even implanting a defibrillator inside his chest would just be buying us a little more time; it wouldn't be a cure. Regrettably, the only real solution is the one I've outlined.'

'But a *heart transplant*,' I said the words on a hushed whisper, as though to speak them louder would invoke a curse. Which was ridiculous, because weren't things *already* just about as terrible as they possibly could be? 'But David's still so young. He's healthy.'

'And these are huge factors in your husband's favour. We would have every reason to hope for, and expect, an extremely satisfactory outcome in a case such as his.'

I shook my head, still grappling with the shocking diagnosis. 'And if he *doesn't* have a transplant. Then what?'

Mr Beardsworth said nothing, but his eyes spoke volumes. I could feel the sob tearing its way through my throat, determined to escape. Silently the consultant slid a box of tissues across the desk towards me.

'But his *heart* . . . ' My voice trailed away. To the cardiologist the heart was just a pump, an organ, an admittedly failing one in David's case. But to me, just talking about removing it felt as though the very essence of the man I loved would go with it. As much as I tried, I couldn't separate the two. 'It's just . . . it's just such a big thing to get your head around,' I explained from behind a wad of tissues.

'I do understand, completely,' the consultant assured. 'It's a lot to take in. But each year around two hundred patients in this country undergo a transplant. Surgically, the procedure isn't as complicated as you might imagine. The difficult thing, after we've fully assessed David's suitability as a candidate, will be waiting for a donor heart.'

'Does he . . . does he know?'

The doctor nodded gravely. 'Even as sick as he is, your husband has a clear grasp of the situation. He asked me outright if a transplant was a consideration, and I saw no reason not to tell him.'

'How did he take it?'

'As well as anybody ever does,' said Mr Beardsworth with a sad smile. 'It's a lot to absorb. For *both* of you.'

I could feel the acid pinprick of tears at his compassion. I closed my eyes until they went away. I needed to hold it together, now more than ever.

'Many of the necessary tests have already been done; the remainder will be carried out immediately. But my strong recommendation is to place him on the Urgent Heart Allocation Scheme, which will give him priority should a heart become available. Until then, he will need to remain in hospital.'

'He can't come home? Not at all?' Even to my own ears, my voice sounded as lost as a child's.

'I'm afraid not, Mrs Williams, he's just too unwell.'

'Can I see him now?'

'Of course,' said the doctor, getting to his feet and waiting as I scrabbled to mine. I almost lost the tattered remains of my composure, when he laid his hand on my arm in a kindly gesture as he led me from the room. 'I am most dreadfully sorry that I can't offer you more at this time. But please keep strong and stay positive. It's important to keep David stable, emotionally as

419

well as physically, while we wait.'

For someone to die, I completed silently, feeling the weight of the words descending on me like a boulder. David's battle would be to hang on to his life, until someone else lost their own.

★ ★ ★

I took a moment to compose myself before opening the door to his room. I breathed in deeply a couple of times at the threshold, as though I were a diver preparing to jump into dark and unknown waters. My game face was in place as I opened the door. David was awake, his eyes fixed on the entrance expectantly. He'd been waiting for me.

I faltered for just a second at the sad look of apology in his eyes as I crossed the distance between us. His lips felt familiar beneath mine, but there was no strength in his kiss. I straightened carefully and sat as close as I possibly could beside him, careful not to tangle myself in the tubes that were supplying him with additional oxygen.

'How are you getting on with that cute doctor?' he teased wheezily.

As ever, I took my lead from him, and pulled a small face and wrinkled my nose. 'I swapped him for a senior consultant.'

'Oh yeah? Was that wise? He looks kind of old for you.'

'I like them old. They don't run so fast when you chase them.'

David tried to laugh, but the effort made him gasp, and the machine readings around him spiked and beeped in warning, making the nurse at his bedside frown disapprovingly at me.

It sobered us both.

'I'm so sorry, Charlie girl. This isn't how it's supposed to be.'

'It is what it is,' I said sadly. I gripped his hand and bent my head to kiss his knuckles. 'But if you keep scaring the life out of me like this, then I warn you, I may have to divorce you.' The nurse looked horrified, but David just smiled weakly.

'No you won't. Till death us do part, remember? I just didn't figure I'd be fulfilling my part of the deal quite so soon.'

Rage flooded through me, not at him, but at life, fate or whatever it was that was leaching the fight out of him. 'Don't you dare talk like that. No one is leaving anyone here.'

David's beautiful blue eyes were full of pain, not at what he was going through, but for what it was doing to me. 'I just want you to be okay, Charlotte. Whatever happens.'

'Nothing is going to happen,' I refuted obstinately. 'You're going to stay right here until they find you a new heart, a good strong one, and then you can spend the next sixty or so years apologising for frightening me so much.' I gripped his hand in both of mind. 'This is a blip, a hurdle that we just have to get over and then get back on track. I don't want to hear any more talk about death or being apart. You owe me a trip to New York, and I intend to claim it.'

David shook his head, his thick, dark hair making a scratchy sound against the starchy pillows. 'So you knew about that, did you? I should have known better than to try to keep a secret from you.' I tried to smile, but somehow it never quite made it to my eyes. 'Okay,' David continued, making a vow we both knew he had no control over. 'No more flat-lining, I promise. No more going towards the light.'

'Was that what it was like?' I asked hesitantly, terrified to hear him speak — even jokingly — about how close I'd come to losing him tonight.

'No, honey. It wasn't like that at all. There was no brilliant light, no tunnel. Just darkness.'

'How disappointing,' I said, trying to match his flippant tone, but not really succeeding. 'I'd always imagined there'd be some sort of welcoming committee, with everyone you've ever loved and cared about waiting for you.'

David's eyes were tender as they went to mine. 'Everyone *I*'ve ever loved or cared about in the world is right here in this hospital,' he said gently.

His words were truer than he realised, and the guilt at what I was concealing from him hit me like a physical blow. He read it on my face. I should have known that he would.

'Charlotte, what is it? What's wrong?'

I took a deep breath, dreading what I was about to say, but knowing I had no choice. The time of secrets was past.

'David . . . there's something I have to tell you . . . '

Ally

They entered through the swing doors together, shoulder to shoulder, as though they needed that physical contact to get through this. I'd only been gone for a few minutes, taking the stairs down to the floor below, where I'd seen a drinks vending machine. I was walking back down the length of the corridor when I looked up and saw Joe's parents standing just inside the entrance to the ward, like shell-shocked survivors of a bomb blast. They looked lost, they looked scared, and frighteningly, they looked so much older than the last time I'd seen them. I broke into a run towards them, and the sound of my booted feet flying over the linoleum made them turn in my direction.

'Ally,' cried Frank, his voice quavering in a way I don't think I'd ever heard before. I threw my arms around the joined entity that was my in-laws, and they clung to me. I knew Kaye was crying even before we broke apart. I could feel it in the trembling shudders that ran through her bowed shoulders. She'd spent most of her life convinced that something dreadful was going to befall someone she loved, and there was absolutely no satisfaction in finally having that prediction come true.

'Hush now,' Joe's dad urged, reaching in his pocket with his free hand for a perfectly laundered handkerchief. That was when I noticed that, quite out of character, Joe's parents were holding hands, their fingers wound so tightly around each other that I could see the white-boned knuckles through their skin.

'I didn't expect you to get here so soon,' I said,

directing my comment at Frank, and allowing Kaye a moment of privacy to dab at her face, where her tears had washed tiny rivulets through the layers of powder and blusher.

'That driver you sent certainly knew his stuff. He made short work of the journey and drove through the storm and snowdrifts like they weren't even there. I couldn't have got here faster myself.' I sent up a silent word of thanks to Max, who was himself somewhere over the Atlantic Ocean by now, on his way to reach my side. The small pieces of my world were coming together like a jigsaw. Albeit one with a hugely important part missing.

'How is he? How's our boy doing?' asked Kaye anxiously.

'There's been no change, I'm afraid. He's not woken up yet.'

Kaye made a small moaning sound, and my concerned eyes flew to Frank's, wondering whether I should have played down the severity of Joe's condition. I saw, the grimset determination in my father-in-law's jaw, which was in sharp contrast to the sparkling over-bright sheen in his eyes. I felt a moment of pure panic. They were old, and both of them had been unwell recently. To be honest, I wasn't sure if either of them was strong enough to cope with any of this.

'I want to see him,' said Kaye. 'Will they let us see him, do you think?'

'Yes, of course they will,' I assured her, putting an arm around her shoulders and drawing her closer to my side. Kaye had always been slight, petite even, but when had she become so frail? It felt like I was holding on to a bundle of bones wrapped up and held together only by the thick wool of her winter coat.

I began to steer them both towards Joe's room. 'I should warn you that they've got him hooked up to an awful lot of machinery.' Kaye's eyes widened in fear. I kissed her cheek and smelled the same Lily-of-the-Valley perfume that she'd worn for as long as I'd known her. 'I have to keep telling myself that every scary piece of equipment is there to help him,' I whispered into her short grey curls. 'They're doing all they can for him. He really is getting the best of care.'

Kaye nodded fiercely, not trusting her voice, while beside her Frank responded in an unusually gruff tone. 'That's good. That's how it should be. That's what we need to hear.'

Although I'd tried to prepare them, I don't think my words had even pricked through the miasma of panic that had engulfed them since they'd received my call all those hours earlier. Were they able to deal with what was waiting for them on the other side of the door? Was any parent? The only thing I could imagine that could possibly be worse than having Joe in this situation, was if it were *Jake* lying in that hospital bed instead.

As the door to Joe's room swung open, I saw their reaction. I felt it shimmer through the air like a shock wave from an explosion. They reeled backwards, and instinctively clutched at each other, their faces wearing identical looks of fear and despair.

Surprisingly, it was Kaye who gained control

first. 'Oh Joe,' she breathed, the folds of her face softening. She appeared to hesitate for a moment, so I took her arm and together we went to his bedside; the woman who'd loved him from the moment he had entered this world, and the woman who'd loved him from the moment he had entered hers.

Kaye reached for his hand, the way she must have done a thousand times when he was a boy, when he'd been afraid, or in trouble, or lost. He was all of those things once more on this terrible night, and I saw a strength and determination glitter in her eyes as she looked down on her only child. There was an inner core of strength, a seam of iron, running deep within the woman who had raised the man I loved, and I don't think I'd ever really appreciated that before. With her free hand she began to straighten the perfect un-rumpled bed covers, pulling and twitching them and flattening out an imperceptible crease from Joe's pillow. She paused with her hand by his head, before gently stroking the thick, sandy hair, and it felt as though three decades had rolled away and I was witnessing a long-remembered nightly ritual. I was suddenly overwhelmed with the need to touch my own son's hair in just that way. Joe and Jake were both my touchstones, and without them I was lost, alone and adrift.

From the foot of the metal-framed hospital bed, I heard Frank clearing his throat several times, before quietly blowing his nose. 'Do you know . . . do you know yet what happened, Ally? How he ended up in the water?'

I nodded sadly. 'A child was in danger on the ice. Joe rescued him, and then went back for their dog.'

Frank shook his head, his face a mixture of pride and despair. He reached out and awkwardly patted Joe's leg through the woven hospital blanket. 'Oh, son.' When he looked back at me he was crying quietly. 'I thought it would be something like that. That he was being brave and unselfish. That he was helping someone in trouble.'

'He doesn't know how to be any other way,' I said with quiet pride. 'You taught him well, Frank. You both did.'

Joe's parents shared a look, and suddenly I felt like I was intruding on something that belonged to just the three of them. 'Look, there's only supposed to be two visitors at a time by the bed, so why don't you both spend some time with Joe and I'll wait in the Relatives' Room; it's just down the corridor.'

I don't think either of them heard me leave, and when I looked back Frank was standing beside his wife, his arm around her shoulders as they stared down at the man who meant everything in the world to them, willing him to come back to us.

Charlotte

I saw Ally disappearing in the direction of her husband's room with an elderly couple, who I assumed must be Joe's parents, because I'd seen photographs of her own family years ago, and it

427

didn't look like them. For a moment I envied her, this time for the close family network and the support that gave her. The knowledge that Veronica would probably be here within the next twenty-four hours, no doubt intending to oversee every decision about David's care, was no consolation and certainly no comfort. Even the indomitable Mrs Williams wouldn't be able to improve her son's condition. Whether David recovered — or not — was now in hands far more powerful than my mother-in-law, although I very much doubted *she'd* accept that.

I hadn't been expecting Ally to return to the Relatives' Room, and from the look on her face as she opened the door, she clearly hadn't been expecting to see me there either.

'I . . . I thought you were with the cardiologist?'

Ally looked tired, and drained. The night had been long and gruelling, and I'm sure I looked no better. I glanced at my watch. In a few hours it would be dawn. The hospital would soon be switching seamlessly into daytime mode. Cleaners would be pushing mop-laden trolleys, ancillary workers would be bringing the patients their breakfasts. Staff would be coming in to work, chatting mindlessly about last night's TV, the forthcoming holiday season and the latest celebrity gossip. Yet Ally and I were stuck inside an entirely different world from them. A world where normality was now crash carts, oxygen masks and life-support machines. A world where husbands, who were meant to grow old and grey beside you, could suddenly be gone for ever. A

428

world where the lines between friend and enemy had become strangely blurred.

'I was. Then I was with David.'

Ally paused for just a beat, her eyes frightened before asking quietly, 'How is he?'

She had every right to ask, and it wasn't just because of the connection that would now link her to my husband for the rest of our lives. 'He's going to need an operation,' I said. It was as much as I was prepared to share with her for now. She already had far too much of what was mine within her hands.

'Oh. Will that be today?'

'Not unless we're extremely lucky,' I replied bitterly, shocking myself with my reply. I looked away to hide my guilt, as I realised how quickly everything you think you know about yourself can be stripped away. How the sudden death of a stranger can fill you with hope, instead of with sadness.

There was a long moment of silence, and I wondered how much longer we would both continue to dance around the subject that hung suspended in the air between us.

'You told him, didn't you?' Ally's words were more a statement of resignation than a question. I wanted to be angry, I felt I had *the right* to be angry, I just didn't have enough energy left to carry it through.

'About your little boy? About Jake? No, I didn't.'

Ally's face looked as though all her Christmases had come at once. 'You're not going to tell him?'

I sighed deeply and shook my head. 'No, I'm not.' I paused and met her eyes. 'You are.' What little colour that the night hadn't bleached from her face, drained away. 'But you're not going to tell him yet. He's not strong enough. I don't want him to know anything about his child until after the operation.'

I saw the challenge in her eyes at the words '*his child*'; it was there right along with her obvious relief at the temporary reprieve.

'So you didn't tell him that we'd both been here all night?' Ally questioned cautiously. There was hope in her eyes. It didn't stay there long.

'Oh no. I told him. He knows that you're here.'

I closed my eyes for a long second, remembering the expression on David's face when I'd told him that impossibly, and unbelievably, his former girlfriend was here in this very hospital on this night. And it was only when I stepped cautiously back into our past, that I fully understood that the bonds that kept him tied to her were still there. For they'd risen up from the earth, and felled me like a trip wire.

Ally

Nervous didn't even begin to cover it. Terrified even fell short of what I was feeling, as I stood outside David's room, my hand fisted, preparing to knock on the door and walk right back into my past. Of course I could simply have said '*No*'. I could have told Charlotte that I had absolutely no desire to see David again, much less talk to him, but then I'd have been lying not just to her, but also to myself.

I'm still not sure I completely understood her reasoning. 'Unless they move Joe to another ward, it's inevitable that sooner or later David is going to see you here. I just want to make sure that nothing about that encounter is likely to shock or upset him.'

'So what you really mean is, you want to *manage* the situation?' I'd said.

Charlotte had looked surprised that I would find this strange. But then I found the whole situation strange. Would I have wanted one of Joe's old girlfriends at his bedside? No, of course I wouldn't. Unless I thought that might help him in some way. If that were an option, I'd have happily invited the devil himself to sit beside him.

'The cardiologist said it was important to keep David stable. So all I'm trying to do here is avoid him having any . . . *unexpected* . . . surprises, until he's strong enough to deal with them.' Her substitution of the word 'unexpected' for 'unpleasant' was practically seamless. I let it pass. 'But remember, there mustn't be any mention at all about Jake. Not yet,' she had warned. That one I had absolutely no trouble in agreeing with.

'Come in.' The response came from a nurse and that threw me for a moment. My hand was damp with perspiration and slipped a little on the doorknob as I twisted it open and entered the room. The most positive thing I could think, was that David looked marginally better than he'd done the last time I'd seen him that night. But given that a nurse had been performing CPR on him at the time, that wasn't saying a great deal.

My steps faltered, halting me just close enough to the door that I could turn and bolt if necessary. I suppose that was why my hand remained upon it, holding it open.

'Ally.' One word, just one, and the years fell away. The door slipped from my hand and I walked towards his bed.

'I've imagined this moment many times over the years . . . I thought I'd covered every possible scenario . . . but I never pictured it would be like this.' Unexpectedly my eyes filled with tears at his words, because they were mine too. 'You look the same,' he said in a weak parody of the voice I remembered so well.

I smiled faintly, but didn't say what I was thinking, which was '*And you look like Jake, the little boy you know nothing about*'.

'How are you feeling, David?'

'I've got to say, I've had better days.' He inclined his head towards the vacant chair beside his bed. 'Will you sit down?' he asked, sounding so exhausted it made the nurse leave whatever task she was occupied with and return to her patient, eyeing the readings on each of the various pieces of equipment David was connected to.

'You must remember not to exert yourself, Mr Williams,' she cautioned.

I slid quickly into the chair, feeling the rebuff

had been directed at me. I wanted no responsibility for making him worse.

'Just for a moment then,' I qualified. 'I can't stay long because I have to get back — '

'To your husband,' David completed. 'Joe? That's his name, isn't it?'

It was beyond weird to hear his name on David's lips. 'Yes, Joe,' I replied, aware that my face and voice changed, softened and mellowed, whenever I spoke of him. That wasn't just because of the current situation. It had always been like that, for as long as I could remember.

I saw something surprising flash across David's face as he recognised the expression on mine, and it took me a moment or two before I realised it was probably the same look I had once worn whenever I spoke of him.

'I understand he's been quite a hero. The nurses have been talking about him all night.' Hearing him speak about Joe, even admiringly, made me feel strangely flustered and defensive. There was a merging and overlapping of the past and the present; there was a paradox here that I didn't know how to deal with. There's probably a very good reason why people lose contact with their first loves, because if the tumultuous and contradictory feelings battling within me were anything to go by, it was far too dangerous a game to become involved with.

'Is he making good progress?' David enquired, and I saw the genuine concern in his eyes. I looked away quickly, the way you do when staring at the sun. His eyes were the only thing unchanged and vibrant in his face. They were, as yet, untouched by his illness, and instinctively I could see nothing but danger in allowing myself to look deeply into them once more.

'I don't know,' I replied sadly. 'Not yet. Everyone just seems to be waiting for . . . something. No one has really told us that much.'

'I'm sorry,' he said. And it sounded as though he meant it.

David paused for a moment, waiting until the nurse had left the room, after assuring him someone would return shortly. 'Is he good to you? Is he a good husband?'

About that, at least, I could sound positive. 'He is. The best. He's wonderful.' David's eyes closed for a long moment, so long that I actually wondered if he'd fallen asleep in mid-conversation. When he opened them again, there was a gentleness within them. 'Good. I'm glad. I'm glad that you're happy. You deserve that.'

I fiddled awkwardly with my hands, realising that I had unconsciously been turning my wedding band around on my finger as we spoke, as though it somehow brought Joe into the room with us as an actual physical presence. However ill he was, David's powers of observation were still acute. He smiled gently at my hands, which I forced to be still.

'Any children?' he asked conversationally, and it was just as well I wasn't the one hooked up to a cardiac monitor, because the reading would have gone clear off the scale.

'Just the one. A little boy.' David nodded absently, and I knew then, without a doubt, that Charlotte had told him nothing. I hoped Jake,

434

who considered himself far too mature to be called a 'little boy' any more, would forgive me for the term, which I knew had made him sound much younger than his actual years.

We fell silent, each in our own way trying to find a footpath through the minefield of topics that neither of us was talking about. David took the first tentative step.

'It's been so long since I've seen you, not since . . .'

'The night of the ball,' I completed.

He nodded. 'You and Charlotte . . . has it been alright tonight, meeting up like this?'

'Well, I haven't slugged her again, if that's what you're asking.'

He looked shocked for a moment at my reply and then began to laugh. The readings on his monitors changed from gentle zigzags to something which resembled a range of mountain peaks. I glanced at the closed door, expecting at any moment a worried team of medics to barge through it.

Unthinkingly I grabbed for his hand. 'Are you alright?' I asked, my eyes flickering to the monitors, which I couldn't read properly, before returning to his face. He had laughed so hard that a single tear had escaped from the corner of one eye, and the urge to reach over and wipe it away was irresistible and unnerving.

I felt his fingers fold around mine, and it was so different from Joe's hand, and yet so achingly familiar that I could feel a schism slowly begin to rip within me. The past and present had no business being here, in the same place. And yet they were.

435

'I love her, you know. I love her very much.' It wasn't an apology. David didn't owe me that.

'I know you do. I can see that. I think, perhaps, I saw it before you did.'

His smile was slightly twisted. 'She's scared of you, you know. She puts on this big tough front, but beneath it, she's scared that I've still got feelings for you.'

And there it was. The moment when the question *And have you?* was just lying there, waiting to be picked up and asked. But I wasn't going to go there. I couldn't, and I wouldn't.

'Would it be very weird if I asked you to look out for her, if . . . if anything happens to me?'

'Yeah, it would be,' I said, shocked on more than one level that he would ask me that. 'Surely you both have family and friends for that? I'm probably the last person in the world Charlotte would choose to turn to.'

'Her family are about as warm and welcoming as mine,' David said by way of explanation. 'My brother's the only one she gets on with, and he lives in Australia these days. And as for friends, well . . . let's put it this way, we've got an awful lot of acquaintances.'

I wasn't used to feeling sympathy for Charlotte, and I didn't know how to deal with the emotion. Her situation was so vastly different from my own. Instead, I switched the subject. 'Besides, you're going to be out of here in no time, aren't you? Charlotte said you were having an operation?'

There was something in David's eyes that troubled me. It took me a moment before I could name it. It looked a little like defeat. 'Maybe. Who knows. Nothing is certain; it's just a waiting game.' His eyes went to mine, and this time I didn't look away. 'It's funny, I always thought *you* were the one who broke my heart, but it turns out I've done a pretty good job of doing that all by myself.'

'I'm sorry Mrs Williams, I'm going to have to ask you to — ' A nurse, one who had been attending to Joe earlier in the night, broke off in confusion as she walked in and saw me holding the hand of the only other patient on the ward that night. The one who *wasn't* my husband.

'Oh, I'm sorry,' she said, her voice trailing away, as she glanced at our hands, and then looked back down the corridor towards Joe's room. She was so comically perplexed at finding the wrong woman at David's bedside, that she addressed the rest of her comments to the clipboard in her hands. 'We need to prepare Mr Williams for some further tests that Mr Beardsworth has ordered, so I'm afraid I'm going to have to ask you to say your goodbyes and step outside.' She backed out of the doorway, still looking confused.

David smiled. 'What's the betting she's now hot-footing it down the corridor to see if Charlotte is sitting by Joe's bedside, holding his hand?'

I wanted to laugh, but even more than that, I wanted to cry. Perhaps it was something to do with the nurse telling me to say my goodbyes to David. Perhaps it was finally acknowledging that those had been said many years earlier.

'Get better,' I said, rising to my feet and squeezing his hand one last time before laying it back down on the mattress.

'I'll try,' David assured.

'Don't die,' I told him, trying to make him smile with black humour, and ruining it all by sounding as though I was about to cry.

'Going to do my very best not to,' he promised. 'Take care of Charlotte,' he asked again, as I reached the doorway to the corridor.

I turned around for one last look, before quietly repeating his own words. 'I'll try.'

★ ★ ★

My phone vibrated against my hip bone as I headed back down the corridor. I glanced through the glass into Joe's room, and saw his parents were still with him, so I pulled the device from my pocket and headed for the stairwell to take the call. The word 'Home' was illuminated on the screen.

'Jake, honey, is that you?' I asked in a panic, glancing at the wall clock and seeing it was only a little after six in the morning. Alice wouldn't be calling at this hour unless something was wrong. But Jake might.

'No, Ally, it's Mum,' said the reassuring voice of my mother. Her presence in my home at this ungodly hour made no sense, unless Alice had summoned her in an emergency.

'Is Jake alright? Is anything the matter?'

'Jake's fine,' soothed my mother, and just hearing her familiar placating tones brought me

438

closer to breaking down than I'd been all night. I hadn't realised how much I needed her with me until this very moment. 'I couldn't sleep, well not just me, your father too,' she said, her own voice sounding a little more hoarse than usual. 'Eventually we gave up trying and just piled into the car and drove to your place. I've sent that lovely neighbour of yours back home to get some sleep. The poor woman spent the entire night sitting awake in a chair outside of Jake's room, in case he woke up and needed her.'

That was so typically Alice, that a small smile of gratitude found its way to my lips.

'So fill me in, sweetheart. What's the news on Joe?'

'None,' I said sadly. 'There's been no change yet.'

'Oh,' said my mother, summoning up a thousand alarm bells in that one small word. Suddenly it wasn't a parent at the end of the line. It was an experienced ex-nurse, one who had spent many years working in intensive care wards.

'That's bad, isn't it?' I questioned anxiously. 'They're not giving me any information. They keep talking about waiting and giving things time. But what is it they're not saying? Mum, you have to tell me.'

'Ally, calm down. The doctors can tell you far more than I can. I don't know anything at all about Joe's condition, and it's been years since I last worked on the wards. Don't go getting yourself into a panic now.'

It was probably a good twelve hours too late

for that particular piece of advice.

'Is Jake awake yet? How is he? Has he asked about Joe? What do you think we should tell him? Can you and Dad stay at home with him today, because I don't think he should go to school, do you?' The words came tumbling out of my mouth like boulders in a landslide. If *I* could hear the strain and anxiety in my voice, then it was an absolute certainty that my mother could too.

She did. 'Ally, take a breath and slow down.' I tried to do as she instructed, but my panic was like an escaped pony that had been tethered up tightly for so long, it didn't want to be reined back in. 'Jake is fine. He's with your father right now, they're making some toast for all of us before we leave.'

'Leave? Where are you going?'

'We're coming up to the hospital. Jake's worried and he needs to see his Daddy, and he needs to see you too.'

'Oh Mum, I'm not sure that's such a good idea. I don't think they even allow little kids to visit patients on this ward, and if Jake saw Joe like this it's really going to frighten him.'

'Ally,' said my mum, her voice soothing and patient, 'he's *already* frightened. Terrified, in fact. He's an intelligent little boy, and his imagination is running riot. However scary you think it might be for him, it's important that he sees it with his own eyes. It will help him process everything.'

Suddenly it felt very much like I was talking to an experienced nurse, rather than a loving grandma. 'But he's only seven years old. What if it's all too much for him to cope with? Joe's in a coma, Mum, he's hooked up to a ton of machinery. He's not even breathing by himself yet.' I'm surprised she managed to decipher the end of my sentence, because it was lost in muffled broken sobs.

'I think that's precisely why he *has* to be there, why we *all* should be. For Jake, for you and also for Joe. And don't worry about their visiting rules. In cases like this, it's important to allow children to visit their parents, if they want to.'

It was hard to know what scared me most: my mother's quiet insistence that our family should reunite, or hearing her refer to her much-loved son-in-law as a 'case like this'. The need to shield your child from anything that could hurt them is inbuilt in every mother. And when shielding alone isn't enough, then it's a mother's job to try to prepare them for the worst of all possible outcomes. I was doing that. And so too, I realised, was my mother.

'How soon can you get here?'

★ ★ ★

I passed Frank in the doorway to the ward. He was wiping his eyes with the back of his hand, and hadn't noticed me doing exactly the same thing, as I headed back to Joe's room.

'I'm just going to fetch us all some tea,' Frank explained gruffly. 'The nurse said we can use the staff canteen.' I nodded, recognising his need to be doing something, anything. 'We'll all feel better with a hot cup of tea inside us.' As much as I wanted to believe in its curative powers, I knew there was only one thing in the world that was going to make me feel better. And it wasn't tea. Frank nodded, as though confirming his own words. 'Yes, well, three cups it is then.'

I had taken two steps away from him before I paused and called back after him. 'Actually Frank, could you make that four?'

★ ★ ★

Kaye looked up with a sad smile as I slipped back into the room. 'How are you holding up?' I asked, gently squeezing her shoulder. Joe's mother gave a tired shrug, the fragile bones undulating beneath my hand. Her eyes were fixed on her son's face, as she replied. 'I don't know, Ally. Better than Frank is doing, I guess. He's not coping very well. He's like Joe, he needs to be doing something, helping in some way. It's hard for him, just having to watch and wait.'

'I just spoke to my parents. They're on their way here, and they're bringing Jake with them.'

His other grandmother turned towards me then, her eyes softening with love. 'That's good. Good for Jake, and good for all of us.'

I sighed, and went around to the other side of the bed and bent to kiss Joe's cheek. It felt warmer than it had done all night. That had to be an encouraging sign, didn't it? Was this the first indication of improvement that the doctors had been waiting for?

'Did you hear that, Joe? Jakey's on his way. You

don't want to still be asleep when he gets here, do you? Wake up now, sweetheart. Please wake up.'

'Maybe when he hears his little voice . . . ' Kaye sounded as though even she was struggling to believe her own words. I reached across the bed and squeezed her hand. 'He'd do anything for that boy. If there's anything in the world that can reach him, it's Jake.'

Charlotte

I took the tea she gave me gratefully. The news . . . well, I didn't take that quite so well.

'Here? Do you think that's a good idea? For him, I mean.'

Ally bristled physically, like an indignant porcupine, and I could hardly blame her for that. After all, what did I know about children? Nothing. Absolutely nothing.

'I think, as his mother, I'm the best judge of that.'

I bit my lip on all kinds of rejoinders that would blow our current truce to smithereens, as most of them would have brought into question her ability to determine what should — or should not — be told or kept secret.

'He needs to see his dad. *Joe*,' she added, quietly emphasising the name. Ally wasn't being exactly subtle. 'Don't worry,' she continued, 'I have no intention of letting David see him, or know he's here.'

I nodded. I wasn't about to start an argument,

but I *was* worried. Because if Jake looked as much like David in real life as he did in the photograph I'd seen, Ally was fooling herself if she thought she'd be able to keep his parentage secret. Somehow I didn't think she'd even considered that.

'Well, I just thought you should know, that's all.'

'Thank you for telling me.'

I waited until she had reached the door before I found the courage to ask her the one question that was burning through me like corrosive acid. It had been, since the moment she had disappeared into my husband's room. 'How did things go, with David I mean? Was it alright?'

She turned slowly, and looked at me for a long time, as though she were replaying their entire conversation in her mind. A small furrow appeared between her brows at the memory and part of me was dying to know what he had said to her, and the rest of me was far too scared to ask. Had he told her how he felt about her? How he'd always felt? I looked around the Relatives' Room in the bleak early morning light. It was a hell of a place to learn that you were 'the other woman' in your own marriage.

'It was fine. He was fine . . . well, obviously not fine physically. This operation he needs, it sounded serious. Is it?'

There was little point in lying. She could just as easily overhear a member of the medical team talking about it. 'Yes. Very serious.'

Ally looked shocked, and I realised then that

444

David must have played down the severity of his illness. For her protection? Possibly. Old habits always were the hardest to break.

12

Ally

He smelled of peanut butter, toast and little boy.
I inhaled it deeply, drinking it in like an addict.

'Mum, you're squishing me,' he complained.
Reluctantly I released him. I leant back on my
haunches, keeping us at eye level.

'Sorry, sweetie. I'm just happy to see you,
that's all.'

He grinned back, then seemed to remember
himself, for his smile faltered a little. 'When
Grandma said Granddad and I had to wait here,
I thought maybe you were going to come down
with Daddy?'

The wind was bitter, and although it had
finally stopped snowing, it was really far too cold
to be in a children's playground. But when my
mum had suggested it would be better for Jake if
I met him there, rather than inside the hospital, I
hadn't questioned her judgement.

'I thought maybe it was going to be a big
surprise, that Daddy had got all better.'

I exhaled slowly and heavily, looking up into
my father's eyes, as he stood protectively behind
his grandson. Where did I begin? How could you
prepare a small child for something like this? It
was wrong on so many levels. I wasn't equipped
for this.

'Oh honey, Daddy's still not feeling very well.'

My own dad looked down at me, and the sympathy on his face almost ripped apart the stitches that were holding me together. 'He's still . . . he's still asleep at the moment.'

'Still?' shrieked my seven-year-old to the empty playground. 'But it's getting light now and everything. He's *always* up first, before everyone. Has he been asleep since *yesterday?*'

I nodded, and watched the thought process flicker behind his eyes. As young as he was, Jake clearly realised that what I was saying was far too peculiar to be okay or normal.

'Yes, he has. You see, he did a very brave thing yesterday and he helped a little boy who was in trouble, but it kind of hurt him, because he was in really cold water. So his body has gone into a very, very deep sleep.'

'So it can get better?' Jake prompted, putting forward the only solution his mind was capable of supplying.

I hesitated for just one second too long, I don't think Jake noticed, but my father did, because he quickly interjected for me. 'That's right, my lad. You got it.'

I looked away, anxious that those perceptive blue eyes wouldn't read what was hiding in mine. I focused my attention on the tall, snow-covered slide, staring so intently that my eyes began to water from the effort. At least that's what I hoped Jake would think.

Finally I took a steadying breath and rose from my crouched position, taking hold of Jake's thickly mittened hands. 'Grandma explained to you that there's all sorts of funny machines in Daddy's room?'

Jake nodded impatiently, anxious for the first and only time in his short life, to leave a playground. 'I know all that, Mummy. Grandma says he looks like an astronaut in a rocket ship. Like he was going into deep space to another galaxy.' I sent up a silent prayer of thanks to my mother, with her ability to demystify an ICU ward to a child, and to *Star Wars* for making it something they could understand.

There was nothing left to say. No more preparations were going to make what was coming any easier. 'Let's go and see your dad then, shall we?'

Jake nodded happily, hopping eagerly from foot to foot as we stood at the pedestrian crossing waiting to go back through the hospital gates.

★ ★ ★

There was a lot to take in in those moments when we arrived back at Joe's room. To begin with, his parents and my mother were no longer in the room beside him, but were waiting in the hallway. Two doctors were examining Joe, their faces poker-player blank as they spoke. The tape had been removed from Joe's eyelids, and in turn both doctors gently lifted a lid and shone a light directly into his eyes. The nurse said something to them and they glanced back through the glass, noticing Jake, who was still busily greeting his other grandparents and had not yet seen we were already at his father's room.

I didn't like the unreadable expressions on the

doctors' faces as they nodded solemnly to each other. But even more than that, I didn't like the one on my mother's, who had been carefully watching their examination through the wall of glass.

'Mrs Taylor?' said the tallest of the white-coated doctors as he exited Joe's room. Both I, and the woman who had held that title for even longer, looked towards the medics anxiously.

'Yes. That's me.'

'We're going to come back in a little while to re-examine your husband, and then we will hopefully have some more information for you and your family.'

More stalling. More not telling me anything. Had it not been for Jake tugging impatiently on my hand I would have challenged them for answers straight away. But right at that moment my priorities were elsewhere.

'Daddy!' cried Jake, breaking free from my hand and bulleting into the room like a greyhound on a track. He got within half a metre of the bed and screeched to a halt, so abruptly that his plastic-soled sneakers squeaked noisily on the linoleum floor. His blue eyes widened as he looked at Joe, then at the tubes, wires and instruments, then finally at the bellows-like machine, undertaking the task his lungs had temporarily forgotten how to do.

None of the adults spoke as we silently filed back into the room behind him. We watched his small dark head turn to study each strange and alien object in turn, trying to make sense of something no child should ever have to see. I

449

turned in anguish to my mother, suddenly not at all sure that she'd been right about this. Her gentle nod of confirmation showed no such doubts. I guess she'd seen this all before.

'See, Jake,' she said gently, laying her hand upon his shoulder. 'Just like I told you. It's like *The Enterprise* or *The Millennium Falcon*.' He nodded solemnly, and I don't think I have ever been more impressed by my own mother. Jake had the coolest grandma ever.

Jake took tiny pigeon steps until he reached the side of the bed. Very tentatively he extended his arm and laid his hand upon the foot-shaped pinnacle hidden beneath the blanket. His small hand clasped Joe's ankle and he gently shook it backwards and forwards.

'Shake a leg, Daddy,' he whispered, repeating the words Joe roused him with each morning. 'It's time to get up.' He repeated the action several times, muttering the words under his breath like a precious litany. Finally Jake raised his head, looking at the faces of the people who loved him most in the world, before settling on mine. 'It's not working. I was so sure that's what he was waiting for.'

His eyes fell to his own cuddly toy, still sitting like a sentry at the foot of the bed. In a rare display of anger, my usually sweet-tempered child pushed the toy over, toppling it to the floor. 'Stupid Simba,' he muttered in disgust. I bit my lip, because that was the only way I was going to keep the sobbing from starting.

Jake gripped hold of the tightly tucked-in blanket covering his father, and slipped his

450

fingers through its open-weave holes. Before any of us could stop him, he hauled himself up onto the mattress, wriggling like a worm up the bed towards Joe.

'Jake — ' I said softly, but my voice was lost under the nurse's reproving tones.

'I'm sorry, but children aren't — '

My mother stepped in front of the nurse who was approaching the bed, presumably with the intention of bodily lifting my child from his father's side. 'It's fine,' she told the younger woman firmly. Turning to the bed, my mum expertly lifted and repositioned the medical paraphernalia to allow her grandson uninterrupted access. 'He just wants to cuddle his dad. I'll make sure he doesn't disturb anything.'

The nurse appeared uncertain, but my mother looked meaningfully into her eyes, and the nurse looked back at her, and I swear there was some unspoken conversation taking place, one that only they could understand.

'Oh well, I suppose there's no harm in it.'

My dad put his arm around his wife, and I don't think I imagined the look of pride in his eyes before they both looked down at Jake, who had now manoeuvred his way past all obstacles and was securely nestled against the immobile length of Joe's body. He laid his head on Joe's chest, which was rising and falling in perfect synchronicity with the respirator.

'Daddy, I know you're like a superhero for helping that other boy, but I really, really wish that his own daddy had gone into the water instead of you. It's not fair that you got hurt just because you were helping him.' Our son looked up at me, before sliding his arm across Joe's body and clinging to him like a limpet to a rock. He reached up to whisper into Joe's unhearing ear. 'I still need lots of help too, Daddy. I don't know how to do that special knot on my shoelaces.' His voice dropped even lower. 'And we're making Mummy that Christmas present, and you know I can't finish it by myself.'

Very gently I leant over the bed, laying my arms around the two men who were all I had ever wanted or needed. I heard Kaye begin to cry softly, before Frank led her gently out of the room, but I didn't turn around. I just kept holding on to the people I loved, praying that this wouldn't be the last time the three of us would be joined in this way.

Charlotte

I had just emerged from the Ladies', where I'd gone to splash some much-needed reviving cold water onto my face, when I heard the voice of a child. For just a single cowardly second, I considered ducking back inside the room I'd just left. But before I could, they rounded the corner and there stood Ally, holding the hand of the son that should have been mine.

In the flesh, the remarkable resemblance to his natural father was even more astounding. This was the same face, the same eyes, the same *everything* that I'd seen in numerous professional family portraits of David as a child, adorning the walls of his parents' home. Perhaps there were also albums somewhere, filled with more relaxed and fun-filled family snapshots rather than those posed ones; jumbled memories of Christmases, birthdays and holidays, although — knowing David's mother as I did — I somehow doubted that.

Thoughts of Veronica brought with them a feeling of gut-wrenching panic. I had no idea of her precise location, or even whether she was back in the country yet, but she was definitely on her way. And I had absolutely no way of knowing how she'd react if — or when — she saw her son's face reproduced in perfect detail on this small child's. I surprised myself with an inexplicable and unexpected urge to protect him from that encounter. Even more surprising, was the urge to protect Ally too.

'But *why* do I have to go to the zoo with Granddad? I want to stay here until Daddy wakes up.' There was just the trace of a whine behind the young boy's pleas.

'Sweetheart, you know that Daddy might be asleep for . . . well, for a long time yet, and you're only going to get bored and restless having to sit around in this boring old hospital all day. Besides, if you go to the zoo with Granddad, just think of all the exciting and wonderful things you'll have to tell Daddy when you come back later this afternoon. And Granddad said he's really looking forward to going. He hasn't been to a zoo in years, not since *I* was a little girl, and it would be such a shame to disappoint him.'

I liked the way Ally spoke to her child. She

didn't talk down to him, she just reasoned with him. Would I have known how to do that? No, of course not. I wouldn't have had a clue. I could negotiate a deal worth hundreds of thousands of pounds, go through a contract with a fine tooth comb, but I had no idea how to talk to a seven-year-old. Something that was just about to become abundantly clear, I realised, as they drew to a stop in front of me.

'Charlotte,' said Ally, her voice measured and controlled, but I saw the way her eyes flashed a protective warning and saw too the way she had unconsciously placed her body slightly in front of the small boy's. I'd seen that manoeuvre scores of times, but usually only on wildlife documentaries. It was the classic pose of a mother animal protecting its young; something else I knew absolutely nothing about.

I tried to smile and look relaxed, but I think I failed on both counts. I could feel my heart beginning to pound, and it was quite a shock to realise how nervous I had suddenly become. 'Hello. You must be Jake,' I said, my voice falsely cheery. I held out my hand to my husband's seven-year-old son.

Jake looked at it curiously for several moments, and then his eyes went to his mother, questioningly. I looked down at my own hand, still stupidly extended for a handshake. Ridiculous. Totally and utterly ridiculous. No wonder the boy looked bemused. Who greets a child of that age as though they'd just met them in the boardroom? A woman totally ill-equipped to be a parent, that's who.

To be fair, Ally did her best not to make me look stupid. 'Jake,' she urged gently, nodding towards my extended hand. 'You know what to do.'

His hand felt unbelievably soft and smooth within mine. And so small.

'Who is this, Mummy?' Jake whispered, as though I might not be able to hear him in the otherwise deserted corridor.

'This is Charlotte, she's one of my old friends from when I was at university,' Ally explained. I have to hand it to her; she didn't even hesitate before the word 'friend'.

'Is she here to see Daddy? To wish him better?'

Ally's eyes went to mine, and I read the unspoken plea within them.

'No, Jake. I didn't know your daddy was in this hospital. I'm here because my husband is sick too.'

Jake looked comically surprised at the coincidence, and it was such a miniature replica of a look I'd seen so many times on David's face that a small gasp got away from me. 'He didn't get hurt saving someone as well, did he?'

I shook my head sadly. 'No. Nothing as dramatic as that. He's just got . . . a poorly heart.' Was that too much of an over-simplification for a child of his age, or just about right? I was working in the dark here.

'Oh,' said the boy thoughtfully. 'Well, that's sad. I hope he gets better soon, then perhaps he and my daddy can share a room and then they'd both have someone to talk to.'

Ally and I exchanged an identical look.

'Well, maybe,' I said.

Ally placed her hand propriotarially on Jake's shoulder. 'Come on now, Jakey, Granddad will have got the car by now. It's time to go.'

'I'm going to see lots of animals at the zoo today,' Jake informed me conversationally. 'My granddad is taking me, but I really wish my dad could come along too.' I felt an ache deep inside me.

'I'm sure your daddy would give everything in the world to be able to take you to the zoo.'

I heard Ally's sharply indrawn breath at my words. I dropped down to a crouch, bringing myself to eye level with her child, wobbling a little on my over-priced red-soled designer heels. Yet another example of my unsuitability as a parent. What mother would wear shoes this impractical? 'It's been really nice meeting you, Jake. I hope I'll see you again one day.'

Ally didn't say anything, but the look she threw over her shoulder as she began to lead her son down the flight of stairs was a curious mixture of apprehension and gratitude.

Ally

I fell in love with Joe through Jake and because of Jake. Not because I needed a father for my child. If that was all I was after, I knew perfectly well where to go. No, it was rather that Jake threw a light onto Joe, onto the man he was, the man I wanted to spend my life with. I'd have seen it myself, sooner or later, but because of

Jake I just saw it much sooner and more clearly.

It was there even before our son was born. I can remember the first glimpse I had of my own future; it was on the day when Joe had given me a lift to the baby equipment store, where I was going to look at pushchairs. Yet again the cheap second-hand car I'd bought was back in the garage for repairs, a place it seemed to reside far more often than it did with me.

'It's no problem, I'm going to the bank anyway,' Joe assured me, removing a bundle of bills from a sealed envelope and sliding them into his wallet. For the last few weeks he'd been working each evening on another private job, and I was surprised at how empty the house had felt without him. It was as though something drained away from the place during his absence, leaving it sepia-coloured and curiously bland until his return. I dismissed the fanciful notion as yet another peculiar by-product of my pregnancy, right up there with heartburn and the need to visit the loo at least three times a night.

Joe pulled up in front of the shop, and while retrieving my handbag from the footwell I saw his eyes follow an approaching couple as they walked arm in arm towards the store, before the automatic doors slid open and swallowed them up. I straightened in my seat and noticed the trace of a frown marking the otherwise smooth space between his brows. It deepened as he observed a second couple standing on the pavement, their faces pressed close to the glass as they studied a window display of vintage cribs.

'Well, thanks for the lift. I don't know how

long I'm going to be, so why don't I just catch the bus back.' I expected him to drive straight off, but instead he unfolded his long frame from the van and walked around to the passenger door. 'Joe, honestly, you don't need to come in with me,' I protested, as he held out his hand to assist me from the vehicle. It was getting harder to do anything gracefully these days, given the size of my bump and the unexpected loss of my centre of gravity. Low sofas and cars were definitely the worst.

'I know you don't *need* my help,' he said, and there was a teasing trace in his voice, directed I'm sure at what he saw as my over-developed independent streak. 'But the bank's open for at least another hour, and I'm in no hurry. I'll just hang around by the door until you're done.'

Only he didn't. I'd left him waiting at the front of the store, while an assistant had led me towards the section of modestly priced foldaway buggies. I could feel Joe's eyes on both of us as we walked away, and I felt suddenly unattractive and cumbersome beside the pretty sales girl with her swinging blonde ponytail (*why are they always blonde?*) with the jeans that, unlike mine, were certain *not* to have an elasticated waistband. No wonder Joe couldn't resist staring, I thought as I glanced back at him over my shoulder. He was smiling, but I wasn't sure which one of us was the recipient. Her, I thought.

Twenty minutes later I was no closer to making a purchase. I'd just about decided that I might be better off searching through the local paper for a second-hand one, when I looked up and saw that Joe was crouched beside one of the most expensive pushchairs in the store, running his hands over the chassis, testing the wheels by spinning them beneath his hands, before lifting it from the display and pushing it along the carpeted aisle. He nodded to himself, before returning the pushchair to the stand and then proceeded to do exactly the same with the one beside it.

I hurried over to him. 'Er, Joe, what are you doing, exactly?' I glanced at my watch. 'And shouldn't you have left for the bank by now?'

'In a minute,' Joe replied easily. 'I just wanted to test drive a couple of these.' *What is it about men and things with wheels?* 'I like this one best,' Joe confirmed, nodding down at the extremely luxurious pushchair he was still holding. There was something about seeing his large capable hands firmly wrapped around the handles of the pram that prompted a very strange fluttery feeling inside me. Or was that just the price of the model which I'd glimpsed from the swinging tag? Surely they'd put the decimal point in the wrong place? That thing cost more than my car had done.

'Yeah, well, that's great, but I don't need one this fancy,' I said, feeling a little defensive. 'It's all whistles and bells.'

'Sounds perfect for a musician,' he quipped.

I nodded back towards the foldaway buggies I had been studying. 'One of those will do me just fine.'

Joe wheeled the pushchair back into place. 'Of

course. Whatever you think is best. Anyway, I'm just going to head off to the bank. I should be done in about twenty minutes.'

I took less than half that time to make my choice, but when I went up to the counter to place my order, the assistant looked surprised. 'I'm sorry. I hadn't realised you were buying two.'

'Sorry?'

'Two. Two pushchairs.'

'No. Just this one,' I corrected with a slightly bemused smile.

'But what about the one your husband paid for?'

She was clearly confusing me with another customer. Pretty she might be, but not very observant, I thought. However, when I glanced around the store I saw that I was now the only shopper within it.

'I . . . I don't understand. I don't have a husband.'

An annoyingly attractive blush flooded her cheeks. 'Sorry. Your partner, I mean. He's already paid for the Bugaboo De Luxe. Are you having this one as well?'

★   ★   ★

I'd challenged Joe about it, of course. But he'd been insistent. When I'd protested further, he even claimed it was more of an investment than a gift, and that the wheels of the ones I was looking at would have left marks all over his newly renovated floors. Joe somehow managed to make it sound as though spending the entire amount he had earned from his private job on a pram for my baby was just a sensible preventative measure, one that would save him from repair work in the future. But he wasn't fooling me. Not for a single minute.

★ ★ ★

As I hurried back to Joe's bedside, further memories scurried along behind me, each tapping me insistently on the shoulder as I walked, anxious that they too should not be forgotten.

There was the day when I'd walked down the length of the garden to the large outbuilding Joe used as a workshop, to find him working not on the custom-made cabinet doors I'd been expecting to see, but instead on an exquisitely carved swinging crib. He'd jumped — almost guiltily — when I'd eased open the door, the sound of my entry having been masked by the electric sander he was running backwards and forwards over the rails.

Absurdly, the sight of this man, who had no connection or responsibility to the child I was carrying, bent low in concentration over the beautifully crafted crib made me burst into unexpected tears. Joe turned off the sander and got to his feet.

'Ally, what is it, what's wrong?' I hadn't been able to speak, but instead I had nodded at the tiny piece of furniture, that in less than two months would hold my baby. 'Look, if you don't like it, if you want to get something more modern, I won't be offended. I just saw the ones in the shop the other day, and I thought . . . ' His voice trailed away as I crossed the distance between us to hug him. His arms went easily around me, despite the size of my bump.

'I love it,' I sniffled into the front of his shirt, which smelled of wood shavings, washing detergent . . . and him. 'It's perfect.'

★   ★   ★

But of all the memories clamouring to be heard, one had the loudest voice. It was the one when I first realised the feelings I had for Joe had strayed a very long way from the friendship which had brought me to him. It was several months after Jake had been born, and I had finally moved his crib out of my bedroom and down to the small nursery bedroom on the floor below. Joe and I had spent several weekends decorating the room, painting three walls a pale sky blue, with fluffy marshmallow-like clouds, and on the fourth Joe had skilfully created a beautiful fairy-tale mural. I can remember the odd little look my mother had given me after seeing the room. 'What?' I had asked. She had shaken her head, but there was a hint of a smile on her lips, as though she knew a secret she wasn't yet ready to share.

The baby monitor had crackled to life in the middle of the night at Jake's first grumbling cry, and I had stumbled sleepily from my bed, thrusting my arms into my dressing gown. I crept barefoot down the stairs without turning on the hall light, anxious not to wake Joe, whose room was across the landing from Jake's. But he was already awake. As I padded across the wooden boards I saw Joe, his back to the door, gently cradling my baby in his arms. Dressed only in pyjama bottoms, it was hard not to stare at the interplay of muscles across his naked back and arms as, with infinite gentleness, he rocked my child back to sleep. His voice was low and whispering in the darkness, and so incredibly tender as he soothed the baby. Something happened in that moment, when I saw my tiny infant with his shock of dark hair and bright blue eyes, staring intently into the face of the man who was smiling lovingly down at him. Very quietly, in a voice that would never make it past a choir audition, I heard Joe softly humming the Brahms lullaby I soothed Jake to sleep with each night. And that was the moment, there in the darkness of the hall, hidden from sight behind the thick oak door, *that* was the moment when I fell in love with him.

★ ★ ★

We took it in turns to sit with Joe throughout the morning, although every moment I spent away from his side left me desperately watching the clock, willing the minutes to fly past until I could return. Above the noise of the ward coming to life, I could almost hear the scratchy trickle of sand in an hourglass, slipping through my fingers.

463

When Frank and Kaye returned to the Relatives' Room earlier than expected midway through the morning, I was already on my feet, anxious to reclaim the seat they had just vacated. Frank stilled me with an age-marked hand, which he laid upon my arm. There was an alarming tremor in his hold, and I was worried about this new occurrence. It was my job to look after both of them, until Joe was able to take up that role once more. It was what he would expect, and I did it willingly.

'The doctors are back with him again. They asked us to wait in here. They said they'd come to see us when they were done.'

I heard a slight rustling from behind me and knew, without even looking, that my mother had straightened in her seat.

We sat in silence. Waiting. The table was littered with drained coffee-stained Styrofoam cups, and rounds of unappetising cellophane-wrapped sandwiches, which no one had the stomach to open, much less eat. I had passed one to Charlotte, when she had returned briefly to the Relatives' Room. She had looked at it for a long time, as though she had forgotten what food was, or hunger. Then she had smiled distract-edly, and slipped the packet into her designer handbag, where I could practically guarantee it was still sitting, uneaten.

At seventeen minutes and twenty seconds past ten, my world changed.

The door to the Relatives' Room opened and the two doctors who I recognised as having been the physicians who had examined Joe earlier,

464

stood at its opening. 'Mrs Taylor, I wonder if we could have a word with you now?' I remember waiting for them to enter the room, but instead the younger of the two men looked at me, and everything I didn't want to see was written in his eyes. 'Please come with us. It will be easier to talk somewhere a little quieter with more privacy,' he suggested, as an orderly trundled past, pushing an overloaded laundry cart.

'My in-laws, Joe's parents, can they come too?' Whose voice was that, it certainly didn't sound like mine.

'But of course.' The doctor smiled kindly at the elderly couple.

We fell in step behind them, a reluctant triad, shell-shocked and wounded even before the explosion went off.

'What about Joe?' Kaye cried, clutching at my hand, her fingers bone brittle but surprisingly strong. 'Joe's alone. We can't *all* go and leave him. Someone should stay with him. What if he wakes up and we're not there?'

'*I'll* sit with Joe until you get back, Kaye,' my mother said kindly, and although there wasn't much between them in calendar years, my mother sounded decades younger. But when we followed the doctors as they led us off the ICU ward, I glanced back gratefully at my mum making her way towards Joe's bedside, and saw she was quietly crying. I knew then what was coming. Knew it, in every fibre of my body.

I couldn't tell you what the room they led us to looked like. I have no idea why they deemed this to be a preferable location. Were the more comfortable chairs meant to cushion the blow of what they were about to say? The physicians introduced themselves, but I have no recollection of their names. They offered us glasses of water from a pitcher on a low table, but we all declined. I doubt any of us were capable of holding one without spilling it everywhere. One of the doctors poured water in the three upturned glasses anyway, and the slow splash as they filled was yet another torturous delay, although it could only have taken a matter of seconds.

The wait was agony, made worse because I already knew what they were about to say. I remember looking up at the ceiling, seeing an invisible guillotine about to fall. I needed them to tell me. To tell me right now. To end the awful not-knowing of it all.

'Mrs Taylor, we are most dreadfully sorry. But we are afraid it is not good news.'

'Nooooo.' The word was an anguished wail, and for one horrible moment I thought it had come from me, but it hadn't. The sound was from Joe's mother who was bent double in her chair, her thin, stick-like arms cradled around her body, as though she could protect it from a blow that no woman her age should have to bear. I was aware of Frank leaving his own chair and going to his wife, burying her face against his body. His gnarled fingers threaded like a skeleton's hand through her tight grey curls.

The doctors were kind. It was clear they had done this many times before. They gave us the news in small portions, allowing us time to take in their words. But I felt like a boxer in a ring, defenceless against an opponent who was battering them down with unstoppable blows.

'But he's still *breathing*. We were just with him. Our boy's still breathing. I saw it.'

The doctor leaned across and laid his hand on Frank's shoulder. 'The *ventilator* is breathing for him. It's keeping his heart beating, keeping the blood flowing through his body. But when we briefly removed Joe from the machine a short while ago, he was unable to breathe alone.'

'But he just needs time. He needs more time to get better. You hear about these things all the time. They're on the news. They make the papers. People are in comas for years and years and then, one day they just wake up. And they're fine . . . ' Frank's voice faltered and then cracked. 'They're absolutely fine.'

I couldn't help him, and I knew that Joe's parents had failed to take in all that the doctors had so carefully told us. They hadn't heard, because the reality was just too terrible.

'Please, can you explain it to us again? These tests . . . these brain stem tests you've done. What if they're wrong?'

The two doctors looked at me, shaking their heads sadly. 'We have both independently examined Joe twice now, and regrettably our findings are conclusive. There is no perceivable brain activity. However, we will certainly examine him again, if that's what you wish, although I don't want to give you false hope. Your husband shows no sign of recoverable life.'

Charlotte

I hadn't expected that meeting Ally's son would affect me quite as badly as it did. I needed every one of the five minutes I remained in the deserted stairwell before returning to David. I had to be sure I could trust myself not to run into his room and blurt out something ridiculous like *'You won't believe this, but I've just met the child you never knew you had.'* But when I saw how unwell he looked, I knew there was no way I could risk saying anything that could cause him a single moment of stress or anxiety. When he's better, when he's stronger, *that's* when I'll tell him, I promised myself, speaking firmly over the voice that quietly asked: *What if he doesn't get better? What if you lose him . . . and he never gets to know that a part of him will always live on?*

I pressed my fingertips against my closed lids, as though to dispel the image of a small boy with my husband's eyes, which was burned into the back of my retina like a negative.

'Bad day at the office?' asked David, his hand pulling the oxygen mask from his face as he spoke.

Very gently I repositioned the mask, my fingers lingering in his thick, dark hair. 'You could put it like that.'

'You should go home, get some rest,' David said on a breathy gasp. 'You look tired.'

'You should stop talking nonsense,' I countered. 'I leave when you leave.'

My heart constricted painfully when his eyes

468

went to mine, the love in them threatening to break me. 'How did I get so lucky as to find you?'

★   ★   ★

I was re-filling David's water jug in the main ward when I noticed Ally and her in-laws being led from the unit by two doctors. For no reason at all, I felt my heartbeat skip and quicken, and the sharp taste of bile rose in my throat. There was something about the sad procession that was impossible to ignore; it was there in the droop of Ally's shoulders, and the way she supported the arm of the elderly woman beside her. It seemed almost inconceivable that I should care this much about what was happening to her. But I did.

★   ★   ★

The nurses talking at the desk had their backs to me. I wasn't intending to eavesdrop, and they clearly had no idea I was there, or they never would have spoken so candidly. Their words carried and suddenly the background noise of the ward faded away to nothing.

'He's got a son, you know. Cute little thing. He doesn't look any older than eight at the most.'

They weren't talking about David, I was almost sure of it, but still my footsteps slowed to a crawl, keeping me within earshot.

'Oh, has he? That's terrible.'

What? I wanted to interject. *What's terrible?* But I knew I was likely to learn more by remaining silent than by asking questions.

'Have the family been told?'

'They're doing it now.'

My fingers tightened around the white plastic handle of the water jug, and the liquid within it slopped dangerously. Small trickles escaped from the spout and ran over my hand, dripping down to the floor, and I never even noticed them.

'What will happen now?'

'The usual.'

'God, that's so sad. It makes you want to go home and hug your family, doesn't it?'

'Every time. Every single time.'

★ ★ ★

Tears, unexpected and red hot, rained silently from my eyes as the meaning of their words became clear. I let them fall unchecked. They slid from my cheeks and dripped like raindrops on to the spilled water at my feet.

Ally

'We'll come and talk to you again. In a little while,' one of the doctors said. I got shakily to my feet, then had to steady myself against the back of the chair, for the room was now a centrifuge, spinning wildly around me. I saw Joe's parents flash past, locked together in a grief-struck embrace; I saw the white-coated

470

physicians, their features a blur of sympathy; I saw the door and headed unsteadily towards it. I had to get out of there. I had to leave.

This was what I'd been fearing; it's what I'd been dreading every single second since the policemen had first come knocking at our front door. On some level I should have been better prepared than this. Yet still the shock of it, the realisation that my very worst nightmare was about to become my new reality was almost too much to absorb.

There was a hole opening up inside me, a huge yawning space where Joe belonged, and as much as I tried, as much as I loved him, I wasn't going to be able to fill it or hold on to him, because I was losing him — had already lost him — if what they said was true.

'Can I see him now?' I asked, my voice shaking. 'I really need to see him now. I can still do that, can't I?'

'Yes, of course. Let me take you back.'

But I was at the door before he could reach me. I was through it and half stumbling, half running back down the corridor. Frank and Kaye were temporarily forgotten, erased from my thoughts by the burning need to return to Joe. While I still could.

I collided with a tall figure just inside the entrance to the ward. He was an immobile wall of lean muscle dressed in a dark woollen coat, wheeling an expensive Samsonite suitcase. His arms went around me and I noticed distractedly that his coat was damp. It must be snowing again.

471

'Ally. Ally, slow down, it's me.'

I flung my arms around his neck, his expensive cologne not quite masking the lingering aroma of numerous cups of coffee, nor the musty traces of a man who had travelled halfway across the world to be with me.

'Max, oh Max. You're here. Thank God you're here.'

'How's Joe? How's he doing?'

My mouth was against his shoulder, I opened it to speak, but instead of words a sound came from it, the cry of an animal in pain.

Max gasped, and his arms tightened around me. 'Am I too late? Have I got here too late?'

'There's been no change at all since they brought Joe in,' I replied brokenly. There was a moment of relief on my old friend's face. A moment when — even then — he still didn't grasp what I was saying. 'And there won't be. That's what they've just told me. So no, you're not too late. There's still time to see him . . . and say goodbye.'

★　★　★

We entered Joe's room together and my mother leapt from her chair, her arms encircling me. She rocked me against her, and I clung to her in a way I hadn't done in decades. There was no need to tell her what the doctors had said. She'd known it anyway, even before I did.

'I am so sorry, Ally. I can't believe this is happening.'

'Could we get another opinion? Is there a

specialist somewhere? Anywhere? They don't have to be in this country. We could fly them in from wherever.'

There was a sad smile on my mother's face as she turned to the man she had known since he was a little boy. 'Hello, Max. It's so good to see you again. Thank you for coming. Ally needs you.'

I wanted to pull away from her then, in denial. It wasn't Max I needed, it was Joe. *I* needed him, *Jake* needed him, his *parents* needed him. But none of that mattered, because we were all going to lose him anyway. Soon, horribly and heartbreakingly soon, the people who loved and needed Joe most were going to have to make the hardest decision of our lives and turn off the machines that were keeping him with us.

★ ★ ★

They let us stay with Joe, all five of us, and somehow the suspension of the 'two-visitors-at-a-time' rule was the final underscore of proof that time was running out. Joe's parents sat on one side of his hospital bed, and I sat on the other, my husband's hand clasped in mine, the way it should have been allowed to do for the next fifty years or so. Max was brilliant, getting us whatever we needed, and showing no sign of jet lag or exhaustion. And when he wasn't running errands, he would simply stand behind my chair like a sentry, his hand resting lightly upon my shoulder, just letting me know he was there for me. It helped. A little.

The doctors conducted their third and final

examination just before noon, and I don't think any of us were surprised at the outcome.

'We are so very sorry . . . ' they began, joining our small sad assembly in the Relatives' Room.

'Has everything been done that could be done?' asked Max into the hushed silence left in the wake of the doctors' words. 'I don't want to sound crass here, but if it's a question of money, or — ' The doctors didn't appear to take offence. They were probably well used to the frantic grasping-at-straws by family and friends.

'Mr Taylor's condition was extremely grave from the moment he first got here. Our efforts to revive him have been exhaustive.' The doctor turned in the seat he had taken beside me, and gently laid his hand over mine. His voice softened. 'We've tried so hard to save him, because we know why he was here. A young boy lives, only because of your husband's bravery. We really didn't want to lose this fight, you have to know that.'

My throat twisted to a close, allowing no words to escape, but I nodded fiercely at him through my tears, believing his obvious sincerity.

'I know this is a difficult and terrible time for all of you, but there are decisions that you now have to make, as a family.' My eyes went to my in-laws, who were facing the loss of their only son. On their faces, in their eyes, in everything about them, the sheer *wrongness* of the situation was plainly visible. They were old. They were meant to go first. No parent — ever — should outlive their child, especially not ones in their seventies.

'With your permission,' the doctor continued, 'someone from the hospital will be along to talk to you in a little while. Someone from another team.' My mother, who was sitting beside me, suddenly slipped an arm around my shoulders and pulled me against her. I realised that, yet again, she knew what was coming. 'A member of the transplant team would like to meet with you.' He paused. 'You *were* aware that your husband carried a donor card in his wallet, I assume?'

★ ★ ★

The resistance came from somewhere unexpected, as did the approval. 'I don't bloody believe it. I'm sorry, Ally, they sound like vultures. For Christ's sake, Joe's not even gone and they want to talk to you about . . . about that,' exploded Max when the doctors had gone.

'That's the way they have to do it, son,' replied Frank quietly. Tears were running openly down his face, and he did nothing to wipe them away. 'That's the only way it works. They have to keep everything . . . working . . . until, until . . . the last moment.' His hand groped blindly for Kaye's, and found it.

'I don't know,' I said, feeling the weight of an impossible decision I should never be having to make, cleaving my already shattered heart in two. 'I don't think I can give them permission to . . . ' I gulped, trying to find the words. 'I mean, yes, I know he carried a card, but still . . . '

'It's what he wanted.' Hearing those words

from the woman who had brought Joe into the world was somehow doubly shocking. Kaye reached into her handbag and pulled out an embroidered handkerchief, dabbing it ineffectively at her red-rimmed eyes, before turning to her husband. 'Ever since he was a little boy, not much older than Jake is now. It's what he said he wanted. Ever since Eric. He had to wait until he was older of course, but he never forgot, not once.'

Small fragments of a long past conversation started coming back to me then, twisting and turning through the thousands of other memories. 'His uncle,' I said, realisation dawning, as the details began to crystallise.

Frank smiled, although his tears still showed no signs of slowing. I wondered if they ever would. 'He told you, then? He told you about my older brother, about Eric. He'd been ill all his life, but it got worse when Joe was no more than a lad. My brother never married, never had a family of his own, but he thought the world of our boy, and the feeling was mutual. Eric had a kidney transplant when Joe was about eight or so; it saved his life. From then on, Joe always said that if anything ever happened to him, he would want to be a donor. Quite insistent about it he was, as I recall.' Frank turned to look at his wife, and I could see the image of their small earnest child shining brightly in their memories almost as clearly as they could. It wasn't hard, because he was replicated in almost every last detail in our own son.

Frank closed his eyes, and despite everything I

476

could count the cost of his next words. 'Obviously Ally, you're his wife and you have to make your own decision. But as far as his mother and I go,' he turned to Kaye and she nodded, giving him her agreement. 'Well, we would want to honour Joe's wishes. Let some good come out of this terrible tragedy. Let him do what he's done for all of his wonderful and amazing life. Let Joe help someone.'

★   ★   ★

The woman from the transplant team was quietly spoken, respectful and compassionate, yet meeting with her was — without doubt — one of the worst things I have ever had to do. She explained the procedure in detail, and told us how many people would benefit from Joe's generosity (those were her words, not mine). Up to eight lives could be saved if I said 'yes', she carefully informed me. So that would be nine senseless deaths if I said 'no', I realised sadly, if you included Joe's. But it wasn't just about the maths, I knew that.

Max was the only one to accompany me to the meeting with the Specialist Nurse from the Organ Donation team. Joe's parents, for all their bravery, had quietly declined when I'd asked them. Max held my hand tightly gripped within his own throughout the interview, and I was grateful for the practical questions he thought to ask, because I was hanging on by a thread already stretched to breaking point, and there was still so much to decide. When the nurse produced a large sheaf of papers that would require my signature, I know Max felt my entire body stiffen in terror beside him.

'How soon do you need our answer?' he asked. 'Can we have a day or two to think about this?'

The woman's eyes were sympathetic as she shook her head regretfully. 'I am afraid there's no easy way to say this, but the sooner you are able to arrive at a decision, the better it will be, not just for the organ recipients, but also for you and your family. Obviously no one is trying to rush you into something you are not comfortable with, but the successful outcomes we would hope to achieve from the donation diminish dramatically the longer we wait. Time is against us here and — as always — there are significantly more people waiting for an organ transplant than there are suitable donors. Indeed, on this very ward there is a patient whose own survival depends on him being matched with a suitable donor.'

I froze at her words. I looked at Max, aghast, and for just a moment he didn't understand the look on my face, then his frown of puzzlement turned into a look of incredulity.

'Here, on the ICU? Another patient on this ward is in need of a transplant?' The Specialist Nurse looked more than a little taken aback at my question, or perhaps it was the horrified look in my eyes. 'You don't mean David, do you? David Williams?' The woman was looking distinctly uncomfortable now.

'I'm sorry, Mrs Taylor, but I'm not permitted to discuss another patient's condition with you.

It was insensitive of me to mention it, and I can only apologise.'

I closed my ears to her words of remorse. She *had* to mean David. There *were* no other patients on the ward except him and Joe. So it had to be David she was talking about. David was the person who was in desperate need of some poor grieving family (*but not ours*) making the decision to let a vital part of them (*his heart, for God's sake, we were talking about his heart*) do something incredible after their loved one had gone. But not Joe, never Joe. That was too much to ask of anyone.

Somewhere, from far away, I could hear Max asking the Specialist Nurse the exact question that I never would have been able to voice. 'Are you saying that Joe's heart could go to the other patient on this ward, to David Williams?'

The nurse took a beat before answering, and I'm sure she could feel the intensity of two pairs of eyes glaring at her as she spoke. 'No. No, of course not. There are a great many factors which are taken into consideration when organs are allocated. First and foremost, consideration is given to patients who most urgently need a transplant, but many other things need to match — or be very close — to ensure a successful organ transplant: blood group, age and weight, all of these are taken into account.' The nurse smiled kindly. 'The chances of two patients being on the same ward and one being eligible and suitable for an organ transplantation from the other, well . . . well, the odds of that happening are infinitesimally small.'

Infinitesimally small, I thought, as I took the literature the nurse had handed me and allowed Max to lead me from the room. How infinitesimal? Was that in any way comparable to the odds of finding the man you first fell in love with, and the man you love now both being desperately ill in the same hospital on the same night? Ridiculous odds that defied all explanation or logic were something I had already learned to accept.

13

Charlotte

I walked into the Relatives' Room and stopped in my tracks. I hadn't expected anyone to be in there, and certainly not Ally. If I were in her position I would be spending every single minute at my husband's bedside, not sitting alone in this small room, poring over a sheaf of forms and pamphlets. Only she wasn't alone; I realised that when a blur of movement from the corner of the room caught my attention. A man stood there. He was tall and stylishly fashionable, from his trendily cut hair to his undoubtedly expensive soft leather boots. He looked vaguely out of place, as though he'd been plucked from an environment far more colourful and exotic and dropped into this drab grey hospital ward by mistake.

He spun around and looked at me. I can't say his expression was entirely welcoming.

I turned to the other occupant of the room. Ally had paused, her pen still gripped within her clenched fingers. Her cheeks were damp and her eyes looked defeated.

'Ally, I . . . I . . . ' I had no idea what to say to her. In truth, it frightened me to get close to her, to that raw and exposed pain, because I knew how easily I could be the one in her position. How I still might be. I took a step towards her,

481

aware that the mysterious man in the corner had matched it with one of his own.

'I heard the terrible news . . . about Joe. I'm so very sorry.' She didn't ask who had told me, I doubt that she even cared. I reached out hesitantly, my hand hovering in the space between us, before I laid it upon her bowed shoulder. I could feel the man's eyes scrutinising me like a laser. Who *was* he?

As I leant in closer, Ally swept the forms she had been in the process of signing a little further away from me, sliding them down the length of the low table. But she was too late. Even upside-down I had easily been able to read the heading on the topmost form. The words Organ Donation seemed to leap at me off the page, and in response my heart leapt right back on seeing them. I was suddenly aware of the need to tread very carefully here.

'How are you doing?'

There was so much pain in her eyes it was hard to meet them. It was like looking directly at an eclipse, if you did it for too long, you would do damage. 'Not good,' she admitted.

'If there's anything I can do — '

'We've got it covered. Thank you,' interrupted the man, walking yet another step closer to Ally. There was just a hint of an accent in his voice.

'Well. If you need me to do anything. Get anything for you . . . ?'

Ally nodded and the man bridged the final distance between them, putting his hand on her shoulder, on the exact spot where my own had just lain.

'How's Jake?' I asked. 'This must be so dreadful for him.' It was totally the wrong thing to have said, I knew that instantly from the tightening of Ally's mouth and the small exhaled hiss from her companion.

'Ally and her family will take good care of Jake. You don't need to worry about my godson.' There was something in his words that told me that this man — whoever he was — knew all about David's connection to Jake.

I was silent for a long moment, mentally regrouping. I needed to speak to Ally. I needed to ask her something, and I was pretty certain that I wasn't going to be able to do it with this guy watching over her like a bodyguard. Don't get me wrong, I was glad that she had the support of so many people around her, given the awful way things had turned out, but their presence didn't make it any easier for what I wanted — no, for what I *had* — to do now.

'Ally, I know this is a living nightmare for you. But could I have a word with you?' I paused for a second. 'Alone.'

Ally raised her head. It seemed as though even that was an effort, and for a moment I wondered whether this was the right time to do this? But if not now, then when? There would *never* be a right time for this conversation. It simply didn't exist.

'Whatever you have to say to Ally, you can say in front of me, Charlotte.'

I gasped. Well, he certainly knew every bit as much of our history as I had suspected. I saw the look in his eyes and realised that he knew something else too. He knew what I was about to ask her.

'It's a personal matter. Private,' I said, trying to hold firm on the quicksand I was currently standing on.

'I'm sorry. I didn't travel three-and-a-half thousand miles to be with Ally to leave her alone now. You're either going to have to speak in front of me, or not say anything at all.' His tone made it perfectly clear which option he hoped I would take.

It wasn't going to happen. He was tough, I could see that. But then so was I. And this was too important to let him silence me. I dropped down into the seat directly in front of Ally. I needed her to be able to see my face when I asked this question, as much as I needed to be able to see hers.

It took several minutes before she raised her eyes to mine, waiting. I think she'd needed that time to brace herself. In the seconds that passed before I spoke I looked at her, *really* looked at her. She was the woman he had loved first. She was the one who had claimed his heart before I reached it. And she was the one who had broken it. She lived on in a part of him that I had never been able to reach. He still thought I didn't know this, but of course I did. What wife wouldn't? For years I had resented the pretty brunette sitting in front of me. Resented her, feared her, and at times even hated her. What if their paths crossed again? Would the love I knew he had for me be strong enough to hold him? Or would the ties that had linked him to her prove

484

even stronger? Were his feelings for her reciprocated in any way? Did she still think of him? Did she ever wonder . . . *what if?* Did she still love him? For years I had been terrified the answer to those questions might be yes, she did. Today everything I lived for, everything I prayed for, hinged on the hope that she did.

Ally

It was a bright and cheery room. The walls were covered in vibrantly painted murals. There were toys everywhere, stacked in overflowing colourful crates in each corner, and the floor was dotted with beanbags and vivid neon-coloured cubes to sit on.

I blinked, waiting for the fluorescent lights to finally stop flickering before stepping into the day room. The Specialist Nurse beside me, her hand still on the light switch, surveyed the room briefly and then turned to face me. 'Do you think this will do?'

I looked around the room, imagining it as it must be during the daytime, full of small courageous children from the adjacent ward, ignoring their bandages, plaster casts or drips they were attached to, bravely disregarding their pain to play among the donated toys. I could think of no better location to do this.

I turned to the nurse. 'Yes. This will be perfect. Thank you for suggesting it.'

'I'm happy to stay, if you would like, if you think it might help,' she offered once again. I slowly shook my head.

'I think it will be better for Jake if there are just the people he knows and loves here,' Max affirmed politely. He softened the rebuff with a small smile. 'No offence.'

'None taken.' The nurse consulted her watch. 'Well, I'd best get back to the ICU. You know where to find me if you need me.' She paused at the threshold and looked back at Max and me, standing incongruously in this overly happy, overly jolly room. There was sympathy in her eyes. 'Good luck,' she said gently.

My dad had phoned; he was on his way back from the zoo, bringing with him a very tired and excitable boy. A boy whose world I was about to shatter. It made me want to run; to put as much distance as possible between myself and the dreadful thing I had to do. But I couldn't do that. I owed it to Joe, and the son he had raised as though he was his own, to do this thing as well as I could. I'd sat at Joe's bedside, trying to stretch the last hours we had together to fill a lifetime of memories, and wished I could draw on his strength. *Joe* would have known the words to use, *he* would have found a way to lessen the crippling cruelty of the blow. But for me they remained painfully elusive. I had no idea what to say to my own child. Perhaps it would have helped if my head wasn't still so full of the dreadful conversation I'd had with Charlotte earlier. Although several hours had passed, the scene kept repeating on me, like I'd eaten something bad that refused to stay down.

'How can you ask that of me?' My voice was

shaking with disbelief.

'How can I not?' she had countered.

'Have you no compassion? No sensitivity at all? Can you *hear* how unbelievably cruel it is, even to have suggested it?'

She was crying then. We both were. 'I'm sorry Ally, but I'm fighting here to keep the man I love alive. You'd do exactly the same thing if the tables were turned.'

Would I? Somehow I didn't think that I would. 'Anyway,' I had said, gesturing towards the pile of papers on the table before me. 'It doesn't work like that. Computers decide where the . . . the donations . . . go. There's a register, there's a list of priorities.'

'I know all about that,' Charlotte had replied, and I realised then that this had not been some spur-of-the-moment request. She had done her research. 'But in America they have something called 'Designated Donation', where you can request that your loved one's organs go to a specific individual.'

'Yes, well, we're not in America now, are we?' Max's voice was glacier cold. It was the first time he had spoken since Charlotte had made her outrageous request.

She had thrown him a quick, dismissive glance before turning back to me. 'It's rare, admittedly, even over there. But I've been looking into this; I've been on the internet all morning.' *I bet you have*, I thought bitterly. 'The next-of-kin can make a request, even in the UK. You can ask that David is considered as the recipient, and if his condition is serious enough, if no one else has a higher priority, then they'll try to follow your wishes.'

'These aren't my wishes,' I cried in desperation. 'They're yours. None of this is what I want.' I was breathing raggedly, each indrawn gulp struggling to fill my lungs with enough air to continue. 'I don't want to choose where Joe's organs go, I don't even want to know. Let the doctors decide. That's the way it's meant to be.'

'None of this is the way it's *meant to be*. You're not meant to lose Joe, not like this.' There was real and genuine pain in Charlotte's voice. 'And I'm not meant to lose David. I can't help him. I can't save him. But you *can*.'

'Don't ask me to do this, Charlotte. It's more than anyone should be asked.'

She looked lost for a minute, all her arguments, all her lines of attack stripped away. 'I'm not asking for me. I'm asking for David. If he ever meant anything to you — ' Max made a sound then, like a low warning rumble of thunder. 'And what about Jake? Have you thought about him? Does he really deserve to lose *two* fathers in one night?'

'And we're done,' cut in Max angrily, stepping in between us like a referee 'Okay, Charlotte, that's enough. You've said your piece. I really think you should leave now, before I do or say something I won't be proud of.'

★ ★ ★

Telling Jake broke me. I knew that it would. He had come dashing through the glass swing doors of the day room, my dad several metres behind him. Jake's eyes scanned the room, saw me and then saw the tall shape of a man standing in the corner. 'Daddy!' he cried. Max turned around and I watched the joy on my child's face melt away and then reappear as he recognised the other person with me. 'Uncle Max! What are *you* doing here?'

Max scooped him up in his arms, in a way no seven-year-old would normally tolerate, but Jake flew to him like a miniature torpedo. Somewhere mid-hug, mid-gleeful exclamations, the oddness of it all filtered through to my far-too-observant child. Max slowly lowered him back onto his feet, but Jake's eyes didn't leave his face.

'Why are you here? Mummy never said you were coming. We always know when you're going to visit us.'

Max's eyes went to mine over the top of Jake's thick shock of dark hair. Very slowly Jake turned to me. 'Is it because of Daddy? Is Uncle Max here because of Daddy being on all those machines?'

He saw me hesitate. Saw me swallow deeply before answering. 'Yes, sweetie. Uncle Max came because I told him how sick Daddy is and he wanted to be with us. To help us.'

'Help us? Why do we need help? Daddy just needs to have a bit longer to sleep and then he'll wake up. And he'll be all better again. That's right, isn't it?' Jake turned to my father who was standing by the door, his face stricken. Finding no response, Jake turned back to his godfather with less certainty in his voice. 'That's right?' Max looked in actual physical pain. Finally Jake

489

looked at me. 'Mummy . . . Mummy, just how sick *is* Daddy?'

And here it was. The moment no parent, even in their worst nightmare, is prepared to face. I opened my arms and Jake went into them. I wanted to hold him close, to protect him, yet I was the one about to do damage. 'Jakey, Daddy was hurt much worse than we realised at first.'

'He's sleeping.'

A knife went through me, all the way through. 'That's what we thought at first. That's what we all *hoped*. But it turns out . . . ' My voice began to break, and I couldn't allow that. I bit down on my lip, so hard that I tasted blood. I saw Max take a step towards us, but I shook my head and he froze in his tracks. This was my task. Mine alone. 'It turns out Daddy's body was really badly hurt. Deep inside him.'

'He's just sleeping, you'll see.'

A second knife joined the first.

'No he's not, sweetheart. I wish he was, but he's not. Daddy was really brave and he went into the cold water to save that little boy. And now you're going to have to be really brave too.'

There was a long, long, terrible silence. Jake broke it first. 'Daddy's not going to wake up, is he?'

Peripherally I saw both Max and my father coming towards us. There is a need to consolidate, to unite, when something terrible is coming. But sometimes, however many loved ones stand beside you, you can't stop the onslaught from felling you.

'No, Jake. He isn't.'

★ ★ ★

You say goodbye to the people you love thousands of times in a lifetime: every time they walk out of the front door; every time you hang up the phone; every waved farewell. You just never know which of those goodbyes is going to be the last one. You aren't *supposed* to know. Except that we did.

'Tonight?' Kaye's voice was a hushed whisper. 'They're going to do it tonight?'

My arms went around her, and I could feel the tremors running through her insubstantial frame. 'I think they have to . . . if he's going to help as many people as possible.' That was the only way I could think about it, not what was being taken from us, but what Joe was giving to others.

The remaining hours of the day passed by in a horrible state of limbo. I guess somewhere donors were being sourced, families who had given up hope were receiving a phone call, a summons to a hospital somewhere that would change their future. Our own had already changed beyond all recognition.

Late in the afternoon, Frank had subtly motioned for me to step outside of the hospital room, so we could talk. I disentangled my fingers from Joe's with aching reluctance. Every moment spent away from his side was a moment lost, a moment never to be regained.

My father-in-law seemed to have aged at least another decade over the course of the day. His skin was greyer, his eyes more washed out, even his voice seemed diminished. 'Kaye and I have discussed it . . . and I don't think we can stay here until . . . until the very end. I don't think his mum's strong enough to get through that.'

I reached for Frank's hands and squeezed them gently. His skin felt hot and dry, the concertina of wrinkles on them crumpled, like thin sheets of tissue paper. I was worried by how vulnerable he suddenly seemed. It wasn't just Kaye who would buckle if they stayed. They both would.

'I understand, Frank. Really I do. You stay only as long as you can, and when it's all too much, then you and Kaye should just go. Joe wouldn't want you suffering like this.'

Joe's parents said their final goodbyes to their son in private. My mum and dad had taken Jake down to the canteen to buy him something that I was pretty certain he wouldn't eat, and Max and I went to wait in the Relatives' Room. Thankfully it was empty, which was just as well, as my appetite for meeting Charlotte right then was probably on a par with my son's for chicken nuggets and pizza.

'Do you think they'll be alright, Joe's parents?' asked Max, holding my hand tightly in his own.

I shook my head sadly. 'I honestly don't know.' My eyes filled as I imagined Kaye, leaning over the hospital bed to kiss her son goodbye for the very last time. Something sharper than a knife gouged into my heart as I realised that before the evening was through, I would do the same thing.

'The car's downstairs waiting for them. It'll take them back home, or wherever they want to go, whenever they're ready.'

'Thanks Max.' I squeezed his fingers a little more tightly. 'I don't know how I'd have got through today without you.'

His smile was gentle. He raised a hand and brushed a straying lock of hair back from my eyes. 'You're strong, Ally. Stronger than you know. You'll get through this, and you'll help Jake get through this. And when you stumble, when it all gets too hard, we'll be right behind you, to pick you up and put you on your feet again.'

I rested my head wearily on his shoulder, knowing that despite his assurances, the journey to this new and unasked-for life was one I'd have to travel alone. A discreet knock on the door made me look up. The Specialist Nurse from the Organ Donation team came through the opening, with a look of apology for disturbing us on her face. But what she had come to say disturbed me even more.

'I just wanted to let you know that the theatre has been booked for nine p.m. this evening.'

It was impossible not to immediately glance at the clock and do the awful mental arithmetic. Joe had less than two hours left.

Kaye and Frank made a quiet exit from the ward, and I was glad they'd already left by the time my mum walked out of the lift carriage with her arm around Jake's shoulders. It would only have scared him to see the adults he relied on, the bedrock people in his world, so lost and broken. Children aren't supposed to see the people they love flailing helplessly in a sea of grief. The need to be strong for our son was the only thing that was still holding me up.

'Where's Dad?' I asked, scanning the empty lift cubicle behind them.

My mum glanced down at Jake for a moment before replying. 'He's just popped out for a little while. There was something he had to get.'

I didn't even question how odd that was, because my mind was elsewhere. Very slowly I crouched down and placed my hands on Jake's narrow shoulders.

'Grandma Kaye and Grandpa Frank have gone home now, Jake. They said goodbye to Daddy, and I think it's time now for you to do that too.' From my position at floor level I glanced up at my mum. 'Then Grandma and Granddad can take you back home.'

'No.' I wasn't expecting such a determined refusal from my young son. But on this thing, there would be no negotiation; I wasn't going to give in. The trauma of having to witness Joe being wheeled away to the operating theatre would live on as a nightmare memory for me, but not for him. I would do anything to spare him that.

'Jake, I know how hard this is for you. I know how much this is hurting you, because it's hurting me too. But you're going to have to be the best and bravest boy in the world and just do what Daddy and I want, okay?' His eyes lifted to mine at the deliberate inclusion of Joe in my request. I dropped my voice to a whisper. 'Daddy wouldn't want you to stay here all night. You know how sad it makes him when you get upset. Please, Jakey,' I pleaded.

Jake nodded slowly. His brilliant blue eyes, a legacy from his natural father, were brimming with tears for the man who had done such a wonderful job of filling that role for all of his young life.

'I know I have to tell Daddy goodbye tonight, Grandma explained it all to me. I get it Mummy, I do.' I shot a look of pure gratitude at my mum. 'But not yet. Not until Granddad gets back.'

I rose to my feet, and took Jake's hand in mine. Perhaps he needed the strength of all of us to help him. I couldn't strip that away from him, not when he was already about to lose so much more. 'Okay then. We can wait a little while.'

Twenty minutes later my father came through the door of Joe's room. His hair and heavy winter coat were speckled with dissolving flakes of snow, and he was slightly out of breath. In his hand he clasped a small bright red carrier bag from a well-known department store. Jake twisted off my lap and ran towards him.

'Did you find it?'

My dad ruffled his dark hair in a loving gesture and passed him the bag. 'I did, Jake. Although I had to go to three different stores, mind you. Thank goodness they're all open late for Christmas shopping.'

'Thank you, Granddad,' said Jake quietly, his hand already delving into the carrier. I glanced over at Max and saw a look of puzzlement on his face that probably matched mine perfectly.

'What have you got there?' My lips parted slightly in surprise as Jake carefully extracted the purchase from the bag. I didn't need to read

495

the title of the book in his hands. I recognised it from its brightly illustrated cover, and from the many times I'd seen it held within Joe's large strong hands. The last time I'd seen this book — or an older, more dog-eared edition of it — had been yesterday morning. It had been sitting on Jake's bedside table, waiting to be picked up again for the much-loved ritual of the bedtime story. Although we both took turns as narrator, this particular book — Jake's all-time favourite — was only allowed to be read by Joe.

Jake approached the bed with the book tucked under his arm. 'We have one chapter still to go,' he declared solemnly. I think I was the only person close enough to see the slight wobble of his chin as he spoke. 'And I didn't want Daddy to . . . go anywhere . . . without hearing the end of the story.'

I looked across at the other adults in the room with desperate sadness. How do you explain this to a child? I thought we had done so, I thought he understood, but clearly not.

'Jake,' I said gently, 'Daddy won't be able to read you the story, honey. I know he would really want to, if he could. It's just that he can't . . . he can't wake up.'

Jake held the book tightly against his small chest, as though it were a breastplate, shielding him from harm. 'I know that, Mummy. I understand. That's why *I'm* going to read it to him. Just this one time. It will help him sleep better.'

I couldn't speak, it was all I could do to keep from sobbing out loud as Jake once again hauled

496

himself up onto his father's hospital bed. He shuffled his slight body into position and slid one small childish arm around Joe's shoulder, mirroring the way Joe always pulled him against his body as he read to our son. The sound of someone quietly crying could just be heard above the sibilant hiss of the ventilator breathing air into Joe's lungs. I looked up to see who it was, and saw that it was *everyone*. Even the two nurses who were standing discreetly to one side of the room had tears running down their cheeks.

'Now, where were we?' said Jake, copying the words he had heard a thousand times from us. He thumbed through the book until he reached the final unread chapter.

Jake was a bright little boy, he always had been, but the book was advanced even for someone who could read beyond their years. But on this night, the long and sometimes complex words didn't stop him. Running his finger beneath the lines on the page, he read on, occasionally stumbling over a word, but determinedly sounding out the ones that were unfamiliar. I didn't prompt him, even when he faltered, because I knew this was something that he had to do. I realised then, that many years into the future, when he himself was a grown man, Jake would always remember the night when he had read this story to his dying father.

Jake's eyes, unlike ours, stayed dry the entire time that he read. It wasn't until he had finally murmured '*The End*' and slowly shut the book, that he began to cry. Very tenderly he leaned down and kissed Joe's cheek, letting his small mouth linger there one last time.

'I love you Daddy,' he whispered into Joe's ear. 'Sleep well. Sweet dreams.' He was repeating the words Joe said to him each night. I held my breath, waiting to see if he would complete them. 'See you when the sun shines again,' he said, his voice sounding lost, and for the first time, so much younger than his years. He slid off the bed and into my arms. 'I'd like to go home now,' he confessed into the wall of my chest.

My mum was already on her feet and collecting their coats. I kept Jake's face against my body, unconsciously rocking him in my arms, as I hadn't done for years, as my parents both kissed Joe goodbye. Then they each held out a hand and very gently I turned Jake towards them.

He walked to the door between his grandparents, his small head bowed. He raised it once and looked back, then suddenly broke free of their hands and ran back into the room. At first I didn't realise what he was doing as he fell to his knees and scrabbled furiously beneath the hospital bed.

'Jake? What are you doing? You can't — ' I broke off as he emerged from beneath the metal-framed bed with his cherished bedtime cuddly toy in his hands. I'd completely forgotten how he had angrily discarded it earlier in the day. He brushed small specks of dirt from the lion's face and looked deeply into the unseeing plastic eyes, then held out the toy to me.

'Can Daddy take Simba? Will the doctors let

him take it with him?'

'Don't you think you might miss Simba a little too much yourself?'

Jake slowly shook his head from side to side. 'I've got you, and Grandma and Granddad and Uncle Max. But Daddy will be all alone. I want him to keep Simba, so he won't be lonely.'

I took the toy from Jake's outstretched hand only when I saw how important this sacrifice was to him. 'Don't worry. I'll make sure the doctors know,' I promised.

★ ★ ★

I could have had a thousand years to say my goodbyes to Joe, and it still wouldn't have been long enough. To give us privacy, Max had discreetly positioned himself in a chair at the far reaches of the room. That was as far away from my side as he was prepared to go. He was pretending to read a magazine; pretending not to keep glancing over at me, with worried concern all over his face. He might even have managed to fool me, if the magazine he was holding hadn't been upside-down the entire time it was in his hands.

When I heard the click of her footsteps enter the room, I didn't even need to turn around to know that the Specialist Nurse had joined us. 'Mrs Taylor?' Slowly I swivelled in my seat. She had an open and expressive face, and her words were redundant. I knew why she was there. 'Mrs Taylor, Ally, I just wanted to let you know that the transplant team have now arrived. In a little while we'll need to move Joe upstairs.'

Panic raced through me. I'd known this was coming, of course I had. But it was still too soon, decades too soon. My galloping heart beat faster, as though trying to build up enough momentum to race us both out of there, to somewhere where none of this could touch us. But that place didn't exist.

'Do you think I could — ' My voice was croaky, as though the words were rusted within me. 'Would it be possible for me to speak to the surgeon? The one who's going to operate on Joe?'

The nurse's eyebrows lifted marginally and the concern on her face was clear. 'Is this something *I* could help you with? Perhaps I haven't explained everything clearly enough?'

'No,' I assured her. 'I understand everything that will happen. I just need to speak to him before he begins. Would that be alright?'

I had wondered if this request was unusual. I could see from her eyes that it was. Yet she hesitated for only a moment before nodding slowly.

'Of course. Let me see what I can do.'

She was back in minutes. 'If you'd like to follow me, Mr Bertram can see you now.' I got to my feet, and looked anxiously at Joe. 'He'll still be here when you get back,' she reassured.

I remember nothing of the journey up to the floor which housed the operating theatres. I don't remember walking along the empty corridor towards the tall man in green hospital scrubs, who stood patiently waiting beside a pair of swing doors.

He held out his hand to me as we approached.

'Mrs Taylor, my name is Sydney Bertram and I will be Joe's surgeon this evening. I understand that you wished to speak with me?'

I liked him instantly, which struck me as surprising, given the circumstances. I especially liked the way he referred to Joe by name. As though he was still a patient in need of his care.

'Thank you for seeing me,' I began. He waved away my gratitude with a casual waft of his hand. His fingers were long and elegant. Musician's fingers, I thought abstractedly. Then I remembered the work those fingers would soon undertake, and began to cry.

'Is there something you wanted to ask me, Mrs Taylor?'

I shook my head, and fought to regain control. What I had to say was too important to allow it to be lost in incoherent tears. 'I wanted to tell you about Joe. About the kind of man he is. Before you begin tonight, I wanted you to know that he's so much more than just a person who carried a donor card. I wanted you to know that he's funny — really funny — we laugh all the time. And he's kind and thoughtful, not just to his family — but to everyone. I don't know a single person who doesn't like him. He is a truly wonderful man, and he means the world to his parents, to his son, and . . . to me.'

Hospitals are busy places. Operating theatres are booked and surgeries are scheduled with detailed precision. I knew perfectly well that elsewhere within this building medical professionals were waiting to begin their work. Outside, in the dark and snowy night there were ambulances, maybe even helicopters, whose work tonight would only begin when this surgeon's job was done. But no trace of impatience showed on his face as he stood before me, gently inclining his head and listening as I tried to encapsulate in just minutes everything it had taken me eight years to learn and love about the man I was passing over to his care.

When at last I came to a halt, his eyes were kind and warm. 'Mrs Taylor, your husband sounds like a man I would have been honoured to meet and to know. I give you my word, that while Joe is with us, my team and I will treat him with more than just respect, but also with admiration and gratitude. Joe was a brave man when he was alive, but what he's doing now, what he's leaving behind, is even more brave and courageous. As are you.'

I shook my head, but his words assured me that I had spoken for Joe as eloquently as I could. I had told them who he was. I reached into my handbag for a tissue, and felt the sharp edge of a plastic container jab my fingertips. The question came from my lips without thought. 'In films I've seen that sometimes music is played during an operation. Is that something that you do?'

Mr Bertram inclined his head. 'Indeed it is. I personally favour classical pieces, Debussy in particular.'

Slowly I withdrew the thin, flat object from my bag. I had last seen it thirty-six hours earlier, when I'd plucked it from the car's CD player, and replaced it with something more to my liking. The cover glinted brightly under the fluorescent lighting: a guitar, a bale of hay and a discarded Stetson. 'Would it be possible to play this when you are . . . when . . . during — ?'

'It would be my pleasure,' he said, taking the CD from my hands.

'Track four is his favourite.'

'I'll make sure it's playing.'

I held out my hand to the man who I knew I would never see again, and whose face I would never forget. 'Thank you for listening to me.'

'It is us who should thank you and your husband for what you're both doing.' His words were subtly drawing our meeting to a close. 'I should go, unless there's anything else you wished to say or ask, Mrs Taylor?'

The question seemed to hang in the thin rarefied antiseptic air of the corridor for the longest moment in time. 'No, Mr Bertram. There's nothing else. Nothing at all.' I turned and walked away.

★ ★ ★

Three things shocked me when I returned to the ICU. The first was the small cluster of people with *Theatre* stencilled on the back of their green uniforms. They were loitering almost-but-not-quite out of sight beyond the nurses' station. Joe's final cortege had been assembled, and was now standing in wait.

The second shock was hearing Max's voice, hoarse and broken, as he conducted his last one-sided conversation with the man he'd

503

allowed to depose him as my best friend. 'Financially — don't even think about it. Not for a second, okay? That's taken care of, alright?' Max sighed deeply. 'For everything else, all I can promise you is that I'll be there for them. Always. Feel free to send a thunderbolt down on me, if I don't do it just the way you want.'

I walked silently up to my friend and laid a hand on his shoulder. He jumped at my touch as though it were a live wire. 'You shouldn't sneak up on people like that.'

'Why? Because it's bad to hear how much someone loves you?' My hand went from his shoulder to rest on his cheek. I looked into his eyes, which were considerably more red around the edges than they'd been when I left the room. 'I knew it anyway,' I said gently, dropping a kiss on his forehead.

'You should have been here a minute or two earlier, when I promised him I'd take Jake to Nashville as soon as he's old enough.'

From somewhere I had almost forgotten existed, a small sad smile curved my lips. 'Joe would like that.'

There was a long unspoken moment which Max eventually broke. 'Did you say what you had to say to the surgeon?'

I nodded sadly. 'I did.' I took a breath to steady me. 'I'd like to be alone with Joe now.'

Max got clumsily to his feet, banging into both a chair and the edge of Joe's bed as he attempted to cross the room and reach the door. When he turned at the entrance it was easy to see why he'd stumbled. His eyes were blinded by tears.

'Have a safe journey, big guy.'

And there was the last shock, because finally — after a day of tears — my eyes were now dry. I wasn't numb to the pain, but something bigger was subtly edging those feelings aside. It took me a while to realise what it was. Love. I loved Joe too much to make this last moment we would share together full of misery and sorrow. That wasn't how we were. That wasn't us. To tarnish our final moments in that way would be wrong.

Very gently I raised his hand and grazed his unfeeling fingertips over the contours of my face. With my free hand I did the same to his. It felt as though I was sacredly binding our souls together. Imprinting the memory on both of us . . . so we could find each other again.

Behind my closed lids a kaleidoscope of snapshot memories spun past: our first kiss; the first time he had slowly peeled the clothes from my body; how his hands — normally so strong and confident — had trembled when he'd laid them on me, as though I was made of delicate spun glass, beautiful but fragile. The images shifted and I saw again the look in his eyes when I'd come to him. The passion taking us both by surprise. It still did . . . or rather, it had.

Finally the travelling caress of my fingers reached his mouth. I ignored the intrusive plastic tube, choosing only to see the smile that had belonged just to me. I bent to kiss his lips, still so pink, still so warm. They were unmoving, but in my heart and in my mind they were kissing me back, his arms were pulling me towards him and he was holding me close, so very close.

'This isn't where it ends, Joe. Not for us.' My lips brushed his, as I breathed life into the promise that somewhere, against all odds, I knew he could hear. 'I will see you again.'

Epilogue

The taxi pulled up in front of the impressive apartment building. Ally craned forward and looked upward towards the top floor. The glass in the windows of the penthouse suite glinted back at her in the bright June sunshine.

'We're here,' she said to her travelling companion. His head was bent in concentration as he studied the electronic device in his hand. He looked up, pocketed the gadget and smiled at her. They waited until the taxi had pulled away before walking hand in hand towards the elaborate wrought-iron entrance gates. A security camera whirred into life as Ally studied the keypad entry system, searching for the familiar surname. As she reached out to press the top-most button her finger trembled slightly, and it came as no surprise that he noticed that. He watched her very closely these days. 'Are you feeling alright? Are you nervous?' he asked.

She shook her head, and then remembered how they had promised to always tell each other the truth. 'Well, maybe a little.'

'We don't have to go in,' he suggested.

For just a second she considered his words, before once again shaking her head. 'Yes we do.'

★　★　★

Charlotte was pacing. She'd been back and forth to the glass double doors in the apartment's entrance foyer at least ten times in the last half hour. She'd even pressed her ear to the gleaming silver keypad set discreetly into the wall, wondering if she'd be able to tell if it was malfunctioning. Her heels clipped on the shiny marble floor as she crossed to a table which held a tall vase of waxy, cream-coloured orchids, and her mobile phone. She checked the display screen, still expecting to see a last-minute text from Ally cancelling this meeting. There were no messages.

Would she have blamed her if she'd made some excuse not to come? In all fairness, probably not. Despite the many phone calls between them over the last six months, this would be the first time she had met with Ally since that dreadful night in the hospital last December. So much had happened since then. Charlotte wasn't the same person any more, and from what she could tell, neither was Ally. It was hardly surprising. What they'd both been through would have changed anyone.

The new Charlotte was softer than the old one, more tolerant and less exacting. She left work on time these days, and made sure her staff did too. When you get close enough to a yawning precipice to feel the wind buffeting your face, only a fool wouldn't recognise it as the bringer of change. The biggest surprise — for both her and Ally — had been the burgeoning and unexpected friendship that had woven between them. As subtle as a spider's web, neither had seen it forming, but suddenly it was there, gossamer fine

508

but already surprisingly strong.

The screen set in the control panel flickered into life and Charlotte saw the image of her visitors displayed on the wall. The breath caught in her throat. She buzzed them in from the street and then followed their progress on the monitor as they crossed the small courtyard and climbed the steps towards the building's main entrance. She hesitated for just a moment. When she pressed the button beneath her poised finger, she would be doing so much more than allowing Ally entry into her building; she'd be giving her entry into her life too. Did she want that? Could she even handle it? Charlotte closed her perfectly made-up eyes for a long second. Then she pressed the button.

★　★　★

'This is fancy,' Ally observed, as they entered the building and two gleaming bronze lift doors slid open directly in front of them. Her companion shrugged, and Ally wasn't in the least bit surprised that he didn't appear overly impressed. The lift had no buttons. It was programmed to know which of the building's residents had ushered them in and which floor they required. Each storey housed only a single residence.

The glide up to the tenth floor, the penthouse floor, was too short to allow Ally to change her mind, but just long enough for her to question if this was really a good idea after all. The lift came to a smooth, practically imperceptible stop, the doors slid apart, and there stood Charlotte.

The two women hesitated for an uncomfortable moment, before deciding to hug. It was a little clumsy and awkward, but that was perfectly understandable, given the circumstances. Charlotte's eyes went to the person standing beside Ally. He was taller than she had been expecting him to be, and dressed casually in shirt and jeans. If he was at all nervous or wary about this meeting, he certainly hid it well.

This was her home, her territory, yet Charlotte suddenly felt wrong-footed and ill at ease. She'd spent all day getting ready for this. The fridge was overflowing with a variety of food she'd bought from several local delicatessens. There were artisan loaves of bread and an assortment of cream cakes waiting in her kitchen. There was wine in the cooler and a range of soft drinks in the cupboard. She had no idea what to serve or what to buy — so she'd bought everything.

A flicker of movement caught Ally's eye. The apartment was enormous and the huge living area opened out onto a spectacular balcony which ran the entire width of the room. The folding glass doors leading to the outside area were pushed wide open, and a tall dark-haired man turned away from the vista of the city skyline and came towards them. Ally's hand was suddenly gripped by the boy beside her.

'Please come in, both of you,' urged Charlotte. If she said anything else, Ally never heard it; she couldn't hear anything above the thunderous beating of her heart. Suddenly she was racked with doubts about all of this. Was this a terrible idea? Was it far too soon for any of them to be doing this?

David stepped across the threshold from the balcony and into the room. He looked strong, healthy and vibrant. This was not the same man Ally had last seen in the hospital: frail, gasping for breath and hooked up to a barrage of machinery. This man seemed full of life and vitality. For just a single second, Ally wondered if she should resent him for that.

'Hello Ally,' said David gently. 'I'm really glad you decided to come today. Thank you.' Ally inclined her head slightly in acknowledgement. 'And you must be Jake,' David said looking down at his son for the very first time. There was no hand held out to shake, nor arms held open for a hug. Instinctively he must have known that neither greeting would have been appropriate. David's voice appeared perfectly composed, but for the women in the room, who knew him so well, everything he was feeling was there in his eyes.

Jake took a small step forward and stared up at his natural father for a long moment. 'You look like me,' he stated quietly.

David's smile was achingly familiar to Ally. She knew it from her past, from her memories, and she also knew it because it was her son's smile too.

'No, not really,' replied David easily. 'You're much better looking.'

'Ally, please sit down,' insisted Charlotte. Ally had wanted to stay as close to Jake's side as possible, but Charlotte practically folded her into a deep comfortable settee with butter-soft leather upholstery. 'Let me get you a cushion, or something,' Charlotte fussed, hurrying off into another room. Her anxiety to make her guest comfortable was having the exact opposite effect.

For a man unaccustomed to children, David seemed to understand perfectly how not to overwhelm them. He turned his attention to his former girlfriend. 'How are you, Ally? You look extremely well.'

Ally gave a small self-deprecating laugh, dismissing the compliment, but he wouldn't allow her. 'Seriously Ally. I don't think I've ever seen you look more beautiful.'

Charlotte returned to the room, carrying a small cushion in her arms. Her steps faltered for just a moment as she heard David's words, and a fleeting sadness shadowed the smile she pinned in place. 'I agree,' she added. 'You are positively glowing.'

Ally bit her lip, knowing just how hard that must have been for her to say. Charlotte slipped the cushion behind her back and Ally smiled gratefully, as her hands instinctively came to rest against her swollen abdomen. As if she knew it was an important moment, the unborn baby girl within her, Joe's daughter, kicked firmly against Ally's palm. Charlotte saw the movement through the fabric of Ally's dress, and although shock and surprise showed on her face, there was no envy there.

'You look well too,' Ally told David.

'I *am* well,' he confirmed. 'Better than I ever thought I would be.' He paused, as though unsure as to whether or not he should complete his sentence. 'Thanks to you.'

Ally closed her eyes against the prickling tears, and the expensive penthouse flat disappeared and became instead a hospital corridor on a long December night that had tied their lives together irrevocably. She heard the echo of the surgeon's voice. *'Is there anything else you wished to say or ask, Mrs Taylor?'*

She had said no. She had even walked half a dozen steps away before turning back around, as she had always known that she would. *'I've heard there's something called Designated Donation. If it does exist, there's a man downstairs in Intensive Care. His name is David Williams . . .'*

Mr Bertram had made no guarantees at that point. All he had said was that he would look into it. But while Ally was crying in Max's arms on the taxi journey back home from the hospital, David was already being prepped for surgery.

★ ★ ★

David sat down on a wicker banquette on the balcony, and after an encouraging nod from his mother, Jake joined him. 'I don't know what I'm supposed to call you,' Jake said at last.

'David sounds good to me,' his father replied.

Jake, who had been intently studying the laces of his trainers, raised his head and there was patent relief in his eyes. 'Oh, okay. I . . . I wasn't sure if you wanted to be called Dad, or Father, or something like that.'

David glanced over at Ally, and his eyes were

kind. He leant a little closer to his son. 'I'm not your dad, Jake. And I'm never, ever going to try to pretend that I am, or try to take his place. Your dad's name was Joe, and he was a really great guy, and I'm only sorry that I never got to meet him. I know how much you must miss him.'

Jake nodded fiercely, as the trainer laces drew his attention once more.

'But he's not gone, you know, not really. A part of him will live on for ever.'

Jake looked up, comprehension dawning. He raised his hand and pointed towards David's chest. 'You mean in there?'

David's smile was achingly sad as he slowly shook his head. 'No. I mean in there,' he corrected, pointing instead at Jake's chest. He paused and looked over once more at Ally, whose own face was a mixture of surprise and admiration. 'I know you're old enough to understand that you and I are related. Maybe you even know that officially I'm what is called your *biological father*. But your dad was Joe Taylor. He was the one who changed your nappies when you were little, made you better when you were sick, and picked you up when you skinned your knees falling down.'

'He did all the gross stuff,' confirmed Jake.

David laughed softly. 'Yeah, but he did the good stuff too. He played with you, he had fun with you, and he helped make you into this smart, super, amazing boy that you are today. And that's how he gets to live on,' David concluded quietly. 'Because he lives on in you.'

Ally had no idea if David's words had been rehearsed or whether they had been just a brilliantly apt off-the-cuff sentiment. It didn't matter. He had struck exactly the right note.

'I don't want to be your dad,' David repeated. 'Because whether he is here, or whether he isn't, you still have a pretty amazing man who deserves to keep that title. But what I really would like to be,' he admitted, bending down a little lower to Jake as he spoke, 'is your friend. If you'd let me.'

'I guess that would be okay,' Jake agreed, looking over at Ally and being rewarded with a proud, yet tearful smile.

Jake bit his lip nervously, as he wrestled with a question he didn't know if he should ask. 'Can I . . . can I see it? The scar from your operation, can I see it?'

'Oh Jake, I really don't think — ' began Ally, struggling to get up from the couch which had all but swallowed her in its cushions.

'It's okay,' said David quietly. His eyes went first to Charlotte and then to Ally in reassurance. 'I don't mind.' He got to his feet and brought his hands up to the line of buttons of his shirt. His strong tanned fingers slowly released each one from its fastening, inch by inch exposing his muscular torso. He didn't shrug out of the shirt, just opened it wide enough so that the narrow line down the centre of his chest was visible. The soft dark hair which covered him and arrowed down towards the waistband of his jeans, had not grown back over the long red line, although the skin appeared perfectly healed. Jake slid off the seat and went to stand before him, his eyes transfixed on the scar.

'May I touch it?'

David nodded. Ally and Charlotte exchanged a look. Ally's hand unconsciously went to cradle her bump, but the other reached out to the woman standing beside her. Charlotte gripped it tightly.

David made it easier for Jake by dropping down to a crouch before him. Jake's hand bridged the last small distance between them. Very tentatively he placed his index finger at the top of the red scar line and slowly ran it down the length of the healed breastbone.

'Does it hurt?'

David shook his head. 'Not any more. It's a good heart. A really strong one.'

Jake nodded, as though this was something he had always known. He ran his finger once more up the line, slowly, almost reverently. Under his young fingertips the heart beneath his touch pounded strongly.

'Hi Dad. It's me,' he whispered.

Very gently David covered Jake's small hand with his own. 'He hears you Jake, I know he does.'

★ ★ ★

It wasn't a conventional family. It certainly wasn't a normal one. But as the three adults looked at each other over the head of the young boy, they each recognised that that is what they were. A family. For years their lives had been tied together by destiny and by fate in ways that were

516

at times too incredible to believe possible. But somehow every moment of strange serendipity had been leading them here. To this time, to this place, to these people, and this future.

Acknowledgements

I have come to realise that when you type 'The End' after you have finished writing a book, it isn't the end at all; it's actually the beginning. Because that is when some very talented individuals take over and turn your words into the book you always hoped it would be. I would like to thank my wonderful editor Jo Dickinson and every one of the dedicated and enthusiastic team at Simon & Schuster for their warm welcome and for helping to create something very special.

I am also very fortunate to have not one, but *two*, amazing agents without whom none of the incredible things that have happened to me over the last two years would have taken place. As ever Kate Burke and Diane Banks, you are beyond outstanding.

I remember back when I was at school (and we are talking a *long* time ago) that my English teacher always used to say, 'Only write about what you know'. Good advice perhaps, but I haven't entirely stuck to it! Instead I found people with the expert knowledge I was lacking to fill in the (many) blanks for me. Patiently, they explained everything I needed to know. I listened carefully, nodded a lot, and then began to write. But if, after all that, I've *still* managed to get things wrong, please accept my apologies, because the mistakes are entirely mine, not theirs. (This is why it is okay to let me write books, but you really don't want me as your doctor!)

So to Hazel and Mark, thank you for not only being the most incredible friends in the world, but also for being at the end of my numerous email enquiries. Your combined help with all things skiing, avalanche, penthouse apartment, and heart-condition related was invaluable. (You're still never going to get me on a pair of skis, though!)

Thanks to Rachel Boyd for her medical input and for pointing me in the right direction. I just know you're going to make a great doctor, chiefly because you don't laugh when someone asks you something totally ridiculous.

One of my favourite scenes is the one at The Rink at Rockefeller Center in New York. When my good friend Kim told me the story of how her daughter Faye and boyfriend Ben got engaged there during a Christmas trip, I just knew I was going to have to 'borrow' it for Charlotte and David. Thank you both for allowing me to share your romantic moment with everyone. And yes, you really *can* arrange to propose to someone on the ice.

On a more serious note, I would not have been able to tell this story effectively without the assistance of NHS Blood and Transplant. Their website was my daily reference point, from which I gained just a tiny insight into their remarkable achievements. I would particularly like to thank one very patient and knowledgeable specialist nurse, who spoke with me at length about transplant and organ donation, because — more than anything — I was desperate to get this right. I am in awe of all the dedicated medical professionals involved in these life-giving surgeries, and even more so, of the countless families who bravely donate their loved ones' organs. I am not ashamed to admit that I was frequently in tears reading their very moving accounts.

I normally thank my immediate family for their love and support, but on this occasion, I would like to single out my son Luke for his particular help. Luke (like Ally) was a music student at university, he too plays the piano and the trumpet (he even depped a couple of times for Moonlighters). Ally's musical talents were created as a sort of homage to Luke, the only member of our family who isn't tone deaf. He got used to some pretty strange questions along the way, although perhaps none quite as surprising as, 'If you were a woman, and a musician, what would you like to listen to while giving birth?' That one got a single word email in reply: 'What??!!!'

I cannot end without thanking Ralph, Kimberley and Luke for being my biggest fans and most honest critics. You encouraged me, when you were the only ones who ever read what I wrote. And you are still encouraging me, every single day. You are, quite simply, the best.